The Fragrant Ones

God bless you, Christie!

A. R. Kimber

Luke 1:45

A. R. Kimber

ISBN: 1494810247
ISBN 13: 9781494810245

For my father, who read the Scriptures to me every day, and my mother, who led me into the Kingdom.

"I tell you the truth, wherever the gospel is preached throughout the world, what she has done will also be told, in memory of her."

—Jesus, Mark 14:9

1

*J*eb wasn't dead yet.

He wasn't dead yet, but Jennifer found herself in a state of constantly memorizing him, in the same way that she'd recall her deceased mother: he would appear in full-color vignettes on a screen in her mind, like movie previews. No plot. A few action sequences with gunshot punch lines or spurts of profanity, depicting angst or despair.

They were impossible to ignore. If she tried, if she made a point of trying to think about something else, she would hear his voice in her head. She would hear his words, every one of them, reverberating, like the words the boys in the back row would teach her before catechism class when she was a kid: various one-syllable words depicting genital organs or bodily functions that would bounce off the walls of her brain while she tried to recite her prayers.

In her mind Jeb remained in a glorified state. She willed him to be perfect; she refused to think of him in any other way, even though her senses were confronted, almost daily, with the erosion of his flesh. She could smell his unwashed body and his breath, like sour milk, and his bed pan, which wasn't cleaned often enough. His apartment reeked of hashish and incense and pee, as if it was inhabited by a hippie or holy man who was long past caring about mundane matters of housekeeping or personal hygiene. She approached him reverently, as if he were the incarnation of a fallen deity. His eyelids quivered slightly, but did not open. His mouth gaped and each breath was accompanied by a sucking noise, more like a gasp, while he slept.

She placed her stethoscope on his left, naked pectoral. He had been in the habit of shaving his chest. Now, most of his hair had either fallen out or stopped growing. But on the screen in her head she could see his torso as she had seen it the first time, lean and tanned, extending out of a pair of short, black gym shorts, the sheen of sweat or oil (it would be like him to oil it) accentuating the dips and dents of his abdominals.

It was at a party, crowded and swinging, *blasting*, as he would say. In the backyard of one of the summer rentals on Heck Avenue, someone had hung a mirror ball and strung Christmas lights. Jeb had mounted a picnic table, and was dancing to a throbbing disco opus by Grace Jones. From the corner of the yard she and Vina had watched the others crowd around the table, urging him on, even the gothic-looking ones who dressed like *Rocky Horror* and normally kept an aesthetic distance between themselves and the rest. "Go, baby go..." they had chanted, arms extended, wanting him, wanting a piece of him. His long, straw-colored hair had swept over his face, so she couldn't see if he was mocking or accepting their adulation. His grinding dance was lewd and belligerent, but his timing and form were mesmerizing. At the end of the song he had lowered himself into their grasp, and within moments the black shorts were waved overhead like a flag of victory. With no small effort he had disengaged himself, resentful that his spontaneous performance had incited such vulgarity. She heard him say, "You assholes—I ain't Jesus." One of the more blatant ones held on, rubbing himself against Jeb's thigh until he pushed him to the ground.

"He doesn't get it," Vina had said at the time. They were alternately licking salt off their thumbs, sucking lemons, and downing shots of Tequila, so Jennifer sensed a profound insight coming. Vina was always more philosophical when drinking.

"What? Who?" Behind her sunglasses she had not taken her eyes off Jeb, but she didn't want to be so obvious, not to Vina.

"His power. He has this power over them. He's always surprised by it."

Jennifer, watching him, could feel it too. Somewhere inside her a dark hole widened, a gaping sinkhole. She craved him heavily, and deeply.

"Fags love me. Women like me," he said, crossing over to them.

"We love you, honey," Vina answered, and kissed him full on the lips. "This is Jennie."

He wore a G-string, black and shiny. Jennifer had seen similar things in a Chippendale calendar, but never *live*. He pulled his shorts on and then looked at her. "Do you love me, Jennie?"

She imagined her fingers tracing the outline of his oblique muscles and was suffused with a longing to pay homage to him. She was like an aesthetic, who, having grown weary of a world that contained so much mediocrity, had suddenly discovered a thing of unsurpassed beauty. Her relief at finding such a prize, combined with the level of alcohol in her blood, felt bigger than lust. It felt like worship.

"I—I've been admiring you. From afar."

He smiled and came closer. His chin had a hint of beard, his lashes were thick, he had a high forehead and cheekbones, and pouty, rock-star lips. His eyes had the guarded expression of a child who has suffered shame. They were hazel or green, with specks of gold. He was perfect. A cross between God and Adam. She could smell him: rum, cologne, sweat. He put his arm around her.

"Yer neck's kinda red," he drawled, exaggerating his southern inflection. "You a redneck girl?"

She put her hands on her neck. It felt hot. Everything did. She could feel her scalp and her armpits and her crotch sweating. If he kissed her she would hyperventilate.

"So, um—are you, gay? Or bi?"

He smiled again, as if she had said something very amusing, and then he put his mouth next to her ear.

"I'm *omni*."

Vina heard, and laughed. They touched their plastic cups together, which broke the enchantment, but Jennifer had been converted from that moment.

Dancer. Painter. Lover. Beautiful boy. My mentor. He taught me the meaning of life. She could already hear them eulogizing him, citing his gifts and attributes with their annoying North Jersey intonation, and saying *like* in the middle of every sentence. He and Vina referred to them as *the girls*. Jennifer thought of them as his disciples; there were always two or three of them hanging around his bed, brushing his hair, rolling his joints, and feeding him milkshakes or soup.

They all looked the same to her; she could never remember who was who. Occasionally, when she walked through the main room of his apartment where some were working on a quilt piece they were making in his honor for some political demonstration, two or three would glance up, their eyes rimmed with lines of sorrow and fatigue, and give her a nod before they went back to their labor of love.

She did not fit in. She was too healthy and balanced, and not eccentric or artistic. She had a large bust and wide hips. *Voluptuous*, as Michael, her occasional lover, had told her. She wore her hair in a ponytail, and had clear skin and good teeth, like her mother's. *Straitlaced*, Vina had said once, and she had felt annoyed.

"I have my vices…" she had mumbled, at the time, but she really didn't, compared to them.

It was better when she came straight from work, still in her uniform, with a stethoscope around her neck. They liked her to be *medical*—probably Jeb did too. It was hard to know why else he'd want her there at this point, but he would ask for her, he'd mumble her name, at least once or twice a day, and if she didn't show up after a couple of days one of them would call her, grudgingly, resentful that Jeb would ask for her when they were all there. She would arrive, with almost religious devotion to attend him, the way supplicants in Eastern lands would patronize a local temple or shrine of a regional, lesser-known god.

"Hey, you. When d'you get here?"

She jumped at the sound of Vina's voice, and turned to see her pulling off her black pea coat, her bracelets clinking, a cigarette poised daringly on her lips.

"Uh—half hour or so."

Vina slid into a chair next to his bed. Jen felt a familiar shield going up inside herself. When they were both inebriated there was no one more interesting and philosophical, with the exception of Jeb himself, but that was ancient history. As it was, Vina led a bipolar existence between inebriation and sobriety, and Jennifer much preferred the drinking Vina.

"Vina, I've told you. You shouldn't smoke in here."

Her eyes narrowed. She took a long haul and let it puff out of her nostrils before she dropped her cigarette and stepped on it. Then she cozied up to Jeb.

"How's our boy, huh? How you doing, baby?"

His breathing slowed for a second and they both expected him to stir. Vina's voice, low and roughened from years of smoking, had that effect on him, and she was proud of it. On Christmas Day she had lain next to him for hours, intoxicated and singing clever, obscene renditions of the traditional carols while rubbing his back. She'd got him to laugh a few times. It was a bit much for Jen though. She'd left the room and found Kevin in the kitchen, looking for something to eat. She'd made him some Kraft dinner and sat with him while he ate it, wanting to leave, but unwilling to abandon him while his mother was thus preoccupied and three of the disciples were hanging around, also drinking, and watching a soap opera. If they'd had any decency, they'd at least put on cartoons for him.

"How's Kevin?"

Vina glanced at her suspiciously, and then looked back at Jeb. "He's with his dad. Why?"

"Just wondering." *I asked how, not where.* "Last time you said he was having night terrors or something."

She shrugged, unwilling to discuss it. Jen surmised that the crisis had passed, and that it was less about Kevin's nightmares than about their inconvenience.

Jeb sucked in his breath suddenly, causing them to start. He blinked, and then stared straight ahead, like a man being forced to confront a hard fact. The whites of his eyes were a dull yellow. His gaze shifted back and forth between them, as if he could not decide who was more deserving of his attention. After another second he blinked wearily at Vina, and he painfully attempted to smile at her, which made his goiter protrude. A raspy utterance that ended in "baby" escaped his lips, and both women bent over him on cue, as if he had expressed a need for prayer.

"One more time, honey…" Vina cooed.

Jen felt cowed by their symbiotic relationship, and wondered, for the hundredth time, if they had been lovers. "Oh, honey, it's way beyond that..." Vina had told her once. "It's a spiritual connection. I saved him. That's the only way I can explain it to you or anybody."

"Love on me, baby..." His face contorted. His eyes pooled and on her side Jen saw a tear slide down his temple and into his ear. She quickly turned toward her purse and coat, which were draped over a stack of canvases.

In a moment Vina was off the chair and lying next to him.

"I'm right here, baby. Right here with you."

Jennifer felt a dull, sick pain in her gut and got up and collected her things.

"See ya, Vina. Take care, Jeb." She did not wait for either to respond. On her way out she closed his front door a little louder than necessary, so he would know for certain that she had left.

Outside she stood beside her car, her eyes focused on the wan light from his window. The snow had started again and the frigid flakes stung her eyes and cheeks. Her mother had died in February too, with the stuff floating down outside her hospital window. She bent her head back, as if inviting the minute, frozen spears to assault her face.

No two snowflakes are congruent. Scientists have photographed and studied hundreds of magnified snowflakes on frozen slides. To date, they have never found any two that are identical.

The driver's side lock was jammed. Last week it had become frozen, and she had stabbed it with a screwdriver, so now it didn't work. She jabbed it a few times with the key and then went around to the passenger's side and slid over. It wasn't worth putting the heater on—she lived a couple of streets away, on Stockton. Her hands were shaking and her teeth were chattering by the time she parked. Clay Peterson had left his car down the street, so she could pull right up in front of her house.

They were like that, the Petersons: always putting her trash can back up on her steps or shoveling the walkway. Rebecca would sometimes bring up homemade zucchini muffins or beef barley soup, which embarrassed Jennifer, because she never reciprocated with any luscious goodies of her own, although she kept intending to. Sometimes they were noisy. They had five kids with Bible names like David and Rachel, but she never remembered who was who. When they had first come, they seemed like Jesus-hippie types, part of an unfamiliar but benign fringe group that was typically drawn to the Grove. Over time she had come to see that they were fairly normal, aside from the home-schooling, which Jen considered countercultural as well as counterpro-ductive. They were decent and considerate, which were rare traits in the human species. And they paid the rent on time.

On her way up, she glanced through the window and could see them silhouetted against the fireplace. The whole family, God help her, was singing—with the oldest boy playing the guitar. Singing. It was too hokey, almost laughable, except for the fact that Jordan—she thought it was Jordan, or was it John-Mark—had Down syndrome, and Bee-Bee, another adopted one, was "delayed." So she didn't laugh. She felt her throat tighten. Their small cat, Olympuss, suddenly brushed against her boots, and meowed loudly at their door, which caused a nameless longing to surge inside her. She quickly stepped over the animal, and proceeded up the stairs.

Without turning on any lights, she poured a glass of wine, and seated herself by the large front window, her usual perch, especially when it snowed. The image of Vina curled next to Jeb caused the sick pain to rise within her, but she forced herself to contemplate the snow. She waited for the peaceful feeling to come over her, the "Christmas warmth," as her mother had called it. Without warning she was back in third grade again.

Now, class, I want each of you to come up with your own snow-flake design. Watch how I fold the paper. There are twenty-seven of us. Imagine each of us making snowflakes from now until we were all very old, never using the same design twice. Imagine all the snowflakes that fall every time it snows. Imagine all the designs.

Inside her a black hole widened. She focused intently on the snow, but the usual sense of wonder and peace evaded her. When she was eight years old, the "Christmas warmth" (she kept it there because she didn't know what else to call it) had healed her, and made her feel right again after her father had left them for good. She and her mother had both grieved, privately, in separate rooms, then Mommy had made hot chocolate and shortbread cookies with a maraschino cherry planted on each one, reminiscent of Rudolph's nose. They had sat by the window in silence, sipping and munching and watching the snow. The room was dark, the night was bright, and the lights of their tree made large confetti dots on the smooth snowbank below their window. Her mother had put *The Messiah* on the phonograph, which she only did at Christmas. *I Know that my Redeemer Liveth* was playing at low volume, and she experienced a peace that both comforted and revived her, and it caused her to believe the snow had a divine quality. She would play in the snow, and lie in it, gazing at the tiny crystalline shapes on her mitten. She would eat it. Once she sat by her window and drew thirty-two snowflake designs before she ran out of ideas.

The Snowgod by Jennie Boughten. No one is sure why there are no two snowflakes the same. Scientists say it is because of how the wind and moisture form them, but I think there is a Snow god. He is not the god you pray to or eat in mass. He just makes snowflakes all the time, even in the summer. I think he must be a nice god. He would never send anyone to hell. All he cares about is sending pretty snowflakes down on us.

But it was different tonight. Tonight the starkness was menacing. The sky glowed with an unnatural, eerie light. The snow looked too pure, too white; it was blinding, and she struggled to keep watching it. At the same time, she had an irrational desire to go out and lie in it and have it bury her. She pictured the Peterson kids finding her under the snow the next morning. She pictured her body heavy with snow even on the inside; somehow it would penetrate her skin and fill a fetid, dark place within her with its pristine coldness.

"That's a crock o' shit," said Jeb's voice in her head. He had said it when she had told him once about snowflakes. It had made him angry, for some reason. She was watching him work; specifically, she was watching his hands and the muscles in his forearms. He'd been stretching a canvas, and he stopped stapling and looked at her.

"How the hell does anyone really know? Maybe after a few thousand or million, the designs replicate themselves. God only knows."

"Exactly. Like a *Snow god.*" Just saying it aloud made her feel like a martyr, unwilling to recant even under the torture of his scorn. She felt her face flush. He watched her for a moment, and then he said, "Sometimes I think you're weirder than Vina, with all her goddess shit."

But a few days later he had handed her a sketch. It was done thoughtfully, in ink and watercolor, like some of the ones piled on his worktable. At first glance it looked like a typical crucifixion scene: a Jesus-like figure in a loin cloth, arms extended, except that there was no cross or blood. Instead, there was a fountain of snow coming out of a hole in each upturned palm. The Jesus-guy was nicely built and had long, blond hair. He was looking down, watching the snow fall to the earth, which was depicted as a globe far below. *Jennie's Snow-god*, he had scrawled underneath.

"He looks like you," she told him when she saw it.

"Yeah. A self-portrait." He looked annoyed. He looked like he wanted to grab it back and shred it. "Throw it out if you don't like it."

"I do like it. I love it. Thanks." She did too. She liked the way he had drawn the Snow god's face. The expression was neither judgmental nor ethereal—rather, he seemed forlorn—like a god who had been passed over for more important deities like Zeus or Allah and was hoping to be rediscovered. It was the only piece of his art she had. She couldn't afford his real work. It was also the closest thing to a gift he had ever given her.

Later she had shown it to Vina.

"Ridiculous," Vina said, studying it. "It's absurd. Trust me, it's a piece of shit. God, he must have been wasted when he did this." Jennifer had rolled it up and stuck it in a closet after that. Vina knew more about art than she did, especially Jeb's art, since she sold it.

She turned on the light, intending to retire, when someone outside knocked. It was Vina. They stared at each other for a moment, without smiling.

Vina exhaled a puff of smoke into the cold air.

"Got any more of that?" she said, pointing to Jennifer's glass.

"Sure. It you put out the butt."

Possibly it would be better with Vina here. At least she wasn't going to stay with him all night.

"I'm kinda glad you came by. I was getting into a weird funk."

They sat sipping, watching the snow, and Vina kept her mouth shut for a while, but Jennifer knew she'd loosen up after a few glasses. They would ease into familiar territory, talking about Jeb, and it would soothe them, and Jennifer would feel like they were almost friends, like there wasn't actually a strong, mutual distrust between them. She knew that they would go their separate ways after Jeb was gone, but in the meantime his life, precarious as it was, kept their lives fused.

II

*R*eumah survives by remembering.

Crouched by the side of the road, she closes her eyes to focus inwardly on her collection: shining moments of unadulterated joy, dark moments of searing pain; each one fragile as an eggshell. She chooses this or that one, and spends her hours contemplating its meaning, like a merchant mesmerized by an exquisite pearl.

This one took place on the last day of her cousin Sarai's wedding feast. She remembers the guests gathering in the shadowed courtyard, the lamps being lit, and the musicians picking up their instruments. Moments later her aunt appeared, giddy with wine and excitement, and waved the bloodied cloth overhead, with a shout that was something between triumph and grief. Some of the grandmothers dabbed their eyes, and the older men swayed slightly, befitting the emotion of the moment. Her mother had looked at her from the across the terrace, where the older mothers were sitting, as if to say, "Hurry, Reumah! I want my turn!"

She pretended not to see, and turned her full attention to the musicians, who had started playing the nuptial songs. "Not yet, my mother," she whispered to no one but herself. "I want to dance at many more weddings before my own."

She looked to where the men were seated, and saw her father's eyes on her. They exchanged smiles. "My lamb," he would say, if he was next to her. She was his only daughter, and his youngest child, after two sons. Already there had been a proposal for her hand—she and her mother had watched from behind the curtain while her father shook his head at the visitors.

"Simeon, my friend…she's still a girl at her mother's side…she is not ready to be a wife." Her mother had scowled and gone back to her cooking pots.

She began to sway, and the other girls joined her. Soon the musicians' hands blurred across the strings, and the drummer's head was thrown back, his eyes closed. Reumah became oblivious to everything but the pulse of his instrument. The undulating ring of daughters widened, the music increased in pace and intensity, and the men ceased their wrangling and murmuring—the dancing girls could no longer be ignored.

Reumah had always been beautiful. When she was a girl, her aunts and grandmothers had clucked and fussed over her, and her mother had constantly chided and coaxed her toward modesty, as if her beauty was a flaw to be concealed. In mixed company, her brothers stood near her, sullen and protective, while their friends tried not to stare at her dark eyes, the glistening hair that fell straight to her waist, the tilt of her throat when she laughed.

"She's a vibrant bloom amid pale lilies," her father had told her mother once, after a wedding feast, speaking loudly enough for Reumah to hear.

"Don't speak in such a way, husband. You will make her vain, and then what good will she be to any man?"

She was in her fourteenth year when Sarai had married, and she knew that more than a few pairs of admiring eyes were on her. The ring of dancers broke apart as the musicians began a new song, and she found herself in the center of the group. The tempo took possession of the crowd, and soon the courtyard vibrated with stamping feet and clapping hands. She spun and twirled, sensing waves of envy and admiration surge toward her from the guests. Even the older women had risen to watch. Her bracelets flashed lamplight onto their faces and her veil and hair lifted like wings. Glibly she imagined them almost worshipping her. She had drawn the attention of all; they would not forget the daughter of Rabbi Nicodemus. When the bride and groom were announced, she ran over to her father, and she took his arm to steady herself.

"Father," she said, trying to get her breath, "Father, why do the old people cry when the nuptial cloth is presented?"

A servant passed with a flask and her father refilled his cup. "To you, my beautiful one," he said, taking a gulp. "May you marry well, and have many sons!"

Reumah laughed.

"I'm in no hurry to leave your house, Father, as you well know. But please…tell me the answer…"

He did not answer quickly, but she was used to that. She fixed her eyes on the bride's jewelry and waited for him to speak.

"They cry…because they are old, Reumah…and they have yet to behold the messiah. Think about it. When the cloth is presented…it means another virgin of Israel has become a wife…and perhaps the mother of the Anointed One, which should be the hope of every God-fearing bride when she marries…They cry because they long to see it…but perhaps you are too young to understand…"

She had stopped listening, because she was staring back at a young man who had fixed his dark eyes on her. He was smiling slightly at her; she could see the white glint of his teeth. He whispered something to a companion, and then they were engulfed by the bridal party. His gaze had left her with a shaky, quivery sensation that she could not name. It was as if a small creature inside her had been awakened. In terms of male beauty, he was her peer; one could have mistaken them for twins.

"Father," she said, grabbing his sleeve, "Father…who is that dark young man…the one by the groom? Do you see him? The one who is now laughing? Do you know who that is?"

Her father squinted in the lamplight, and his mouth parted slightly.

"Ah, yes…I see him now…that young man…his father is a scribe, and the elder brother is likewise, in training. But he, I understand, is a disappointment. He works as a money-changer in the court of the Gentiles. I imagine he finds that a more lucrative business." He did not attempt to mask the sarcasm in his voice.

"But his name, Father? Do you know his name?"

"A moment, and it will come to me. Yes. His father is Simon. His brother is Zerah. He is…Judah. Or perhaps Judas."

Judas. She felt disappointed that such a striking young man should have a common name. But as is the nature of names, it would take on the persona of the one who held it. It was a small white dot on the horizon of her mind that would become more luminous with time, until its sharp, bright point would penetrate her soul and continue its orbit, leaving a hundred unanswered questions in its wake.

"Hey, girlie…are you sleeping?"

A rough voice startles her, and the edge of a sandal nudges her leg. The golden hours of the past break apart and the pieces drift back to the hazy edges of her mind. She opens her eyes, and out of habit, looks first at his feet. They are crusted with sand and smell of dung. Slowly she stands up, fighting the dizziness that has plagued her of late, and avoids looking at his eyes.

He comes to her regularly—a small-minded, idle man. She recognizes the way he holds his hand over the part of his cloak that covers his money pouch. A tax collector. Most of them are.

Moments later he is grunting and heaving above her, and she can smell stale food in his beard. The familiar loathing, the acrid bile of hatred rises in her throat until she has to bite her lip to keep from screaming. She longs to press her fingernails into his eyes, into all of their eyes, until they are blinded with pain. She wants to kill them all, and then surrender to the God of heaven who has punished her with such a life for the sins of her youth.

But not yet. Not as long as she has one drop of hope, as real as her father's last and most costly gift to her—an alabaster vial of spikenard. Like her defining memories, she holds it sacred, her one valuable earthly possession; its purity transcending the black hours of her daily existence. He had given it to her secretly, as a provision after her divorce. It is well worth a year's wages, but she has never broken the seal, nor can she contemplate the thought of selling it. She will take it to her grave. It's all she has of him, the sole vestige of his love, and in her heart it bears the hope of his forgiveness.

3

Sometimes Jennifer wonders what her mother would have thought of Vina. Probably she would have warned her not to spend too much time with her—a divorced woman was always suspect, especially with a name like *Vina*. Her mother's name was Phyllis and her friends had names like Bea and Ruthie and Gloria, and they were married to men named George or Russell or Ed. "Vina?" her mother would have said. "Never heard of that. Is it foreign?"

There is nothing about Vina that would have put her mother's suspicions to rest, and Jennifer thinks this may have been why she was drawn to Vina, without really wanting to be. Vina is moody and enigmatic, and Jeb's disciples are intimidated by her. She's slender and tidy, and she wears her glistening dark hair in a perfectly shaped bob that is impeccably trimmed every eight weeks without fail. Her nails are perpetually manicured, and Jennifer has never seen her without makeup.

She knows very little of Vina's past, except that she had kicked her husband out the day after Kevin's second birthday because of his repeated infidelities. The balloons were still up. "*There was this piñata, it was bright yellow, a giraffe. It was hanging by its ass from the ceiling fan. The neck had been bashed off, and you could see the paper mache coming out, like guts. I sat on the couch and drank Jack Daniels and stared at that thing until I thought I'd pass out. It wasn't so much the affairs he was having. I had had a few dalliances myself. It was that he just couldn't handle me. I was too smart for him or something. I think he was afraid of me. In the morning I told Kevin, "'You see that giraffe? That's me and Daddy. We broke apart last night.'"*

Vina had sold her house, and opened *Vamporia*, in Red Bank. It smelled of incense—jasmine or eucalyptus or some other exotic scent that Jennifer couldn't identify. It was a small place, dim and crowded with an eclectic array of housewares and accessories: jungle-print bar stools and ceramic tiles with Aztec designs or French words scrawled on them, a couple of chunky chandeliers that, to Jennifer, looked like something a kid in junior high would assemble for a science fair project. There were masses of peacock feathers, like small trees, gallantly displayed in vases of cobalt and amber, and resin floral sculptures featuring large, distended petals which, even to Jennifer's untrained eye, surely fell under the category of "lesbian art." In the middle of the sales floor was an antique bidet piled with silk cushions in garish colors—orange, chartreuse, fuchsia, and violet.

Jennifer had been lured into Vina's shop in the same way that she had been lured into all the other small shops in all the other quaint tourist towns of the Jersey Shore. Regardless of the wares in each window—French-milled soaps or antique dolls or Battenberg doilies or scented candles—all were irresistible to her, and the ordered beauty of each window display created a longing inside her that was difficult to name. Inevitably she would find herself drawn in, as if she were addicted to an unknown substance that permeated the atmosphere of each tiny seashore boutique. *Vamporia* was a high-end boutique, which both titillated and intimidated her, and Vina had seemed sophisticated and arty—two qualities that Jennifer felt were especially lacking in herself. She had emerged, a half hour later, carrying a shiny red shopping bag containing a lime-colored silk pillow, a small bottle of scented oil called "Nard," Vina's business card, and an invitation to a "compelling" and "pivotal" art show, featuring a local artist from the Jersey Shore. She was forty-five dollars poorer, but nevertheless much refreshed and stimulated. Predictably, the pillow looked better in *Vamporia* than on her futon, but Vina had seemed to like her, and when she learned that Jennifer lived in the Grove, had also invited her to the party on Heck Avenue, so it was worth it. If she had never met Vina, she would have never met Jeb, and the best part of her life, she always believed, began and would end with Jeb.

"So," Vina says. Her glass is empty and she looks around for a place to set it. Jennifer flushes. She can always rely on her apartment to look its cluttered worst on the rare occasions when Vina drops by. There is a coffee stain on the lime pillow. She hopes Vina won't notice.

"So," she says again, setting her glass down on an end table that contains some of the numerous snow globes Jennifer has collected over the years. Vina glances at them and then quickly looks away, as if she is determined not to notice things that will offend her artistic sensibility. "How much longer, you figure?" All their conversations now revolved around Jeb.

"I don't know when he stopped taking his pills. At Christmas I would have given him about a month. Here it is, February."

"His time has not yet come." She takes a long, shaky breath, as if needing a cigarette. "I believe he will come back."

"Excuse me?"

Vina looks back out at the snow. "I've been thinking of him coming back—you know—as something else. Like, an eagle or a German shepherd. At first I wouldn't know it was him. But after a while I'd know, somehow. I would just know."

Her hands are still. Usually they splay out elegantly, waving around while she talks. "Nail-speak," Jeb had called it, his term for how women gestured when they had nails to be displayed. He had, on occasion, behind her back, aped Vina doing it, which had remained a private joke between himself and Jennifer.

"You mean like reincarnation?" Jennifer suppresses an urge to snicker.

"Precisely." She toys with her bracelets for a moment, and then looks at Jennifer, "What do you think will happen to him?"

Jennifer is convinced that there has to be some kind of god up there, some kind of Nature god. In kindergarten she had first wondered, fingering the green shoots that had sprung from the lima beans she had planted only days before, in a Styrofoam cup. Later, gazing at photographs of snow crystals in third grade she became certain of the Snow god. In ninth grade she had been astounded at the complexity of a single plant cell under the microscope. On different occasions she had tried to imagine a Nature goddess, or some kind of primeval, multibreasted Mother Earth goddess, but she always came back to the Snow god, and she persisted in thinking of him just as Jeb had drawn him: a celestial hippie-Jesus that looked exactly like Jeb. In her mind, he peacefully hovered over the planet without a cross, and snow instead of blood swooshed from his palms.

There must be thousands of gods like mine, Jennifer had, on occasion, reasoned to herself. *One religion was basically the same as any other. Try hard. Worship something good and be a good person, whatever that means to you. Hope that your good deeds outweigh your bad ones on some cosmic scale.* She held a strong conviction that one's faith should be a private affair. She cleared her throat.

"I think the main thing is...what does Jeb believe? I mean...he's never talked that much about his personal beliefs...what he thinks about...you know..." and as soon as she had said it she saw them suddenly, like the movies that kept playing in her head, sitting at a table in the *Pink Lincoln*, eating seven-layer nachos and imbibing their second round of margaritas. Vina was particularly animated. Her cheeks were flushed and she was coming back to earth after a weekend retreat with some touring guru who was from Sri Lanka. "He named us," she was telling them. "*It was so spiritual. He went around to each one of us, and put his hands on our heads, and gave each one of us a name.*" She paused, as if for dramatic effect, and then continued. "*It all has to do with our divine roles, which was the whole point of the retreat.*" She pulled some peach-tinted papers from a folder, and pushed them across the table. Jeb nudged Jennifer's leg under the table as she read the title. "*Your Cosmic Space: Discovering your Divine Role on Earth.*"

"'*Yer cosmic space, huh?*'" She intuitively knew that the phrase had already taken on a crude rendering in his mind, but to his credit he resisted. "*Well, well. So whatdy'he name you?*" Jeb asked, *not impolitely.*

Vina started, as if surprised by the question. "*Well, it's not that simple. I mean, it's a sacred thing...he's a divine agent, and he's...he's...defining you. He's like, an avatar, like Joan of Arc or Shirley MacLaine.*"

Jennifer feigned sudden interest in the dessert menu. "*In other words, you can't tell us. Well, that's OK. We have that kind of stuff in* the Catholic Church too. Confession and all that. It's all confidential. Between a priest and a...a..."

"'Lay person?' Isn't that what you call it?" His eyes were widely innocent, but Jennifer could read him. They shared a compendium of private, off-color jokes. She nudged him under the table.

Vina sighed a long, motherish sigh.

"You guys don't get it. You're comparing my experience to conventional religion. Hey, I grew up Catholic. Nothing but rules and edicts and guilt. Do this, do that, pray the rosary and your sins will be forgiven and all that shit." She rolled her eyes and took a long sip of her frothy pink drink. "No, this is new. This is real, it's powerful. Hell, I felt something, I swear to God. Or whoever." She took another sip. "You make your own rules, and your god lives in here, and your god lets you do whatever you need to do to create your own destiny." She patted a spot directly over her stomach to indicate the current residence of her god. Jennifer quickly looked down to keep herself from looking at Jeb. She knew if she did she would never stop laughing. She excused herself to go pee.

"Nothing. He thinks nothing happens. Dust to dust, that's it. His soul will live on in his art. Case closed." She fingers her bracelets, and then suddenly laughs. "Although once...when he was blasting the Rolling Stones...once he said he believed in Lucifer...like *he's* someone we should pay more attention to, have some sympathy for." She pauses, and then when Jennifer doesn't speak, she continues. "I personally find that intriguing...that's definitely an idea I am pursuing...I mean, with regard to the funeral and such."

Jennifer says nothing. She feels as if Vina sometimes functions on a higher plain, and she feels incapable of responding, especially about his funeral. Vina had told her once that the bond she had with Jeb went beyond lovers, or marriage, or friends, or family ties. "It's spiritual..." she had said. "We're soul mates."

"I believe in the god within us," says Vina, as if she has read Jennifer's mind. "I believe in what binds us to each other, all that is, the good and the evil, it's all divine. That's our religion—mine and Jeb's. All those who believe in us are with us." She pauses, as if waiting for Jennifer to sign up or convert or indicate that she was getting it.

"I'm not sure what I believe in. I don't pray to Jesus or the saints or the Virgin Mary." She feels a pang of guilt when she thinks of the Snow god. She could never say it aloud though. She had told Jeb, and he had mocked her. But then he had given her the sketch, so in a way, she had a spiritual connection with him too. But she would never tell Vina.

Vina's eyes become narrow, like she is studying her. Again, Jennifer has the suspicion that Vina can almost read her mind. Vina is spiritual. She has some kind of mystical knowledge that no one can debate, but her religion, whatever it is, seems dark and sinister, and Jennifer cannot accept that Jeb has any part in it. She feels sure he would never stop laughing if he could hear this now.

"Listen. Listen to me, Jennifer. You don't need to *pray* to the Virgin Mary. You become her. Or Venus or Kali or Asherah or Sophia; take your pick. You gradually embody her power and authority. Everything else you've been taught is a lie. The priests and the nuns and the pope and all the fucking TV preachers with their white suits want to keep you in the dark, keep you from knowing, from having the power and wisdom you could have…"

Jennifer stares deeply into the snow. To be polite she tries to make it look like she is pondering Vina's instructions, but her brain instead produces the image of Jeb, stretched out on her futon and grinning at her behind Vina's back. She shrugs her shoulders and tries to keep from smiling.

Vina sits back and gives a tired little wave, as if she has uttered a prophetic revelation, and the effort has been wasted on a blind and unbelieving pagan.

After a few minutes, she stands, as if to go, sways a bit, and then sits down again. "Listen, I need a favor."

Instantly the shield inside Jennifer goes up. Change his meds. Get some doctor to write a prescription, stronger stuff. He needs a bath, do you think you can…

"…babysit Kevin?" she is asking.

"Kevin? I—uh—I guess so. Why?"

"I want to stay with Jeb…you know…just in case. Just for the weekend. I'll come get Kevin in the morning."

"What about his dad?"

"It's not his weekend." She gets a look, then, like her skin has suddenly become brittle. "Hey, if it's too much to ask..." she stands again, to go.

"Oh, God, of course not. It's fine. Really."

She feels exhausted, like a huge hand is pressing down on top of her head, like she is dying too. Along the way, she had fused her spirit or her soul or some other huge part of her identity to Jeb. Vina perceives it. At the moment of his death, some part of her would be dead too. She would become as hollow and fragile as a painted egg.

IV

bba. Abba!

Reumah wakes to the sound of her own voice. A full moon beams through the latticework of her one small window, making a pattern of stripes and crosses on the dirt floor. For a moment she forgets where she is.

They had been in a fishing boat, on the Sea of Galilee, headed toward Magdala to visit some relatives there. She was only nine or ten years at the time, but she could still remember how suddenly the storm had come upon them, and her mounting fear at the sight of the white-foamed waves spilling over the sides of the boat, as if they contained an evil force, intent on her destruction. She had screamed for him, but the sound was whipped away by the wind before it could reach him. In her panic she had stood in the heaving boat, lurching toward him, and then felt herself slamming into an empty oarlock, with the iron taste of blood in her mouth.

Sometime later, when the darkness had cleared, she found herself in his arms on the rocky shore. She gazed at the sky, which was a beguiling blend of gentle blues and pinks, and the sea, which glimmered calmly in the setting sun.

"Abba, my head is hurting. What happened?"

"A storm, my lamb. It came up suddenly. Even experienced fishermen have been known to drown in them. It is the nature of this sea." He spoke slowly, as if doubtful of what had really happened. "We are survivors, Reumah! You and I. Even the fishermen are thanking the Master of the Universe for delivering us."

He did not customarily display affection toward her in public, as it was considered improper for men of his standing, yet he continued to hold her for some time, apparently forgetting the purpose of their trip. The weight of his arms around her, the feel of his beard against her forehead, scratchy, like goats' hair, the sea arrayed in sky-colors before them had filled her with a joy and a relief that caused her to sob. It was as if a carefully constructed aqueduct somewhere inside her head had unaccountably burst, and she could not contain it.

"Save your tears, Reumah. We are both alive." But he said it gently. She shifted in his arms, and put hers around his neck.

"I will always love you, my abba. No matter what I do in this life. I will love you to the day I die."

She turns to her side to keep her tears from running into her ears. Her head is heavy with fever, and there is a throbbing ache somewhere below her ribs. *The sentence of death is on me,* she thinks. The final punishment for her sins. Lying. Adultery. Breaking the Sabbath. On the Day of Atonement she had eaten twice before remembering—she, who had once marked the days on the wall of their house, with her father smiling his approval.

Master of the Universe...I am scum to you. Send me your worst. A short, painless death would be too kind. I should starve. I should rot. She says it into her head roll, but feels sure he can hear her. She imagines his spirit hovering somewhere near the earth, perhaps deep in the temple's holiest place.

The moon rises with the hour, illuminating her sparse room. Gradually she becomes conscious of a smell, like rotting fish. Rising on her elbow, she sees the pot containing her blood-soaked rags. In her weakness she has not been able to wash or go for water.

Menstruous rags, so says the prophet, is our righteousness before the Holy One of Israel. She remembers her father's sonorous voice echoing in the synagogue, and women and girls next to her, behind the curtains, clucking their tongues that a man should speak of such things in public. Her mother had not spoken to him for a week.

Bloody rags. They had marked almost her entire life, dividing the months, and widening the chasm between her bright girlhood and her present darkness.

There had been no blood on her first day as Zerah's wife. She had opened her eyes to see her mother's face, puffy from lack of sleep. Dim streaks of light appeared on the walls behind her.

"Reumah. The cloth. Let me have the cloth." The words came in a raspy whisper. She squinted, sleepy-eyed, at her mother, not comprehending. Zerah slept heavily beside her, exhausted from the wedding festivities.

Her mother persisted. "The cloth, Reumah! I must have the nuptial cloth."

A cold fear enveloped her as the implication of her mother's request took form. She had not thought of it before. Her longing for Judas, and the pain of his betrayal, had made the weeks leading up to her wedding a blur. It had not occurred to her to worry about a few spots of blood.

Her mother sighed angrily. "Reumah, wake up! Don't you know what day it is? I must have the cloth!"

She rose slowly, without answering. The fear had settled in her bowels, and she had an urgent need to relieve herself. When she returned to the bed, her mother faced her, with something close to panic in her eyes. She was holding the white linen cloth. It was wrinkled, but unspotted.

"Daughter. I want the truth. Was the marriage consummated?"

It had been. Briefly the image of Zerah dutifully mounting her, half-asleep and smelling of wine and roasted meat, drifted across her mind. It made her want to laugh uncontrollably, or else scream.

Instead she said calmly, "Of course, Mother. What do you think?"

The sound of her mother's hand smacked hard against Reumah's cheek caused both of them to look over at Zerah, but he did not stir.

Her mother took a step closer. "I'll tell you what I think. I think you could not save all that beauty for one worthy man. Spiteful, shameless girl! Depriving your husband of his lawful privilege, and your mother of her moment of joy and pride." She caught hold of the ends of Reumah's hair and twisted them around her wrist, bringing her face within inches of her own. "I will have my moment of triumph, Reumah, even if I have to cut my own flesh to put blood on that cloth. You should thank me. I have saved you from shame and even death!"

She did not fear her mother's wrath. It was a fitting conclusion to what her life had been as her daughter.

What she feared was her father's displeasure, which her mother knew well. At the door of the bridal chamber she turned back to Reumah, and pointed to her, still clutching the incriminating cloth.

"Your father will know what a fool he was to call you his little lamb."

"Reumah, are you happy?"

They were standing on the roof of her new home. Below they could hear Zerah's loud laughter above the other men's voices. Judas had not come, although he had been invited. Her first banquet had gone well: she had managed the two servant girls, the young goat had been roasted well, and her loaves had been fragrant. Domesticity had settled on her like a heavy mist. Zerah was jubilant. He felt the envy of his unmarried friends, and the pride of his relatives. His wife was beautiful, submissive, and she could cook. He had married well.

She had come up to the roof, weary from her toils in the kitchen, with a single oil lamp, which had been quickly extinguished by the evening wind. In a moment he had come up behind her, the tread of his sandals so familiar she was not the least bit startled by his voice.

"I am—" what word to use? Restless? Bored? How could she tell him of her nameless longing—he, who had painstakingly made all the arrangements of her life to ensure her greatest happiness?

"I am content, Father." She managed to smile, hoping he would see it in the dim moonlight and be satisfied.

He gazed outward at the nearby houses, gray-white in the moonlight. "Forgive me, daughter, but there is a matter that weighs heavily on my heart. You are pale, and there is no spark of joy in your eyes, as should be in the eyes of every new bride." He sighed heavily, reluctant to continue. A feeling of dread rose within her. She found it hard to breathe.

"Reumah." He turned to face her. "Is it true what your mother tells me?"

She said nothing, so he went on. "I do not wish to speak of such things, but a father's blessing on his daughter's marriage is essential to its happiness and success. It is like the blessing of God. Therefore I urge you, my daughter, to tell me the truth."

The truth was a perpetual ache inside her. She longed to pour it out, like dirty water onto the dust, and have her father's forgiveness. But would he? Already his low voice was changing into the authoritative rabbi's voice she knew so well from the synagogue. No—she could not chance the withdrawal of his nuptial blessing, or worse, the sting of his rebuke. He was her beloved father, but he was also a teacher of the Law.

"Reumah—I will be blunt. Your mother spoke to me of pouring wine on the nuptial cloth in order to save our house from shame. Of course I did not believe her at first...I know she has a tendency to... exaggerate your faults. But...after seeing you tonight...her words are haunting me." He faced her. His eyes strained in the darkness to read hers, which were cast downward.

She could not make any words come. She would take her secret to the grave. But she could not keep herself from trembling.

After a long pause, he sighed deeply, as if under a great strain. "Reumah, my daughter. Please tell me the truth. Was it Zerah? Could he not restrain himself until the wedding night? Please tell me it was Zerah. Already you are stabbing my heart."

She began to sob softly, hoping he would accept her tears as an answer, as well as an indication of her remorse.

It worked. He drew her close. The smell of his clothes and the shelter of his arms made her want to leave her life with Zerah immediately and go back to his house. But it was not possible. Marriage was a sacred duty. He had taught her that from her girlhood.

"Never mind, my lamb. Such things happen. As beautiful a garden as you are—I cannot blame him for not being able to wait to...browse among the lilies...like King Solomon and his Shulamite..." He smiled at her. "He paid a great price for you, after all. And the betrothal was legally binding."

Afterward she thought, *it wasn't a real lie*. She had not spoken it. She had spared them both the pain of the truth. Her father would believe the best about her; he could not bear to do otherwise.

But wringing out the bloody rags in the wash basin, month after month under her mother-in-law's scrutiny, proved her wrong. The Master of the Universe had set his curse on her.

5

*M*ichael has left a message on her answering machine.

"Hey, lady…they've grounded most of the flights out of Newark because of the snow…I was thinking I'd come by…I'll call you again before I leave the airport. Uh—OK. See ya. I hope. Bye."

She considers. Part of her wants to see him. He is not Jeb of course, nor ever could be. Jeb, she thinks, is a gleaming white unicorn in a herd of horses, but Michael could easily be considered a prize stallion, valued especially for breeding purposes. He could stir her blood a little. She'd shower and put on some makeup. Then she'd tidy up the apartment and change the sheets. That was usually the best part of it—getting ready. He'd show up at her door, still in his uniform and smelling of musky cologne and he'd drop his bags and they'd start making out right there and then end up on her bed, like in a soap opera, making all the appropriate moans and sighs. Then they would go over to *Sal's* or the *Pink Lincoln* to eat, and he'd talk about Phoenix or Atlanta or wherever he had been, carefully leaving out certain details, she was sure, and then they'd go back to her apartment and have sex again. Usually he'd be gone by the next afternoon, but sometimes he's stay for the weekend, and by Sunday night she'd be weary of him, weary of the dance that was their relationship.

She calls Vina to tell her.

"Ah, your pilot friend…I didn't realize he was still in the picture…"

It's none of your goddamn business. Aloud, she says, "Well, I don't mind…I mean, it might be a little weird for Kevin…but I'd do my best to make sure he wasn't uncomfortable in any way…"

"Oh, God, no. Of course not…I'll just have to find someone else… anyway, Jeb's doing a bit better today, so I'm not as worried as I was last night…"

"Really?"

"Yes, really. He seems to have rallied. I even fed him some ice cream."

"Well, that's good to hear." Her jaw tightens, as well as her hand on the receiver. They never, never called her when he was doing well. "OK, so…as far as Kevin…if you're really in a bind…"

"Honey, I'm never in a bind…there's always someone…it's just that Kevin seemed to prefer you. Consider it a compliment."

Jennifer hangs up and throws her wine glass across the kitchen, forgetting that it is a clear plastic goblet suitable for patio entertaining. It does not shatter, but the wine spatters onto the wall and the floor. It looks like someone has been stabbed.

Later, much later, when she can't sleep, she turns to look at Michael, her eyes wide in the semidarkness, wondering what it would be like to have him here for the rest of her life. He is breathing moistly through slightly parted lips, but he's not a snorer, thank God. His hair is still thick and he's nicely built and not excessively hairy and she runs her fingers lightly over his left arm, shoulder, and chest. She feels certain that other women, mostly flight attendants, sleep with him, and undoubtedly find him attractive.

Her mother would have liked Michael, or at least would have liked the uniform and the steady income, with benefits, not to mention the free flights all over the country if they had married. Surely she would have expected Jennifer to have married him by now—they've known each other for almost three years. *What's holding that boy up?* Her mother would say. She would have been surprised to learn that neither of them has ever hinted about it. But then, her mother wouldn't have known about all the little things, the annoying things that she felt were smothering whatever spark of romance or passion had gotten them together in the first place.

His lukewarm showers, for instance. How could you even get clean? The way he checks his stocks in the paper and then acts resentful if I don't seem interested. The way he talks with food in his mouth. The way he always wants to know what I paid for something: a pair of sunglasses, a spare tire, a coffee table. The way he complains about every goddamn thing—the tolls on the parkway and the weather and taxes and prices and movies and TV commercials and airline food. God, I'm so sick of hearing it. The way he pokes his fingers into me like I've got some kind of ignition system—just stick the key in and away we go.

Itemizing his deficiencies causes her to remember a game she and her girlfriends played in junior high. Long past midnight during slumber parties in one or the other's basement, they would verbally assemble the perfect boy, taking a part or two from each of the boys they all knew—Jeremy's wavy hair, Joey's voice—which had already deepened—Tim's blue eyes, Hugh's laugh that you could hear from down the hall. They would take only the best parts, and sometimes she pictured the discarded boys, strewn about a gym or a soccer field, each of them missing something the girls had taken—this one bald, another devoid of speech, still another without eyeballs. Of course one of the smuttier girls would name *those* parts, and usually these were hewn from their gym teacher, Mr. Parelta, because he wore tight shorts, rather vainly. They would all laugh, because they had all been thinking it but no one had wanted to say it. The discarded boys in her brain would laugh too, but more from relief.

She's wide awake now, so she decides to pore over old boyfriends, going back to senior high, to see if any of them had parts worth salvaging. *Mommy liked Steve because he was charming, and had a nice haircut and had taken me to the prom. I liked him too, until I saw him in the mall that time, making out with Monica. Phil was another cutie. That was fun, until he got tired of blowjobs. I wasn't ready to go all the way. After a while he stopped calling. Daryl was the lucky one. He had those sexy eyes. That started out fine. He even said "I love you," in the back of his dad's Nova. I thought I'd marry him! Then I got that foul-smelling discharge. I told Mommy it was period problems, and she believed me, never questioning why I'd need antibiotics. That was the end of that. I tried to be more careful after him. Vince. Oh, God, Mr. Romance himself, until I discovered his "S and M" magazines. God, that was scary. I couldn't get out of there fast enough. Then Richard.*

The only bookish guy I ever had. Met him in the library, like a real college romance. He played the violin, and was teaching himself German. German! He had nice sideburns. We'd smoke a couple of joints, everyone did back then, and then we'd make out. That was weird. He'd get me to come, and then he'd go into the bathroom and jerk off, with the door locked. He claimed that sex was a very private thing for him. Good god! Maybe it was all the Freudian shit he read.

One by one she picks them up, scrutinizes them, and lays them down again, along with all the other discarded boys with their missing parts.

You're It. Above the pile of discarded young men her favorite rises like a phoenix, like a gladiator stepping on the bodies of his vanquished opponents, and stands before her, golden and blond and chiseled, like her old Malibu Ken doll, but with tattoos and much longer, brushable hair. *But you're missing some stuff too. Don't think you're perfect*, she says to him.

Yeah? Like what?

You're...mean. You use people. You have no love in you.

He would laugh and laugh if she ever really said that. He would tell her that people liked to be used, at least by him.

Once, long ago, before he got really sick, he called her on a Saturday morning in late September and asked her to go to the dunes, way down south. Just the two of them. This is it, this is it, she figured. She found it hard to breathe. She made them a lunch and put on her pink bikini with the little gold buckles on the hips, and they drove for an hour, barely talking. She didn't care. All she could think was that she'd be under him, or maybe on top, and he'd be inside her, finally inside her, filling her empty spaces, and then they'd fool around in the waves and maybe sleep for a while, and then do it all again.

But when they got there she noticed he had his sketch pad and graphite pencils and he told her that he wanted to draw her, nude, in the dunes. It took her awhile to get the other pictures out of her head. *You got great tits* was pretty much all he said but she let him sketch her for more than two hours, until he said he was tired, and after that they went swimming, and after that, they ate her lunch, and then...then they were lying on the blanket next to each other, and she thought again, this is it, this is it…he had his face down in his arms and his hair was in a ponytail and she brushed it aside and started kissing his neck.

"Forget it," he said, without lifting his head.

"What? Why d'ya mean?"

"I ain't gonna fuck you. Just forget it."

"Why not?" the taste of the roast beef sub they had eaten rose in her throat.

He looked at her then. "I only fuck for money. Or dope. Or if I need a big favor. You know that."

"Well…let me see what I have…" she was only half-joking, reaching for her purse.

He looked at her again. "Forget it, Jen. You can't afford me. Anyway…nah, just forget it."

"Anyway what? What were you going to say?" A stray cloud appeared from nowhere and eclipsed the sun, making her shiver.

"Nothing. I'm doing you a favor, that's all…you'd be real sorry after."

She had gone down to the waves then, and sobbed until she threw up. She sat there all afternoon while he slept. Her tears and her puke and her fantasies washed away in the surf.

If you weren't dying…if you were totally healed and had your strong body and rock star hair and unforgettable face again, and if you were still funny and creative, but also kind…and protective and loved me and wanted to always take care of me and would never, ever cheat on me…you'd be the perfect man and I would follow you to the ends of the earth and do anything, anything for you and give up everything just to be with you.

She gets up for tissues, and hears Rebecca Peterson moving around down below. She figures it's Rebecca, who seems to require only five hours of sleep. She tries to imagine what she's doing. She pictures herself going down there. What would she say? *I heard you were awake…? Wondered if…if what?*

Rebecca is quiet. She must read a lot, because when they moved in Jen saw that there were piles of books, important ones, not the thick romance novels her mom used to read. She probably thinks a lot. She's mysterious, like a nun. Maybe she prays.

The thought of Rebecca down below, awake and watchful in the night, thinking or reading or praying, is weirdly comforting to Jen, like when she was a kid going to sleep and she could hear her mother in the living room, chuckling over Carson and clinking her spoon against her ice cream bowl. She finally sleeps.

VI

The well is situated outside the village, just beyond two low hills, but it might as well be on the other side of the city. Her body is burning with pain and fever, and the sun is merciless. She always goes at noon; the village women never come out at this time.

A small dog suddenly runs up behind her, barking and snapping at her heels. Panicky, she turns to kick it, and the water jug topples, smashing on the stones of the path. The frightened animal retreats, whimpering.

She wants to lay down right here. They will find her sooner if she's beside the road than if she dies in her bed. She has made preparations: the precious vial, sealed and inscribed with her father's name, is enclosed in a pouch, tied on a thong around her neck. Her legs buckle and she sinks to the ground, the dust filling her nostrils.

No, the well. Get to the well. If she is near the well, someone might give her a drink, out of pity. It might be enough to revive her. Perhaps a compassionate merchant, or a Levite, stopping for water, will discover her, and be able to take word to her father. Perhaps he will come just in time, and take her back home, and she will be restored…

Master of the Universe, have mercy on me…get me to the well. She half crawls, half climbs the two hills, then collapses against the stones of the ancient well. The sun overhead makes only a slim shadow of it, which she curls into, infantlike, and closes her eyes. Her mouth feels swollen from thirst and she can feel her pulse pounding in her ears. Pain shoots from the top of her head down through her neck and back.

Only her lips move. *Master of the Universe...deliver me.* He has done it before.

> "*Make no mistake, I will come for you.*"
> "*What if you can't find me?*"
> "*Stay near Bethlehem...I will find you, never fear.*"

Of course, she had believed him. She had clung to him, in the darkness of the roof with only the stars illuminating their embrace, long after Zerah was asleep, and his words had quenched the fear of her impending trial and divorce.

After Zerah had divorced her, she found work in the kitchen of an inn. The beleaguered innkeeper's wife had hired her out of desperation, not kindness. The gossip had spread, and most surmised her situation knowingly. She was given a small pallet in the corner of the scullery. The day's leftover bread was her sustenance, along with a few pilfered figs when she could get them. She was sure he would come soon, that it would only be a month or so, and then he would come for her. She kept her head down, and spoke only when addressed, but it wasn't long before the innkeeper noticed her. He came to her at night, his features all but hidden in the pale light of the lamp he was carrying.

"I have a room for you upstairs," he whispered.

"I'm content with my place here, sir," she had answered carefully, with a feeling of foreboding rising in her belly.

"Don't be foolish," he answered. "You're young, and very pretty. Why should you hide in here, smelling like garum? Come with me. I can give you better food, clothes, a private chamber, in return for a few small favors."

She felt suddenly cold, though the night was warm. "Your wife hired me...to work in the kitchen...she would not take kindly to—"

"Let me worry about her," he answered harshly. In the lamplight she could see his eyes narrowing. "Listen to me, girl. Make your decision. Either you come upstairs with me, or you find yourself on the streets, at the mercy of beggars and thieves. Which will it be?"

A hostess, he told his wife. The merchants who traveled a long way needed to be refreshed with the sight and company of a pretty girl, and revenues would increase. During the day she was permitted to sleep late and bathe luxuriously. In the evenings she poured out wine for his guests, and brought them bowls of scented water for washing, and almost every night for the first month the innkeeper would come into her small room, bringing her sweets and little presents in an attempt to get her to laugh or smile. Thereafter he tried unsuccessfully to get her drunk, and finally he forced himself on her, within earshot of his wife, who of course, despised her. Soon he hated Reumah too, with the particular hatred of a man who has pleasured himself with a beautiful girl but has failed to win her regard. He grew weary of her, and told her that she would have to service the gentlemen who could afford to pay. In a moment of clarity she understood why her father had given her the vial of costly perfume. A dream of his face tormented her, and she felt sure that she would go mad with grief and self-loathing until she heard a voice that must have come from inside her head, but it was so alluring and commanding that she had turned, as if someone next to her had spoken.

Hate them. Just hate them…hatred will sustain you. And this she did. She would smile with cold civility, if at all, but inside she would scorn their naked, tumorous parts, their vacuous eyes, their pathetic, insatiable need for her flesh. She imagined herself opening like a snare, trapping their seed—the essence of their manhood—leaving them maimed and inert, like lepers. She despised them.

Not long afterward her cousin Sarai had come to her at the inn, carefully veiled and avoiding Reumah's eyes. "Your father wishes you to leave this town at once. He asks that you respect your family's good name, and not bring further dishonor on him."

So he knew. *Abba, don't be angry. I couldn't sell your vial, your last gift to me.* She would obey him. She would die in the street before bringing more shame on him.

At dusk she had crept out, intending to go to Bethany or even farther into Galilee. A centurion riding in a chariot had slowed his horse, curious at the sight of her.

With an undisguised leer, he told her to crouch down by his legs. She put her small bundle next to her, and held on as best as she could. Minutes later the inn and then the town and all that was familiar disappeared. She felt no fear. Her head felt hollow, devoid of any thought save her father's request. He had spoken of her, at least. He had known about her, which meant he must have asked about her. Obeying him, even at the risk of her life, gave her more peace than she had felt in all the weeks of waiting for Judas. The thought of Judas was a sharp pain, and she could only hope that whatever had detained him from coming to her was legitimate. She had heard a rumor that he had left his father's house to become a disciple of a young rabbi who had the gift of healing, but she felt sure they had mistaken him for someone else.

She kept her eyes on the hairy legs of the centurion, which were next to her face, and listened to the steady hoofbeats up ahead. She would start over again, where no one knew anything about her. Whatever her father might hear of her in the future would be good.

The sun had completely set when the driver pulled his horse to a halt. They were in a marketplace. Two men, a father and a son, were shuttering their small shop.

The centurion approached them. "Your lives for this horse," he told them curtly.

"But, sir—we were just about to leave for the night—"

"Do as you're told!" he cracked his whip at them. "And see that it gets some water."

She had known there would be a payment due, for his service. *This will be the last time.* He shoved her toward a darkened, narrow alleyway. "On your knees," he said, and pushed her down by her shoulders.

She tried to spread her cloak, but he suddenly grabbed her by the hair. "I haven't got all night, woman."

"Sir, the ground is cold...if you will just allow me to spread my cloak..."

"Stupid girl. You think I'm going to put my cock into the cunt of a Jewish whore? It's a cesspool." He loosened his belt.

Now she understood what he was asking. She had done it before—and hated it. "Please, sir—I beg of you—" She stared up at him in the darkness, feeling the stones cut into her knees.

"What are you, a mule?" He thrust the hilt of his sword against her lip. She felt it split, and tasted blood. He grabbed her head with one hand, and held her hair with the other. "Open your mouth—wide—or do I have to cut it open?"

His stream of urine hit her full in the mouth, and then her face. She could hear him laughing as she gagged and retched, until black tears from her kohl-rimmed eyes had coursed down her cheeks and onto her tunic, leaving small, dark spots. She collapsed, sobbing onto her cloak and heard him say, "A latrine—that's all you whores are good for..." before he moved on. An hour later, even after she had drank deeply from the village well, she kept gagging, and an acid taste filled her throat and her nostrils. Eventually she had fallen asleep, sobbing and shaking, not caring if she lived until morning. In the middle of the night someone dropped a cloak over her. At daybreak, a woman came to reclaim it.

"My father took pity on you," was all she said. "You may have a room at our inn if you are quiet, and tidy, and can do some cleaning and cooking. You will have to bake your own bread, and fetch your own water." She did not ask her for her father's name, or if she had a husband.

"May the Lord bless you—and your father—for your kindness," Reumah had answered, bowing her head low to the ground, not knowing what else to say. Then she stood up as quickly as her stiff limbs and back would allow, and helped the young woman fill her water pots. As they were carrying them back to the inn, the sun edged over the horizon, bathing the whitewashed town of Bethany in pale rose and ochre. The Master of the Universe had spared her life.

"Simon. Let's give this woman a drink."

Startled, Reumah opens her eyes, and sees a pair of dust-coated feet in worn sandals. One of his toenails is missing.

She tries to sit up, but is overcome with dizziness. Suddenly a man is so close to her she can smell him—a mixture of sweat and grass, like someone who has slept in the fields. A shepherd, perhaps. He lifts her to a sitting position—how strange to feel a man's arm around her in such a way in a public place—and places a flask to her mouth. She can't see his eyes. The sun is behind him and his face is hooded. Beyond him there are some others. Even in her delirium she can see that they are embarrassed by his close proximity to her.

Reumah drains the flask, and it is filled again: water from the well, mixed with some wine. She hears her father's voice in her head. *Hagar in the desert...the angel of the Lord showed her a well, and she and Ishmael were saved...such a strange little story...I have long puzzled over it...how unsearchable are his ways...that the Most High should let himself be seen—and named!—by our father Abraham's Egyptian concubine. Now Reumah, were you listening? What was the name—the one Hagar gave to the angel?*

"Lahai Roi."

The men behind him turn to look at her, and she realizes she has said it aloud. Perhaps he is a rabbi. Twice a rabbi had come to her, had paid her to sleep with him, but always after dark, and never with his disciples. Afterward he had wept with guilt, and his remorse touched a nerve inside her with the sharp pang that she was an accomplice to his sin. She told him bluntly not to visit her again.

This one, however, is not dressed like a rabbi, and his men seem too old to be students.

The drink has been restorative. She reaches for the well to steady herself, but to her surprise, he helps her to her feet. "Thank you, sir. You're very kind." She lowers her eyes coyly, and adjusts her veil.

He steps over to where the other men are and takes some things out of a basket. "Go home and eat this," he says, holding out to her a barley loaf and some dried fish.

Reumah stares at him, trying to see his eyes. It must be a joke. They will burst out laughing at her naiveté, she is sure of it. The man will want some degrading payment for showing kindness to her.

But he continues to hold the food out to her, while the others shift impatiently behind him, obviously uncomfortable that he has taken this much notice of a woman like her in broad daylight.

Slowly she takes the food from his hands. For a brief second his fingers touch hers, and she feels her cheeks coloring, as if some intimate secret has passed between them.

"Please, sir...may I ask your name?" she says finally, feeling unsettled, like when the scar of an ugly wound is exposed.

Under the shadow of the cloth, she can see a smile above his beard. "Daughter, you have already spoken it."

He's crazy, she thinks. *This is not a normal man.* She walks away quickly. When she gets to the first hill, she breaks into a run, clutching the vial and the food to her bosom.

The teacher watches her go, and then he turns back to his disciples, scanning each of their faces in the sunlight until he locks eyes with those of Judas. They contemplate each other for a moment, as if each discerns the other's thoughts, and then Judas turns away.

In the dim light of her room she pulls the bread apart gently, as if it had been blessed, still seeing his hands holding it out to her. When the first bite is in her mouth, she stops, suddenly realizing that the fever has left her body. The pain is gone.

7

Late at night, Rebecca works on her storybook. That's what the kids call it, "Mommy's storybook," as opposed to her published novel, which unfortunately has not sold well here in the States, but has done better in Europe, oddly enough, and, when it was translated into French, in places like Morocco, where it is being sold on the black market. The kids are not very aware of Mommy's novel because it predates them, and not even Rachel has read it, although they have agreed that she will be allowed to have her own signed copy on her eighteenth birthday. But the kids like her storybook, and to Rebecca that's more important, because she wants it to be relevant to them. She has a storybook for each of them too.

When she was pregnant with Rachel, someone had given her a baby book that was more like a scrapbook: in addition to all the usual spaces and fill-in-the-blanks for baby's pertinent information, there were pages with small keepsake pockets and colored miniature envelopes and *glue-photo-here* sections to delight any reader but certainly the subject herself in later years. Rebecca was enchanted. She loved the idea of recording the hazy, early years for each child, combined with tangible evidence to support the tale: hospital ID bracelets, deflated Welcome Baby balloons, newspaper clippings, hair-sprayed bits of dried flowers, and birthday candles alongside coordinating photos of cake-smeared toddlers in their highchairs.

It's been difficult, of course, to keep it up, especially with the younger ones, but Rebecca has worked hard to ensure that all five books are full of party photos and potty-training awards and cute drawings as well as sweet, funny, or remarkable quotes that she thought were especially poignant. Each child's book has a page of blessings, written by caring relatives and friends, and all of them have the verse in which Jesus says, *Are not the very hairs of your head numbered?* underneath a lock of baby hair taped securely into the opening pages, except for Nathan, who didn't grow any hair until he was almost three. Besides the conventional biographical data of dates, weights, birthplaces, and so on, Rebecca has written detailed information on how their names were chosen, and specific Scriptures God gave her while she was carrying them, or, in the cases of Beulah (Bee-Bee) and John-Mark, while she was waiting to hear from the adoption agency.

Once, after an especially productive session, she had flopped back onto the bed and said to Clay, "It's like a sacred rite...does that make any sense?"

"I don't know. What do you mean?"

"'We will tell...the next generation...the praiseworthy deeds of our God...' That's what I'm doing, I think. Like the patriarchs of old, handing down the laws and stories through the oral tradition...only I'm making it tangible...I'm putting it in books for them."

"Ah, like memorials. Altars. Bethel and Shiloh and such."

"Yes! Exactly. Reference points."

"Maybe you should make one for yourself."

So it had been Clay's idea. She only works on hers at night though, just in case.

Just in case she hits a roadblock, amid all the cutting and gluing and journaling, and becomes overwhelmed with the pain and beauty of her story, and has to stop and weep and pace and pray and worship and weep some more, mostly happy tears, but still. She has to be alone. Clay would understand, but the kids would think it strange.

She gets up to stop the kettle before it screams, and pours the water over a bag of chamomile tea. She checks on Bee-Bee, and gently pulls her thumb out of her mouth. John-Mark is damp with sweat; she pulls his comforter off and leaves him with just the sheet. In their bed, Clay has fallen asleep with a heavy, hard-cover book on his chest, *Megachurch Megacheats*, which she carefully removes, along with his glasses. She turns the light off.

When she gets back to the table with her tea, she hears the floor creaking upstairs, and listens. Twice she has heard Jennifer crying up there, and she had to stop working because she felt so powerless. The fact that they're both awake, often at the same time, makes her wish she could know her better, but Jennifer remains withdrawn. The few times she's brought something up to her, in a neighborly fashion, Jennifer seemed anxious to have her leave. Polite, but not warm. A sweet enough smile, but in her eyes a look of darkness, like guilt or smothered despair. Rebecca knows, because she's seen it in her own eyes, in her pictures.

She flips her book back to when she was bat mitzvahed. Her parents had never been religious, but they liked the idea, and anyway, lots of people were doing it, it was new. Her grandparents on her father's side said it was ridiculous; they had never heard of girls being bar mitzvahed, but her mother's mother thought it was a lovely idea. Why should the boys have all the fuss? Of course, they told her, it's this or a big sweet sixteen party, make your choice.

She had chosen the bat mitzvah, because, truthfully, she didn't have many friends, and you needed to be popular to have a successful *Sweet*, as they called it. Moreover, she was intrigued by the idea of learning some of the Torah, and the religious aspect of the event held more sway over her than the celebration, but this she kept to herself.

But when she looks at her eyes in the pictures, she sees the darkness that came after she read the Torah, because after she understood some of the law, she understood that she was guilty, and from then on she became obsessed with the concept of Atonement, and fearful as well, because her parents almost never went to synagogue, and would not have understood her questions. When she told them she wanted to go, they rolled their eyes and muttered they should have never had the bat mitzvah, because it had filled her head with archaic notions.

A few pages later, there are pictures of her with her modestly attired swim team at the Jewish Community Center, but these always make her remember a boy who is not in any of the pictures. His name was Ari, and he tutored a younger boy in the same room in which Rebecca did her homework while she was waiting for her mother to come pick her up after swim practice. Ari was sixteen or seventeen. Rebecca thought he was intensely handsome, certainly the most compelling boy she had ever seen. She correctly guessed that he attended the yeshiva, because he did not go to her high school like everyone else she knew. His eyes were deep and black, and he wore a yarmulke and long side curls, which he wound around his pencil while he explained algebra to his young pupil. More than anything else, Rebecca wanted this boy to notice her. In the locker room after practice she would put on lip gloss and brush out her hair, but Ari remained oblivious.

One day she saw some of his friends slap him on the back, like he had done something good, and she overheard that he was going to Israel, to study. The next week she gathered her courage and walked over to him, carrying her books demurely in front of her chest, because she surmised that he would find her more appealing if she looked modest and bookish.

"Excuse me…um…I heard you were going to Israel…"

"Yes?" He looked up at her, without curiosity, and she felt certain that behind his dark eyes his soul possessed sacred truth passed down from ancient rabbis. The young pupil looked up at her as well, his eyes large behind thick glasses.

"I…I envy you…you must be very excited…" She hadn't thought about what she was going to say.

"You wish to go to Israel?"

"Yes. Very much." In truth, she had never thought about it until this moment.

"Well, then. Ask your parents." He shrugged. "We must work now."

The next week he was gone, and Rebecca went into the girls' bathroom and sat on a toilet and cried silently and furiously. She wasn't sure why.

At the dinner table that night she told her parents that she wanted to go to Israel as soon as she had finished high school. "To study?" her mother asked.

"No. To live." Her parents said nothing, only glanced at each other. She saw her father smirk, because he was sure his graduation gift would deter her. He was planning to buy her something that no one else's kid had, except for the Kauffmans' daughter Francine, who had the latest of everything: a car.

There are only three pictures of her on the kibbutz, if you count her ID badge. There was little time for pictures, because everybody worked, very hard, all the time. Avrum, her boyfriend at the kibbutz, had taken the pictures of her, on a rare occasion when they both had the same day off. She's wearing long khaki shorts and a light-blue embroidered blouse from India. Her hair, which had not been cut since she left New York, hung over her left shoulder in a long braid. Her eyes are squinting in the sunlight, but the darkness was there too, because she remembers how it felt. One of the sabras told her that she never smiled; another told her that she was a good worker, which was the highest compliment you were likely to receive. Most of her assigned work was in the large, shaded yard and garden next to the industrial-sized kitchen. They kept hundreds of chickens, and they ate chicken almost every night, and she got sick of chicken within days. After she left Israel she never ate poultry again, although she still loves falafel.

When she wasn't working she went to the reading room, but she grew weary of the mostly political news magazines and books on agrarian economies that dominated the shelves. There was also a large section of feminist books, some literature anthologies that featured writers such as Camus and Sartre and Albee, and some philosophy and psychology textbooks that some students had left years before. All these she perused until she discovered a sparse collection of books on religion. These also turned out to be disappointing: there were two volumes with crispy pages that seemed to be about the Torah and ancient Israel, but they were written in Arabic, and Rebecca's Arabic was not sufficient enough to make sense of them. She asked the reading room attendant if there was anyone available who would be willing to translate some of the text for her. The attendant, a taciturn, heavyset man with a condescending air, told her he would try to locate someone after dinner, and he put the books on a small shelf next to his desk. He went back to his newspaper. Later when she was leaving the room, she glanced at his newspaper. It was in Arabic. When she returned the next day, the dusty books were gone from the shelf, and a different attendant insisted he had no idea what Rebecca was referring to.

The other books in the religious section were bland texts about Judaism and various world religions, but they were more about cultural distinctives, and Rebecca was more interested in what people believed than what they ate or wore.

Only one picture had caught her interest. In a section on Christian extremism, there was a full-page photo of a man who had had himself crucified, sort of, in Jerusalem, in 1969. For about twenty minutes he had allowed himself to be hung up on a large wooden cross with iron hooks digging into his wrists and feet, which were bleeding. There were dozens of people below the propped-up cross. Some of them looked like they were sneering and some of them looked like they were weeping and some of them just stared in a blank, stunned way. The man himself was a bearded, hippie-type, and his face was grayish-white, with blue-tinged lips. You could see the outline of his ribcage, because he was naked except for a pair of frayed, denim cutoffs and a crucifix around his neck. He did not look holy. He looked unwashed and stoned. Rebecca stared at him for a long time. She tried to envision herself at the scene, but she could not imagine what she would do. Or think. When no one was looking, she ripped the page out of the book, folded it, and put it into her back pocket. She never went into the reading room again.

Now she contemplates the photo, carefully mounted in her storybook. This is where she always stops. She has to walk around and pull herself together. There are no pictures for the next part.

There are pictures in her head, but they are hazy. Years ago she would pretend she had dreamt it: two of their friends had gotten engaged, and a group of them went out for drinks, because the kibbutz had a strict no-alcohol policy. She remembers it was warm, and she was wearing a white denim miniskirt, a wine-colored embroidered blouse from India, and large silver hoop earrings, which her mother had sent. Avrum had not liked her outfit. He told her it was too *plebian*. They had argued, and he had not stayed long. She was getting drunk and then she was drunk, because she had had so little experience with alcohol. And then she was in a room that smelled like hash, and the sheets were dirty and crumpled, and her skirt was pushed up around her hips. Two of them had fought over which would go first, but she was sure there were three, one after the other, like she was a urinal. They each put themselves into her and grunted and groaned. She remembers trying to scream and no sound came out. She remembers trying to move, but her limbs felt detached and refused to comply. She remembers feeling wet warmth spread beneath her and she knew she had peed or bled.

An unidentified woman drove her to the gated entrance of the kibbutz the next day, but nothing was the same. Avrum, despite all his talk of an egalitarian utopia, wanted nothing more to do with her. She told the two sabras who were in charge of the single women's dorm, thinking they would help and understand. They told the merakez, and then there were meetings, with her and without her, but in the end, they said there was nothing they could do since she had left the compound and knowingly put herself in danger, and they certainly did not want the police coming in to investigate; it might destroy the unity and trust of the entire community, and she wouldn't want that to happen, would she?

She left not long after that, conscious of a growing hatred and despondency. She hung out in a run-down section of Tel Aviv with a group of artists and musicians who were stoned most of the time. One night she made love with a gleaming, dark-skinned drummer and then afterward found a machete under his bed. She knelt over him, the knife poised, with an unaccountably strong compulsion to slit his throat while he slept. *Thou shall not kill* flitted through her brain, and she went into his bathroom and locked the door and sat on the toilet, trembling, until dawn. Sometimes in the middle of a party she would find a telephone and attempt to call her parents, but they had moved to Boca Raton, and she could never remember the phone number. Once she took LSD and felt demons clawing at her throat. She knew they would kill her. A man with blood dripping from his face and hands appeared, walking toward her, and the demons went away. She didn't drop acid again after that.

On Yom Kippur she rode a bus into Jerusalem with a guy named Thomas who told her that it was "trippy" to get high and then tour the Church of the Holy Sepulcher. She smoked a couple of joints with him and then felt light-headed, because she had previously decided to fast until sundown. They waited over an hour to get inside the large, arched doors, and she felt her body weakening. It occurred to her that the Christian god might be angry at their lack of reverence. Once inside the ancient walls, it was cooler and smelled thickly of incense. *Spikenard*, one of the nuns told her. When they got to the Stone of Unction, she knelt down and wondered what it would be like to be Catholic. She was intrigued by the idea of making a confession.

Feeling increasingly weak and disillusioned, she began to cry quietly, her head resting on her arms on the ancient stone slab. Thomas soon deserted her; tour groups came and went, still she stayed, weeping softly, without knowing why. It was as if the air was permeated with the prayers of thousands of pilgrims from the centuries before her, prayers for mercy and forgiveness and healing, prayers for the living and prayers for the dead, a great spiritual force pressing on her. She could not move. She felt weighted with guilt and anguish, as if years of unatoned-for transgressions that had been committed by her and against her had slowly been lowered onto her frame.

In a moment of clarity she looked up and stared at the mosaic of Jesus, supine and anointed for his burial, and said, not aloud but mentally to him, "Please make atonement for me." And then she blacked out.

When she came to, there were three girls and two guys clustered around her—students from an American seminary, she soon found out—giving her water and a package of smoked almonds. One of them was Clay.

She has left much unwritten, but the part about the Stone of Unction she has written on the page next to some postcards of the church. That mosaic of the anointed Jesus became the inspiration of her novel, but she didn't know it at the time. At the time, she barely knew anything about Jesus, and less of the women who followed him around and loved him and anointed him for his burial, but in due time she found out, and she wrote her thesis about those women, who became like personal friends in her mind, which then served as the basis of her novel. After the church postcards there are photos of her baptism in the Jordan River, surrounded by Clay and her new friends, who are singing. After that she will mount more pictures of herself and Clay, their wedding, of course, which her parents but none of her grandparents attended because she was marrying a *goy,* and then the pictures of all their favorite professors and friends from the seminary.

She looks closely at her eyes in the pictures after the Jesus postcard: gray and serious as ever, but the darkness is gone.

The faint sobs of a woman are heard from above her, and Rebecca stops every thought to listen. Her heart beats faster, and she places her head on her arms over her book.

Yeshua, have mercy on Jennifer too.

She prays the same thing every night.

VIII

*A*s the long shadows of the late afternoon stretch over the court-yard, Reumah sits in her usual place behind the large water pots, drinking a cup of diluted wine and absently eyeing some children who have captured a large locust. Each week the innkeeper, a widower, places a few coins in her hand, and lets her have a pallet in a small room in exchange for some cleaning and laundering duties. The mea-ger income is barely sufficient for her to buy bread and have enough money left over to buy oil for her one small lamp, so sometimes, at dusk, she goes out, heavily veiled and with her eyes rimmed with kohl, and looks deeply into the eyes of the men on their way from the mar-ketplace, until one of them follows her back to her room. The next day she will go and buy some olives and a bit of cheese or salted fish. On rare occasions, when she has been amply rewarded for her services, she will treat herself to a bracelet or a hair ornament.

Go home and eat this.

The way he said it, like her father would, expecting to be obeyed. He must be a teacher, she decides. She wants to see him again. She wants to find out if he is truly a healer, or if it was simply the water and food that revived her. After all, she was weak from hunger and thirst. On the other hand, she had fever and pain that have disap-peared. Perhaps the bread had medicinal qualities. She has heard of such things: conjurers and healers that use herbs and roots to treat sickness. But she has never met anyone who was immediately healed or soothed by them. And the bread itself had not seemed unusual—it was fresh, and filling, and certainly better than the gritty loaves she was used to, but not extraordinary in any way. She wonders if he will teach in the local synagogue, like the temple priests and rabbis that come from the city.

On the other side of the courtyard a woman is lighting lamps and singing with a frail voice that drifts thinly on the breeze. It causes Reumah to momentarily forget the strange teacher, and she strains to hear the song, which sounds like a child's play song, but she can't discern the words. The children stop and listen as well. Levi, a boy of about three years, shows her the captured locust, and grins up at her.

A man must have a son, or he is not a man. Zerah had said it to her defensively, almost apologetically, in the third year of their marriage. They were standing on the roof, watching the children play in the street below. Often she would go up and watch them, not longing to have one, as her mother-in-law suspected, but rather to be one. How she longed to be a singing, dancing girl in the shadows of her father's house again!

He could have said worse things to her: *a cold stone, a dead fish is what you are to me.* She did not love him, and he knew it. In the early months of their marriage he had misjudged her aloofness for modesty and made allowances for it. But he had since grown resentful, and their days at home were full of reproachful silences. Only at feasts and festivals, among his friends and family members, would his spirit temporarily revive. From across a crowded banquet hall or courtyard she would watch him, laughing and talking, with his wine cup held aloft, and she would try to draw out from her heart a drop of affection for him, but it was in vain. Her capacity for warmth and fondness, that which they called "conjugal bliss," had been destroyed in the moment of her surrender to Judas, although she little suspected it at the time. How easily he had pierced her—like a dagger into a honeycomb—and left in her soul an oozing wound that would not heal. Daily she could sense her spirit seeping out of her, like the blood draining from the sacrificial animals she had seen on Passover and the Day of Atonement. *The life of the creature is in the blood*, her father had told her repeatedly, quoting from Leviticus, when she wept over the young lamb or goat. *It is the blood that makes atonement for one's sin.* She did not question the truth of it.

"She is cursed of God. The seed of Zerah falls on barren ground." Her father-in-law's pronouncement had silenced the entire council of the elders. Just beyond the group of men she perceived the nods of agreement from her mother-in-law and some of the other women. But she would not take her eyes off her father. She could see his eyebrows twitching beneath his headdress, and occasionally his whole body would sway, as if he were in pain or prayer. He would not look at her, and had remained silent during the entire debate. When he opened his mouth to speak, it seemed to her that the entire world had stopped to listen.

"We must be careful what we lay at the feet of the Almighty. If the wife of Zerah—" here he paused, again swaying for a moment before continuing. "If the wife of Zerah is truly cursed of God, as her husband and father-in-law believe, then perhaps there is a sin for which she must give account. If the sin is confessed and atonement is made with the acceptable sacrifice, undoubtedly the curse would be lifted, and the blessing of children would follow." His shoulders slumped, as if the speech had exhausted him.

There was some murmuring and headshaking, then the senior elder called for silence. "Our brother speaks wisely. After all, the God of our fathers is one of mercy as well as judgment. Therefore, we must give the wife of Zerah the opportunity to confess and make atonement for her transgression, if that is the case. Wife of Zerah…is there a sin for which you must make atonement?"

Up to that point they had discussed her case as if she were not present, with careful, formal words, no doubt out of deference to her father. Now, they all turned to look at her, all except him.

Abba, my abba—please look at me. Why do you not regard me? Am I not still your daughter?

She lowered her eyes. Only her hands moved in her lap, one rubbing the other, back and forth. Zerah shifted uncomfortably beside her. She knew that he had already set his eyes on Junia, the daughter of one of his cousins, to replace her. Junia was a plump, dark-eyed girl who laughed easily. His growing fondness for her had been especially apparent at the last family wedding. How inconvenient it would be for him if she were now to confess her sin, and make atonement, and have the Almighty open her womb!

But no atonement could be made for her sin, she knew. The punishment for premarital infidelity and adultery was death or divorce, depending on the mercy of the husband.

Please, my abba, please look at me. If you would just look at me... with love in your eyes, I would tell the whole truth, the truth I tried to hide from you...

She looked toward him again, and sensed that he was struggling to avoid her gaze. She saw his shoulders shift slowly, as if he were taking deep breaths. The sight of it gave her boldness.

"Yes." Her voice sounded like a girl's compared to the sonorous tones of the elders. "Yes, there is a sin that has not been cleansed from my soul." She returned her gaze to the ground before her. From the corner of her eye she could see Zerah's hands clenching and unclenching.

There was a rustling and murmuring again, then one low voice clearly spoke above the rest. It was her father's. Her inside parts contracted at the sound of it.

"Wife of Zerah, I charge you—give glory to God, and confess your sin." She looked up, and his eyes were on her, but they were not the eyes of her father. They were the eyes of a judge.

A dark wave of bitterness engulfed her, followed by a moment of clarity. He could have extended to her the compassion of a father or the judgment of an elder. It was impossible for him to do both. He had made his choice, and the entire council had witnessed it.

She could not speak. She could not look at him or any of them. The penalty of death now seemed preferable. Throughout the months of her marriage to Zerah, she had often longed for her girlhood, but never for death. Now everything had changed, because death was preferable to a life without her father's love. Quickly she veiled her face to conceal the hot tears that wet her cheeks.

They judged her silence as rebellion, and after a few minutes of debate, granted Zerah the right to issue her a certificate of divorce. She kept her head down until it was over. When she looked up again, Zerah was gone, and she watched the others walk toward the synagogue, their white headdresses rippling in the hot wind. She knew her father by his gait, which was slow and almost limping. Her eyes followed him until she could see him no more.

They said she could take her clothes, and whatever food she wanted, but none of the jewelry, and of course, not any of the servants. She set a cloth in the middle of her marriage bed, and placed the collection of her bridal jewelry in it, knowing full well that in a short time it would grace the neck, nostrils, forehead, earlobes, wrists, and ankles of Junia. In doing so she felt an unexpected relief, as if the weight of the jewelry itself had been too much for her to bear, and now she was relinquishing her burden to another. As a girl she had longed for the day when she would be adorned with the glittering jewelry of a bride; it occurred to her now that she had never felt particularly attached to any of it.

There was no sign of Zerah or his parents when she left before dawn the next day. The house was deathly silent, and the few servants that were awake regarded her with a mixture of awe and pity before turning away. Clearly they had been instructed not to speak to her. She set out carrying a large basket of food and a bundle of her clothes, deciding after a moment's deliberation to walk toward the marketplace, in the opposite direction of her father's house. Her mind was blank, as if the dark wave of her father's judgment had drowned any emotion that either her past or her future could evoke. She kept her head down, putting one foot in front of the other.

She had not proceeded far when she heard the sound of someone running behind her. She turned, and a man, panting from a hard run, stood before her. After a moment she recognized him as Elias, her father's steward, a man who had been with them since her girlhood.

"I did not think you would leave this early..." He wiped his brow and caught his breath before continuing. "When I stopped at Zerah's house, they said you had already left."

"What is it?" she asked, at the same time noticing that he was carrying a small package. She tried to ignore a seed of hope that had cracked open at the sight of him.

"I was instructed to deliver this to you." He handed her the small package. She saw his face contort momentarily, as if he was endeavoring to remain businesslike, as her father would have expected him to.

She wondered why her father had sent his trusted steward—a man beyond the age of forty—instead of one of the household servants to run after her. Elias seemed to be waiting for an answer from her. He clasped his hands in front of himself, as she had seen him do countless times in her father's presence before receiving instructions.

Reumah studied the package. Elias had known her all her life, yet she was unwilling to open it in front of him, for fear of betraying any emotion. It had a hard, elongated shape that was less than a cubit, and weighed slightly more than a *kab* in her hands.

"Elias…what did he say? What were my father's wishes concerning this package?"

"He said, 'Tell her to be wise…to remember all that I have taught her…and do not neglect the tithe.'"

So. It was money or some valuable to ward off her destitution. She knew she should feel gratitude—in spite of everything that had happened, her father seemed determined to provide for her—yet she felt overcome with disappointment.

"Was there…did he say anything else?" she asked, not without some bitterness.

Elias hesitated, as if unsure how to respond. "He—he did not say anything else…only that I should make haste."

They stood there for another moment, neither looking at the other, neither willing to conclude the conversation. Finally Elias spoke again.

"Reumah…perhaps I should not speak…but I will tell you…your name is always on his lips."

"On his lips? He speaks of me? To whom?"

Why did he not speak my name in the council? Why was my name not on his lips then?

"To God. He sits by the window facing the temple, and he prays, with his shawl over his head. I read his lips…" Elias looked down as if slightly embarrassed at this revelation of her father. "Your name is on his lips."

The image of her father praying toward the temple on her behalf tore at her, and her anger dissolved. She clutched the package tighter.

"Elias. Please thank my father for this provision…" she felt her throat tightening, and she swallowed before continuing. "And please tell him—that I—that I will not forget the words of the Law as he has taught me." She bent down hurriedly, and retied her bundle to accommodate the package.

"I will tell him your words, just as you have spoken them. I—I should go now—he is no doubt wondering why I have not returned." He bowed deferentially to her, even though they both knew he no longer had any obligation to her.

"Good-bye, Reumah."

She watched him until she could no longer see him, and then immediately untied her bundle, annoyed at her lack of restraint. Carefully she removed the package, all the while imagining her father's hands on it. The thought of his handprints on the cloth now mingled with hers overwhelmed her, and by the time she had opened it there were fresh tears on her cheeks.

Inside the wrapping was a vial, made of pure alabaster. There were markings carved onto it that indicated it contained an ointment of spikenard, which had been prepared by a master perfumer—she recognized the name—especially for her father. It was an ointment used in palliative care, and in preparation for burial. *His* burial, she realized with a sharp pang in her stomach that was a mixture of awe and grief.

Once before she had felt the same perplexity: the day he had announced her bride price to Zerah's father, Simon. There had been a collective gasp from the small group of men that had gathered in their house, and her mother had stomped up to the roof and thrown down a pot in her anger.

Simon had fussed and fawned, but her father had refused to negotiate. "Her price is far above rubies..." he had murmured, more than once. In the end, Zerah's determination to have her prevailed over his father's reluctance, and they had agreed.

Only Judas had remained impartial at her father's announcement. There was a disinterested, polite expression on his face, as if he were flattered that her father assumed his family was completely capable of producing the extravagant amount, and he had remained silent, as if he considered the negotiations—one-sided as they were—to be petty, like marketplace wrangling, and himself above them. Instead, he had looked directly over to where she stood, peering from behind the curtain, and smiled at her, fully knowing that she had been watching him. She immediately drew the curtain and felt her cheeks burn.

The memory of that day, together with his costly gift that she was now holding, flooded her with such an intense love for him that she sat by the road for possibly an hour, alternately swaying and crying. Finally she had risen, and continued down the road, away from him, but strengthened by the knowledge of his love, and the hope of his forgiveness.

The sound of a girl singing is suddenly next to her, on the other side of the large water pots. Reumah turns to see who it is, and her eyes widen at the sight of Anna, the ward of the innkeeper, a cousin's daughter or cast-off niece whom Reumah has seen rarely. Anna's face is crooked on one side, her mouth and left cheek are drawn up as if they had been stitched together to her eyelid. The girl limps tortuously, and Reumah had assumed she was a mute, and feebleminded as well, because she has only ever heard faint noises come from her, like the coos of a dove.

She is directly behind the pots now, reaching up to light a lamp. Reumah stands up, transfixed by the sound of Anna's voice.

"Anna! Anna—is that you?" The singing stops, and the girl turns to Reumah. In the pale lamplight they regard each other without speaking.

"Yes—it is I, Anna. Who are you?" her voice is so soft that Reumah strains to hear her.

"I am Reumah. I live here, at your master's inn. Over there, just off the courtyard."

"Oh, yes. I—I have seen you." She glances downward, as if knowing that Reumah, for all her beauty, has a less-honorable occupation than lighting lamps.

Reumah peers at her curiously, aware that the girl doesn't seem to be limping, and surprised at her being able to speak. Something has happened to her.

"I heard you singing…I didn't know you could sing…I mean…What is the meaning of your song?"

Anna puts down her lamp oil and steps over to Reumah in a girlish, springy way. She stands directly in front of her and lowers the veil from her face and head. At the sight of her, Reumah takes a step back, and drops her cup.

Anna laughs, not unkindly, at Reumah's look of shock. "I am singing a love song. I made it up—I swear, it came from my heart. I could not do less for the one I love."

Reumah's hands are over her mouth, now she clenches them over her heart, which is pounding, as if she herself is about to be drowned in the same wave of love. She whispers her next question, already knowing the answer.

"And the one you love...is the one who healed you?"

Anna puts her hands on Reumah's cheeks, startling her. "He did this," she says. "He looked into my eyes—no man has ever looked into my eyes. If they looked at me at all, if was with pity or revulsion. But he looked at me, and then—you will not believe this, but it is the truth—he kissed my forehead, and he said, 'Little sister, your faith has restored you...go in peace.' Immediately I felt something break loose inside me, and I could speak...I could smile...I could sing! Now I can't stop singing!" She laughs and wipes her eyes, delighting in Reumah's surprise.

"And the one who healed you...what is his name?"

Anna's eyes cloud for a second. "I heard someone call him, 'the son of David.' Others have called him 'the Anointed One.' Beyond that, I don't know. But I am going to find out. This much I know: I was in a dark prison of pain and despair, and he has set me free. For that, I will love him forever."

She resumes her song, waves happily at Reumah, and goes back to her lamps.

The son of David. The Anointed One. Lahai Roi. How can it be? He did not refute the names. Perhaps he is not simply a teacher or healer. Perhaps he is a prophet, like Elijah, or Ezekiel.

Quickly she veils herself, and goes out onto the road toward the marketplace, scanning the faces of the men that go by, but desiring to see only one.

9

*I*n the golden moments before she becomes fully awake, she dreams of Jeb. She dreams that he is here, that they have a life together, and they wake up in her bed every day. They'd live downstairs—the Petersons would be gone—and upstairs, her apartment would be his studio. And he'd break ties with Vina, and his best work would be created while living with her, because she'd be his model and his muse and the missing piece of his life. She dreams that he is now in the kitchen, making coffee, and that they will drink it in bed, and read the *Times*, and that this is their normal weekend routine, and they have been doing it for years.

The dreams are in one part of her brain; the other part of her brain attempts to dispel the illusions, like an obnoxious child bursting bubbles with a dirty finger. For one thing, she has never seen him drink coffee. The few times she happened to be with him in the morning, he drank chocolate milk. Also, he wouldn't be interested in reading the *Times*—unless it contained an article about him. Furthermore, he never planned to live in the Grove permanently, and certainly not with any woman, not even Vina. Vina had delivered him—to hear her tell it—from Klaus and the bathhouse scene, and if he hadn't gotten sick, he'd have probably moved back to Manhattan by now. Jennifer wasn't sure who Klaus was, but his name had come up occasionally in conversations past, and it seemed to her that Klaus must have been the embodiment of Satan himself. "I wanted to liberate him from all his past associations so that he could begin new work in complete tranquility," was what Vina had told Jennifer. So Jeb had settled in the

Grove, but it is, in fact, Michael who is in the kitchen making coffee, and judging by the aromas, frying pork roll too. He is singing with Bruce on the radio—*Born in the USA*.

Behind her bathroom door and overhung with her hand-laundered lingerie, is a calendar that a couple of girls at work gave her when they found out she was dating a pilot: each month features an actual, professional pilot, almost naked, beside, in, or under some kind of airplane. *The World's Sexiest Pilots*. All airline logos are carefully blurred. February's pilot is Norwegian. He is clad in tight black briefs and a pilot's cap, and stretches out invitingly in the cockpit of a 747. She contemplates his blond, shoulder-length mullet, and then drops her eyes to the date below. An unsettling thought begins to surface through the sludge of her dreams and is accompanied by a pervasive nausea. Her period is four days late.

She stands for a moment, trying to steady herself, and then throws up in the toilet. She flushes and then cleans it, and then sits on it, because her bowels are also in revolt.

Sometime later she enters the kitchen, wrapped in her robe, and sits opposite him.

"Hey, babe." His mouth is full of scrambled eggs and pork roll. "I was thinking of maybe driving down to AC. We could have dinner and stay overnight. How about it?"

Before she can answer, the sound of clunking footsteps is heard on the stairs outside, followed by a flurry of knocking. Michael looks at her. "You expecting someone?"

"No…" she gets up and pulls her dressing gown tighter. *Vina would call if…surely they would call and tell her to come right over. He would want her there. He's made that clear. He had Vina make a list.* It has to be the Petersons. Who else?

It's the boys. David and…she can't think of the other one's name. Framed by the door, they almost look like twins, although she knows they're two or three years apart. They have the same mullet haircut, but the younger one has freckles. The older one will definitely need braces.

"Hi," she says, after a pause.

"Hey, mister—" the younger one starts, before the older one—David—cuts him off.

"I'll ask him…" He mutters, and then looks toward Michael. "Um—we were just wondering—could we wash your car?"

Michael looks at her, as if needing a direction. Jennifer shrugs.

"Um—no. I—uh—just had it washed. Thanks anyway."

"But we saw a cardinal crap on it," the younger one says.

"He doesn't care what kinda bird, Nath." David says. "Anyway, it was a plain old sparrow."

"Was not. It was a cardinal. A female."

Michael gets up from the table and their mouths close. "Show me where," he says, stepping toward them. For a moment they both look uncomfortable at the sight of him in jockey shorts and a T-shirt.

"Um—on the trunk. We could wash it for ya. We're good at washing cars. We wash my dad's car all the time." Jennifer tries not to laugh at the implied comparison between his BMW and their dad's old Ford.

Michael follows them out the door and down the stairs. *Idiot*, she thinks. *Forty-three degrees and he goes out in his underwear to see the bird shit on his car.* She switches off the radio. At that moment she realizes that she can't handle the rest of the day with him, let alone the rest of the weekend.

She makes herself a cup of tea, not really wanting to drink it, but for the comfort of warming her hands. Mommy always had tea. *Put the kettle on, willya, hon? And grab us a few cookies while you're at it.* They would sit at the kitchen table after school, her mother reading *Woman's Day* or *Redbook*, her tea on one side, the cookies nearby, Mallomars or Oreos or Lorna Doones. The house would be quiet except for her mother's sipping and crunching, and the rattle of the cookie package. It was their weekday ritual. Jennifer would wordlessly stir her tea, not really drinking it, and dunk the proffered cookies into it until she could feel a thick mush at the bottom of her mug. Her mother would pause every few minutes to address her. *Oh look at this, honey…even supermodels have cellulite…they've got a low-fat chocolate cake here, made with apple sauce…oh Lord, look at this outfit on Cher…ham and potato scallop, my, that looks yummy…*Jennifer would stare into her mug, watching the remains of the drowned cookies disappear. *A bunch of my friends are going braless,* she would say to her mother, but not aloud, just in her head. *A boy tried to put his hand up* *my sweater today. Two girls came from another school to beat up this girl in fifth period for messing with one of their boyfriends. This really cute boy in algebra asked me if I wanted to smoke pot with him after school. I told him I had a dentist appointment. But what if he asks me again? Mr. Leiderman taught us all about the f-word 'cuz we're read-*ing Catcher in the Rye. *He said it's a perfectly good English word with Latin roots. He made us all repeat it five times.* She wondered what her mother would say if she spoke it aloud. The mush at the bottom of her mug or something else made her gut feel uptight, so after a while she would go upstairs and flop on her bed and pick up the snow globe that she kept on her nightstand. She would turn it over and over again, and watch the tiny white particles of fake snow resettle onto the little plastic cottage, covering the minuscule flowers and grass until only the lamp post could be seen. The knots in her gut would gradually unwind, but she would feel guilty about leaving her mother alone, down in the kitchen, eating cookies. She could hear the cellophane of the package crackling. Her mother would finish the cookies and take a nap on the couch until it was time to start supper. For some reason, Jennifer couldn't do her homework until her mother was napping.

"Hey, Jen, ya got some Windex or something?" His pants are on, and he's pulling a sweater over his head.

"You have to go." She sets her mug on the table.

He puts on his sunglasses and gazes at her. "What?"

"I need you to go."

He takes his sunglasses off and sits down on one of the kitchen chairs. "What's wrong with you? What's going on?"

"Nothing's wrong with me." She can hear the edginess in her voice. "Nothing is wrong with me. I've had a rough week. I just want some time to myself."

"You never said so last night."

"I was happy to see you. Honestly."

He sits there for a minute, not believing her, but unable to discern the truth. Then he gets up and takes a turn around the room.

"You have other plans, I guess."

"No."

"The hell you don't."

"Michael, please."

He stops directly in front of her. "It must be that psycho artist. God, isn't he dead yet? I can't believe you still hang around those freaks. A bunch of fags and pot heads that paint and sew and play with clay, for Chrissake. Aren't you afraid of catching their disease?"

She tastes bile coming up her throat. It's as if he's mocking her religion. In another moment she will throw up. Instead, she gets up and puts her mug in the sink. "The fact is, I'm sick. I threw up before—just before in the bathroom."

"Why didn't you say so?"

"I don't know! It's embarrassing. I guess I drank too much."

He studies her for another long moment.

"Ok, fine. I'll go. But I'm gonna call you later."

He says it like a threat.

Dear Mommy in heaven, what should I do? Please tell me what to do. I know you wouldn't want me to kill it. Please help me. Amen.

For a long while she grieves in bed, and wishes there were prayers to the dead. You could ask your mother for advice, for instance, instead of bothering God. For that matter, if your lawyer or your accountant or your auto mechanic died, you could ask them to send you advice or suggestions, as needed, and they would be only too happy to help, because now they were dead, and living up there in heaven, with not a whole lot to do. They would feel happy and generous and helpful because they were, in fact, relieving God of his many duties, and besides, it felt good to benefit mankind, when they had pretty much lived for themselves the whole time they were down on earth. God working himself out of a job, is pretty much the way she would have set up the system if she had designed it.

She picks up her old snow globe and absent-mindedly turns it upside-down and then right again. She seriously considers offering a prayer of petition, but can't decide if it should be liturgical, or made-up. A made-up one would be more difficult, but which would be more effective? She is certain that God is pretty pissed off at her by now, and the Snow god, although benevolent, is primarily concerned with snow. She considers the Blessed Virgin, who also had an unplanned pregnancy, but she already knows what Mary would tell her to do. Then again, her baby was Jesus—who would mess with that? If she prayed to Jesus, would he answer? Her ideas of Jesus encompass a sleeping, haloed infant in a manger, or else a disjointed, languid man, perpetually hanging on a cross. Both seem equally ill-equipped to offer her any divine assistance.

Mommy, can you hear me? Can you answer me?

Nobody said "died." They said, "Your mother passed," like she had passed them on the street, or in a shopping aisle. They said, "I'm so sorry...I'll say a prayer for her."

Jennifer had said them too, the prayers for the dead. But she couldn't sleep and she couldn't stop wondering, because her mother had not received the final sacrament. Father Donnely had not been able to get to the hospital in time for her last hour.

In her mother's last hour, Jennifer had been ten minutes away, starting an IV for a hepatitis patient in the next building. She had never forgiven the C-fourth nurse for not paging her sooner.

After a few months she had stopped going to mass, and then she decided to go see Father Donnely at St. Joseph's, but he was on medical leave. There was a young priest there instead, fresh out of seminary, she guessed, because he had pimples or possibly untreated rosacea on his cheeks. He had an earnest, formal manner, and after a pause, invited her into the study, which was technically still Father Donnely's. They stood awkwardly for a moment, and Jennifer cleared her throat. "It's about my mother...my late mother..."

"Was she a parishioner here?"

"Yes. Always. Father Donnely knew her well."

"Ah. Well. Why don't you sit down?"

They both sat down. "Sir...I mean, Father...my mother had a tough life. She grew up poor, one of six kids. My dad left us when I was eight. She worked her—she worked hard to put me through school. She kept boarders and sold Avon and Tupperware. She wasn't perfect. After my dad left us, she started eating too much, and eventually it killed her. But she was a good person. She always went to church. She did what she had to do. I can't imagine that she's not...you know...in a better place right now."

"Of course, uh—Miss?"

"It's Jennifer. But she didn't, like, have extreme unction, or last rites or whatever...you know what I'm saying?"

"Uh—OK. What happened? Was there anyone with her?"

"Well, yes, there was, actually. A patient care specialist. Hold on a minute." She retrieved a small paperback book from her purse. It was her mother's book and her mother had been holding it at the time of her death. Her mother had specifically asked for it, a few days before, and Jennifer had retrieved it from the drawer of her nightstand. At the time it was new, and her mother's bookmark—which was a coupon for chocolate syrup—was almost to the end of the book. There is a hazy picture on the front cover depicting some dark, Middle Eastern woman with her hair blowing back. Jennifer had never read the book. She figured it was another romance novel that her mother was fond of picking up at yard sales for a dime apiece. She still had boxes of her mother's books in the attic.

"This lady—her name was Leticia—was with her. She said something about *repentance*, which I thought was strange. I mean, that's not a word you hear every day, right?"

"True. It's not in everyday use."

"Well...that lady...she gave me this afterward...after she had been with my mom." She handed him the small, soft-cover volume, which smelled like Woolite, because it had been in her underwear drawer.

The priest examined the first page, on which there were two shaky letters, like the scrawls of a child. One looked like a *J* with a lower-case *e* next to it.

"I'm not sure I understand..." he said, his eyebrows forming a ridge. "This lady...this PCS...was she a Catholic?"

"Nope. A Christian, I guess...but of the born-again variety." Jennifer had not felt the need to tell him that the woman was an expansive, black grandmother who sang hymns while she wiped asses and changed soiled bed sheets. "She had one of those fish pins above her name tag...you know the ones. Anyway, I don't think she was Catholic, but she was, um, fervent, if you know what I mean. She told me that my mother had 'prayed to receive Jesus.' I figured that was as good as final unction or whatever. Right?"

"Oh, chile, she's wi' da Lawd," Leticia had said, hugging her in the hallway outside the room. *"It happen so quick...she prayed to receive Jesus, and Jesus couldn't wait to take her...he just scooped her up in his arms...and lis'en...lis'en, chile...she prayed for you too...she prayed for you to receive da Lawd Jesus too...I'm just sayin..."*

Leticia had smelled sweet, like honey butter or syrup. Her mother had probably loved her. Jennifer had stood there, like a statue, holding her mother's book. She could see her mother's form, under the sheet. She let Leticia hug her, as if the hug would detain her from having to go in to the room, and lift the sheet.

The priest was still examining the letters. She wondered if he would insist on keeping it, as evidence of some kind. But he handed it back to her.

"Those small marks...they were made by your mother?"

"Yeah. I'm sure she was trying to write something to me but in the end, I guess that was all she could do..."

"Of course. It seems to be a word—your name, perhaps—or else Jesus..."

"I suppose." Jennifer flushed. She had hoped he wouldn't ask. "Letitia told me she was trying to write *Jesus.*" Couldn't it just as easily been J-E-N?

Damn it, why couldn't she have been there? Why not Father Donnely, at least? Why some bustling, overzealous born-again nut?

"I see." He had risen at that point. They mumbled a few pleasantries, he saw her to the door, and she turned, still expecting him to say something about her mother. A verdict, of some sort. Where the hell did he think she was?

"So...you think she's OK? I mean...you think she's up there...you know...*in heaven?*"

"Of course. Why wouldn't she be?"

"Well...it sounds like she changed directions there...at the end... like, switched to "born again" or something..."

"I'm fairly sure, based on that person's account...your mother died as a Christian."

So what? How could he be sure? How could anybody?

In the late afternoon she buys a pregnancy test, but not in the Grove's Drug Mart, since they knew her mother and they've known her all her life and she can never buy any sex-related products there for that reason. She heads out of town toward Asbury Park and passes Jeb's place on the way. Vina's car is there.

When she returns, the instructions say that she has to wait until morning to test her pee, so she sets the kit next to the toilet. She rummages through the fridge and carefully eats some applesauce, feels squeamish again, and lies down.

Ten minutes later she throws up in the toilet. When she's done throwing up, she grabs the stick out of the kit and holds it under her pee, thinking *why not*, and thinking too, *if it's negative, I'll go buy another one and do it again, to be sure.*

But the little plus sign on the tester stick turns pink, and she sits for a few minutes, resting her head on the counter next to the commode.

Mommy can you hear me?

Back in her bed she picks up the snow globe again. She shakes it and watches the snow drift down, onto their little cottage, which is warmly lit from within, because now there is a fireplace, with a comfy, cushy rocker, and they take turns, her and Jeb, rocking the baby.

X

The brightness of a full moon illuminates the courtyard and has made it impossible to sleep. Reumah, drawn from her pallet by its intensity reclines on the narrow bench near her room. Her body is weary from the day's work, but her restless mind spins with old memories and then snaps back to Anna's love song and healing.

Underneath a shrub that grew near their house, she had once found a dove with a broken wing and showed it to her father. The frantic fluttering and terrified eyes of the bird had filled her with fear and awe as she watched her father bend down and gather the creature into his hands.

"Stay here, my lamb. I will take care of it."

"Father, what will you do?" she had clung to his arm.

"Reumah, the poor creature is suffering. It would be a kindness to end its life."

She had wept as if her heart would break and begged him to save it until, sighing deeply, he agreed to set the broken wing with a small stick and a few strips of cloth. She made a soft nest for the benumbed creature in a basket, and placed it in the shade of the shrub. For three days she watched over it and poured tiny drops of water and honey into its beak. The following night she awoke to the rasping sound of growling dogs and she thought of how her brother Aaron would be in trouble again for neglecting to fasten the latch on the outside gate. The next day she found, to her horror, the basket empty, and a few blood-stained feathers. When her father returned in the evening, her eyes were swollen from weeping.

"Ah, Reumah. We cannot keep alive what the Almighty has determined should die. We cannot grant relief to those he has destined should suffer. We should have let it be…or perhaps killed it quickly and with mercy when it found shelter in the shade of our house."

But this man—this healer. What would her father say? He had power—not just to heal, as he had done to her, but to restore, to recreate. Anna's face was now lovely and unbroken. Her spirit had been released from darkness, and she who had barely uttered sounds could not keep from singing now.

She felt compelled to know. Was his power given to him, like the Spirit of the Lord that had come upon the ancient prophets and judges? Would her father believe it? Or would he say it came from a more insidious source—the prince of demons himself, who had also been granted power for reasons known only to the Almighty?

Back and forth her mind ranged, trying to make sense of her father's teachings and what she had seen with her own eyes and felt with her own heart.

Lahai Roi. You have already said it. She had eaten the bread he had given her and felt her body recover; she had seen the beauty of Anna's face and heard her song of devotion. In spite of all she knows to be true of her father's lessons, she cannot prevent a surge of hope from rippling inside her: of being restored, not her face or her voice, but her soul; of being forgiven, not temporarily, with a bloody animal, but irrevocably; not just by her father, but by the Master of the Universe himself.

The moon rises and makes large shadows of the water pots beyond her bench. She closes her eyes for a moment or maybe an hour until the sound of singing awakens her. Abruptly she says "Anna?" but the voices are many and farther away this time, coming from the hills beyond the village.

She listens, and gradually it comes to her: the ancient festival for Jepthah's daughter. Every year the virgins of the villages and towns go into the hills for four days to commemorate the daughter of Jepthah, who was sacrificed because of her father's rash vow. Reumah had gone for three years in a row before she became Zerah's bride.

She sighs deeply. It was five harvests ago. A night like this night, it was. She and her friends had gone up into the hills to the appointed place beside a cold stream and laughed and drank sweet wine and ate almonds and raisin cakes. The older girls would divulge age-old tales and secrets of their elder, married sisters, secrets of blood and birth and the marriage act. There would be gasps of shock and more laughter and then one or another would pick up her tambourine and the dancing would start. The dancing would go on and on until it reached a frenetic crescendo and then Mara, a young widow, would begin the lament for Jepthah's daughter, and the wailing would go on sometimes until daybreak. Some of them would drink too much and some would fall into a trancelike state and eventually all would fall asleep before the smoldering fires, but always Reumah could feel she was being watched, even as she collapsed on her blankets. The unmarried young men of the towns—mostly brothers and cousins—formed a loose shield around them and stayed at a respectable distance, but it was no secret that they would inevitably creep closer, with only the large bonfires between them, to survey the dancing girls, gleaming in the firelight. The girls knew they were being watched, and danced as if they weren't. They closed their eyes and swayed and circled and spun and clapped their tambourines and shed their outer garments until they were almost naked. They felt safe—they had only to scream, and all the brothers would come to their defense at the slightest impropriety or encroachment. Any young man who was ever so bold as to approach one of the virgins would have soon wished he were dead.

And yet—he had come for her.

On the third night, when the wailing was over, most of the girls had collapsed before the fires, some of them still moaning and swaying on their knees, most of them asleep. Reumah felt her face burning from the fire's glow, and she had crept over to the brook to get a drink and splash water on her cheeks. The moon shimmered on the water like a blade of lightning. She stood watching it for a moment, as if in a dream, and suddenly he was beside her, with his hand over her mouth to keep her from screaming.

"Don't scream. I won't hurt you. I promise."

He had whispered it in her ear, and she had believed him. He had led her by the hand to a secluded place behind a large rock, and that was surrounded by a hamlet of ancient olive trees, as if he already knew the place well. He turned to her, and spoke in a low voice that made her tremble.

"There, now. You're not afraid, are you?"

She was afraid to speak. She had never been alone with any man, and could think of nothing to say.

"I've watched you for three nights. Did you know? I had to talk with you. That's why I came. Reumah, you know I'm in love with you. I've seen you look at me."

She felt her knees buckling.

"I'm sorry—I have to sit—"

"Of course. Forgive me. You're weak from dancing and lamentation. All for a nameless girl that lived a thousand years ago. The festival would have ceased centuries ago, if it didn't afford such tantalizing sights for the young men of the villages. I'm certain we look forward to it as much as you do." He laid his heavy cloak down and she sank onto it. He immediately sat next to her, and took her hand.

"Reumah, tell the truth." He gazed at her, unwaveringly, and she felt her blood pulsing in her head. "Are you in love with me, as I am with you?"

"How can you ask such a thing when you know I'm pledged to your brother?"

"My brother..." he picked up a stone and threw it into the darkness of the tree trunks. They heard a dull thud where it hit. "My brother seeks to own everything that I want. It's not enough he's the firstborn and will inherit my father's wealth and position. No. That's not enough for him." Even in the semidarkness of the olive grove, she could see his mouth twisting into a hard sneer. "He watched me. He saw how I looked at you at the wedding that day and that's when he decided he wanted you."

"What?"

"You doubt me?"

"I—I don't know. I thought...I felt sure he must feel something for me—to pay such a price..." she was suddenly hot with embarrassment.

After that, there were words whispered, his lips almost touching her cheek, words that told her that she rightfully belonged to him, and more words that become a blur in her memory, because she was exhausted, and wanted to sleep, but also to know the end of this encounter. After that, the words stopped, and she can remember the outline of his head and shoulders above her in the moonlight, his dark hair, damp with the night air, hanging over her and the taste of his breath, like cloves, when he kissed her, and his lips moving downward along her throat and his fingers loosening the ties of her nightdress, while she said *no, no*, but he took hold of her softest parts as if he already owned her. She remembers the moon, because it had suddenly disappeared behind a cloud that had come out of nowhere, like the hand of God plunging them and the olive trees into thick darkness at the exact moment that Judas had covered her mouth with his kisses, to stifle her cry as he pierced her.

What if she had screamed?

They would have caught him. They would have killed or banished him, at best. Zerah would have broken the betrothal with a certificate of divorce, and his father would have insisted the bride price be returned. She would have remained an unmarried woman in her father's house for the rest of her days. The young girls would look away and the women would cluck their tongues; her mother would loathe the sight of her.

So she had not screamed. Not then, and not when he approached her again, in secret, on the roof of her married home, in the cool night air.

"My brother sleeps deeply," he had said the first time.

"You must go!"

"You saw how much he drank…"

"Judas, please! Think what would happen!"

"One kiss."

"And then you will go?"

"I promise."

But he had not done as he promised. Even as she protested and strained against him, his hands had deftly lifted the hem of her robe, and her flesh yielded to his even as her heart raced in panic. Thereafter each time he came to visit them he would laugh and jest, and dip his bread in the sauce at the same time as Zerah, and insist on pouring the wine. At the end of the meal he would say, "Allow me to thank my brother's wife," and he would place a cake of dates in her hand, and press her fingers meaningfully. It was his signal. And late, late in the night, when Zerah was breathing heavily beside her, she would rise from her bed and go up to him on the roof, thinking always that it would be the last time, knowing she was trapped, but not knowing how the end would be.

One night a servant girl with her lamp had found them there, and the three of them had stood in surprised silence for a moment, studying each other in the flickering light. Judas was the first to speak.

"Well, girl? What is it?"

"A thousand pardons, sir. My mistress—your mother—is not well. I came to soak some cloths to cool her fever. I did not think I would find anyone awake at this hour—" She glanced at Reumah, and then looked away quickly, which helped Reumah recover her speech.

"Indeed, I have had some trouble sleeping myself. I have had a nightmare, and came up to clear my head, so as not disturb my husband." She looked directly at Judas. "Thank you, dear brother, for your reassuring words. They have eased my mind." He had smiled at her. She hoped the girl would not see the two cups of wine that she had placed on a ledge, nor their cloaks arranged on a nearby bench.

What would he have done? She often wonders. What would he have done if they had been really caught? Each time he spoke less, and risked more, as if the risk itself was as much pleasure as the act. Each time she begged him to be careful, not to expose her needlessly, but her words went unheeded. Until the last time, when he had promised to come for her, she could not think of their adultery without fear and self-loathing.

And what if he doesn't come for her? Almost a year has passed; still he has not come. She closes her eyes and thinks again of the Healer. Without knowing why, she ascribes to him great power. She imagines that he has power not only to heal bodies and souls, but the tangled lives of men and women.

"Reumah."

Her eyes open widely at the sound of a man's low voice. He is standing near to her. She rises quickly, and stares at him. It is not difficult to discover his face in the brightness of the moonlight, though he is hooded, because she knows him better by night than by day.

11

On Sunday she considers going to church. She hasn't gone in almost five years. She thinks of making a confession. Surely a priest would confirm the decision she's edging toward. She hopes it's not the young pimply priest, because he might remember her. Father Donnely has *passed on.* She wonders if he's met up with her mother. She can picture them having tea and cookies on her heavenly porch, like they did in the Grove.

Probably a priest will recommend a Bible study group or a support group or some literature, if nothing else. Something that would bolster her and keep her resolved. She doesn't relish the idea of getting involved with a group or a Bible study, but she feels that she must do it, as a first, important step to becoming more circumspective and responsible. She must atone, in a sense, for her negligence.

The phone rings while she's putting on her mascara.

"Jennifer?" It's a foreign-sounding man. He says her name like "Zhen-ee-fair?"

"Yes?"

"I am Jean-Denis." He says it like Zhon-Denee, with a French intonation.

"Who?"

"I am with Jeb. He asks to see you."

"Oh, God. Is he all right?"

"Yes, yes. He's very good today."

"Wow. OK. Tell him I'll be right there."

Jean-Denis, it turns out, is the hospice nurse that is currently attend-ing him. He is gloved and masked, and is adjusting an IV drip when she arrives. Jeb is watching him. She carefully sits on the edge of his bed, pretending to take professional interest in the IV, but she is really think-ing how providential it is that no one else, not even Vina, is there. At that moment she knows she will tell him, but not yet.

"You're a good man…" Jeb says, his voice barely a whisper. "No pain today."

"OK, I make you relax. I am in the next room. You call me." He surveys Jennifer for a moment and then motions for her to follow him.

"You are his girlfriend?"

"Uh—no. Just a friend. Why?"

"Just to be sure. You understand, I think…absolutely no sexual relations of any kind, not even kisses. No fluids to be exchanged… saliva, semen…you understand?"

She laughs awkwardly. "Of course, of course. I'm a nurse myself."

"Ah. You have a mask?"

"Uh, no…but it's OK. I'll be very careful." She returns to his bed and sits next to him. He is curled up on his side, ensconced in pillows.

"He's a beautiful man," Jeb says to her slowly, as if talking too loudly or quickly will cause a rupture somewhere. "He's from Haiti, you know. Klaus loved Haitian men. They're so dark and shiny, he would say. Like ebony." For a moment he grimaces, as if remembering some uncomfortable truth, and then he smiles crookedly at her. "I never had much use for niggers when I was younger, but I've come to appreci-ate them." He tries to laugh, but it comes out like a cough. "Come lie beside me."

If she hadn't ditched Michael yesterday…if she had left for Mass a few minutes early, like she planned…she wouldn't be here with him now, alone, except for Jean-Denis, who hovers like an attending angel in the next room. She feels like she has received a divine blessing, but she doesn't know who to thank, because she didn't actually pray to any known god. She curls her body as close to his as she can, and carefully places her arm around him. The back of his neck smells clean, almost medicinal. Jean-Denis must have bathed him. It occurs to her she hasn't felt this happy in months. The radio is playing so low she can barely make out the song, *Wild Horses*. Outside the day is overcast, with strong winds that rattle the old, multipaned windows. A humidifier bubbles congenially on the other side of his bed. She wants to hear him talk some more, but if he wants her to lie next to him in silence for the rest of the day, she will do so.

After a while she is sure that he's sleeping, but he suddenly stirs.

"My old man told me that God hates fags."

She rearranges herself so that she can see his face better. She never knows how to respond to statements like this, and it makes a knot form in her stomach. Vina would know.

"And my mama figured out a long time ago that God likes men better than women."

Silence again. Jennifer wishes they could just keep lying there. After a moment she says, "Want me to rub your back?"

"Who the hell would want a God like that? Would you?"

"Come on, it's not worth getting worked up about."

"Answer the question."

"Of course not." She quickly determines that she will not mention anything about going to Mass.

"Why do so many people like God, for Chrissake? This whole town is into God."

"No it's not. You know that."

"It's got a cross sitting on top of it like the American flag on the fucking moon. Like it's been conquered. Like God owns it or something." Underneath her hand she can feel his blood pressure going up.

"Stop—you're getting all worked up. Please."

"I hate this town." It looks like he has tears, but his eyes are runny sometimes, so she's not sure. She passes him a tissue from the nightstand, but he ignores it.

"God hates us. He fried Sodom. It's in the Bible."

"Why should you care?"

"I personally don't give a flying fuck. I'm just saying."

"Are you sure you're gay?" It occurs to her suddenly that she's never believed it; otherwise, why would she have hoped? How could she have been so obsessed with him? She views his sexual deviations as just that…he veered off the path here and there, but it's not who he really is.

He stares at her as if her eyeballs have evaporated.

"What?"

"I mean, really—like deep, down. How do you know what you really are? How do you know you're not just being what other people say you are?"

He gazes at her for another moment, and then he closes his eyes. His breathing slows, and she assumes he is dozing, but abruptly he begins to talk again, in a phlegmy whisper. She wishes he would clear his throat.

"Nobody knows they're gay at first. I sure as hell didn't. I knew I was special, but only because of my art. I was doing my own thing, I was minding my own business, I wanted to be a great artist, which is why I was drawing myself naked in front of an old mirror I had dragged into my room. I remember my old man asked why I put it there and I lied and told him that I needed to see things from different angles when I drew 'em. He got this sneery look on his face. Fact is, it wasn't my idea; it was Donald's, my art teacher's. Donald was a flaming faggot but I didn't care 'cuz I thought he knew everything about art, and I wanted to learn. Now I'm thinking he probably just wanted to see the pictures I drew of myself, but I didn't think that then. At first it was weird, drawing my own prick and having my eyes watch me, but after a while, I got used to it. Like, sometimes when I looked into my eyes it felt like there was some spiritual entity looking back at me." He tries to laugh and ends up coughing again. "Vina would say I had discovered the god inside me, or some shit like that, but maybe it's true."

Jennifer forces a laugh. "So—you fell in love with the god in the mirror? And that made you think you were gay? Wasn't there some mythological guy like that?"

"Narcissus. A Greek guy. Figures." He takes a deep breath and waits for a moment, as if pacing himself. "Anyway. I had this friend named Tommy. He was older than me, and he had already flunked outta school. He lived down the street in a dumpy, white-trash house and almost every day he'd come over with his old man's girlie magazines under his shirt, say hi to my mother, and come into my room. We'd look 'em over and whack off, y'know, separately, in the can. One day Tommy says, *Hey, let's see if we can hit the mirror.* After that it got to be a game, to the point where I had to keep paper towels and Windex in my room to wipe the cum off the mirror. Then one day I come into my room and he's found my sketchbook, which I kept under my mattress, and he's looking at all the goddamn naked sketches of me, and he says, *God, you're really something...and I'm so goddamned ugly...* only he says it like he's really distraught. So I sit next to him and I didn't know what to say, because the fact is the guy *was* ugly. He had squinty eyes and a big space between his front teeth and a white, paunchy body with zits all over his back and his ass too, as I later found out. Next thing I know, Tommy is sniffling, and after a while he says, *Hey, Jeb, can you do me a favor? You're my best friend...*and I'm looking away, feeling bad for him, so of course I say, yeah, sure, anything. And then he says, *Can you jerk me?* I sit there for a whole minute thinking. First I was thinking about my mother down the hall watching her soap opera. Then I was thinking about a line, like there was a line, and I was about to cross it, and I'd never be able to come back. Part of me wanted to back away from the line, y'know? But part of me wanted to see what would happen, 'cuz it was just so wicked and evil, at least from what I'd been told, but I knew I'd always wonder if I didn't do it. Then I said, Naw, Tom, I don't think so. *Just this once,* he says. *No one will ever know. I swear to God.* And he keeps his head down and unzips his pants, and next thing I know, I'm doing it."

He stops speaking, but Jennifer wants to hear more.

"So that was it. Your first, like, experience."

"Yeah. Sometimes I wonder...if I had never done that with Tommy..." and he stops again.

"What about girls? You must have had girlfriends." Not too many, she hopes.

"They were always coming on to me. They'd shove notes in my locker or my pants. *I want you sooooo bad. Meet me in the gym where the mats are...*stuff like that. A guy in the library says to me one day, *Hey, Jeb, what's that in your pocket?* He pulls out some panties that a slut named Melanie had stuck there, and the whole fucking library erupts. I got sent to the principal and my old man told me I was *burning* *with lust* and beat me with his belt, but not as bad as usual 'cuz then he figured I was into girls and that was a relief to him, so I figured I might as well screw around. I lost my virginity to Lisa Beth, my driving instructor. She was twenty-three. I did the usual fucking at the drive-in and the prom and all that, but I couldn't get into it."

"You couldn't get into it?" she says, smiling coyly in the old way they had.

He rolls his eyes. "Couldn't get into, like, relationships. Girls were so needy and whiny, like my mother and sister. They'd look at me with these eyes that said they expected me to be some strong, manly guy that would take care of them, and deep down, I wanted one of those guys too—for myself, I mean."

He stops again, as if trying to determine how to make the best use of his remaining strength; what to tell her, what to leave out. She wishes he would sleep now, so she could digest some of this. But after a moment he goes on.

"It felt weird at first—Tommy's prick in my hand, but after a while I got used to it, like everything else. Around this time my old man was always looking for a reason to beat me. All I'd have to do is forget to flush or leave a plate in front of the TV, and he'd get his belt going and whack me till I made some noise. My mama would cry and beg him to stop and he'd say, *Spare the rod, spoil the child, Ellie.* One day me and Tommy are on my bed and suddenly I hear my old man, I hear him coming down the hall—he and my mama are home early from some meeting, and I hear him coming, I can still hear his church shoes clomping on the wood floor outside my door, and I hear him clear his throat and I'm scrambling to get my jeans up, and I kick Tommy's pants under the bed and shove him in my closet. Daddy comes in and takes a look around almost like he's sniffing out my sin, and I hope to God he doesn't smell Tommy's sweat 'cuz I sure could. *Why is the trash can still out on the curb?* he says, kinda snarling. And I say, Sorry 'bout that, Daddy, I must've fergot…and he looks around again (I swear I could hear Tommy breathing in the closet), and he takes a step over to my desk and sweeps all my stuff—pencils, pens, graphite, ink, oil tubes, palettes, brushes, rags, gesso—all of it, onto the floor—Christ, what a mess—and then takes off his belt and starts beating me across my bare back."

She can feel him trembling slightly now.

"Stop now. Don't say any more. Please, Jeb." She kisses him gently on the ear and again on his temple.

"Finally it's over, and he leaves to go watch Walter Cronkite, and I pull open the closet and there's Tommy, white like paper, and he's shat all over my sneakers. Get rid a'those, I tell him. God, what a smell. But he's whacked-out, blubbering and saying, *Ya gotta get outta here, Jeb, ya gotta come with me, I'm gonna find us a place*. And he does too."

"Stop, Jeb. This isn't helping." She gets up and takes his pulse and his temperature, hoping to distract him. She doesn't want to hear anymore. One thirty-two over eighty. Too high. One hundred point three, which is pretty normal for him now. She goes out to tell Jean-Denis, who returns with her, and checks his vitals again.

"How you feel?" says Jean-Denis.

"Like a drowning man. It's my lungs."

"You have pain?" He places his stethoscope on Jeb's chest.

Jeb inhales and exhales, inhales and exhales; coughs. He coughs violently for a minute and Jennifer gets some water. He takes a sip and then lies back on the pillow, smiling weakly at Jean-Denis.

"Go get some lunch for yourself. I'm good. The steroid does the trick."

"You want something?" Jennifer asks, feeling hungry herself.

He turns to look at her. "I want to tell you the rest."

Jean-Denis glances at her with the barest suspicion. "Do not let him be upset. He will cough too much."

"I'm trying." She plumps the pillows between his knees and under his head and fluffs the one he holds against his chest. She adjusts his blanket and moves the tissues and the ice water and his nebulizer within easy reach. Then she folds herself next to him again, and takes hold of his hand. It feels dry and papery, like an old person's, which makes her feel like crying, because he's only thirty-two.

"OK. Tell me the rest, if it makes you feel better."

"It makes me feel better. Tommy kept his promise, like I said. I left home after high school. My mama kissed me good-bye on the front porch, and my daddy yelled out *Yer kissin' an abomination, Ellie*. Tommy found us a place to live with these two guys, Brian and Leon.

Brian was this big guy who lifted weights and drank a lot and never said too much. I think he was a bouncer. Leon was a model, a real model who flew around the country doing photo shoots. I think we were mostly living off Leon's money. Everything was fine, at first. I was happy to be out of my old man's house, and these guys seemed OK, especially Leon. After a couple of weeks they decided they didn't want Tommy around anymore 'cuz he ate and drank too much, so they kicked him out. He stood on the porch crying and yelling *Jeb, c'mon— come with me. Jeb's mine, he's mine*, and he'd call me on the phone all the time, crying and saying, *yer mine, c'mon, I got you outta yer house, I saved yer ass.* But I had it pretty good, living with those two. I got no place else to go, I'd say to Tommy. *I'll find us a place*, he'd say. OK, you do that, I told him. After a while he stopped calling and three years later I found out that some guy had screwed him in a motel, and afterward Tommy had taken the guy's tie and hung himself in the fire escape stairwell."

"Oh, god."

"Yeah." He motions for the ice water and takes a sip before resuming. "Problem was, Leon was away a lot, and I had a job in a restaurant, but business was slow, and they kept cutting my hours. Seems every time I was in the apartment, Brian was there too, and it was makin' me jumpy. What I really wanted to do was paint, but I didn't have enough money to buy my stuff. Meanwhile, my ass would be sticking out of the fridge and I'd turn around and Brian would be starin' at it, or I'd come outta the shower with a towel around my waist and it's like he was sittin' there the whole time, waitin' for me."

His voice is slowing, and then he stops, and puts his arm over his eyes.

"You OK?" she says, watching him carefully. His arm stays over his eyes.

"One night, it's real late and I come outta the shower and he grabs the towel off me and says, *Time you started earning yer keep around here, boy.* He pushes me onto his bed and I start yellin'. *You just relax and quit that hollerin' and everything's gonna be fine.* He's got this big jar of Vaseline next to his bed...I was screamin' into the pillow...it hurt, god, it hurt so bad...my ass felt like it was busted open and when I got up there was blood and shit all over the sheets, and I was shakin', and I couldn't stop shakin'. *Won't be long yer gonna come beggin' me for more...*he tells me, real snidelike. After that, Leon came in, which is when I realize he had been there, Leon had been there the whole goddamn fucking time. He comes over and hugs me, and he says, *You're not a virgin anymore, you sexy bitch,* and *C'mon, I'll help you soak your ass,* and he's already got a bath run for me, like he's my mother or a fucking nurse..."

Under his arm he is crying and she pulls it away gently but he can't stop and now he is hacking and sobbing at the same time, which is precisely when Vina comes in.

"Oh my god, oh my god...where the hell is Jean-Denis?" and then she is yelling at Jean-Denis in the living room and Jennifer is trying to soothe him but she can't, it's almost as if he's crying harder now, because Vina is here, like a kid with a scraped knee who doesn't cry until his mother sees it.

"Goddamn, this is what I get for leaving him...everybody get the hell outta here." She stares straight at Jennifer.

"He called. He asked to see me."

"He's on painkillers. He's not in his right mind. I thought you knew that."

"He wanted to see me."

"Right." She steps over to Jennifer and bends her face close. Jennifer can smell the tobacco on her breath. "Because I wasn't available. Now I am. So you can go. Your shift is over." She is imperious, and Jennifer can feel herself withering.

When she gets in her car she realizes she is crying, and she can't decide if it's because of all he said to her, or all she didn't say to him.

XII

She had imagined, during long nights when sleep evaded her, that she would first gaze at her, renewing his admiration of her face, and then perhaps trace her lips with his fingertips before he took her in his arms. She had imagined that they would make love almost immediately, instinctively and intensely, and speak afterward. She had imagined that he would explain why he had been delayed, and then after many reassuring words and meaningful glances, they would make love again, more slowly. But it is nothing like she had imagined.

He gazes at her with detached recognition. His eyes then move around her, surveying her living accommodations in the semidarkness. His expression is more like that of a soldier completing an assigned mission. It is almost as if he has come to her against his will.

Nevertheless he has come.

She leads him to her small room and lights the lamp. He glances behind him quickly before stooping at the low door. For a few minutes they watch the flame, and neither speaks. She tries not to look at him, but out of the corner of her eye she notes his clothes, which are dusty and frayed, and his feet and hands, which are not clean. She wonders if he would be insulted or relieved if she brought him a basin and a towel.

He sighs deeply, and then, unexpectedly, lies back on her pallet. She gathers up her head roll and places it beneath his neck.

"You are weary. Perhaps you should sleep."

"I have no wish to sleep."

"Are you hungry? I have some bread here in a napkin..." She was saving it for her breakfast.

"I am not hungry."

Her heart sinks at his coldness. For so long she imagined herself saying *Why did you not come as you promised?* After another pause she speaks, with the barest reproach in her voice.

"Why did you come?"

He sighs deeply again, and then says, "The Master sent me."

"The Master?"

"The Master. The Teacher. The Rabbi. Call him what you will."

"I don't understand."

"Reumah, are you blind and deaf? The entire countryside talks of nothing else. The healings, the miracles, the mass feedings, the demons screaming as they are exorcised. Surely you have heard something of him?"

Her mind gradually absorbs the meaning of his words.

"So...it is true, after all. I heard it said...that you had become one of his disciples..."

He laughs softly. "You did not believe it, of course."

But she cannot laugh, only wonder. "How can it be? What made you choose to follow him?"

"Ha! I did not choose him. He chose me."

"What? How can it be?"

"It was about a year ago. I was in the outer court. He was teaching in the temple. A crowd gathered, as usual. The people hung on his every word. 'What did he say? Tell me again?' said an old man next to me. I went closer to get a better look at him, but I could hardly see him because of the crowd. I had a sense of his power even then. Men, women, even children—they stood there, with eyes fixed on him. A child was brought before him—a small girl whose hand had been burnt in a cooking fire. At once the Master stopped teaching. The crowd was silent except for the screams of the child which echoed against the columns. The Master took her into his arms. No sooner had he taken her hand into his when it was healed. The girl's crying stopped abruptly and the Master gave her back to her mother. The people surged around the girl and her parents, and the Master immediately backed away from the crowd, as if he had done something wrong rather than something good."

"But how did you—"

"I'm getting to it. After that I pressed my way through the crowd, but he eluded me. Eventually I went back to the court of the Gentiles, and suddenly he was there—directly in front of my table. I stood up and bowed, as if he were one of the teachers of the law, though he was not dressed like one of them. *Sir, may I be of service?* I said, wondering what could possibly have made him come to me. He didn't answer at first. He looked at me for a moment, with a sad, perplexed look, as if I had offended him in some way, though of course I had never laid eyes on the man before, so how could that be? *Leave this,* he said, sweeping his hand over my scales and my accounts. *Leave all of this, and come follow me.* It was unnerving. Behind him was a ragtag group of four or five men; none of them looked very promising, I can tell you. They looked like day laborers or fishermen, poorly educated and poorly dressed. They smelled like it too. Hardly the sort of company I care to keep. *Sir,* I said to the Teacher, *I am not worthy of you.* Again, he did not answer immediately. It was awkward. Now that I know him, I am accustomed to his silences; he is often in prayer, but how could I have known that when he simply stood there with his somber eyes on me? *Nevertheless, I have chosen you to be my disciple.* It was as if God himself had placed an obligation on me. I felt compelled to obey. I don't know how else to explain it. And so, here I am."

A thousand questions fill her mind. The rest of the night, she thinks, will not be sufficient to learn all she desires to know.

"You said you know him. What sort of man is he?"

"He's a man, like any other man, and yet not like any other man. He is subject to hunger and sickness. Strange as it sounds, I have seen the Healer become ill from eating bad fish. I assure you, there was nothing divine in the way he vomited. He is subject to exhaustion. I have seen him sleep soundly through thunderstorms and pelting rain on the open sea. I have seen him frustrated—mostly because a certain few of our number remain dense and close minded despite his teaching and miracles. I have seen him eat and sleep and sweat and pray and weep and sigh and fast and keep vigil. He is a man who lives wholly in every moment. He regrets nothing. His mind is never idle."

"Does he keep the law?" She is thinking of her father.

"In essence, yes. But he has little regard for the traditions of our elders."

"I wonder if my father knows about him."

"I assure you, every learned man and teacher of Israel knows of him now."

"Is he well versed in the law and the prophets?"

"I have never known a teacher so familiar with our holy books. It is as if he himself wrote them."

Surely her father would commend him for that! It is what he loved best and respected most in a man.

"Is he very serious, then? Very scholarly?"

"He is never anxious. Certain things make him laugh. The stories of children. Or watching a man curse his donkey or a woman smacking hungry hands away from her fresh-baked bread. Last week, a dark-eyed beauty in the market winked at Thomas, one of our men. He was so taken with her that he tripped over a cart and dropped all our bread in the dust. We were furious but when we told the Master, he laughed uproariously and seemed to think it was very funny."

"Has he—a wife?"

"No. He lives like one of the Essenes."

"But surely he has loved some woman? Or some have been in love with him?"

He stops and looks at her in the lamplight. "Why should you care?"

She glances down, feeling her face become heated. "Women care about such things."

He lies back down again, and contemplates their shadows on the wall. "He's a strong man, though not very handsome, if you must know. Aside from his eyes, his looks are rather disappointing for such a charismatic leader. Quite common, really."

"I suppose his wisdom and power outshine his physical imperfections."

He looked at her again, almost suspiciously. "You have not seen him, then?"

"I have not seen his face."

Her answer seemed to satisfy him. "As to women, he admires their beauty, as any man would. But he does not become—inflamed. I have seen women come to him after dark to offer themselves. I don't know what he says to them, but within seconds they leave, their faces white with holy terror, as if aghast at what they were about to do."

And what about you, she wonders. Surely some of the women have offered themselves to his disciples as well...surely their eyes had lingered on the face of her lover, and lusted for him...

"I suppose this new life of yours...is what kept you from coming to me?"

"Naturally. It is as I told you...I feel compelled to obey him."

"You said he told you to come to me...what does he know of me?"

"He knows many things—hidden things. He reads the secret thoughts of men, it seems."

"You told him nothing about us?"

"Not a word."

Her mind spins at the scope of his power. To be able to discern the thoughts of a man...or a woman. Surely he is a prophet of great magnitude.

"What did he say to you?"

"You have dealt treacherously with her...you have been like Laban with our father Jacob. I warn you, Judas—unless you turn from your evil ways—it will be better for Laban than for you on the day of judgment."

The rebuke still pounded in his mind, like hammer blows, but he does not repeat it to her. Instead he replies, "He instructed me to... attend to your needs...so that you would not be forced to...compromise the principles that you have been taught."

She wants to believe him, but his words sound rehearsed. She lowers her head. "You don't love me anymore."

He sighs impatiently. "I have other priorities now. Is that so hard to understand?"

"What is to become of me?" She tries to control the tremor in her voice.

"Stop this! You will be provided for. Here." He tosses her a small sack that contains a handful of denarii.

"I don't want your money! I want your name...I want you to marry me, and take care of me, so I can walk through the marketplace and go to the synagogue without the women clucking their tongues after me! Surely the Master would bless our union! Then you can go to him, and follow him around the countryside, if he so wills, only make me your wife first!"

"I shall not. I cannot! I shall live as he does—without a wife or any other comforts of home. It's only right."

They are silent for a few moments. She turns away from him and weeps softly.

"Reumah, I must go."

"Will I see you again?"

"I will come again, I assure you."

"Ah. Words I have heard before."

"Indeed! And here I am." There is anger in his voice.

He stands, and pulls his cloak about him. She does not attempt to help him. In the pale light some of his face is shadowed, and he seems older, or darker, as if a sinister aspect of his character has been momentarily revealed.

"Reumah—the money?"

"What of it?" She still clutches the bag.

"Well? Do you want it?"

"It's all I have of you."

"Well, then. Use it well. I will bring you more when I can, but I am not a rich man, you know. Especially now."

She knows he expects some token of gratitude: to take his hand, and kiss it, perhaps, like a child receiving a coin from a benevolent father. But she turns away from him, and he leaves without speaking again. She watches him go through the gate of the courtyard, glancing this way and that, and then she looks toward the sky. White-yellow streaks of fiery light in the eastern sky herald the new day, but her despair is too deep for hope or prayer.

13

As soon as Jennifer leaves, Vina softens, like ice cream left on the counter. She sits next to Jeb on the bed, and dismisses Jean-Denis from the room with a shake of her bracelets. After a moment's hesitation, he obeys her.

"Here, honey. Drink this." She holds a cup with a straw, which contains a protein shake.

"Vina." His voice has been reduced again to a laryngitis-type whisper.

"Do as I say."

"I want to die as an artist."

"We'll talk about it later. Drink."

"There is no later for me."

"What the hell were you doing with her?"

"Don't be mad." Their words overlap and they each have their own brand of power, but Vina is stronger now, as she was at the beginning, and he knows it.

"I want to go down as a great artist."

"Of course." She places the protein shake on the night table, and crosses her arms and her legs.

"I'm saying—I don't want to be remembered as a big-time queen."

"It's too late for that." The foot that's crossed over her leg begins to jerk.

"I could marry Jennifer."

"God, you're insane!" She yells it, and Jean-Denis comes to the door. She waves him away again, and puts her long index finger, which has some kind of Egyptian scarab ring on it, on Jeb's chest, and licks her lips.

"What did she say to you?"

"You know she would do it."

"Where is this coming from?" Her voice is becoming louder.

"When they interview you after I'm gone—reinvent me. They'll believe you." In his mind he imagines his father, alone and enfeebled, reading about him in a foul-smelling nursing home somewhere down south. He begins to cough violently again, and Vina turns away, apparently disgusted. She crosses to the window, and motions to Jean-Denis. She gazes out at the house across the street while she talks to him.

"…some kind of sedative, maybe?"

"That is not necessary right now."

"I disagree. He's very agitated. His mind is troubled."

"That is to be expected, Madame."

"No, you don't understand. That girl that was here—Jennifer. She upsets him. Make sure that she is never left alone here with him again."

"I will do my best, Madame, but I must comply with the wishes of the patient, as much as possible."

"To hell with that. He's got dementia. I have the power of attorney. Do you understand what I'm saying?"

"This is not dementia."

"Clearly he's not in his right mind."

"He is very clear—"

"God damn it—"

"—and this is usually a sign that the end is coming. I have seen it in other patients. A period of clarity when they are spiritually awakened, as if to prepare for their final hours…" His voice trails off, because Vina has held up her hand. They look over at Jeb. He has stopped coughing, and is listening to Jean-Denis.

"Come…" he motions to Jean-Denis, who then crosses over and sits on his bed. Vina stays by the window.

"Soon…after I sleep a bit…I want to make a confession."

"I should get a priest?"

"No…no." He coughs violently again, and Jean-Denis lifts him up from behind and holds a cloth gently over his mouth.

"I want to make it to you."

"I will get you a priest."

"Just you. When I'm ready."

"OK. You rest now."

From the window she watches him curl up on his side and close his eyes, at the mercy of Jean-Denis, or anyone who could walk into his room and put some crazy idea into his head. One could just as easily put vodka or vinegar in his IV. How easy it would be, really. Only the strong prevail. Of the many things Vina hates, weakness is the worst.

He had not seemed weak, but aloof and slightly detached from reality the first time she had met him, which was in Florenzio's gallery, where she worked, on the Lower East Side in '74. Klaus had come in first, and immediately asked if someone could hang up his fur coat in a back room. She handed it to Christine, her assistant, and then introduced herself as Davina Paranoy, which was the name she went by back then. Klaus monopolized her the entire time even as she kept glancing over at Jeb, who was dressed all in black: cowboy boots and Stetson, studded shirt and leather jeans. The hat and boots added five inches to his six-foot frame and his straw-blond hair hung wavy and loose to his shoulders. He was hard to miss. Jeb had merely nodded to her, then removed his sunglasses and spent the entire time studying the three pieces of the exhibit that Vina hated, because they were done by a photographer who had told her that he wanted to be the next Mapplethorpe, and she had a particular disdain for wannabe artists.

Klaus was looking to purchase, and he was one of those clients who had to give his opinion about every piece in the gallery. He would not let her stop listening. He had two large gold rings on each hand, and his nails were buffed. He wore a dark leisure suit and an unbuttoned shirt to advertise his gold necklaces, and a sapphire-blue silk scarf, which he occasionally stroked with his right hand. With the left he smoked a long cigarillo and waved it around while he pontificated. He barely made eye contact but she thought she detected traces of eyeliner around his lashes.

Eventually they moved around to where Jeb was still standing, in front of a group of photogravures that featured images of polished male torsos and buttocks.

"Your quiet friend seems fascinated with the Moraux prints..." she ventured to Klaus.

A look of distaste came over his face while his eyes scanned the pieces. "Yes, well. *Chaque' un a son gout.*" He edged over to Jeb and nudged him significantly, as if to move him on. "What these lack in originality they make up for in poor taste," he told Vina over his shoulder, which was trailed by a puff of smoke. "Have that girl bring my coat."

She gave Klaus a catalog and her card as they were leaving, and she agreed to have lunch. Out of the corner of her eye she observed Jeb take another catalog from the silver basket on the counter. Brady, her other assistant who was just returning with a bakery box of brioche, held the door for them and stared, openmouthed, as Jeb slid himself into the limousine.

"He's a beautiful young man," he gushed to Klaus, before Vina could stop him.

"Yes," Klaus said, exhaling through his nostrils. "He's the son I never had."

As soon as they were gone, she walked back over to the Moraux prints and contemplated the three images that he had found so entrancing: the first featured the chiseled upper body of a young man whose arms were bound, crucifixion-like, by leather thongs at his wrists. He was blindfolded and his mouth was open slightly, as if he were trying not to breathe through his nose. Three hands, two male and one female, smeared a dark muddy substance on his torso. She knew it wasn't intended to be chocolate. The next piece featured the sculpted back and buttocks of the same model, apparently. Words tattooed on his tailbone read, "EXIT ONLY." A small arrow below the words, also tattooed, pointed southward to the crevice of his butt. The third piece showed him naked again, from the waist up, looking directly at the camera. He was wearing makeup. A very dark-skinned man, also naked and greatly muscled, embraced him from behind, one hand encircling his throat. The young man's long hair blew back over the dark man's head, and there was a mesmerizing expression on his face: lust and cruelty, like Nero or Caligula, in the curve of his mouth; rage and despair in his kohl-rimmed eyes. They were the eyes of a slave.

"Oh, God, it's him." Brady had come up behind her.

"Of course," Vina replied, although she had just realized it herself.

"I'm lusting," Brady said, his mouth filled with brioche.

"He was staring at himself the whole time? What a prima donna," said Christine, who had also come over to look.

"Maybe." Vina tapped her pen against her lip. "Maybe not."

Christine snorted contemptuously, which was a habit of hers, and she went to answer the phone. Brady gazed for another minute and then went to make cappuccino in the back room.

"Maybe he's trying to find himself." Vina said, but no one heard.

"Maybe you're still trying to find yourself," she says, stepping back to his bed. He opens his eyes. "But it's too late. You are who you are, and everyone knows who you are."

"Who?"

"Everyone!"

"No, I mean…who am I? Who do people say I am?" She has to bend her ear over his mouth to hear him.

"Oh honey, you're like a messiah to them. Compelling. Controversial. A gay artist with a tortured soul. Your work speaks to them. And now, on top of all that—a martyr."

But his eyes have closed again, and he is drifting away.

Klaus had chosen Grimaldi's for lunch, and she wasn't surprised or disappointed that he brought Jeb along.

"This is my Johnny," Klaus told her. "Have you met?"

Vina felt certain that she had met him somewhere other than the gallery. "Not formally," she said, and held out her hand.

"Hi," he said, and he shook her proffered hand in a lax manner. She wished that he would take off his sunglasses, but their table was next to a sunny window and the light seemed to bother him. Another patron, a young man she recognized as a model and soap opera actor, came over and kissed Klaus's hand. Then he nudged Jeb and whispered to him, and the two of them left the table. Jeb was wearing white flared jeans and a shiny black shirt. He had on platform shoes. His hair was parted in the middle and the two sides blew back off his face like wings when he walked. Everyone watched him go by.

She and Klaus ordered martinis, and Klaus ordered a rum and Coke for "Johnny." After about twenty minutes he returned to the table and took a sip of his drink. His nostrils were runny and red and Vina quickly began to despise him. While Klaus talked, he sat with his long legs stretched out under the table, sniffing and wiping his nose, and he kept looking around the dining room, as if nervous that someone else might recognize him.

"So. How did you two meet?" she said casually when Klaus stopped talking to swallow one of his escargot. Her eyes flitted back and forth between them.

"In San Francisco," Klaus told her, and picked up another snail, apparently unwilling to say more.

"Did you work together?" Although she knew better.

"It was at the Sledge." It was the first time Jeb had spoken directly to her.

"I beg your pardon?"

"The Sledgehammer. It's a club." He put his sunglasses on the top of his head.

"Ancient history..." said Klaus, and she could tell he was about to change the subject.

"I was working on a mural behind the dance floor—"

"We have business to discuss," Klaus said.

"You're an artist?" Vina asked, doing her best to keep a sarcastic edge out of her voice.

"You don't believe me?"

Vina immediately looked up from her salad. His eyes stared straight into hers, and she never, never forgot it, because they held an astonishing amount of anger, and something of a threat as well. Neither of them looked away until Klaus cleared his throat.

"Johnny. Eat your soup."

Vina did not want to jeopardize eighteen-hundred dollars of commission, so she switched back to Klaus. Jeb ate the *au gratin* from his onion soup, and then pushed it away and lit a cigarette.

Toward the end of the meal, when she felt certain that she was nearing the finish line of the deal with Klaus, he stood up and turned to Jeb.

"Come to the men's room." He glanced at Vina, and then back at Jeb.

"I'm fine, Pops. You go ahead." He was on his third cigarette, and the smoke was getting to Vina.

"Your hair. It needs some attention."

"I'm gonna finish my cig." He blew a perfect smoke ring, and fixed his eyes on Vina. A dark look passed over Klaus's face, but he left them.

"I know who you are," he said simply.

"Of course you do," she said, and a small warning light began to flash in her head.

"No," he leaned forward and lowered his voice. "I know who you really are…you're that dominatrix who does those Satanic rituals with the fucking suits who pay you to whip them."

She glanced around the room, and then leaned toward him, maintaining a stiff smile.

"I have no idea what you're talking about."

"You have an inverted crucifix tattooed between your shoulder blades."

She reached over and picked out one of his cigarettes, lit it, and blew the smoke out past him. It gave her a moment to think.

"Apparently we have some mutual friends."

"I have pictures." His eyes bore into hers.

"Ah, yes. You said you're an artist." Her brow went up when she said *artist*.

"Photographs of you. And a certain judge…rather nasty, actually."

By the time Klaus had returned she had agreed to meet him at their gym at 10:30 on Monday, which was when Klaus was in the steam room. She picked up the bill and shook Klaus's hand. Then she turned to Jeb and smiled widely.

"Very nice meeting you, Johnny. I hope to see you again soon."

She figured she would hire some thug to pour acid on his face.

They sat at a table in a café that adjoined the spa. As soon as she sat down, he slid his chair next to hers. One would have thought they were a couple. She noted with satisfaction that his hands were shaking. He kept them both on the *Times* in front of him, and gave her the barest glance of the grainy photos, which were concealed between the folds of the paper.

"Isn't there some kind of law against bloodletting?" he murmured into her ear.

She smiled, and glanced nonchalantly around the room.

"You could get more from the gentleman," she said, crushing out her cigarette.

"I don't want money."

She glanced at him. "What do you want?"

"I want you to sell my art."

"It must be shit if you have to blackmail me."

"That's not all. I want you to get me away from here—from the whole fist-fucking scene. I want you to get me away from him. I need to be where I can work."

"Well, leave then. Find an agent. Why do you need to involve me?"

He took her hand under the table, and squeezed it so hard she almost screamed.

"I'm his fucking concubine. He owns me."

"Don't you ever touch me again." Her voice came through her teeth.

"I can't take a shit without him watching."

"And you thought I was kinky." Her hand was still throbbing.

"Who do you think I stole the photos from?"

She lit another cigarette. "Go on."

"He was going to blackmail you to get the pieces he wanted. He had at least five picked out, including the Moraux, oddly enough. You'd be left with nothing, lady. *You'd* be paying Florenzio for years—just to keep these riveting shots of you and the judge from surfacing."

"You're lying."

"You're not the first. He preys on your type."

He glanced at his watch, and then gathered up the *Times*.

"I'll be here next week."

In the end, it was his art that saved both of them. She flew to San Francisco, and called the bathhouse and club owners who had commissioned him. Only one, the owner of the Sledgehammer, returned her call. Her high heels clicked across the dance floor in the early morning off-hours, and then stopped short when she saw his mural, which was a shockingly irreverent interpretation of Michelangelo's *David*. When she returned to her hotel she made a long-distance call to an old friend in Denmark. The following Monday morning, Klaus came out of the steam room and discovered that his Johnny and four hundred dollars from his wallet had disappeared.

Jeb was on his way to Amsterdam, and the fatal photos were shredded and burned in Vina's own kitchen sink. She watches him sleep for a few minutes, and then signals to Jean-Denis, who watches at the door.

"I want you to call me if he has any visitors. Anybody at all."

"Yes, Madame."

Vina wasn't taking any chances. She owned him now.

XIV

There are women too, Reumah learns. There are women who follow the Master, and Reumah has seen them. Three times she has gone out to hear him preach, following the crowds up into the hills surrounding the city. Three times she has returned late in the evening, exhausted, but unable to sleep because of his words, which, on leaving his lips, are borne on the wind to reach even the most reluctant ears in the crowd, as if assisted by a divinely appointed breeze. Three times she has strained to see his face and failed; at night when she closes her eyes, the faces of the women come before her, even while the Master's words echo in her head, much like her father's.

The women are called *The Fragrant Ones*, because they exude the scent of spikenard. Their perfume permeates the crowd of onlookers, and even the blind beggars are able to discern when they are near. They are mostly older women, her mother's age, perhaps, except for one, who is only a few years older than Reumah. They seem to her like ministering spirits, with their scented veils blowing out behind them as they fan out into the multitude and gather the crippled and the blind and the aged and the little ones into their arms, bringing them near to the Master for blessing or healing, as needed. Some of them carry baskets of bread and dried fish, or cakes of figs or raisins, and place the food into the hands of clamoring children and pleading beggars and impoverished widows, gently urging and smiling, quieting the tumult with soothing words.

Once, as a girl, Reumah had seen a leprous man, and the sight of his filmy eyes and gnarled hands had given her nightmares. The youngest of *The Fragrant Ones*, however, does not recoil at the sight of crooked limbs, swollen tumors, foaming mouths, sightless eyes, oozing scabs, or any other uncleanness, not even leprosy. Reumah has watched her, climbing over a low hill to approach a ragged group of lepers who huddle far away from the crowd, exuding the stench of death, their corpselike faces shrouded and their blistered flesh barely concealed beneath filthy rags. She watched in horror as the young woman placed her clean hand in the crooked paw of one, and pleaded with him to accompany her to the Master, but he could not overcome his fear of the crowd.

Most have followed him from Galilee, Judas tells her.

"From Galilee? So very far? Where do they stay?" she asks him when he returns to her one night. It is always at night.

"Mostly in the city, at the home of Mary of Magdala, or else at the house of Lazarus of Bethany. He has a large house with extensive gardens and plenty of rooms—and money." There is a note of cold disapproval in his voice, as if he would make better use of Lazarus's wealth if he could. "He is a master perfumer, as were his fathers before him. He and his sisters are among the Master's closest friends."

"Ah, that explains the perfume. Which ones are the sisters?" She is astounded at the idea of the Master counting women among his closest friends.

"Why should you care?"

"Please—please, Judas. Tell me. Which are his favorites?"

"Why do you ask? Do you intend to become one of them?" He glances at her sharply.

"I—I'm curious, I suppose. A man having women as friends—it seems—unseemly."

"It is unseemly. And unmanly." He sighs impatiently. "He's a great leader, and powerful. You have no idea of his power. And yet he sacrifices precious hours of sleep to pray. You've heard him preach—he's a brilliant orator. He could hold court with Herod himself! Yet he wastes his words on the dull ears of the ignorant masses and expends his great power healing every hapless invalid that crosses his path." He places his head down into his hands, and runs his fingers back through the long curls of his hair, as Reumah herself used to do when they were lovers.

"Listen to this: a month ago we were resting quietly in the shade of the ancient groves, eating our noonday meal, and a group of a dozen mothers with twice as many squalling children approached us, determined to have the Master bless their noisy offspring. Naturally we told them to leave because the Master was resting, and then suddenly he stood up and rebuked us! Rebuked *us*! We thought we were doing him a favor! The flies gathered on his unfinished food while he sat there for the next hour, coddling and murmuring prayers over the babies. Of course none of us got the slightest bit of rest with that babbling swarm. I tell you, we were none too pleased."

She shivers at the iciness in his voice. In her dreams, Judas becomes the Master's closest friend. In her dreams, the Master urges him not to delay in marrying her, and then in their married home, he becomes their most frequent guest. In her dreams, he removes the stigma of her barrenness with one touch, and then blesses the baby sons that are born to them...

She takes a breath and carefully says, "You should not be angry at his kindness."

He shifts his weight onto his elbow, and gazes into the lamp. She has noted that he hardly ever looks at her directly, and seems to have lost interest in her allurements. Aside from giving her money, and having the comfort of her presence and her bed, he seems to have forgotten that they were lovers.

"I am angry," he says slowly. "The fact is, I am wiser and more learned than all the others, especially those from Galilee. Ha! Illiterate riffraff they are, good for catching our fish and building our fires on cold nights. They sit there with their mouths agape, hanging onto his every word, as if God himself were speaking. If ever one of us was suited to be taken into his confidence, it would be me. And so I have tried to urge him, to persuade him to use his power for a greater good, but he is deaf to my counsel. I wish he would argue, at least. But instead, he just shakes his head and looks at me with great sadness in his eyes. I hate it. I hate that look." He claps his hand over a small beetle that has crossed the dusty floor, and feeds it into the flame of the lamp, which produces a vile odor.

"But he's given you charge of the money…how fitting that is! He must deem you worthy of his trust. That's an honor, surely."

"An honor. Ha! There again is something I can't fathom…he had Simon—a man who has bread for brains—catch a fish that had a gold coin in its mouth. He then used it to pay their taxes! He could turn water into wine and have gold appear in the mouths of the fishes we eat, and yet he chooses to rely on the charity of his friends. It falls to me, then, to bow graciously as I accept a handout from Lazarus…or Joanna, the wife of Herod's steward. Can you imagine? A woman giving money to me! Utterly humiliating. I hate it. I'm disgusted."

His jaw is locked in anger, she can see veins in his neck, and she is troubled at the menace in his eyes. Was it always there? She tries to remember him as he was, before the time of her trouble, but her mind is clouded, because it was always night. It occurs to her that she has only known him intimately under the veil of darkness, and she wonders now if she has been deceived as to his true nature, which is a thought so unsettling that she immediately pushes it to the furthest corner of her mind.

"You are weary…and discouraged," she says carefully. "Perhaps the Master is testing you by giving you this mundane task—perhaps he is about to give you a more important position or responsibility—but he is just now testing your loyalty."

He suddenly rises to a sitting position and looks at her directly. They contemplate each other briefly, and then she flushes and looks down at her hands, which feel cold in spite of the warm night air.

"Why do you insist on defending him?"

"I—I'm not defending him! I'm just trying to understand—"

"You're a woman. You understand nothing, unless I explain it to you. You don't even know him."

"I want to know him! Explain him to me, then."

"How can I when he explains nothing to me? He gives no defense of his actions, and expects us to believe everything he says. I have not the heart for it."

Her spirit caves under the vehemence of his words. The pain of longing for him to want what she wants, and love what she loves, closes in on her, and for a moment she cannot speak.

"Please, Judas. Please, may I meet him? Will you not bring me to him? Just once?"

"I see no reason for that."

"I would like to thank him, at least—for healing me when I was so sick."

"Yes, yes. You and a thousand others. He's a busy man, Reumah. He chooses whom he will allow near him."

"And he has chosen you! And yet you are cold to him."

"That's my business!"

Suddenly he takes her arms and pulls her toward him, and his eyes become narrow.

"You shall meet him, Reumah. You shall meet him when I determine the time and the place. Trust me, you will not soon forget it. In fact, you may well regret it. So do not plead with me again."

She shivers in fear at his words, and attempts to change the subject.

"And what of the women? May I not meet them? Surely you would not object to me meeting them…"

"'The Fragrant Ones?'" he says it with a sneer. "They are extremely preoccupied with their service to the Master, as you have seen. I doubt they'd have time for idle chatter, unless you suddenly developed a case of blindness or leprosy."

But she cannot let go, because of the longing that has taken hold of her.

"The youngest one—she appears to be slightly older than me. May I not make her acquaintance? She seems so kind…can I not at least greet her by name?"

He lets go of her arms, then, and nods with a look of sudden insight.

"Ah, yes. She is kind…and beautiful. Don't you think she's beautiful? She has the most delightful smile, I think."

The way he says it causes a different feeling to spring into her heart.

"I suppose so…in her own way."

"That is Mary. She is the younger sister of Lazarus. She is one of the Master's favorites, and full of virtue. She is known throughout the region for her good works. And her purity."

The meaning of his words is not lost on her. She suddenly loses the desire to meet any of them, for surely they would discern immediately what kind of woman she is.

Yet the longing remains. Hours after Judas has left her, the longing remains, and becomes the central preoccupation of her mind. More than anything, even more than becoming the wife of Judas or bearing his child with the Master's blessing, she would like to be Mary. She would like to be one of *The Fragrant Ones*.

15

*J*ennifer makes it back to her own apartment, to her own toilet, to throw up. Not much comes up, and it occurs to her that she hasn't eaten anything all day except a bowl of cornflakes. She rummages through her fridge and fries two pieces of pork roll and two eggs, makes herself some tea, and sits down at the small table next to the window. She looks out and sees Clay Peterson, his face raw with cold, coming home with two bags of groceries. She looks down at the sweating pork roll and overcooked eggs on her plate and pushes it away. She wonders what it would be like to have a husband that would buy groceries and carry them into the house. A provider. "Here, honey—picked up a few things on my way home." It seems like a fairy tale. In real life, she thinks, women are the providers. In real life, they are the ones that carry everything—grocery bags and shopping bags and diaper bags and handbags—the ones that make food appear on the table. The men and the kids come eat it, wipe their mouths, and go away again. In real life, women answer to the need of the moment.

He called me, she thinks. *He practically demanded I come over. I'm supposed to say no to a dying friend's wish?*

If only he would say it to Vina. If only he would say, just once, *I want her here. I need her here, just as much as I need you. More so.* Why couldn't he? Why didn't he stand up to Vina?

It was like Vina owned him. Maybe she did. When he had returned after two years in Europe, he was exhausted from overworking and numb from exposure to the virulent gay nightlife of Amsterdam. Vina had met him at the airport and brought him to Red Bank where she lived with her new husband. To hear Vina tell it, he was almost dead.

"Dead?" Jennifer had asked her at the time. "You mean literally, dying?"

"No, spiritually. He was a shell—a zombie. Like a mannequin. He barely spoke."

Vina had fed him and let him sleep, on and off, for three days, and on the third day he woke up and said, "Are we near the ocean?"

So she had driven him along the shore, and stopped in Ocean Grove for lunch, but he wasn't hungry. He wanted to lie on the beach, he said.

Vina walked up and down Main Street, poking around the little shops, and Jeb lay on the beach, face down on his arms, not sleeping but barely moving. After an hour she came back to check on him. He had taken off his shirt and scrunched it up to make a pillow out of it. He did not speak when she poked him with the edge of her toe and asked him if he wanted anything. She left him and went to look at rental properties.

It was a Saturday, and there was a Gospel choir singing in the pavilion on the boardwalk directly ahead of where he lay. The words of "Leaning on the Everlasting Arms" and "Nothing but the Blood of Jesus" and a few others that he recognized from the churchgoing years of his childhood drifted down on him. He remembered standing next to his mother in the pew while she sang and smelling her lilac-scented perfume. He never liked to sing, and she would nudge him from time to time, and lower the hymnbook to his eye level. He remembered cracking his knuckles, out of sheer restlessness as the preaching went on, and his father scowling at him. Sometimes when the sermon seemed interminable he would study the hats of the ladies in front of him, starting with the first row, and give them a grade based on overall impression. Most of them got C's. Two rows in front of where he sat was an elderly lady who wore the same hat every week: a white-trimmed navy-blue straw hat with a bunch of small red cherries perched precariously on the brim. One Sunday he fantasized about making a peashooter and hitting the cherries off the hat, one by one. The idea produced an uncontrollable shudder of laughter from deep inside him. His mother placed her hand on his knee, but he couldn't suppress the ripples of mirth that took control of him. Soon his sister, who was sitting next to him, began to snicker as well, only her laugh came out as a snort, and this made them both laugh harder. His father glanced at him, with daggers in his eyes, and Jeb left the pew, red-faced, on the pretense of going to the men's room. He had not been able to sit for two days after his father had dealt with him. From then on he hated church, and church people, and decided he did not care for their God either, who, in his mind, seemed determined to squelch anything fun, using violence, if necessary.

The sun was warm but not too hot, and the old hymns and the ocean and the wind caused him to lapse into an almost hypnotic state, as if a huge but gentle hand was pressing him into the sand, imposing rest on his depleted soul. He could not move or open his eyes. Nor did he want to. He thought he might be dying, and he felt completely calm about it.

He thought he'd be dead when Vina came back. He thought his spirit would have leached out of his body and sunk into the sand or flown out over the waves and there'd be nothing but a corpse when she returned. But suddenly her feet in beaded sandals were next to his face and he looked up, squinting, and said, "I want to live here."

"I know," she answered. "I found you a place."

She had found him a large, well-lit studio apartment in town, and used her own money for the deposit. She helped him move in and set up and told him to "focus on healing" and not to worry about working for a while. "When your energy has returned," she told him. She brought him aromatic candles and incense and meditative music and called him every day from Red Bank to see if he needed anything. Most times he just wanted pot or cash. He could get chocolate milk or cigarettes or toilet paper from the local shops. He'd buy a croissant sandwich or a slice of pizza or some ice cream from any of the cafes on Main Street, and he'd sit at one of the bistro tables along the sidewalk and eat without enthusiasm. He'd kick at the bold pigeons that pecked under his chair.

Sometimes he went to lie face down on the beach, his head on his arms, but most days he walked through the town to the park at its center, in front of the big auditorium that had stood for more than a hundred years and had been the center of the town's spiritual foundation. He spoke to no one, although he was greeted frequently. He avoided eye contact, although he was regularly gazed on after he had passed by. His hair had grown long, and he would go for days without shaving or changing his clothes. He began to look like one of the transient people who frequented the area. He slumped on a bench in front of the large airy edifice and contemplated the cross mounted above it, and every day the incongruity of having a cross illuminated by light bulbs on top of a Victorian-era building irritated him more and more. It reminded him of his father, who had put crosses all over the house, even above the toilet, like God was watching even when you took a piss. He thought how his father would like this Christ-haunted, church-dominated town—"God's Square Mile," as it was nicknamed, and he thought how his father would be astounded that he was living there. So every day he thought of his father, and every day a black, ugly, menacing beast grew inside him, and the beast inside is what got him back on track, he told Vina.

One day he didn't answer the phone, no matter how many times she called, so she drove down and he was stretching a canvas. There were a dozen sketches on the table and floor and she stood there watching him for twenty minutes without a word.

Finally she said, "What do you need now?"

"A car," he answered, "to truck all my gear."

"OK," she said. "What else?"

"Some dumb slut with big tits to pose for me. Just try to find one without an agent, OK? I hate dealing with agents."

That's exactly what he had said, but Vina had never told that to Jennifer.

It didn't take him long to ask her, after the party on Heck Avenue. He called her in the middle of a Wednesday. She had worked a twelve-hour shift the night before and was half-asleep when she answered the phone. She sat up and tried to make her voice sound more mellow and sexy. She could feel her pulse in her neck.

"Jennifer," he said. "That you?"

"Uh-huh."

"You remember me? From the party?"

"Sure. How could I forget you?" and she laughed in what she hoped was a throaty way.

"Well, good. Vina tells me we're neighbors."

"Uh-huh. I think so."

"Was wondering if you could drop by…"

And he had shown her around, and shown her a bunch of his sketches and then some of the larger canvases. He stood so close to her she could smell the fabric softener from his freshly laundered T-shirt. She could feel his breath on her neck. He popped open a beer for each of them, and then he asked her how she felt about posing.

"Posing? Me?"

"Yeah. You know. Be my model."

And she had laughed and blushed and thought about the dimples on her butt and the two pockets of pudge above her hips and a few dark areola hairs and said quite firmly, "I don't think so…"

"We'd pay you, of course."

"We? Whose we?

"Well, Vina handles the money."

Which gave her a clue, then, as to their relationship, but it also made it easier to say no to him. If he had simply asked her to climb into bed with him, she would have kept her clothes off afterward, and he could have drawn, painted, or sculpted her to his heart's content. She would have done it for free.

Not long after that they got her drunk. She didn't know they were getting her drunk on purpose, but that's what they did. They were at Vina's place in Red Bank. Vina had made it sound like she was having a party, but it turned out to be just the three of them. Vina was pregnant with Kevin, so she said they'd have to drink her share. Jeb sat next to Jennifer on the white leather couch, with his arm around her, and squirted schnapps into her mouth with a water pistol.

"Come on, do it sexy."

"Wha? What d'ya mean?" she could feel herself sliding into the phase of still knowing what she was doing, but not caring.

"You know what I mean. Fellate it."

And she did.

"With your eyes closed. Like you mean it."

And she did.

Vina started taking pictures but she didn't care because he kissed her full on the mouth, then, with his lips tasting like schnapps too, and it felt like all her bodily organs were sinking down to a place between her legs.

She didn't remember very much after that. She didn't remember taking off her blouse or the rest of her clothes, but there were pictures to show it. But she didn't see the pictures till much later, when it was too late.

She didn't see the pictures or find out anything until his big show in Hoboken.

That night they picked her up and they were dressed like rock stars, both of them. Vina wore a vintage black lace dress with padded shoulders and a rhinestone brooch and four-inch heels and a small hat with a black fingertip veil that concealed most of her face except for her scarlet lipstick and faux beauty mark. Jeb wore champagne-colored satin pants and shirt, and platform boots and a leopard-skin coat. The top of his hair had been cut, styled, and gelled into spikes above his head, and the rest of it hung thickly over his shoulders, mullet-style. His makeup had been professionally applied. Jennifer felt dismally underdressed. She had borrowed a black leather jacket from a friend, and was wearing it over a red satin blouse and black jeans and boots, but compared to the two of them she felt frumpy and provincial. The blouse was a bit tight, and she knew without look-ing that it was gaping between the buttons. She had concentrated on her hair. Now it was so teased and sprayed she felt like it had become separated from her head and was hovering above her like a dark cloud.

They were in a stretch limo, and the limo picked up some other people too, and everyone was drinking and laughing and talking. Jennifer tried to keep up, but she had the sense that she was becom-ing invisible.

When they got there, when they emerged from the limo, there were cameras flashing and it was so crowded she felt like she had left her body and was watching from a point in midair. Afterward, when she thought about it, she decided her brain had done this on purpose to keep her from panicking, because some other part of her already knew what was coming.

There were wall-to-wall people—bizarre, human oddities of neither sex, it seemed, with vacuous eyes and sardonic mouths. They were mostly dressed in black or purple or red, and they surged around Jeb, who gleamed in his clothes and was taller than all of them. For some reason he had not let go of Jen's arm. Vina kept to his other side.

It might have been three hours or fifteen minutes or all night—she did not know—when she stood with him and Vina and the crowd in front of a large painting and his mouth was next to her ear, and he said, "Here's the little surprise I wanted to show you…" and she looked at it for a few minutes, because it did not sink in at first.

On the card next to the canvas it said "Blowjob" and she saw the card first, because it was written so crisply in black and white, and her eyes took in the words before they could absorb the images he had painted. Her mouth froze into a stiff grin while her brain tried to make sense of the image of herself—it most definitely was herself, there was no mistake and the entire crowd seemed to understand that—herself naked and performing fellatio on a gun, a loaded gun, apparently, since the trigger was cocked, and a man's hand was shoving it into her mouth. She took a step closer, and she recognized the hand, because it was his hand, his perfectly formed and skillful hand, shoving the loaded gun into her mouth.

His face was still next to hers and he kept holding her and saying something but her ears were ringing and she felt so hot and she saw herself again, from above, sinking down and down and wishing she could haul herself up and get herself out of there. That was what she remembered. She had no recollection of moving, or leaving, or coming home that night.

At first Vina left messages on her recorder—polite messages, asking her to call and hinting that she was entitled to a stipend. She did not return her calls. A week went by and Jeb called. She replayed his voice saying, "Hey, Jen…what's goin' on? Git back to me, OK?" four times, but she did not call. She drove by his house a few times, saw Vina's car there occasionally, and kept going. She was moving forward, she felt. She was leaving him behind, and instead of pain or passion there was numbness anytime she thought of him. The wound had stopped bleeding. It was getting smaller.

It would have scabbed over, and healed completely, she was sure, had he not called her two months later.

Two months later he called her, two months after the show, and begged her to come over. He begged her. Told her he was sick.

"I'm going to die…" is what he said.

"Aren't we all?" she said coolly.

But she had gone over, and walked into his apartment, and a bunch of the disciples were there, and some of them were crying. She had the sense that she was in a bad dream. They took her to his bed and then left her there with him. He gazed at her for a minute, and then she looked away, because she could not believe how different he looked from the last time she had seen him. He was a pale, shrunken version of himself, like a wet dog after a bath.

"I done you dirty," he said.

"Yeah. You're no friend of mine."

He sighed. "In the drawer there…over there. That's all the pictures, I swear. Take 'em."

So she took the pictures out of his drawer—all the pictures Vina had taken. There were eight or nine of them, mostly topless, sucking the water pistol, with her eyes half-closed, but then there were two of her spread out on the white leather couch, full-on vulva shots. For some reason this did not bother her as much as the fact that they had put her high-heeled boots back on. She thought about killing Vina. Poisoning her with a controlled substance, she figured, would be the easiest.

"C'mere…" he said.

"I hate you. You and her."

"C'mere," he said again.

"What do you want from me?"

"I want you. Don't leave me. Gimme another chance. Please."

"The hell I will."

"Come on." He moved to make room for her, and patted the sheets next to him. She obeyed.

"What's wrong with you anyway?"

"Fucking T-cells betrayed me."

"What?"

"Have to have more tests. Has to do with my T-cells."

He put her arms around him, and he snuggled his head next to her breasts.

"Just stay for a bit, OK?"

She had never seen him cry, but he must have cried then, because she could feel her bra getting soaked where his face was on her shirt. And that made her want to cry too. After a while he fell asleep, and she heard some of the disciples quietly coming in, whispering, and leaving, but she kept her eyes closed and her arms around him.

She kept her arms around him all night, until dawn, when she carefully disentangled herself because she had to pee so badly. She came back to his bed and watched him for a few minutes in the pale light and was struck by how much he looked like everyone else, like any other guy she had spent the night with. She felt something change. Whatever she felt for him before had somehow slipped into a different category now, and she couldn't define it, but she knew she would never again turn her back on him.

She sits at her table with her tea, now cold, and knows she would do it all again, the same way. She would never refuse him. She figures she would die for him, if she could.

XVI

*M*ary begins each day at sunrise. As the pale rays of the dawn seep through her window and infuse her bedchamber with a faint golden glow, she rises and opens the shutters to face the light. The gardens are just beyond her window, and in summer the scent of roses and jasmine fills her nostrils as she stands with upraised hands to pray.

Blessed be the name of the Eternal Father, Lord of heaven and earth, the Most Holy One who dwells in unapproachable light. I praise you for shining your light on my soul and redeeming my life from Sheol. Sanctify me by your truth. Redeem your people Israel. Restore those who are yet in darkness. Deliver the ones that have been abused and trampled and afflicted…

So she will remain, for the better part of an hour, before joining her brother and sister and the rest of the family for a breakfast of bread and cheese and figs. After that there are almost always guests to serve, and this she does with cheerful efficiency, going from person to person, the scent of her perfume lingering, like a sweet memory, even after she has left the room.

Her widowed sister, Martha, remains by the cooking fires, patting out loaves of her fragrant bread, and directing the two servant girls, who scuttle and scurry to please their mistress, for she is a righteous woman, known everywhere in the village and beyond for her healing arts and generous gifts to the poor, and they count themselves blessed to be in her household.

Martha has never been idle, but sometimes, for a moment, her eyes rest on her younger sister, attending the guests, talking and laughing among the servants, and her heart is caught up in unending wonder at the miracle of her sister's restoration. She is twelve years older than Mary, and recalls the darkness of her birth and childhood as much as any mother would, for so she became when their mother yielded her own life moments after the baby girl was born.

Mara, meaning *bitter,* was the girl's first name, and it was bequeathed to the infant shortly after her birth. Not only was she deprived of her mother's tender caresses and milk, but the tiny girl's face was deformed by a severe harelip and cleft palate, and the midwife had fainted at the sight of her. In the dark hours that followed the tragic birthing, Martha had tried to find a nurse for her afflicted sister, but none of the young mothers would give suck to the child, for they feared that their own babies would be thus cursed or contaminated. The baby daughter's affliction made suckling impossible anyway, and in despair her family begged the Almighty to take the frail infant quickly to himself and end her suffering. Their prayers apparently went unheeded, and the baby's piteous cries blended with the wailing of the relatives and neighbors who had gathered to mourn the dead mother.

Martha had taken the baby into the large workroom at the back of the house, where the perfume was made, to escape the pitying looks and whispering of the crowd. An entire wall of the workroom was lined with shelves filled with pots of crushed myrrh, cassia, and orris, and on the worktables there were urns brimming with fragrant oils and aromatic unguents, the smell of which overpowered her senses, so that her prayer was unspoken, but nevertheless ascended from her heart along with the pungent scents of lilies and Damascus rose.

Master of the Universe, will you not pardon me if I stifle her cries with the heavy cloth of my robe? Why? Why would you crush our mother, like these pale lilies, to give this baby life, only to have her die of hunger? Please forgive me for the ideas I am having…it would be a mercy to all of us, would it not?

At that moment her Aunt Salome had come in, with a concoction of goat's milk and diluted wine and honey. "Give me the child…" she commanded, and proceeded to drizzle the fluid into the baby's mouth with a reed. "You see?" she said after a few minutes of the painstaking feeding, "This is how you must do it, Martha. And may the Master of the Universe give you both strength."

The child thrived, first on the goat's milk, then on the bits of bread that Martha would first chew, and then gently place into the tiny crooked mouth. The older women called her "Little Mother," and dabbed their eyes, and at her marriage three years later they invoked many blessings on her for wealth and sons. Though Mara clung to Martha's knees, and pleaded incomprehensively through her tears, her new husband would not have the afflicted sister in his home. "She is not mine," he said. "The children of my house must be mine. She must remain here with her father and brother." His lack of mercy seared Martha's heart, and the pain of it remained for all the years of her marriage. Many times, when her own little sons cried out for her, she would hear her sister's voice in her head, calling her "Aerta...Aerta" in the peculiar way that Mara had uttered her name.

When their father died, she returned to his house for a few weeks, and was appalled at the sight of her sister. Now a child of eight or nine, Mara was too thin, and her dark hair was matted and unkempt, her fingernails were long and blackened, her tunic was filthy. She spent her days in the garden collecting flowers, or in the workroom, shredding the blooms, minding no one except Lazarus, and no one minding her. Her speech was comprised of odd, erratic murmurings that blended into the daily noise of the household, like the roosters at dawn or the clatter of pots in the kitchen or the babble of servants in the courtyard or the dogs that howled at night.

"Mara! Mara, it is I! Your 'aerta...' do you not remember me?" Mara said nothing, but contemplated Martha with large, unflinching eyes as she allowed her elder sister to bathe her, and clean her clothes, and put her hair to rights.

Martha begged her brother Lazarus and his young wife, Caliah, whose hands constantly caressed her belly, enlarged with their first child, to have mercy on the little sister who could not help herself, but she feared that the new baby would leave little room in their hearts for Mara's special needs. "To be so afflicted...and no mother to soothe you...think of it," she pleaded earnestly. At the end of her visit, it was the elder sister that clung to the young one and wept.

She bore her husband three sons, and when Perez, the eldest, was in his sixteenth year, her husband clutched his chest one morning, stumbling in pain, and never stood up again. *The pride of his heart has killed him, and made me a widow,* Martha thought, but she never spoke the words aloud.

When the time of mourning was over, she begged leave of her father and mother-in-law, requesting that she be permitted to return to her brother's house. Lazarus had sent her word that his wife was greatly weakened from bearing their third child, and he feared for her life. He did not mention Mara, and Martha was filled with apprehension as she made her way back to Bethany with her youngest son, a boy of twelve, and two devoted servants who had pleaded to be allowed to go with her.

Her brother rejoiced at her return, but soon retreated to the back of the house, where he spent long hours working, and, Martha suspected, purposely avoiding the disorder of his home. Donkeys and goats wandered freely about the courtyard along with her brother's young sons, whose faces, hands, and clothes were grimy with dirt. His wife, Caliah, did not leave her bed, but spent her days weeping, sleeping, and suckling her infant daughter, who was sticky and foul-smelling for need of a bath. The servants had become slack in their work, and the kitchen was rank with the odors of rotting scraps of food. Mara was nowhere to be seen. Martha longed to question her brother, or the servants, but she dreaded the answer she might receive, and so said nothing.

By nightfall the entire house had been swept clean, the children had been bathed, their clothes washed, and the servants had been reformed. The lamps were cleaned and filled, and burned brightly around the family members as they reclined at the table to eat the meal that Martha had prepared.

"You are a righteous woman," said Lazarus to Martha, as he chewed gratefully on the bread she had baked. "I am blessed to call you 'sister.' What can I do to repay your kindness? What gift can I give you?"

"Two things, my brother," Martha said without hesitation, for she already knew. "Two things I ask of you, and may the Lord move your heart to grant my requests."

"My heart is already moved to grant your requests…please speak your mind."

She moved closer to him so that her words would not be heard by the others. "Allow my son, my youngest son, to become your apprentice, and work with you until he has learned your trade. That is my first request."

Lazarus eyed the boy carefully, who was at that moment arm-wrestling with his own son.

"Done," he said. "He shall be as one of my own, and a brother to my sons."

"Thank you, my brother. May God reward you for your mercy."

"And what of your second request?"

She took a deep breath, because uncertainty had filled her heart. "Promise me—promise me, my brother, that I will always have a roof over my head and food enough for my daily needs."

He put his cup down, and raised his palm toward her. "Before the Lord, I promise you, as long as the Almighty gives me life, you shall never be without food, shelter, or clothing."

He picked up his cup, and raised it to her, but Martha did not respond.

"Come now, eat and drink, Martha! You shall be provided for."

"Since you have shown kindness to me...may I also plead for our sister? I do not know what has become of her, and my heart is filled with fear as to what you will tell me regarding her."

His eyes clouded and he set his cup down. After a moment he got up from the couch, reluctantly, and told her to follow him. Her heart pounded as he brought her to a narrow door that led to a small room off the garden. The door was locked from the inside, and she knew without him telling her that her sister was on the other side.

"She comes out only at the darkest hours of night...right before dawn," he whispered to her.

"What? Why?"

He glanced away. "The children...even the servants...are afraid of her...I'm sorry, Martha...I know you loved her, but...she is not the same...her mind has become...darkened..." His voice broke off, and he said no more.

"Leave me," she ordered. "Leave me be." He backed away quickly, and as soon as he was gone, she put her hands and her head against the wooden door. "Mara! Mara, it is I! Please open the door for me! Please, my sister...open up for me! I have returned for you..."

But the door stayed latched, and there was no response.

Then came the night, about a month later, when Martha was awakened by the sound of strange speech, like a foreign tongue that she did not recognize. She sat up in her bed, straining her ears in the darkness. From beyond the courtyard she heard a rooster crow, and then the sounds of a woman's odd, babbling voice came within range of her window. Her heart knew before her eyes did that it was Mara.

She sprang to her window, and pulled open the shutters. The moon was bright enough for her to discern the dim shapes of shrubs and trees in the garden, and the scent of the flowers engulfed her. Within moments she had left her room and moved through the courtyard to a gate that led to the enclosed garden. She stood for a moment, uncertainly, before calling out her sister's name. Minutes passed, and there was no response.

"Mara! Please come to me...it is I, Martha...please show yourself to me."

After another long pause, there was a rustling nearby, and a pale figure stepped out of the shadows and crept, barely upright, toward Martha.

With her heart pounding, Martha held out her hand toward the stooped figure in the moonlight. "Come to me...don't be afraid... please come to me..."

But she would not approach any nearer, so Martha stepped carefully toward her. When she was close enough, she quickly took hold of her sister's hand, and then her arm as well, because immediately Mara cried out, as if in pain, and attempted to escape. The two sisters struggled frantically for a moment, one desperate to run, the other desperate to hold fast, and the latter proved to be stronger and prevailed.

"Please...I just want to see you..." but she did not perceive immediately that being seen by anyone was what the young woman feared above all else. Mara turned her head abruptly and cords of tangled, dark hair, more like the feathers of a raven, fell over her face. Martha pushed them aside, and gasped at the sight of her sister.

Even in the dim light she could see that her face was puffy from lack of sleep, and dark circles spread below eyes that were dulled with pain...and something else. For a fraction of a moment the younger sister beheld the elder before turning away, but the one glimpse of her eyes and the scent of her breath was enough for Martha to discern the effects of a powerful narcotic substance.

"Oh, my own sister, what has become of you? Let me take care of you...I am here now...I will help you..." but her words might as well have been death threats for all the effect they had. Mara struggled in her grasp until she was forced to let her go. With a heavy heart she watched the pale figure retreat into the shadows.

The next day she accosted Lazarus in his workroom.

"How dare you?" she demanded. "How dare you allow her to take poison? Do you gather and distill the deadly blooms for her as well?"

Lazarus sighed deeply. "She gathers them...in the hours before dawn...when the scents are most powerful...but yes, Martha, it is I who distills them for her...and makes the substance that has become her food and drink...what else could I have done for her? She was in pain, Martha...constant pain...by the time she reached her fifteenth year, her mouth was swollen from her misshapen gums, and her teeth gave her unrelenting pain...she was going mad, I tell you...we all were...it was an endless nightmare..." He did not tell her how the idea of poisoning her food, for the purpose of forever ending her suffering, had haunted him for weeks before he had come up with the solution that could at least temporarily relieve her suffering. He had not counted on her body needing more and more of it, and now he was exhausted and overworked from producing Mara's substance, as well as filling the orders of his prestigious clients.

In the seclusion of her bedchamber Martha had wept and prayed before her window. She covered her face with her hands, and the words of her prayer were unspoken, though her lips moved.

I look to the hills from whence comes my help...my help comes from the Lord, Maker of heaven and earth...why will you not save her? Why did you spare her life as an infant, only to allow her to sink into the darkness of Sheol? Does the Lord take pleasure in the death of even one of Israel's daughters?

She raised her eyes to survey the hills of Judea, and though she did not know it at the time, the Teacher was descending at that moment… coming down from the hills, into the village of Bethany, to the house of Lazarus.

She had already heard of him. His reputation as a gifted rabbi—whose words and teachings surpassed those of the most prominent of Israel's teachers—as well as his healing powers, had preceded him, so that by the time he entered the village, a huge crowd of followers and onlookers surrounded him. She assigned Tobias, the steward of her brother's house, to go immediately into the marketplace and implore the Master to dine with them.

"Make obeisance to him," she instructed. "Do not allow him to go anywhere else. We will begin preparations immediately."

Around the twelfth hour of the day he entered their courtyard with his disciples, and the entire household, with the exception of Caliah and Mara, who remained out of sight, bowed low to greet him, as per Martha's instructions. After an awkward pause, the servants picked up their heads, one by one, surprised and amused at the lack of splendor that they had supposed their esteemed guest and his entourage would possess. The Master was hardly distinguishable from his disciples, who looked as dusty and weary as ordinary men returning from a day's hard labor. Nevertheless, Lazarus and Martha stepped forward and bowed low before him.

"We are honored to have Israel's greatest teacher in our home. Please abide here as you see fit…my house is yours," said Lazarus.

"Blessings on you, and all who abide here," he said. There was a quality in his voice that immediately stopped the murmuring of the servants. He turned his smile on Martha. "We are grateful for your hospitality. I assure you, our mouths have been watering since we smelled the scent of roasting meat and baking bread." He knelt down next to the younger of Lazarus's sons, then, who had chosen that moment to approach his father's guest.

Martha remembered him for the rest of her days. Years later she would tell her grandchildren every word he had spoken, exactly what he had eaten, the way he had looked into her eyes whenever he addressed her.

"It was as if he could see inside my soul," she would say. But most of all, she would tell them, and anyone else who would listen, how he had drawn her aside long after the meal was over, and most of the men had fallen asleep on their couches.

"Where is your sister?" he had asked her.

Martha had looked at him in shock. No one had told him, as far as she knew.

"My Lord...please do not count her rudeness against her...she is unwell."

"Take me to her."

He had stood at the door, just as Martha had, and knocked repeatedly, but Mara would not open it to him.

He came again with his disciples, much to the delight of the entire household, and each night, when the meal was over, he went away from the crowd, and knocked repeatedly on Mara's door. He did not forbid Martha from accompanying him.

"Little sister...open the door," he said with his head against it. Martha stood, holding her breath, praying that her sister would open to the one who she was sure could heal her, but the door remained shut.

On the third night, after he had knocked on the door again, he turned to Martha.

"When does she come out?"

"Only at night, my Lord. She...visits the garden...just before dawn...but..."

"Very well, then. Do not fear, Martha. God has heard your prayer."

When the cock crowed at daybreak, Martha, who had been sleepless for most of the night, ran to the garden. At the gate she stopped, almost fearful, and then pushed it open. There was the Master, looking down on her sister, who knelt at his feet. Mara's hair, which now hung in long, shining ringlets, covered her face, and Martha ran over, knelt down next to her and pushed it back.

For the rest of her life she would tell of that moment. To know Martha was to know the story of that moment. Years later she would describe the scent of the flowers and the sounds of the birds and the feel of the wet grass that she knelt on when she pushed back Mara's hair, and saw her face, newly healed, for the first time. The two women stared at one another, wordlessly, and when Martha placed two fingers on her sister's soft, full lips and shining teeth, Mara began to laugh and cry all at once.

Then she spoke, and her words came forth effortlessly and with perfect clarity. "A man came into the garden...I didn't know him...but I knew his voice. He told me that I would be Mara no longer, but Mary. And then he healed me."

Martha turned immediately to prostrate herself at the feet of the Healer, but he was gone.

17

She dreams that she is standing outside his house, and her teeth are chattering and they are not letting her in. Vina and all the disciples are inside and they are not letting her in. She is banging and knocking and yelling because she knows something has happened, but they are not letting her in. After a while there are flashing lights, and uniforms go in and drag him out, hanging between two of them, his feet leaving a trail of slime and his flesh greenish-gray and blistered and his head lolling to one side with the eyes of a frozen fish.

Her own scream awakens her. Lately she has been keeping her mother's last book under her pillow and now she takes it and presses the slim paperback against her cheek and takes a few deep breaths. Her heart slows down. She can smell her mother's hand lotion.

Mommy, can you hear me?

She studies the cover as if it might contain a clue: *The Fragrant Ones* by R. F. Friedlander. She opens the cover for the hundredth time, and reads the words of Jesus, *I tell you the truth…wherever the Gospel is preached throughout the world, what she has done will also be told, in memory of her…*from the fourteenth chapter of the Gospel of Mark, above the diminutive scrawling of her mother's pen. She has no idea what woman Jesus is talking about, or what she did. For all she knows it may have been his own mother, but in her mind, she ascribes the words to *her* mother's last act of writing below his words, because clearly her mother meant a name to go there, and it was truly the last thing she did. She wipes off the page where her tears have spattered and brushes her fingers over the wobbly *Je*. She decides that her mother would be more approving of her praying to Jesus.

Jesus…the Jesus who said these words that my mom liked…please let me see him one more time…please let me say good-bye to him… please…um…amen.

She hopes that Jesus, wherever he is, is watching, and paying attention, and she closes her eyes and clasps her hands to show him she means business. She is pretty sure he knows who she is since her mother is up there, but she can't be sure he will answer her. Why would he?

Which is why, after she has blown her nose and wiped her eyes, she is stunned by the jarring ring of her telephone.

It is Jean-Denis. Jeb wants her—wants her to come as quickly as she can.

She replaces the book under her pillow.

Thank you, Jesus…you didn't have to do that…thanks a lot…

But she can't help but wonder. Maybe it was a coincidence. But what if it wasn't? What if he was really listening? She tries to think. Did she pray aloud? Or did he read her mind?

Is he *really* there?

"Please…please don't disturb his spirit," Jean-Denis says to her when she gets there. He eyes her suspiciously.

She tries to think what that might mean. Vina would know, of course. She tries to think what Vina would say.

"I've come to…to…commune with his spirit," she says.

"Ah, that is good. Yes."

It feels like she has passed a test.

"You love me?" his eyes are closed when he asks her and his voice is a phlegm-coated whisper.

"Yeah. Sure I do." She lies next to him and pulls the blanket up over both of them. The yellowish, papery skin of his face is tight over his jaw and cheekbones. His brow bones and chin have become prominent. She can picture his skull with very little effort.

"Really love me?"

"You know I do."

"How do I know?" He turns his bleary eyes on her, and she can feel her stomach tense.

"I would do anything for you." She says it, and there is no turning back.

"Really. Anything, huh?"

"OK, within reason...not something that's going to land me in prison or a hospital...or the morgue." But she says it without conviction. Her future life without him appears as a highway stretched out in the middle of Kansas, flat and endless, with a horizon devoid of lights or scenery.

"So you wouldn't die for me?"

"Oh, God. Why would I have to?"

"Let's just say...say that you dying would save me somehow... would you do it?"

She feels like saying yes. She pictures a large balance scale, with his side infinitely heavier than hers. It would make sense: offering up the lesser soul to save the great one. Except for one thing.

"No."

"So your love has limits, then."

"There are other issues."

"Yeah? Like what?"

"Like...I'm pregnant."

"The hell you are."

"I am. Truly. Was going to tell you when I was last here."

He moves slightly. She is conscious of him shrinking away from her.

"So. You're screwing behind my back."

"What?"

"You heard me. All the girlie boys out there...the ones who wait on me and love on me—they took a vow of celibacy, you know. Did you know that?" There is an edge in his voice and it goes a bit higher.

She highly doubts it. She has seen pairs of them, once or twice, all flushed and glazed coming out of his bathroom, or embracing supinely on his couch while he sleeps, or french kissing and blowing smoke into each other's mouths while they pass a joint.

"Why would they do that?"

"Solidarity." He says it from a lofty moral plain and she feels guilty, but says nothing for fear of upsetting him. The vision of him, swallowed by death and forever out of reach, comes back to her. They lie in silence for a few minutes. Her intestines clench and unclench, like a fist flexing for a punch. Finally he stirs himself to speak.

"Kill it."

"Why?"

"You said you would do anything for me."

"How would that help?"

"It's the principle."

"I don't know what you mean."

"You said. You said you love me."

"I do! But—"

"Do you love me most of all? More than that thing inside you?"

She stays silent beside him, her mind racing to think of a way out. She has no concept of loving what is inside of her, and yet, pitted against her love of him, she suddenly feels rigidly protective of it.

"While I'm lying here, suffering, trying to suck down my last few gasps of air…you're out there…spreading yourself for your fuck-buddy pilot and carryin' his bastard…"

"Oh my god, it wasn't like that! I didn't do it on purpose! You mean everything to me. You know that."

"Then, prove it."

Last time, it had been a boy. They never told her, and there was no way she could have known, but her heart knew it had been a boy.

He would have been a mulatto boy, and that, more than anything else, would have upset her mother, who had firm convictions about the respective races mating and reproducing from within their own kinds. She had been working at the hospital for three years when she conceived the child, who was the product of a casual alliance she had formed with another nurse. A *male* nurse, she would have had to explain, because it would have been difficult for her mother to conceive of a nurse who wasn't a woman.

Byron was his name. He had been there longer than she had, and flirted with all the women, but especially the white women. His low, placid voice belied his dark, restless eyes, and he wore his hair in corn-row braids that were gathered in a long ponytail. He would lean over the counter while she worked and drum his fingers on her paperwork to get her attention and then cluck her under the chin or lift her necklace to admire it, and her skin would feel hot under his touch. Invariably he worked the same nights as she did. Three times they had gone out for breakfast after the night shift was over, and he had winked and grinned at her while they ate their eggs, and pressed his long legs against hers under the table, and then they had gone back to his apartment in Asbury Park. He was the tallest man she had ever slept with.

By the time she found out, he had moved on to someone else, and she decided immediately. But almost the whole first trimester was sandwiched between deciding and actually going to do it.

The entire event had become vague in her mind, like a hazy dream that is recalled on awakening but forgotten within minutes. It was as if her brain had refused to absorb the experience entirely, but had instead selected a few vivid details, which had become stubbornly rooted in her consciousness and made no sense to her.

She had no recollection of any conversations with Byron about it, for instance, and yet she felt, rather than recalled, that he had driven her to the clinic, helped her fill out the paperwork because her hands were shaking, and driven her home hours later.

She could remember two women. One was gung-ho and freckled and bustling and stayed near her side the whole time. The other was dark and Asian and was stationed between her legs, which were in stir-rups. She was quiet and efficient, with her eyebrows drawn together. The women didn't say much once it started, and the room was so quiet that the soothing New Age music that drifted from the PA system seemed suddenly loud, and almost drowned out the muted voices of children playing in a school yard nearby. She remembers a long clear tube turning red and hearing herself moan when the cramps started. She remembers throwing up afterward, in another room, and crying because she felt so weak and dizzy. She remembers seeing a few other girls, shuffling slowly down the hall in red-stained hospital gowns, ashen-faced and silently weeping. The atmosphere of the entire place seemed heavy with anxiety and pain. She wanted her mother. She asked them to bring her a phone. After a long time they brought her a phone, and plugged it into the wall and placed it on the bed beside her. She tried to pick up the receiver, and it felt like a fifty-pound dumb-bell. She dropped it on the floor. They took the phone away.

She has little recollection of the days that followed, except that her mother thought she had the flu, and her period, at the same time, and brought her trays with toast and tea or ginger ale with ice cubes and a pink plastic straw. Every time her mother came in, she wanted to blurt it out. But the words weren't there, not even in her brain, and her mother would say, "You rest now, honey," and close the door softly behind her.

After a week she was back at work, and she felt fine. She chatted with the others and attended to her patients and filled out paperwork and even saw Byron a few times. He winked at her as he passed, and whistled as he continued down the hall, and she felt fine. Christmas passed uneventfully, and she started going back to the gym. At home she sat with her mother watching the news. On her twenty-seventh birthday the Iranian hostages were released. The new president was on the TV and her mother cried because he spoke so movingly. It seemed the entire country was celebrating.

Her life felt small and unimportant, and nobody, not even her mother, was paying attention, and she was fine with that.

Her mother had been lying down a lot, and her blood pressure was bad, but Jennifer kept monitoring it, and her mother kept taking her pills, so they weren't worried. Her mother gave her the shopping list and asked her would she mind? She said sure, and when she got to the store, she pulled out a shopping cart and the front of the shop-ping cart, the part where the baby sits, said DO NOT LEAVE CHILD UNATTENDED, and she stopped breathing.

She started breathing again but it took all her concentration to keep taking breaths and waves of terror swept over her and her heart was pounding so fast and so loud she could feel it in her head and her neck and she ran back to her car and put her head down on the steering wheel. She could not move. It was like a huge, dark hand was pressing on her, forcing air out of her. After a while she drove home and told her mother she had lost the list, which was partially true, because she didn't remember where it was. She didn't feel so good, she said. They had oatmeal for dinner, and she couldn't eat.

I'll have to avoid shopping carts for a while, she figured, but it was too late. There had been a kind of rupture. It was as if a large sinkhole had unexpectedly opened inside her, and she would have to take precautions to circumvent it.

It made no sense. Her friend Melissa, who had graduated with her from the nursing program, was now hugely pregnant. Jennifer was unfazed. She brought chocolate-covered strawberries to Melissa's baby shower because strawberries were the theme of the shower to match the baby's accoutrements. She felt giddy with a sense of liberation and relief that it was Melissa, and not her. She drank two big strawberry daiquiris and laughed loudly at all the dirty jokes and was one of the last to leave.

A few months passed and she felt fine, she told herself. She went out all the time with the girls from work and they would drink until they couldn't stop laughing at everything. Mostly they would laugh at each other, stumbling in and out of the ladies' room and into taxis afterward. Sometimes she had dates but not with anyone she couldn't live without. She liked it that way.

It got so that she hardly thought about it. When she did, she congratulated herself that she was working and going to the gym and getting in shape and having fun. She assured herself that she was doing well. It had been a bad dream. It was like it had never happened.

It's like it never happened. She had come out of the shower and was sitting, wrapped in a towel, on the bench in front of her locker at the gym. She was smoothing moisturizer on her legs, which were nicely toned, and the room was quiet except for a Billy Joel song drifting down from speakers in the ceiling. She became conscious of a small gurgling noise. She looked over at the next bench and there was a bare-backed woman with a ponytail sitting in a hunched position, and the noises were from her. She was about to ask the woman if she was all right, when she saw something on her back. It took her a few moments to recognize it as a tiny hand.

It was a tiny, twitching, dimpled, pink starfish of a hand. It was connected to a small, chubby arm, which wriggled while its owner sucked contentedly.

Jennifer watched, like she was in the audience, and the woman and her infant were on stage. There was a sunbeam brightening the entire bench on which the woman sat, and her hair and skin seemed to glow with warmth. She felt sure now that it was God's voice singing "I Love You Just the Way You Are" to the woman, and she felt her intestines lurch with a stabbing pain that felt like jealousy, but worse. She wanted to stop staring, but she couldn't pull her eyes away. She told herself to breathe, and breathe, and breathe and soon the room was spinning and she found herself on the floor, barely covered by the towel, and two of the gym ladies standing over her. One was offering her water, and the other was saying, "She don't look so good..."

They had to help her get dressed because she was shaking so badly, and they said they would call an ambulance, but she insisted that she was fine, really fine, it was just the shower, she shouldn't have taken it so hot. *Little fainting spell*, she told them. *I'm a nurse. I'll be fine...thanks.*

She lunged into her car and drove around for fifteen minutes before deciding that she would see a priest. She didn't know why she hadn't thought of it before. *Confession is good for the soul*, Mommy would say. She pulled into the parking lot of St. Denis's and directly in front of her, directly in front of her eyes, was a car with a bumper sticker: large blood-red letters on white.

Abortion is murder.

The tires of her car screeched as she wheeled around to pull out of the church parking lot. Two blocks later she stopped at a red light and saw another bumper sticker depicting a heart monitor going flat. She looked down at her hands. They were shaking on the steering wheel. She pulled into the parking lot of a Quick Shop and saw on the back of a station wagon, another image of a fetus, incased in a red circle with a slash through it. She did not read the words.

She bought a chicken salad sandwich and a diet Pepsi, and drove east to the boardwalk, intending to eat her lunch in her car, in the warming sun. But when she got there she jumped out of the car and ran down to the beach and sat down on the sand in front of the waves.

The glare from the sun made her eyes hurt. A cold breeze off the water blew over her and she could not stop shivering, but she could not leave. She put her head in her arms and her arms on her knees and cried to the ocean until she could not cry anymore, because it seemed that only the ocean was big enough to hold all her pain.

"I can't go through that again." Her voice is shaky, but inside she is sure. She looks straight at him to make sure he's heard.

But he's not listening. His eyes reveal that another idea had taken hold of him.

"Naw…I got a better idea."

"What?"

"You'll say it's mine."

"What?"

He fixes his gaze on her, and she detects a glimmer of madness in his expression. It's not the first time she has wondered about his mental faculties.

"Tell them the kid is mine. Tell everyone."

"You're crazy. No one would believe that."

"Make them! Swear it, Jen. Swear to me now. The kid is mine."

"Right. And I'm the Virgin Mary."

"Swear it to me. Swear you'll do it. It's all I ask of you."

She studies his face, his eyes, his mouth, hoping for a clue, trying to unlock his motivation. She tries to think through the implications, but they swirl away from her, like a tornado abruptly changing direction.

"OK. If that's what you want. But no one will believe it. You know they won't."

"They'll believe me. They swallow anything I say."

She sighs. "OK. It's your kid." Inside her head she sees her golden dream, coming true.

"Swear it."

"I swear. It's your kid, and that's what I'll tell the world."

He closes his eyes, completely exhausted by the exchange. "Now I know."

"Now you know what?"

"You really love me. Let me sleep now."

He must have seen into her head and decided to give birth to her dream, which will save her and the child from becoming completely insignificant. She wonders if Jesus did it.

But it feels like a lie.

XVIII

She wakes slowly, from a dark place, like coming to the surface of a lake after being submerged in its murky depths. She wakes to the sound of women whispering. Her eyelids are swollen and dry, and she thinks for a minute she is back in the hills, surrounded by the other girls, after Judas had come to her. Something has happened to her.

Something has happened to her, and they must know. She squeezes her eyes shut to evade their scrutiny. She knows that her tunic must be creased and dirty, as if she has slept in the dust, and her braids are tangled. The odor of his sticky seed between her thighs, like day-old fish, rises to her nostrils. Surely they know.

Something has happened to her, and she becomes conscious now of a hand on her bare arm, and a voice, a grandmother's voice, falls on her, reciting a psalm of Israel's great shepherd king. The ancient words flow through her ears and her mind, and if the psalmist had intended them to permeate the deep trenches of the human heart, he would have seen his purpose accomplished. All her life she has heard the voices of men, and especially her father, reciting the holy scriptures, but rarely a woman, and never this woman. Still half asleep and without opening her eyes, Reumah trembles like a wounded bird.

"He gathers the exiles of Israel…he heals the brokenhearted and binds their wounds…," intones the grandmother's voice over her. It is a low, tranquil voice, edged with sorrow and deepened with the wisdom of her years.

A storm rages inside Reumah for some moments and then passes. She lacks the energy to sustain her grief. Another moment passes, and she opens her eyes. She notices the woman's hair first because there is such an abundance of it. From beneath a crown of coiled, gray-streaked braids, more rippling tresses flow out over her shoulders and down to her waist, like a cape. Reumah has never seen so much hair on one woman's head.

For a few seconds, she contemplates the older woman, whose eyes are still closed in concentration as she recites, before becoming aware of another woman nearby. It takes her a few moments to remember. The younger woman hovers near the bed, silently respectful while the older one speaks, yet watching Reumah with interest. When their eyes meet, she smiles quickly and reassuringly, and suddenly Reumah remembers.

It is Mary. And this must be the home of Lazarus, her brother. And probably—although they bear no familial resemblance—the one reciting the psalm is Mary's mother.

They brought her here, because something happened, and now Reumah remembers.

She remembers he came to her, very early this morning. She was still asleep, and when he knocked, rather urgently, she fumbled with the latch and was surprised to see him. She remembers the sky behind him was still dark, but in the east, there was a pale glow on the horizon.

"I must have you…" was all he said, and he immediately began to unfasten her cloak.

At first she resisted. Oh, if only she had resisted more! Her arms and legs and spine were stiffened with the night's cold, and she pulled her cloak about her.

"Let me first light the brazier. I am cold."

"Please, Reumah. It's been too long. I was not made to be celibate. Please let me have you…" and he began to kiss her, almost violently, as in the days on the rooftop, which now seemed like a lifetime ago.

She despised herself for still wanting him. She despised herself for her weakness, but as soon as his hands were under her tunic and the scent of his hair and his skin filled her nostrils, she forgot her self-loathing and surrendered willingly to him. She enclosed him in her arms and legs, drawing from him as much pleasure as she relinquished, and closed her eyes, thinking, as she had many times before, *surely this* *will be the last time...I must remember it...*Thus passion and despair blended simultaneously and at the height of her rapture, the words, "My love!" escaped her lips, and tears sprang into her eyes.

They must have heard her. They must have heard everything, including the exultant groan of Judas as he released himself into her, because suddenly there were two large men in her room, and a hand smothered her scream. It was Judas's hand.

"Just go quietly...and all will be well." He said it into her ear.

"What?"

"You heard me. Cooperate and all will be well. You must trust me on this."

They were holding her, and she struggled and started to scream again. A sharp slap stung her face, and she gazed at him, uncomprehending. His voice now was cold with cruelty.

"Listen to me, woman, and listen well. You know as well as I do you live a fruitless existence. Can you deny it?"

Her mind could not absorb his meaning. She did not answer. He proceeded.

"Today I am giving you a chance to do something useful—if you cooperate. Today you will be part of something bigger...a catalyst for a change...thanks to me and these men, you might be the start of a revolution...an overthrow of Rome and the deliverance of our people... think of that! Wouldn't your father be proud!"

"I don't know what you mean!" she screamed, and he raised his hand to slap her again.

He put his face next to hers and spoke to her as if she were a child. "It's a setup, actually. A forced confrontation...not really about you at all...part of my much larger vision..."

Her tongue and throat were so dry, she found it difficult to speak. She forced herself to look into his eyes.

"I loved you," she said, almost choking on the words.

"Ah, yes. That was your sad fate."

He said it as if she were about to die.

At any other time, the sight of Herod's temple, resplendent in the first rays of the rising sun, would have moved her beyond words. She had visited the temple only a few times in her life, with her parents, and the sight of it had stirred her like the sight of a bride adorned for her wedding. The large, gruff men whose daggers could be clearly seen walked on either side of her, and told her that Judas had paid them handsomely to bring her there, but that was all they told her. The idea of seeing her father in the outer courts, by some miracle, crossed her mind, but soon fear and exhaustion prevented her from thinking of anything but placing one foot before another. She tried to pray, but the words in her mind stumbled one on the other, like her feet over the rough, rocky road that led uphill toward the city.

The sun had fully risen by the time they arrived in the outer court. She begged them for water, which they gave her, and a piece of bread, but the bread was like sand in her mouth. She could not swallow.

And then it happened.

There was a signal—she saw it—one of the men gave a signal to a long-robed teacher of the Law, and suddenly she was engulfed by a crowd of Pharisees and lawyers and teachers.

She remembers crying out for her father, and then harsh voices commanding her to be silent in the court of the temple of the Most High. A voice next to her ear had whispered that her father was not there, and no one but God could save her. She remembers the front of her dress being ripped apart, while her hands were tied behind her back so she could not shield her bare breasts from the crowd. It was a huge crowd. She felt her knees buckle under her, and they half-carried, half-dragged her.

And then the crowd parted and she stood before him, before a rabbi who sat so calmly, it was as if the noise and commotion had escaped his notice. The drumbeat in her head drowned out any other sound, and a slight wind blew toward her, bearing the combined odors of incense and of slain animals. Reumah knew now that her sin had reached its fullness, and the entire multitude fell silent, convinced that they were about to witness the judgment of God on a sinful woman.

The rabbi looked up.

He looked into Reumah's eyes, and though she had never seen his face clearly before, her heart sank with recognition. Her entire body trembled uncontrollably as if she had been stricken with palsy. Her lips moved in a prayer for the Almighty to let the ground open up and swallow her.

One of the leaders, a member of the Pharisees, said in a voice loud enough for the entire crowd to hear, that she had been caught in adultery, and did the esteemed teacher think she should be stoned, according to the Law of Moses? What was his judgment?

For the rest of her days she would hear the cold, condemning voice of the Pharisee, and the silence that followed. Instead of answering, the Teacher stooped down and began to write in the dust of the temple floor.

He wrote on the stones, and in that moment her father's voice, reciting the ancient patriarch's words, came to her.

Though he slay me, yet will I trust him…

A strong breeze blew over her and loosened her long hair, causing it to fall like a curtain over her face and breasts. Though her outward form still trembled, her heart became calm, like the pool at the base of a fountain that suddenly ceases to flow.

Though she was sometimes asked, in later years, how long the moments of silence continued, in which her life hung between judgment and mercy, between death by stoning and life by pardoning, but she could never recall for sure. She remembered that he sat up, and spoke to them, but her mind could not absorb the meaning of his words. She remembered that there was a shocked silence that followed his words, and that they fell like hammer blows on the crowd of her accusers, which were made up of Israel's best teachers and lawyers, but they had no rebuttal. Instead, they began to disperse, in their usual custom, with the oldest ones leaving first. The younger ones looked daunted and embarrassed, and murmured to one another uncomfortably while they waited for their turn to leave.

Much of the crowd began to disperse as well, disappointed at the lack of drama. Still she stood, shaking, and waiting for his verdict, which she realized now was the only one that mattered. He had been writing in the dust again, writing the same words, she thought, over and over. He straightened up and looked at her again. There were deep lines in his face, and his expression was a combination of controlled anger, and aching weariness. Her gaze settled on his feet.

"Woman—where are all your accusers? Has no one condemned you?"

"No, sir." Her mouth was so dry she could barely whisper the words. She did not think he had heard, and she opened her mouth to say it again, but then he spoke.

"Neither do I condemn you. Now go freely, and leave your life of sin."

The words were not out of his mouth before the women had surrounded her, and loosed the cord that tied her hands, and covered her torn dress with a cloak. They coaxed her to walk with them, but she kept stumbling in weakness and confusion, and then somehow they carried her. At one point a troubling question came into her mind, and out of her mouth, and they stopped.

"They said adultery…but I am not married…and yet…they knew… in my heart and in my past…I have been an adulteress?"

They did not immediately answer, and she searched their faces. There were four of them, four of The Fragrant Ones. Finally the one called Salome looked deeply into her eyes and said, "The one who betrayed you is married."

"No! No, it cannot be!"

Down she went again, sinking into the dust of the road, and one of them just as quickly sat down next to her, and placed her arms around her.

It was Mary.

She trembles now, remembering too clearly and the one called Mary, again, kneels by her side. They gaze at each other and Mary says,

"You are safe now. Please don't fret. You are safe."

"Where am I?"

The older woman has stopped reciting and opens her eyes. They are the darkest eyes Reumah has ever seen. Her left one shifts slightly outward, giving the impression that she can see two things at once.

"You are in my home, child, in the city of our God. And welcome. I am Mary of Magdala."

"Thank you. May God bless you for the mercy you have shown me today." She is at a loss to know what else to say to the older woman, who is like one who should be listened to, rather than spoken to, like a revered grandmother. She turns back to Mary.

"And you—are Mary the younger?"

Mary smiles. "I was called *Mara* at my birth, and the one who gave birth to me is no more. But your feeling is correct—for this lady has become my mother, and the mother of many daughters. Now come… eat and drink, and then if you are able, you can bathe."

Bread. Fish. Wine. Water, a basin, towels, and a fresh robe. It is a simple, well-made robe, and beautifully embroidered. Reumah fingers the embroidery while Mary arranges her hair. She wonders if this is what it must be like to have a sister. Her throat tightens so that she can hardly speak, but she must ask.

"Why are you doing all this for me? For a woman…like me?" she cannot bring herself to look at Mary in the mirror. The older lady has been called away.

"A woman like you? Oh, my dear…" Mary stops braiding for a moment. "Reumah—don't you know what the Master wrote in the dust of the temple court?"

"No. I never saw."

"Oh! I thought you knew! Little sister…we all understood it…it was his verdict."

"His verdict?"

"Yes—the Master wrote, 'Today you shall become a Fragrant One.'"

19

She does not think in terms of life insurance or making a will or even a scrapbook. She does not think about where her child will go to daycare or school for that matter. That will come later. Instead, she gets three books from the library. They all have to do with having a healthy pregnancy and bearing a healthy baby. On the way home from the library she stops at the drugstore to buy some multivitamins. At the checkout, where the magazines are, there is a decorating one featuring "Terrific Rooms from Tots to Teens." She buys the magazine. After that she stops at the grocery store and buys skim milk and orange juice and decaffeinated coffee. She doesn't normally drink skim milk, or orange juice, or decaf, but she is determined to make some changes.

She is in the middle of an article in the decorating magazine about how newborn babies respond to black and white patterns, when there is a knock at the door. She rises, unthinkingly, to open it.

It is Clay Peterson.

It is Clay Peterson, and she is sure that his eyes zero in on the pregnancy books on her coffee table. She considers telling him that she is planning to work in obstetrics, but he seems preoccupied.

"Hi, Clay."

"Uh, hi. Was wondering if I could ask you…uh…about a bookshelf."

"A bookshelf?"

"Yup. The boys and I—" before he can finish, his sons come bounding up the stairs behind him.

"Hey, Dad, did she say we could do it?" It's the younger one. Their names are David and Nathan—but she can never remember which one is who.

"Uh—haven't asked her yet, son…why don't you guys wait down-stairs…you can start making a list of stuff we need, OK?"

Jennifer smiles at him. "Guess there's a project under way, huh?"

"Uh—just wanted to check with you about building another book-case. It'll be on that back wall—behind the couch."

"Sure. I don't mind."

"You sure?" He seems reluctant to leave, as if he wishes she would put up a little resistance or ask some questions about it. He rubs his jaw for a second, as if trying to buy time.

"I'm fine with it. As long as you don't paint it purple or some crazy color."

"Heh heh. Nope. Maybe stain the wood a bit. Or maybe just leave it bare." At the word "bare," their eyes meet for a half second, and she swears his cheeks flush.

"OK, then. Well. Have fun with that."

"Yeah. Thanks." He turns to head out the door. "You'll have to come see it when it's done."

"OK. Sounds good."

"Give it the landlady's seal of approval, y' know?"

"Ha-ha. Yep. Will do."

He nods at her and disappears down the stairs. If she didn't know better, she'd think he had a little crush on her.

She returns to the couch, but she doesn't pick up her magazine right away. Instead, she thinks of Clay buying wood and nails and brackets with his boys, and guiding their hands on the electric saw. She imagines him, with his ashy, unkempt hair falling over his protective goggles, plying an electric drill, and she smiles. She tries to imagine what it must be like to have a man in your house all the time, noisy and busy and preoccupied with manly projects, and her mind goes blank.

Her father had served in the air force as an aircraft mechanic. She knew that much. She had also figured out, not by anyone telling her, but just by doing the math, that he had gotten her mother pregnant before they were married. She had no idea how he felt about marrying her mother, but it was the fifties, and that's what people did in the fifties.

She figured they were happy for a while. If not happy, at least content. Her mother inherited the house in the Grove, and her dad fixed it up. Her dad could fix anything, her mother had told her, because it was one of the few things she would tell her about her dad on the rare occasions when the subject came up. There seemed to be much more that could not be told. There were questions that hung in the air, waiting to be asked, but Jennifer never asked them, and so they were never answered.

He acquired a reputation as one of the best mechanics at the shore, and his specialty was emergency vehicles, her mother had told her. It got to be where they pretty much only called him, because why waste time trying to take it anywhere else when you knew Jack could fix it every time? And if Jack couldn't fix it, well, it was probably time to scrap it. So Jack's Emergency Repair was on the bulletin board or Rolodex of every hook-n-ladder company from Cape May to Sandy Hook.

"He made a lot of money," her mother told her. "He had a monopoly." And Jennifer would picture the board game, which she had only ever played at the houses of some of her friends, and picture her father, driving his truck past assorted game pieces and over the variously colored properties, going round and round the board, passing GO, collecting money, and avoiding jail.

Once when she was nine or ten she had found a stack of blank invoices, imprinted with *Jack's Emergency Repair*, and showed them to her mother, and her mother said, "Oh…oh…put them away somewhere…oh, I don't know…" She was at the kitchen counter, making something, and she quickly returned to her onion chopping. Jennifer had carried the invoices, still in the box from a local printer, up to her bed. She stared at the words, *Jack's Emergency Repair*, and she wondered if it meant that he repaired emergency vehicles, or if it meant that he would come in an emergency. Or maybe it was supposed to be both. She wondered if her dad was clever that way. She put the box of invoices under her bed.

She was four when he bought his boat. She remembered the boat, which he had named *Lady Liberty*. She thought it was a good name at the time, and it did not occur to her to ask why he named it after a statue and not her mother. He took her for a few rides on it. She was scared at first, because she had never been on a boat, but he seemed so happy and confident, wearing a Mets cap with his long-ish hair blowing out behind him, steering the wheel and thumping over the waves and laughing to himself, that she forgot her fears and just watched him, because he was like another daddy compared to himself at home. At home he was quiet, and he watched game shows and baseball and *Gunsmoke* on TV. He never watched the news. He hardly ever spoke to her or her mother, but sometimes he would rustle her hair or tug one of her braids when she sat beside him on the couch with her crayons and her coloring book. On Saturday nights in the summer his friends would come over, two or three of them, and they would sit on the front porch and drink beer. Her mother would pad back and forth, in bare feet, with bowls of potato chips and pret-zels for them, or a cutting board full of sliced cheese and pepperoni and Ritz crackers. Her mother seemed happy and pretty and smil-ing when she did this, and so much younger. Also slimmer. Jennifer would fall asleep hearing the men's voices on the porch. It seemed like the other men talked more than her father, and she couldn't make out what they were saying, but sometimes she would hear her father's laugh, and she was happy that he was happy.

The summer she was six he took her to the inlet where his boat was docked and there was a lady in sunglasses waiting there. She seemed to know her father, and to Jennifer's surprise, she joined them in the boat. She sat in the boat with her legs crossed and lit a cigarette and once or twice smiled at Jennifer. Jennifer did not smile at the lady even though she could see she was pretty. And slim. The lady was wearing a cotton sundress printed with bright orangey-pink flamingos with black eyes, and she had large black circle earrings and a matching bracelet. She held her cigarette between her teeth and untied the straps of her dress that had been tied in bows over her shoulders. Jennifer thought her dress might fall down, but it didn't. She smiled again at Jennifer, but Jennifer could not see her eyes behind the dark glasses and she looked away.

On the dock next to some pilings and rope she could see two gulls squawking and fighting over a half-rotted fluke. They were ripping the fish in two, and one gull had a much bigger piece. It made her sick to watch them. The smells of saltwater and dead fish and the dark lady's perfume were making her tummy ache, she thought, and she soon went down below, into the tiny cabin which was her favorite part of her daddy's boat, and lay on the cushioned bench, which was exactly her size, while her dad moved around the boat doing whatever he did before he would rev the engine and plow out away from the docks and onto the open water.

"You didn't like my friend, did you?" he said to her later, when they were driving home.

"She's not your friend," Jennifer said.

"No? How come?"

Jennifer wasn't sure. She only knew she didn't belong there, on her daddy's boat.

"She doesn't come on Saturday night to sit on the porch like Kenny or Mike."

Her father had looked at her and laughed.

"You're a funny little girl, you know that?"

But he didn't take her on his boat again after that. And he was home less and less, especially in the summer. Sometimes he would stay out on his boat all night, and not come home at all. "Fishing," her mother would tell her. Jennifer would lie awake picturing him, way out on the choppy, open sea, trying to catch fish in the dark. She would look out her window at the sky, and ask God to keep him safe.

"It was that boat…that damn boat," she had once heard her mother tell her best friends out on the porch. There were three of them: Gladdy and Bea and Marjorie. Jen had made up a little rhyming song and she used to sing it to her mother for fun:

> Gladdy and Bea and Marjorie…
> Come and sit on the porch with me
> We'll have cookies and we'll have tea…

Her mother would smile and when they were there she'd pour Jen her own cup and put two cookies on a napkin for her before telling her to run along, and Jen would go inside and feel happy because her mother was always a bit lighter when her friends came by, and it seemed like all the problems of the world could be solved by her mother and her friends if they could just sit there on the porch long enough, talking.

But her mother had said *damn boat* and she almost never said *damn*. "He got a taste of freedom…like a sailor…and never wanted to come home." And Jen hoped that her mother's friends would cluck and murmur and know what to do, and somehow they would help her get her daddy back. But for once, they were quiet. She heard Gladdy sigh heavily, and then Bea said something, but she couldn't hear it.

Didn't he miss us?

She was sure it wasn't just the boat. She wanted to go out to the porch and tell them that she was sure the lady in the flamingo dress had something to do with it, like she had put a spell on her daddy that made him forget about her and her mother. She asked God to wait until her daddy was not on his boat, and then make the boat with the flamingo lady on it, sitting with her legs crossed and blowing smoke out of her nostrils, blow up, or crash, or sink.

She resumes her reading but the words have become irrelevant because another thought has crept over her and taken over her brain and she can't shake it off, although she tries. She rereads the paragraph about newborn babies making distinctions between black and white, and faces, but she is thinking of the baby seeing only her face all the time, and never a daddy's face, and she wishes the article would address this issue, because it seems like it might be more crucial. Is there any long-term damage done, she wonders, if a baby sees only a mother all the time, and never a father? Will this skew the child's view of humanity, or affect his or her sexual orientation?

Jeb had both parents.

Jeb *has* both parents, she corrects herself. He's not dead yet. Neither are they, as far as she knows, although he once drawled, when she asked him, "*Might as well be…*"

She closes the magazine and tosses it onto the coffee table where it lands with a slap. She closes her eyes and tries to picture how it will be. She tries to make the picture happy and bright, with her child going around telling her friends, "My daddy died from a terrible disease, but he was an artist...my daddy made pictures that are in museums now..." but the little voice sounds tinny and unconvinced, and larger questions loom in her eyes, questions that hang in the air, questions that are never answered.

She sits for a long time with her eyes closed, and then abruptly stands up, fighting off momentary dizziness. She goes into her bedroom and retrieves her mother's book from under her pillow. She holds it to her nose for a minute, and then drops to her knees.

Jesus...it's me again. I don't know if you can hear me, but...I've made a decision. I'm gonna keep this baby...for now...but only on one condition...and that's where I need your help...I need you to keep Jeb alive...to be the baby's father...I know it's not the way it's supposed to be, but...it's what I have right now...otherwise...well...you know. You know what I'll have to do. I don't want to do it, but...I think you'll understand...I hope you'll understand. OK. Amen.

She stands up, dizzy again for a moment, but then steady.

She feels a trembling in her gut, like a small creature waking up after a winter's hibernation, stirring inside her. It feels like hope.

XX

*I*n the late afternoon, as the cooking fires are being lit, a tall girl of about fifteen or sixteen years approaches her.

"Are you well enough...to fetch water?"

"Yes! Of course..." Reumah answers. She is surprised then relieved to know that the mistress of the house deems her worthy of service, even though it is only to fetch water. "But I am not familiar with the city streets...how shall I find my way if we become separated?"

"Follow the sign of the fish...and the smell of garum," the girl answers, hoisting her jug on her head.

Her words prove helpful. Either because zeal for her task consumes her, or perhaps because she is eager to impress Reumah with her ability to navigate the winding streets to the local well, the girl, whom Reumah soon learns is called Keziah, charges ahead into the crowded passageways of the city. On their return, with their water jugs balanced precariously on their heads, Reumah loses her in a large group of merchants who are dispersing after the day's selling, and afterward she is sure she would never have found her way back to the home of Mary Magdalene if it were not for the pungent odor of fermenting fish.

The entrance to the older woman's home is sequestered in a small, dark alleyway that curves off a wider street. Aged doors and passageways line the ancient street, and these open into homes wherein dwells a large family group that has made and sold garum for generations. Mary of Magdala is related to this family through her mother, although she no longer plies the family trade, and her mother has been deceased for more than four decades. At the entrance to the alleyway is a large fish emblem, and engraved above the doors of the family homes, including Mary's, the emblem is again repeated.

The fish odor is so pervasive that Reumah is faintly nauseous by the time she lowers her water jug inside the entrance of Mary Magdalene's home. She is struck at once with its sudden contrast to the outside world. The dimly lit rooms, though small and sparsely furnished, are cool and scented with an unidentifiable perfume. Embroidered cushions and coverings, the work of a skilled needle, embellish the couches, and there are colorful weavings on the walls. Toward the back of the dwelling is a narrow courtyard where the low ovens are, and she follows the scent of baking bread, carefully carrying her brimming jug.

On entering the courtyard, she stops, and a number of them turn to look at her. There are roughly a score of women of various ages. Some of the faces are vaguely familiar, but most she has never seen before, and in vain she glances quickly around in search of Mary. One of the older women comes up to her, and extends a darkly hennaed hand.

"Come, Reumah…take your place among us. And welcome."

"Thank you…how kind of you." She blushes deeply because she does not know the older woman's name, and feels certain that she should. As if reading her mind, the older woman says, "I am Mary. Another Mary…" and smiles gently.

"Ah. Thank you. I'm sure I shall have no trouble remembering that," Reumah answers, returning her smile gratefully.

Minutes later, when they are sitting down to eat, Keziah whispers into her ear, "That is Mary, the mother of our Lord."

"Our Lord?"

"The Master himself, of course. The Teacher."

Reumah turns to gaze at the woman in surprise, and is instantly struck by the resemblance between her face and the face of the one who pardoned her only hours before. Both possess the signs of weary sorrow and sleepless nights in the lines of their brows, yet both display the fervency of hope in the light of their eyes, and a reassuring smile on their lips, as if they had never questioned the purpose of their existence. *To be a woman of such strength…and to infuse that strength, somehow, into your son. This is indeed a mystery.* Her contemplations are cut short, however, as the mistress of the house enters with two other women, one of whom is her new friend, Mary, and are seated for the evening meal.

"Blessed art thou, Oh Lord, our God, Creator of all, who has given us every good thing to enjoy, and blessed us with this, our daily food..." Reumah has heard similar prayers many times in her father's house, but intoned by Mary Magdalene the prayer seems new, as if she were hearing it for the first time, and she thinks, My ears have heard it many times, but my heart has rarely been thankful for what I have received from the Lord...Her face reddens slightly and she lowers her eyes, because she has the sense that the other Marys can almost read her thoughts, but when she chances to look up, they are talking quietly, and partaking of dried figs, and bread dipped in garum.

Keziah, it turns out, is a chatterer, and Reumah soon wishes she had a few moments of uninterrupted silence to reflect on her circumstances. She wants to ask questions of the Marys, for instance. She wants to know how this house of women came to be, and who they all are, and how they keep themselves.

And I—do I belong here? Shall I abide here? Will they have me?

As if reading her mind, the mother of the Master comes to her, extending her hennaed hand.

"Come, child. Sit here with us, closer to the fire. Your eyes have questions and your heart has doubts. Let us tell you our stories, and then you can tell us yours."

Hours later, long after the lamps have been extinguished, and she is lying next to Keziah and two other slumbering women on a low sleeping platform, the stories of the women tumble over each other in her mind, like waves, and she strains her eyes in the darkness, endeavoring to match each tale with its owner's face and name.

There are two like her, for instance, whose husbands had cast them off because they had not produced sons. One of them had had a daughter, however, and that daughter is Keziah. No sooner had Reumah made this discovery when she felt her heart softening toward the younger girl.

Two women, around her age, have left abusive and drunken husbands. They have changed their names, to avoid discovery, and pray tearfully every day for the sons they were forced to leave behind. The eyes of every woman glistened in the firelight as they repeated their stories.

At least half of the women are widows, most of them older than her mother.

"You will know us by our hands," the mother of the Master said softly. Reumah gasped in awe, as one by one each widow displayed the intricate patterns permanently tattooed on her palm. They were the work of a gifted artist, each one different from the rest. Reumah had never seen such faultless markings, and knew that such skill was generally reserved for the hands of wealthy brides and wives.

"Who…who does this work? She must be commissioned by queens!"

Mary of Magdala smiled. "Indeed. She is called Joanna, the wife of Cuza, who is a manager in Herod's household. Her skilled designs adorn the hands of all the royal brides of the rulers and governors of our land, and she became a favorite in the palace, and married a wealthy man. In Herod's household she lacked for nothing; she indulged her flesh, and gifted herself with every pleasure a woman could desire; even so, her soul was empty, for she cared not for the ways of our people and our God. After her baby son died she despaired of life, until she repented and was baptized, along with her husband, by our brother John the Baptist. Not long after, she came to our sister Mary, the mother of our Lord, and implored her to allow her to apply her skill. *It is such a small thing*, she said at the time. *Such a small thing I can do to honor the mother of the One who has become for me the hope of the ages, and the Savior of Israel.* From that time until now, she has not ceased to adorn the hands of all the widows of our company…all who have placed their hope in the Master, and have set him apart as the Lord."

One of the older widows spoke up at that moment. "While she was cutting her reeds and mixing her inks to do my hand, I said to her, 'I am no longer a bride. I am surely not a queen or great lady. Who am I, that I should be adorned in this way?'" Her eyes gleamed in the light of the lamps, and she spoke slowly. Reumah waited for her to speak, without realizing that she was holding her breath.

"'Hush,' Joanna said to me. 'It is I who am honored…I would do no less for my own mother, were she alive.'" The older woman wiped her eyes on her sleeve.

All eyes became fixed on the glowing embers of the brazier, and there was a natural pause in the conversation, as if each woman held counsel with her own heart. A moment went by, and another, and then suddenly one voice broke out in a lilting song:

My soul glorifies the Lord and my spirit rejoices
In God my Savior, for He has seen
the humble state of His servant…

The voice was so clear and sweet, and the words were so lovely, that Reumah wondered if one of the heavenly beings had descended from the stars and taken its place by the fire. She glanced toward the voice…it was the mother of the Teacher.

"She has a gift for songs," Keziah whispered, as the other women began to join in the song. "She says the Holy One gives her songs in the night…and then she teaches them to us…"

From now on…
All generations will call me blessed
The Mighty One has done great things for me
Holy is his name…

Reumah did not know the words, so she listened all the more. Some of the women blended their voices to harmonize with Mary's, and the resulting sound ascended into the night sky, along with the sparks from the fire. A lump formed in her throat and she squeezed her eyes closed.

"My dear child…let them come…you need not be ashamed of tears in this circle…" whispered Mary of Magdala, who had settled herself next to Reumah. When the song was finished she said, "Now, speak to us. The hour is late, and we have not heard your story."

Reumah's eyes widened. Her heart became a loud drum. She felt its pulse in her inner ears.

"Oh, please, my mistress. I—I should much prefer to hear your story…and perhaps the other ladies who have not yet spoken." She had begun to call them the Three Marys in her head, and as yet their pasts were a mystery to her, for they were the only ones of the group who had not shared. The other women seemed to take this for granted, as if the Marys' stories were so ingrained in their collective conscious-ness that they need no longer be discussed, but only cherished, like the ancient story of the parting of the Red Sea.

"You shall hear our stories in time. They are part of a greater story… and only the Lord himself knows it all, from beginning to end. But now, my daughter…let us hear yours…let us understand what brought you into our company."

She opened her mouth to protest again, respectfully, but all the women had become silent while Mary of Magdala had spoken, and every eye was now on her. The words *my daughter* had touched a deep, unhealed wound inside her, and it was as if the older woman had seen the wound, and poured balm on it. Reumah took a deep breath, and then another, not knowing how to begin. Her hands shook in the folds of her gown, and she clenched and unclenched them des-perately, praying that the words would come, and wishing she had her father's gift for addressing large gatherings.

In that moment, whether it was the thought of her father, or per-haps her silent prayer, a clear voice was heard, and she marveled to realize that it was her own.

"My father is Nicodemus. He is a righteous man, and one of Israel's teachers. From my earliest days, he made known to me the sacred words of Moses, and our prophets, and judges and kings…while he taught my brothers before me, he never forbade me from listening at his feet…"

And so she continued. She told them of her betrothal to Zerah, and the festival in the hills for Jepthah's daughter, and some of the women smiled and nodded in recollection of their own younger days. But all fell silent when her voice dropped, and she told them of Judas. She spoke of him as her lover, and the one whom her soul had loved, and would not speak his name. She told them of her adultery, and her self-loathing, and her barrenness, which she felt was a just punishment, and her divorce. She told them of the humiliations, and the hatred and guilt that first consumed her as she gave herself to men for money: hatred for herself, and for those that used her, and then the guilt that became a dull pain, and then numbness. She kept her eyes fixed on the fire, and felt compelled to reveal all, except for one thing: she could not bring herself to speak of her father's gift, for fear of their judgment. Her mind quickly passed over it. To her amazement, they listened to the end.

"It was as if my soul had died...and then today...as I stood before a great Judge...I thought he would pronounce the sentence of death by stoning for the sins of my past...but instead...he extended mercy. I know not why. All I know is that now I will do whatever he bids me to do...today he has become my Lord, for such is the least offering I can make to one who has extended pardon and forgiveness to me, and restored my life."

As the words, the *least offering* came out of her mouth, she thought again of the vial of perfumed ointment her father had given to her, and again, passed quickly over it. It was too sacred to touch, even in thought.

On her bed she went over everything again...the stories she had heard, and the one she had told. She closed her eyes, finally, and heard the song of the Lord's mother in her head, gleaming through the pain of the stories, the pain of the lives of these women, gleaming like a rivulet of gold in a dark mine. She heard the song until she slept, and woke with it in her head the next morning. The women assembled for breakfast and prayer in the small courtyard, and afterward went to their appointed tasks. Each seemed to know exactly what she was meant to do.

She stood by, uncertainly, wondering if she should pick up the water jug again. Then the younger Mary was at her side.

"Our mother has told me that she will pray and seek to discern the Lord's will for you here, but in the meantime, you shall be my companion. Now come...let us anoint ourselves to go out into the crowds."

So saying she took a small vial and called the other women to her. Reumah gasped when she saw the vial: it was identical to the one her father had given her, with *Lazarus of Bethany* engraved into its smooth alabaster. Again she felt a stab of guilt that she had not revealed her secret to the women, but she pushed it away. Mary unstopped the vial, and instantly the entire room was engulfed in a fragrance she could neither describe nor forget.

It was the fragrance of another world. It was unlike any scent that she had ever experienced, and it evoked images of exotic flowers that grew in faraway lands, or in the ancient gardens of Babylon. It was a fragrance that caused her to sigh deeply, to close her eyes, to feel pleasure and pain at once. It was a fragrance a woman would wear to consummate a marriage, or after the birthing of the first son, or to mourn a husband's death, or to inhale deeply at the end of her own life…yes, more than anything, it was a fragrance that transcended the present scene, as if its source had been specially planted by the Creator himself to evoke memories of Eden and the promise of everlasting life.

Tiny drops were administered to each woman, and each dabbed them on her wrists, or ankles, her temples or between her breasts, as she preferred. The scent, Reumah was told, would last for days, even after bathing.

"To cover the odor of the fish," Mary whispered to her as she pressed Reumah's fingertip onto the tiny opening of the vial. Reumah closed her eyes, and then opened them almost immediately, because she had two thoughts at once.

The first thought was that she was now truly one of The Fragrant Ones, and it felt like the Almighty himself had anointed her.

The second thought was that she had left her vial—her precious vial—in her room near Bethany, and Judas had been there when she was taken away.

21

Over the grinding drone of the electric saw, Clay Peterson can hear his sons arguing. They argue about everything. They are arguing now about who should get to use the electric sander. They expect Clay to remember who used it last, so he will know which boy's turn it is. They expect him to be fair, and it amazes him that they would accept his decision, regardless of who got what. He is momentarily daunted by their belief in his sense of justice, and then he remembers that he used to expect that of his own father.

He attempts to dodge the question by saying he has no recollection of either boy using the sander, which is true, and this unleashes a loud protest, delivered simultaneously, with each of them insisting that they haven't had a turn in months, and Nathan ending with, "I should have my own tools."

I should have my own life. That's what he had told his father, twenty-four years before, only he hadn't actually said it aloud. He had directed the statement to his reflection in the bathroom mirror, when he was almost twenty years old, but he had pretended that he was saying it to his father, and that his old man would absorb it quietly, would actually listen to what he was saying, and for once, not have an answer. His father had never actually heard it, but stating it so emphatically to his own reflection had given Clay enough resolve to leave.

"OK, guys. Let's flip a coin." He turns off the saw and reaches into his jeans and finds a butterfly nut, half a book of matches, the dog-eared business cards of two contractors, four crumpled receipts from Mason's hardware store, a stick of licorice gum that has become unwrapped in the dank darkness of his pocket and has a piece of cat hair stuck to it, and a nickel and two pennies.

"Heads," David, the elder boy says.

"Hey! Why should he pick first?" Nathan says, and then whines, "You're supposed to use a quarter, Dad. This is so unfair."

Clay tosses the nickel, catches it and flips it onto his arm. *Heads.*

"Hah!" his firstborn son yells, and begins to unwind the cord of the sander.

"Hey, sorry, pal—" Clay says to Nathan. "Maybe you can help me with these—"

"No fair! No fair, Dad. You always let him do everything. *Always.* Just 'cause he's older."

"That's not true, Nath."

"I quit. I quit this stupid, goddamned project!"

"Hey! Watch the language!" but the younger boy has slammed out of the back room where the project is under way. They call it the freezer room, because of the large, ancient appliance that dominates the space, but it is also home to Clay's tools and workbench and sawhorses.

There is a pause during which Clay thinks of nothing. And then, unaccountably, he thinks of Jennifer, upstairs, lounging in her white bathrobe with a pink *J* embroidered over the left breast. He wonders if she heard the slam. Of course she heard it. The entire house shook like an old man with a sudden tremor. One day she will have had enough of the noise and the banging and the clamor of his large family, and she will gently and almost apologetically tell them they must go. He doubts he would ever see her again.

"Dad! He cussed! Aren't you gonna do somethin'?"

"I have ears, David. And you have work to do." He removes the plank from the saw, and hands it to his son. "I need some air. The smell of this room is getting to me."

He hasn't had a cigarette in sixteen years. He quit shortly after his marriage, not because Rebecca had nagged him—she had never nagged him—but because they had been so broke. They were both in seminary at the time, and had subsisted on peanut butter sandwiches and Rebecca's homemade soup for almost a year, and she never complained, not even once, which convicted him every time he went to buy a pack. He had had a brief relapse when Rachel was born. He had bought a box of cigars on the way home from the hospital, ostensibly to hand out to his father and brothers, which in itself was ludicrous, since his father hadn't spoken to him in four years, and his brothers were always so busy, he instinctively knew they would never come around just because his wife had given birth to a baby girl. He had smoked one of the cigars as soon as he got home, and by the end of the month the cigars were gone, and he found himself buying a pack of Camels, and he was hooked again.

It was ten times harder to quit the second time around, and the only good that had come from the whole experience, as far as he was concerned, was that he ended up memorizing large chunks of the New Testament and the Psalms, and Bobby Adler had become his best friend.

Bobby Adler had become his best friend about three minutes after they met, which was in the men's room at church. Clay had just smoked outside in the pouring rain, and had walked into the men's room and found a huge man dressed in grimy work pants, sitting on a commode, facing the tank, and rocking on it. Clay had made a kind of suction noise with his mouth…it was a habit he had that gave him time to think before he had to say something.

"Sealing the wax, huh?"

"Most fun part of my job." The big guy stood up. He was six foot five, and hefty too. He squeezed himself through the door of the cubicle. He smoothed back onto his head some greasy grayish-brown bangs that had become dislodged by his efforts with the toilet. He badly needed a haircut and there were pockmarks or acne scars on his cheeks. He stuck out his hand.

"Bob Adler. You?"

"Uh—Clay Peterson." Clay shook his hand—reluctantly—and tried not to think about what Bob's hand might have been exposed to on the job.

"How much you smokin' these days, Clay?"

"Huh?—oh, uh…maybe half a pack…give or take…" Clay quickly edged toward a urinal, and silently resolved not to smoke again in the vicinity of the church, and to stop saying "give or take," because he was actually smoking almost a pack a day.

"Thursday nights. Here at the church. We got a Bible-study group. Just guys with addictions. All kinds of addictions."

"Huh? Oh. Yeah, maybe I'll check it out some time." Clay focused his attention on a cracked tile directly above the urinal.

"I'll pick you up. You live local?" Bob was washing his hands now. There were no paper towels.

"Heck, you don't have to do that…"

Bob stepped over to him. He was still urinating and Bob had put his large wet hand on the back of Clay's jacket between his shoulder blades—had crossed the touch barrier—and looked down into his face. He was a whole head taller than Clay and at least ten years older and he said, "You need to come, bro. I can tell. I'm an old junkie and my brain is cooked, but I can tell things about people—you're a troubled man."

Right then Clay decided he hated Bob Adler, and told him so, weeks later. Bob had laughed. His laugh was a loose, wet, snorting sound. They were in a diner, sucking down coffee and sandwiches between jobs, and Bobby's laugh was so loud that Clay was sure every person in the place had turned to stare.

"That's when I became your best buddy."

His best friend's voice was loud too—and for ten years it had been loud enough to drown out his father's voice that played like a tape in his head.

"What the hell's the matter with you? You're smart. Maybe smarter than Clive, but you're sure as hell smarter than the older two, and look at them. Own their own houses, take vacations, buy new cars every two years. Don't you want that? Why wouldn't you? How can you be my son?"

The tape in his head got worse after he married. It gave his father new ammunition.

"You can't just be thinking of yourself, now. Your wife's gonna be pregnant in five minutes, I can see that. She's that type. Probably gonna want a whole brood. You gonna be renting some dump in Asbury Park with five kids?"

He hated that his father had been right about the five kids. At least they weren't still renting in Asbury Park though.

Jennifer's house is only three blocks from the ocean, which is why they chose to inhabit the bottom two floors of it, and Clay decides to walk to the beach. He thinks of Bee-Bee. He looks up at the house, and magically, she is there, a small dark face surrounded by fuzzy curls, at the bay window. She doesn't wave to him. She squinches one of his undershirts in her hands, which she always does whenever he is not around, like a miniature mad scientist. If he was a better dad—or just more like Jesus, say—he would go in and bundle her up and put her in the stroller. And she would squinch her hands in her mittens all the way to the beach and back again.

He waves lamely to her and then shoves his hands in his pockets and begins to walk, wondering how a person can still get intense nicotine cravings after sixteen years of being smoke-free. Bobby would know. Bobby was ten when his stepfather punched his mother in the face and then him kicked in the stomach when he ran over to her. *Mama's boy*, he sneered over Bobby, who was curled up on the linoleum. He had started smoking pot when he was eleven and was freebasing cocaine by the time he was in junior high. He had tried almost every kind of drug, and had lived more of his years drunk than sober. He had lived in foster homes, in jail, and in US Army barracks. He had had his fingernails ripped out in a POW camp in 'Nam, and he had ended up in a mental hospital. In the mental hospital he had started to eat his bandages, and bang his head against the wall until the plaster was bloodied. Every night, he told Clay, some nurse that he could hardly see in the dark, would come to his bedside and put her hands on the restraints, and pray that God would "release him from the power of Satan, and raise him up to be alive in Christ." On the night before they were going to lobotomize him, the nurse didn't come. Instead, Jesus stood beside his bed and said, "*Bobby.*" Just like that.

"There was a full moon and I could see him standing next to my bed where they had me strapped down, and he said my name, and I knew it was him 'cuz his wrists had scars in 'em. And I said, "You gotta fix me, Jesus. I'll do whatever you want. You're the boss." And that's what he did, bro. That's what Jesus did. The next day the white coats

171

ran all their tests on me and I looked 'em in the eye and answered every question and they shrugged their shoulders and released me three days later. I'd be fryin' in hell now if it weren't for Jesus."

His story was easier to digest in small pieces, and that's how he would tell it to Clay, and to his support group, to various other groups, to entire churches, and to customers whose toilets he unclogged. He would break off bits and pieces of his story and offer them to anyone who would listen, and Jesus was always the main ingredient. And every time Clay heard a piece of Bobby's sordid story—how Jesus had got him out of an abusive foster home or away from a gang of thugs or had gotten him food while he was starving in the prison camp—it made him feel like God was bigger than any pain or problem, and that his life mattered.

At the moment he can't decide what he misses more: smoking...or his best friend's voice.

Clay's father smoked cigars, of course. He smoked cigars and drank whiskey and ate in expensive restaurants and drove a Mercedes and had affairs with younger women who wore perfume and fur coats and called him *Charlie.* He had actually met some of them.

"Can you blame me?" he would periodically ask his four sons, who never answered.

Clay's mother had been a thin, house-bound woman who was chronically ill with an ambiguous nervous disorder. It was impossible to imagine her giving birth even once, yet she had managed to contribute four hefty males to the population whom she had named Calvin, Clifford, Clayton, and Clive, after characters from various romance novels. During his entire youth he had rarely seen his mother dressed in anything other than wine-colored silk pajamas, sitting on her chaise in the sunroom with the Venetian blinds drawn, her eyes and her diamond rings glittering through the haze of her cigarette smoke when he would come in after school.

"Put on *Oklahoma* for me, will ya, sweetheart?" she would ask him. She had a great fondness for Broadway musicals. He would oblige, and sit there for a few minutes, watching her wave her hand in time to the music, with the cigarette smoke trailing after it like an undulating snake. After a while he would say, "OK, Ma...I'm gonna make a sand-wich. Ya want anything?"

She would shake her head, her eyes closed, lost in the swell of the music.

"You're my favorite," she would say in the voice of an aging movie star, when he went to kiss her cheek.

Her only other passion was her orchids, which she kept in a green-house that had been built especially for them next to the sunroom. By the time he was a teenager she was too frail to tend them, so she gave him twenty dollars every week to spray and fertilize them. It was a secret arrangement, and he felt sure his father would have disowned him if he had ever found out. He loved and hated his mother. He didn't know why he loved her, but he knew why he hated her: he hated her because she did not cook or clean or do laundry or even wear clothes like other mothers. His friend Hugh's mother cooked almost every night—stuffed chicken and pot roast and spaghetti—and waited on the family and Clay, in her apron. By the time he was fifteen, he had already made up his mind that if he ever got married his wife would have to be a good cook, if nothing else.

He loved and hated his mother but he hated his father even more, for not loving her. He was seventeen when he realized that he hated a lot of things. One day he took the bronze bust of Wilfred P. Hardwick, the deceased founder of Hardwick Preparatory School for Young Men, and smashed the large glass showcase that housed the trophies and commemorative plaques of Hardwick's most accomplished athletes. He was expelled from the school within hours, despite his higher than average IQ and grades.

"I was bored," he explained to his parents. His eyes took in his sneakers, and then his father's Italian leather loafers, and then his mother's pink angora house slippers. He tried not to snicker at the rare sight of their feet in such close proximity to one another.

"You'll buy your own car now," his father retorted.

In public school he had signed up for carpentry because he thought it would be an easy class to skip. He was wrong. His teacher's name was Shotlander, and he had a plaque on his desk that said, *My boss is a Jewish carpenter*. Clay hated him immediately. By the end of the semester, Shotlander told Clay that he was a natural when it came to tools, and Clay told him that he had hated him and woodworking at first, and they both laughed.

"And now it's your favorite class, right?"

Clay signed up for advanced carpentry, and Shotlander introduced him to the mysteries of cabinetry, and later on, to the mysterious idea of Jesus actually having been resurrected, and currently alive, and accessible. At first nothing changed except that Clay stopped saying *Christ* as a curse word, and started praying to him instead. To his surprise, lots of things happened the way he prayed. On the morning of his nineteenth birthday he woke up and realized that he didn't hate so many things anymore, and that he really liked doing carpentry, and he was convinced that Jesus had something to do with it. His entire life had been redirected.

By the time he was twenty, he had managed to let his father know that he was not planning to go to any university, and he would not be getting his MBA, and that he had applied and been accepted into seminary because he wanted to study the Bible, and be a carpenter as well. His father assured him that he would be disinherited as a result, and also conditionally disowned until he could come to his senses.

"I promise you this—I'm not leaving my money to a religious jackass. You're on your own now. You make your own way from here on."

He had fallen in love with Rebecca, in Israel; before he found out she was a good cook. He had fallen in love with her because she was the steadiest and most peaceful person he had ever met, and because she loved him back. He had fallen in love with her the moment she had turned her large, soft gray eyes on him, eyes that were hungry for truth. He had never thought himself exceptional in any way, but Rebecca apparently recognized qualities within him that had gone unmarked and unappreciated for most of his life. He was amazed that a woman who possessed such rare beauty and keen intelligence would find him desirable, and he was astounded when she agreed to marry him. On the first night of their marriage he had watched her, in a state of joyous disbelief—as if she might disappear if he closed his eyes—sleeping naked beside him.

She brings him good, not evil, all the days of her life.

Bobby had quoted the old proverb the first time Clay had told him about Rebecca. Bobby had trouble sometimes remembering the names of his own kids, but early on he had prayed that Jesus would restore enough of his brain cells to memorize Scripture, and Jesus had answered that prayer, and then some. Most of the verses in Clay's head were in Bobby's voice, because they had gone over them so many times together. He wondered what Bobby would quote now.

He wonders what Bobby would quote, for instance, if he knew that he had not looked away when Jennifer got into her car one evening, wearing a leather miniskirt, and the vision of her thighs, shapely and smooth as butter, had seared his brain, and had become the catalyst for numerous steamy daydreams. He feels sure that his wife would forgive him if he ever had an affair. He feels equally sure that his sons never would.

He sits on the beach before the small portion of the Atlantic that God had allocated to Ocean Grove, and puts his head into his hands, conscious of a surge of fresh grief mitigated with anger. His friend has been dead for four years but Clay has not stopped missing him.

You gotta fix me, Jesus.

XXII

*I*n her mind, Reumah has come to think of them as the Three Marys—a "cord of three" that strongly binds the group of women who follow the Master. She now kneels before them, trembling slightly. Her eyes are fixed on the embroidered cushions on which they sit, the bright colors contrasting with the darkness of their clothes and skin.

"Speak plainly, my daughter. Mary said you became pale at the sight of her vial. What is your secret?"

She takes a deep breath and tries to steady her voice.

"Indeed, I have a secret…I kept it from you…from all of you last night…but clearly the Almighty intends it to be revealed." She takes another breath, finds her voice, and tells them of her father's gift. They are silent for a moment, and then Mary of Magdala speaks.

"Where is the ointment now?"

"I have hidden it…in my room…near Bethany. At least…that's where it was left."

"And the one who betrayed you was there when you left?"

"Yes, mistress." A wave of panic surges within her. The three Marys glance at one another.

"If I am your mistress, then you must do my bidding. You must go and retrieve the precious vial. Mary will summon some of our men to accompany you. We cannot delay. You must go at once."

"I will get the men…and I will go with her." Both of the older ladies nod, and the younger one disappears behind a paneled door that leads out to the courtyard.

Reumah's forehead touches the cushions before them. "How can I express my gratitude? How can I thank you enough for your kindness to me?"

"A gift from a parent is like the name we are given...it must not be taken lightly...especially if it is a gift that was chosen with love and wisdom. It can unlock the truth of our identity. But why did you feel the need to conceal this matter from us?"

Reumah looks into the older woman's eyes, and then back down at the cushions. "I...I don't know...I was afraid. The vial seems almost sacred to me...I suppose I was afraid that you would expect me to relinquish it...in payment for clothing me and feeding me and letting me stay here...or...showing me kindness..." Her voice floundered.

"Whatever kindness we have rendered is out of love for our Master. That is *his* way. We do not force others to share what they have...only to give as they feel led. Go, my daughter, with my blessing. We shall pray for you. Gather what you need...Bethany is not far...make haste. The other women will help you."

Reumah exits from the same paneled door, and both Marys refrain from speaking for a moment, as if needing time to understand the implications of Reumah's revelation. After a moment Mary of Magdala speaks.

"Perhaps you should warn your son."

"I was thinking the same. But surely he knows what Judas is."

"We all know what Judas is...but if he sells Reumah's vial, and suddenly has that much money at his disposal..."

They are silent again, and then the mother of the Master rises.

"I will go to my son. I will tell him what we suspect. He will know what to do."

"Indeed, he will. He is master of every circumstance...do not fret, my sister. No one can force his hand, or take his life. This you know."

"Indeed. No one can take the life of God's anointed one...of this I must keep reminding myself." She smiles gently at her friend, as if to reassure them both, but her thoughts trouble her. Long ago, an aged and devout man in the temple had taken her newborn son in his arms, and uttered an oracle over him that confirmed his destiny. But then he had turned his gleaming eyes on her and prophesied that a sword would pierce her soul. She had never doubted his words nor forgotten them.

Mary of Magdala remains in her chamber for some time. Once or twice the paneled door opens quietly, but when the women see that her head is bowed, her long hair falling over her shoulders like a veil, they assume she is praying, and leave her in peace.

But she is not at peace. For some time she has sensed the presence of darkness approaching her Lord, like a gathering storm, and this latest revelation of Reumah's vial has given her a sense of foreboding. She has no doubt that Judas would have searched her room, and if he found the vial, he would as quickly sell it, and use the proceeds to hire a small army, or bribe some of the governor's officials...but to what end? She is a loss to know what would make Judas think he could somehow force the Master to follow a scheme or fulfill his own ambitions.

Unless Judas has given himself over to the dark deceptions of the Evil One. She herself knows something of being deceived...of exchanging the hard stone of truth for a glittering lie.

She glances down at a small raised scar on her hand...the number seven, branded into her right palm when she was in her seventh year. Her own mother had done it, with two servants holding Mary down as she screamed. It was one of the last memories she had of her mother, and in a sense, her mother's last gift, although, unlike the costly gift that Nicodemus had lavished on his daughter, her mother's gift had been despised by Mary for many years.

Her mother's name was Elliana, and she was a Jewess who had married a Gentile from the city of Magdala. The details of their courtship were imprecise, but a few years after her mother's death, Mary had learned from her mother's old doula that Elliana had been young, and very beautiful, and had been flattered by the attentions of the much older Senchia, who then seduced her. Her father had agreed to give his daughter to Senchia as a bride, but told her that after the marriage had taken place, she would be his daughter in memory only. She had pleaded at his feet on her knees, the old doula had recounted, but to no avail. From the day of her marriage to Senchia she was cut off from her father's house.

"Seven is the Lord's number..."

Her mother had told her repeatedly while she wept and applied balm to the blistered palm of her little girl for several nights after the branding. *"I have set it as a seal on your right hand so that you will not forget your mother's god or her people. You belong to Elohei Haelohim, the god of Israel, my daughter. Do not forget it, no matter what."*

They were among the daughter's last memories of her mother, who had contracted a disease from a parasite that caused her to waste away. While the dying woman's last words should have inspired hope and assurance, it seemed at the time they became an omen of destruction. Her mother died soon after, and her father, Senchia, not long after that, and she became a ward of her eldest stepbrother who feared neither God nor man. Until her first menstruation she did the work of a servant girl in her stepbrother's house, and lived on the uneaten crusts from his table. In her twelfth year she was taken to the temple of Astoreth, to be trained as a *kedesha*. The first week in the temple left her dazed beyond words, so great was the contrast between the neglect she had suffered in her stepbrother's house and the attentions and flattery of the temple attendants...she was bathed and perfumed and given embroidered robes to wear, and the slave girls braided her hair for hours and applied kohl to her eyes. She and the other *kedesha* were fed sweets and wine, and given beautiful chambers to sleep in. But it did not last. One day soon after, she was brought to the great room of the temple that contained a floor-to-ceiling statue of the goddess herself, surrounded by bronze candelabras molded into the shapes of entwined serpents. The smoke from the incense burners and the flames of the candelabras caused shadows to flicker over the statue so that it seemed to slither, even as its eyes stared blankly and its face remained impassive. Mary had gasped at her first sighting of it. Along the walls of the large room were couches separated by draperies that hung from the ceiling, which had been blackened by soot from the lamps and incense burners, making it seem always night despite the slivers of light that came in through small slits in the walls. After some time her eyes grew accustomed to the dimness, and she beheld numerous pictures painted on the temple walls above the couches.

There were no faces in the pictures, only depictions of the private parts of men and women, as well as their arms and legs and mouths, in all kinds of postures and combinations. She was told to study the pictures until she understood what they entailed. The images confused her at first, and then they made her intestines cramp, as if she had a sudden illness, and a strange compulsion to press her thighs together.

"As you have seen, so you must do," the one in charge of the *kedesha* told them repeatedly. *"If you do well to our patrons, it will go well for you…if you will not partake of the sacred acts in honor of our goddess, you will be punished."*

She heard the cries of the other girls when they were taken, one by one, by the highest paying patrons and forced to offer up their virginity in honor of the goddess. Her turn was coming and no amount of pleading or crying kept them from thrusting her into the preparation chamber. She did not eat for two days prior to the bidding so they administered a small leather whip, imbedded with shards of seashells, but only on her shoulders and the back of her neck, so her hair would cover the bloody gashes. When she persisted in her refusal they brought her to a room wherein lived three girls who stooped like lepers under their veils. They did not speak, but when commanded, they held out their hands and feet, all of which showed missing fingers or toes that had been severed. She looked into the eyes of one of girls. They were like the eyes of a dead fish.

"Toes and fingers are not needed to perform the sacred acts of our goddess," the overseer said with a sneer. *"Thus it will be for you, if you do not comply with the wishes of our patrons."*

She did not cry out like the other girls.

She could not recall his face, but only that he was a young lord, very fat and hairy, who put his damp hands all over her. He made grunting noises that reminded her of swine while he thrust his distended part into her until she broke open like the ruptured seal of a perfume bottle, and afterward she believed that the essence of her soul had spilled out onto the linen, never to be retrieved, but rather discarded like urine or blood. She bit her lip against the searing pain of it and looked over at the heavy stone image of the fish goddess and pleaded silently for release, and her mind, it seemed, was also altered at that precise moment. It seemed to her that something else came in, a darker, more rigid version of herself, older and wiser, who was summoned from a distant time as a protective guardian. She felt certain that she had become two persons, and that her spirit guardian had issued from the goddess herself. When the young lord was snoring noisily she tried to creep away, but he awoke. He pulled a silken cord from the heavy drapery that surrounded the couch and tied one end around her throat and the other to the base of the statue and made her crouch down, and put his part in another place and she had the sensation again that she was splitting into pieces, and of suffocating in the cushions, and her soul being obliterated, as if she had become merely one of the faceless figures she had seen on the temple walls. She cried out for her mother but to her shock it was the name of the goddess that came out of her mouth, and the man who humped her like a dog suddenly groaned heavily and fell back, his eyes turning up into his head. With trembling hands she untied the cords, wrapped her robe about her and prostrated herself at the feet of the statue, and when she rose up she declared that her name was no longer Mary, but *Ishtara,* in honor of the goddess.

Within a year they had made her high priestess over the entire *kedeshim,* because her zeal for the goddess was genuine and unsurpassed by any of the other male or female *kedesh.* It seemed that the goddess had smiled on her in return, by sending her numerous other spirit protectors, seven in all. The seventh one came to her in her sixteenth year, at the birth of her firstborn. At her request, the old doula who had served her mother delivered the child and rubbed the screaming, slippery infant, a girl, in salt and swaddling cloths.

"Shall you name her Elliana?"

"No. I shall name her for the goddess, and to the goddess she will be dedicated. Now give her to me."

The old woman's eyes narrowed. "Have you forgotten your mother's god and your mother's people? Are you so foolish as to cast aside your mother's last wishes?"

"She is mine to name!" She cried out to hold the child, and a deeper voice came out of her, like the growl of a bear, intoning the name of the goddess.

"What is the seal on your right hand?" persisted the old woman, the pitch in her voice going high with indignation.

"My mother was deceived! I belong to the goddess only, and she has appointed seven spirits to protect and guide me!"

"Never! There is but one true God, *Elohei Haelohim*!"

So saying, she took the child and ran from the room. Ishtara screamed and screamed, and when the servants had sent for the temple guards, a voice not her own ordered them to show the old woman no mercy. Within minutes the blood of the old doula was shed in the outer court of the temple. They brought the infant daughter, who had fallen onto the bloody stones, to her mother.

"Shall you not taste the milk of my breasts, or gaze on your mother's face even once?" She said to the infant, who lay cold and still in her lap. The servants watching said afterward that her face became hard, and her eyes glittered coldly when she looked at them. "Take the child from me, and let it be said today that I have sacrificed her in honor of our goddess!"

A day later she had a dark vision and foretold of a heavy squall drowning many men and overturning dozens of fishing boats, and in six days, it came to pass. When it became known that she possessed the gift of uttering oracles and foretelling, prominent men from distant towns came to worship at the temple and paid huge sums of money to consult her. A high-ranking general had a vision that he was to drink the milk from her breasts to be healed of a tumor in his thigh, and so he was. Thus it became known that *Ishtara* channeled milk with healing properties from the goddess herself. Not long after, she was sold from the temple—secretly and for a breathtaking sum—to Caesar's palace, and became answerable only to a high-ranking official whose name she was not given.

"Rome is great, and if by your power and wisdom you make it greater, you shall be rewarded by the emperor himself," he told her. And so she had visions, and spoke oracles, and divulged palace intrigues, and whispered into the emperor's ears the secrets and schemes of his enemies and traitors, and she was lavished with jewels and fine clothes and seated at the emperor's table. Powerful men trembled at the sight of her, and paid her obeisance. When the voices began to fall silent, she nevertheless kept up the appearance of having the wisdom of the gods and she uttered lies and invented plots, sending many innocent men and high-ranking women to their deaths. She danced and chanted to the point of exhaustion, she drank the sacred potions, she slashed herself with knives, and fell into trances almost daily. Still the voices of the spirits that indwelled her and gave her prophetic utterances fell silent, and gradually it became clear to all that she had lost her gift.

They beat her to the point of unconsciousness, and would have put out her eyes as well, but one who was merciful advised that she be merely abandoned in the hills of Judea, lest the spirits of the goddess be awakened inside her and aroused to seek vengeance.

She has almost no recollection of the long years that followed; at first there was a steady stream of men that came to her at night in groups from the surrounding villages. They brought her food and drink, and she submitted to the worst degradations their imaginations could conceive for their entertainment. Sometimes the women of the villages would attempt to poison her, a few tried bravely to kill her with knives, but always she escaped their clutches with peals of eerie laughter that echoed through the hills and made the youngest children whimper in fear. In time her hair grew matted into thick feathers and her nails became long and dirty, and out of her mouth came the sounds of a wounded beast instead of words. The men came less and less, and she can recall only the dim interior of a cave, and eating leaves and locusts, and wild dogs licking her sores. One day a man came up to her and asked her what was in her hand. The sound of his voice caused her to brace herself in defense, like that of a leper having his shroud lifted for a glimpse of his ravaged face. She opened her mouth and screamed the foulest words of hell at him. He came to her again, and asked her what was in her hand, and she picked up a stone to throw it at him, but the stone crumbled in her palm. Again the man returned and asked her what was in her hand, her right hand, and she fell at his feet, her body writhing.

"The seal of *Elohei Haelohim*," she screamed in a terrified voice, and the words came out amid a flood of vomit and curses.

"Release her now, and I forbid you to enter her again," the man said to the seven spirits. She felt compelled to kneel at his feet, and he asked her for her name.

"I am called *Ishtara*," she said, looking up at him carefully, and then looking away, because her eyes could not return his gaze.

"Mary."

At the sound of her name from his lips, her mind was restored, and she began to weep, and to worship him.

"Adonai…behold your bond servant. May it be to me as you will."

The women outside the paneled door hear the closing words of her prayer and whisper and wonder why she is so long about it today. They do not sense the darkness closing in on the Master as she does. When she emerges from the inner room her one eye rests on them steadily, but the other eye, which drifts at times to the left, seems to be drawn to a distant sight…a vision of black storm clouds gathered over her Lord, pierced with shards of lightning, and wrathful thunder from the heavens descending on him, like the curses of God.

23

When Bobby Adler had been in his life, it seemed that Jesus had been around more too. It seemed to Clay that Jesus was always in and around Bobby, invisible but powerful, drawing people together and answering prayers and healing brokenness and vanquishing addictions. For some reason, Jesus didn't seem to operate in the same way when it was just him and Clay. Oh, sure, he answered prayers. He had answered a lot of prayers, especially about his kids. Especially Bee-Bee. But as far as Clay himself, it seemed like Jesus had a more hands-off approach, like there were some things that even Jesus didn't want to mess with. Or couldn't. Clay wasn't sure.

He watches the ocean for a while. He watches the relentless waves swell and foam and roll, and thinks about Rebecca asking the kids one evening last summer, when they all sat together on the beach, how the ocean is like God.

"You can only see a small part of him at any one time," is what she said. There was a thoughtful pause among his family members, and he wondered if he should jump in and say something, to show support for his wife.

"Well…God is mysterious like the ocean. There are really deep trenches in the ocean floor that no one has ever seen." That was Nate. He grinned when he heard it.

"Plus it's beautiful and dramatic. You never get tired of being near it." That was Rachel, who was becoming more beautiful and dramatic herself every day. He felt a stab of guilt. It didn't seem fair that his family should be so wonderful.

"It gots fish." That was John-Mark, sitting on Rebecca's lap. David, his astute firstborn son, rolled his eyes.

"How is that like God?"

"Daddy tolded me the fish sign means Jesus."

Rebecca gave David a look. "OK, David. Can you come up with one?"

"Yeah. It changes every day. You never know what to expect. But there's also an order to it that you can rely on. The tides, for instance."

They were quiet then. They were waiting for him. He could feel Rebecca's eyes on him. He was looking down at Bee-Bee sleeping in his lap. It was warm and sweaty where her head rested on his arm. She had one of his undershirts (which she habitually took out of the hamper) around her neck. Her mouth was slightly open, and her eyelids flickered in the light of the setting sun behind them. She hadn't had a seizure in over a month, and his attitude had wavered, with each passing day, between gratitude and fear. He looked at his wife, trying to think of something at least as simple and profound as the observations of his children.

"You could drown in it," he said, after a moment.

He stays by the ocean and he prays by the ocean and when he starts heading back home, he is almost not surprised to see a man, apparently waiting for him, who turns out to be his brother Clive, whom he has not seen since two Thanksgivings ago. They shake hands and contemplate each other. Clive looks rather well-fed and older. There is a ridge of flesh below his chin and above his collar, and an ample belly straining against the buttons of his shirt. He has been freshly shaved and barbered, with his hair parted crisply on the side. He strikes Clay as very businesslike. Maybe gay too; he's not sure, but he thinks it's a possibility.

For his part, Clive says, "You look different, bro. You growing a beard?" His brother looks five years older, and his clothes seem ill-fitted to his lean frame.

Clay sheepishly rubs the two-day growth on his chin, suddenly conscious of the sawdust on his sweatshirt and his stained jeans. His brother is wearing a collared shirt and tie, and his shoes are polished. "Something like that. What are you doing here? You're all spiffy."

"I got a client right in your neighborhood. I'm heading over there now. Stopped at your house and the wife said you were down here."

"Really? I wasn't aware lawyers made house calls. Don't you have some spiffy office in Hoboken?" It occurs to him that he has never been to Clive's office, and this makes him flinch with guilt. He wonders if Clive cares.

"Yeah, well. This guy's kind of special. He's one of our bigger clients and he wants to go over his entire last will and testament—or at least, that's what his agent said. She's the one who called. He's dying. Could be any day now."

"And he lives here? In the Grove?"

"Yep. He's a big-time artist."

"That so? I had no idea. Guy must be very reclusive." Clay feels embarrassed that he wasn't aware of this information. It occurs to him that his world has shrunk significantly since he has become an associate pastor. He never wanted it to happen, but it has. He feels certain that Clive must think this too. There isn't anything else to say. The brothers stand together for a minute, gazing out at the sea, the older one always conscious of a pull toward it; the younger one glancing over it, merely acknowledging its presence. He looks at his watch.

"I gotta go, Clay. Maybe see you a bit later?"

"Absolutely. Come for dinner. I insist."

"Yeah?"

"Yes. Yes! For sure. I'll tell Rebecca we're expecting you."

"Actually she already did."

"Well, then. It's a done deal."

Growing up, Clay had always been his favorite brother. He had never told him, of course. In their father's house there didn't seem to be a vocabulary for expressing emotions. There was anger and guilt and resentment and reproachful silences. There was fear too. But nothing was ever said. It permeated the air that they breathed, like the Lysol his mother insisted that Nancy, their housekeeper, spray throughout the house once a day.

Clay was the only one in the family who had never made fun of him. There was a lot to make fun of: In his younger years, Clive had been a nose picker and a booger eater and a bed wetter. He had been over-weight and underbathed. He was good at math, but no one seemed to give him much credit for it. He was wearing bifocals by the third grade. He didn't play any sports, and he had no aptitude for fixing or building things, like Clay. Once Clay had fixed the lousy reception on the TV in the middle of the Super Bowl while his father and brothers were watch-ing, and you would have thought he had won the game himself. Clive watched them whoop and holler and slap him on the back, especially his dad. He tried to think of what he could do to earn the same amount of approval, but nothing came to mind. He didn't hang out with them most of the time anyway. He visited his mother daily while she sat in her chaise, and she would wrinkle her nose and ask him when he had last showered, or tell him to change his shirt. He knew she preferred Clay. Mostly he kept to himself and read comic books and watched *Star Trek* and *The Twilight Zone*. Real life seemed utterly tedious by comparison.

He had shared a room with Clay. He was tidy and Clay was messy, but he didn't care, because he had nightmares from time to time, and Clay would always wake up and turn the light on for him. They would keep the light on until Clive could fall back to sleep, and Clay never complained. Not once. That, more than anything else, made Clay his favorite brother, because the nightmares had terrified him, and if he hadn't been able to see his older brother laying there, alive and breath-ing in his undershirt with his arm over his eyes in the twin bed next to his, he would have gone insane. At least he felt so at the time. When they got older, he didn't have nightmares anymore or wet the bed, but Clay got into Jesus and went away to seminary and that was pretty much it. It didn't bother him that Clay was "born again" and got mar-ried too young and didn't go to college and all the other things his father said were such a disappointment. He just missed his brother.

He checks his day planner for Jeb's address, and realizes he should have asked Clay for directions to Heck Avenue, although he is twenty-five minutes early for the appointment. He had been to Jeb's place once before for a party about three years back, but it had been at night and someone else had been driving. At that point he had only met Jeb a couple of times, for business reasons, and thought maybe something had crackled between the two of them. They had had a few drinks together and he remembers feeling disappointed that nothing more had come of it, because Jeb would have certainly been the most sexually charismatic person he had ever slept with, man or woman. He had been in therapy for a while trying to figure himself out, and ended up sleeping with his therapist, also a man. After that brief and scorching affair he had moved on, deciding to focus his energy on his career, which paid off, although he was drinking and eating more than he ever had before. He calculated that his overindulgence was a substitute for sex, and the lesser of two evils.

He hasn't seen Jeb Kellon in over a year. He had been asked to come as soon as possible, because "Jeb wants to go over a few things before it's too late." He had heard rumors, but hadn't realized how sick the man was. He hadn't believed until he heard about Jeb that gay sex could literally kill you.

"Thank God I never made it with him," Clive mutters fervently, glancing at the numbers of the houses as he drives along Heck Avenue. "Thank you, God."

Jeb struggles to keep his eyes open, because every time they close a series of vignettes plays across his mind, like previews for a movie that depicts his life. He keeps seeing Sylvain, for instance. He has successfully prevented himself from thinking about Sylvain for most of his adult life, and now an image of the young man, prostrated on the couch before *The Price is Right*, has become permanently embedded on his brain, and cannot be deleted.

He forces his eyes to open and focus on the sleeping form of Jean-Denis, slouched in an ugly armchair next to his bed. The puce-colored armchair is obese, and he hated it from the very first time Vina had brought it over, because, she said, it "worked" with the scheme of the room.

"It's the ugly-fuckingest thing I've ever seen, no lie." He resisted the urge to throw his paint brush at it. Or her.

"It's perfect. I don't tell you how to paint. You don't tell me how to decorate."

"I gotta work here! I don't want to look at that piece of shit every day."

"Hey! Who got you the apartment? And who got all your furniture? And your big clients? And the little presents that you smoke and snort?" There was an edge in her voice, even though she smiled evenly while she spoke.

He had been drinking a beer, which he now threw with all his strength against the living room wall. It left a crater in the plaster. They both watched the pee-colored rivulet flowing down the wall, and the shattered brown glass on the floor for a moment. Then she sidled over and kissed him.

"Just trust me, OK? I'll make it work."

He had never trusted her, but he trusts Jean-Denis now. His clears his throat as loudly as he can.

"Hey…hey, Jean. Wake up, man." His voice is so diminished he can hardly hear it himself. He clears his throat again and tastes the phlegm that has taken up permanent residence in his gullet.

"Jean-Denis…can you hear me, bro?"

Jean-Denis's eyes are closed and his mouth is slightly open. His arms are crossed on his chest and suddenly his head falls limply onto his chest. The abrupt movement causes Jeb to shudder. It's like seeing someone being let down from the gallows. He closes his eyes quickly.

The weird thing is, when he contemplates his own existence after death, a dark curtain falls and he can't seem to focus on the subject. It's as if it's not actually going to happen, or else some force prevents him from thinking about it and he thinks that must be how the human mind deals with it, and that's the way it should be. But for some reason he has become obsessed with Sylvain. He wonders where Sylvain is *right now*, and if he will actually see him on *the other side*, whatever that turns out to be.

That kid watched The Price is Right *every day because he had a thing for Bob Barker. We all teased him about it, but especially me. I don't know why the hell it bugged me so much. Maybe I was jealous. That's so fucked-up, me being jealous of Bob Barker, but it bugged me that this stupid French-Canadian eighteen-year-old kid was obsessed with Bob Barker, when he had me living there, and everyone else was obsessed with me, why wasn't he? He was Klaus's houseboy, you could say. Klaus kept him because he liked him to talk French to his cronies*

*and clean up our shit, especially after parties. He was skinny and girl-
ish and wore Lacoste shirts all the time and had this preppie haircut,
parted on one side, not one hair out of place. I woke up late one morning and he was watching Bob Barker, his big grayish-blue eyes glued to
the TV. I stood there looking at him for a minute, and for some reason,
I got so mad I wanted to kill him. I did the next best thing.*

"Sylvain...come 'ere. I'm gonna fuck your brains out."

"Eh? Pardon?" he said it in French. He kept watching Bob.

*"Sylvain...here. Now. Let's go. I'm the boss when Klaus is out, you
know that."*

*He stared at me for a long minute, then looked apologetically at
the TV, like he was excusing himself politely from Bob, but something
had come up.*

*I made him turn off the TV, and I did it to him, right there in the
living room. I wanted to hurt him bad, and I did. He whimpered like a
girl and he bled on Klaus's white couch. "Clean that up," I told him. I
remember he wiped his eyes with his underwear before he put them
back on and got some cleaning stuff and turned the TV back on, but
his show was over. We came home from a party that night and he had
shot himself through the mouth, and his brains were splattered all over
the mirror behind the white couch. We were both kind of drunk, and it
took us awhile to call the police. While we were waiting for the cops I
remember Klaus yelling, "Who the hell is gonna clean up the mess?"*

"Stop! Stop...you are getting very agitated. You must stop this."
Jean-Denis is behind him suddenly, propping him, and holding him like
one would hold a sobbing child who had had a nightmare.

"I'm not a bad kid...I'm not a bad kid, right?"

"Non...no, you are very nice man."

"Daddy...my daddy put his hand on my shoulder when I was ten...
the screened-in porch was on fire...it was blazing, and I had saved my
daddy's big Bible out of it...and my daddy said, *You done good, Jeb.
You done good.*"

"Yes...yes. You done good."

His eyes are about to close again, but then he sees Clive, coming
into his room. Jean-Denis shakes his head at Clive, as if to say that it is
not a good time.

"The door was open, so I took the liberty…Hello, Jeb…if I'm dis-turbing you…I can wait outside…or…"

Jeb's eyes seem larger than the last time he saw him, or perhaps it's because his head has shrunk down to a skull with yellow skin and wisps of long, thin hair hanging off it. His sunken eyes gleam with unshed tears and fever. He stares at Clive like a terrified child. Clive stands awk-wardly, glances furtively at Jeb, and then at an ugly armchair next to the bed, wondering if he should sit down without being asked. He needs a moment to recover from the shock of seeing Jeb. If Jeb speaks, it will seem like a horror flick: a voice coming out of a corpse. He sits carefully on the edge of the armchair and laces his fingers, trying to buy time.

"Sylvain?" Jeb's entire face contorts when he says the name.

"Huh?" Clive says, looking at Jean-Denis for help. Jean-Denis nods his head vigorously.

"Sylvain…is it you?"

More vigorous head nodding from Jean-Denis. Clive decides he must play along.

"Yes…yes, it's me…Sylvain."

"Come…come here to me." Clive moves himself gingerly to the edge of the bed, praying Jeb doesn't cough or sneeze or cry on him. To his horror, Jeb reaches weakly for his hand.

"You forgive me? For what I did to you? Are you OK now?" From behind Jeb, Jean-Denis locks eyes with Clive, as if daring him to resist.

"Uh, yeah. I'm good, Jeb. I'm OK."

"You forgive me?"

"Yes…yes, of course. I forgive you."

The dying man closes his eyes, almost smiling. Jean-Denis mouths the word, "Merci," and carefully lays him down. Clive gets up slowly, and the phrase, "I forgive you," bounces around his brain while he watches Jeb sleeping for a few minutes, watches his chest rise and fall, watches him suck in every breath with difficulty. He wonders how close he is to the end. He wonders if that was all that was needed to release him to the other side, whatever that is. He decides that forgiveness must be a powerful thing. Maybe the most powerful thing.

XXIV

*H*er brother's house has never been calm, but since the Teacher has become their cherished friend, it seems that hardly a day passes without curious strangers clamoring at the gate, many of them in tattered, filthy robes, and often weak from hunger or sickness or carrying sick children. They beg Martha for a glimpse of him, or to speak to those who are closely associated with him. Most of them simply seek favors, and implore Martha or Mary (when she is there) or Lazarus to plead with the Master on their behalf. While Lazarus has been ill, the weight of the household has fallen on Martha's shoulders, and night after night the ragged strangers present themselves in her mind, especially the little ones, and she is unable to sleep; nevertheless, she wills herself to rise at the appointed hour, drunk with fatigue and weepy with exhaustion, mumbling her daily prayers to the Almighty, and pressing into the day's work.

"He is not here today, but he will come again, rest assured." She hands out cakes of raisins or barley loaves, and then shuts the gate firmly. She says nothing about the banquet. If they knew, they would come in droves, and it would ruin everything.

She escapes to her chamber for one moment to breathe, and to think. She contemplates her reflection in the mirror. Her eyes, normally bright and thickly lashed, appear dull and sunken into her face, which is lined and pale. Her cheeks and mouth trend downward, and there is a layer of flesh under her chin that has appeared, it seems, very recently, along with scattered gray hairs above her temples. She turns away from the mirror to the window, where a hummingbird hovers over some lilies, like a brilliant harbinger, divinely appointed for that moment to cause her to forget her troubles. She tries to focus on the fragile beauty of the tiny iridescent bird, but her thoughts close in on her—clustered in groups, like small birds alighting and settling, only to take wing again.

In the last month, Lazarus had been complaining of dizziness and fatigue. He had been unable to leave his bed for the past week. Two nights ago the fever had broken, and today he had risen at the cock's third crowing, and had returned to the distillery. Almost all of the servants have been called to the back room to clean vessels and utensils and fetch water and bank fires. The arms of her youngest son, Daniel, ache from the hours of crushing petals and roots and herbs with the pestle. Unexpectedly the concentrated buzz of industry throughout the house has shifted focus from the preparations for the banquet—which has been uppermost in Martha's mind—to reclaiming the lost time due to her brother's illness.

"The banquet is tomorrow night! You can't take all my helpers from me!" She pleaded with her brother at breakfast. She had not been able to eat her bread because her intestines were tense and her head was full of the tasks that were as yet undone.

"Martha...I must work when I am able...who knows that I won't fall prey to this illness again? I am sorry, sister...perhaps the banquet can be lessened in some way...I'm sure the Lord will understand...he is a man of deep thoughts, and simple tastes, and I'm sure he will not object if one or two of your usual dishes are not on the table—" His voice dropped off when he saw the look on Martha's face.

The sudden shortage of servants has left her with Naomi, who is primarily Caliah's nurse and doula, and is therefore rarely available to assist with the rest of the household, and Narissa, her maid-servant in the kitchen. She is fully relying on Mary, who is supposed to be returning any minute from an important errand, with another young woman who is called Reumah. Mary had arrived with Reumah yesterday evening from the city. Of course, she could not have known that their brother had been sick in her absence, but Martha nonetheless is irked by the inconvenience of her sister's return with another houseguest when there are few servants to be spared and so much cleaning and cooking still to be done.

The girl, Reumah, is quite beautiful and mysterious. Even in her dusty street clothes, she has the bearing and dignity of a wealthy man's wife, although she seemed submissive and subdued when she responded to Martha's polite questions, as if she feared that her eyes or her expression would reveal a shameful secret. "Her father is Rabbi Nicodemus," is all she got out of Mary, but that was reason enough to welcome the young woman into her home and feed her generously. Normally she would not expect a guest to assist in common household tasks, but out of desperation, she hopes that Reumah will not object to assisting them in the preparations for the banquet.

She had been planning the banquet for two months—ever since she had found out from her sister who had found out from the Master's mother herself—the date of his birth. She had heard tales of the lavish parties and feasts that were held for great men and kings in honor of their birthdates, and the idea had taken hold of her and she could not think of anything else with such ardor and excitement. In her mind, there was no one more deserving of such an honor, and her eyes shone with joy at the idea of creating a banquet, resplendent with music and lights and wine and all his favorite foods, in honor of his birthday. The spacious courtyard has been swept and scoured, and she has borrowed as many benches and tables and couches that could be carried from her neighbors' homes and all have been arranged amid lamp stands and caged turtledoves and vessels of wine and fragrant bouquets.

Martha stands in the center of the courtyard and closes her eyes, envisioning the Master at the central table in the seat of honor, and whispers a prayer.

"Eternal Lord, glorify thy son in our midst as we seek to bring him honor in this place." She wipes her eyes, and turns suddenly at the sound of Mary's voice.

"How very beautiful you have made everything, my sister!" It is the first time Mary has seen the courtyard since her return, and she is stunned by its transformation. The girl, Reumah, stands beside her, biting her lip.

"Yes. Well...I am relieved you have returned. There is much to be done. Was your errand successful?" She glances over to the troubled girl.

Mary steps over to Reumah, and puts her arm around her. Then she looks at Martha. "I am sad to say that it wasn't. We had hoped to find...a cherished belonging that had been accidently left in a room in town. Alas...it could not be found."

At these words, tears start from Reumah's eyes, and Martha steps over to her.

"Now, my dear. You mustn't fret. In the eyes of God, nothing is ever lost...surely he will come to your aid in this matter as in any other."

"Indeed," said Mary, her eyes shining. "And the Lord is coming... no one can be hopeless when he is near. His very presence is a comfort to all who are cast down."

The words are not out of her mouth before Reumah takes hold of her sleeve. "Will you ask him for me? Will you speak to him on my behalf concerning that which I have lost? I am told he can read the thoughts of men...perhaps he knows something of it..."

"When the time is right, you can speak to him yourself. I have never known him to turn away from anyone who sincerely sought his help."

"Oh, I cannot! Please, Mary! I hardly know him...and...the brief encounters I've had with him have been...strained. Please! You are a great favorite with him. Please do this for me, I beg of you!"

Mary gazes uncertainly at Reumah, as if trying to see into her heart.

"I will speak to him, my friend—but not because I am his favorite. I will speak to him because he is merciful."

"Thank you so much!" Reumah's face brightens with hope, even as Martha's darkens.

She turns away from the younger women, and feels like her heart has become a ballast of wet sand. She cannot decide if it is a certain amount of distaste for the young woman who is so preoccupied with her lost item that she will not leave the Master to enjoy his birthday feast in peace, or if it is her reference to Mary as his "favorite." *You are a great favorite with him*, is what she said.

And her sister had not refuted it.

She begins to wipe down the tables in the courtyard with violent distraction, and Mary and Reumah take up cloths to help.

Inside her head she hears a voice of condemnation.
You're a foolish woman…and…old…old.

Years later, Reumah would tell how she had been so nervous before
the banquet that her trembling fingers had been unable to arrange the
braids of her hair, and Mary had come to her assistance.

"Shalom, shalom. All will be well. There is no darkness in the presence of the Lord." She took a bunch of delicate scarlet flowers—the
same that adorned her own plaited hair—and skillfully wove the sweet-
smelling blooms into Reumah's braids.

"How lovely! What are they?" Reumah asked as their delicate scent
reached her.

"These are my favorite—clivia. They are a symbol of beauty, maj-
esty, and purity."

"Oh, Mary! We shall be like royal brides of Solomon!" They both
laughed, and gazed at themselves in the polished silver. With their hair
similarly plaited and adorned, they looked like sisters, and the laughter
eased Reumah's tension for a moment. But only for a moment.

The source of her trepidation, Reumah decided, was the thought of
seeing both the Master and Judas in the same place and time; of being
simultaneously confronted with the powerful presence of one, and the
painful reality of the other.

"Please allow me to stay and help you in the kitchen," she had
begged Martha, and Martha had agreed, after a quizzical gaze. Martha's
cheeks were reddened from the ovens, and her eyes were bright with
a mixture of excitement, anxiety, and exhaustion. She did not refuse
Reumah's offer, and so Reumah spent much of the evening in the pas-
sageway between the stoves and the courtyard, passing serving platters and baskets of bread and bowls of sauce and meat to the servants
who took them into the guests. Her work did not prevent her from
glimpsing the guests as they feasted, and frequently she paused to
take in the scene. There was no sign of Judas, but even if he had been
there, Reumah would have felt safe from him, because the Master's
joyful presence eclipsed every fear.

Years later she would say that the noise of the birthday banquet
was like waves crashing on the shore. The crashing waves were the

tambourines and cymbals and drums, the singing and the dancing, and loud voices punctuated with laughter, especially from the men who were seated about him; between the waves were pauses of silent consideration when the guest of honor held up his hand, and told a story. He was full of stories, Reumah discovered, and she regretted that she couldn't hear them better. Occasionally one of the synagogue leaders would ask a question, and always the Teacher answered with a question of his own, and the learned man would turn to his fellows and mutter uncertainly, or stroke his beard in deep thought. "No wonder the sisters call him 'Lord,'" she thought to herself. He reminded her of an exultant groom amid his wedding guests, except that no bride was present. Her eyes frequently rested on Mary, who had seated herself near his feet, apparently determined not to miss a word that fell from his lips. Mary's smile held constant as long as she gazed on the Master, and it seemed her dark, shining eyes never left his face. She was unabashed in her love for him. Seeing this, Reumah's romantic inclinations were stirred, and she wondered if the Master had ever considered Mary for his bride, and if so, why did he delay the betrothal?

There was a pause in the noise as the guests began to partake of the food, and for a moment Martha stood alongside Reumah, surveying the courtyard with her.

"Mistress," Reumah said, "how joyful he looks."

"Indeed," said Martha, with a smile, and it struck Reumah that she had hardly seen the elder sister smile the entire afternoon. "It is just as I hoped. His joy is my best reward."

"He reminds me of a bridegroom, enjoying his wedding banquet. I cannot help but wonder...can it be that there is no woman who is worthy of him?"

Martha drew herself up suddenly.

"No doubt there are many who would love him dearly and faithfully. But...it is not his purpose to marry...at least...I don't think it is." To Reumah's surprise, Martha flushed deeply.

"I thought—perhaps it is foolish of me—but I thought perhaps your sister had captivated his heart."

Martha turned to her sharply. "My dear girl, you must not romanticize. It is an idle pastime, and no good can come of it. I assure you, neither of them has ever said a word on the subject." She abruptly turned back to the stoves, in the manner of someone who had been insulted. Reumah felt her cheeks flush and a few minutes later, when Martha returned to the passage with a large pot, Reumah bowed down.

"Please forgive my foolish talk, Mistress. I meant no offense."

"None taken, my dear." She sighed wearily. "I am tired from all my efforts and not very patient, I'm afraid."

Reumah held up her arms with a thick cloth to take the large pot.

"No," said Martha firmly. "It's one of his favorites. I shall serve it to him myself." She walked swiftly into the flickering lights of the courtyard straight toward his table. What happened next Reumah remembered for the rest of her life, and imagined that many of the guests did as well.

Perhaps because her arms were aching, or perhaps because her foot slipped, suddenly the large steaming pot slipped from the cloth that Martha used to carry it. It landed on the couch where the Master reclined, and then rolled off and clattered to the floor. The men around the master immediately became silent, which caused the other guests to stop talking and look about curiously. The pungent smell of black cumin filled the air, thick lentil stew lay splattered like mud on the ground, and on the feet of the Master and some of the men who reclined with him, and on Mary, who had been seated near his feet during the entire banquet. Mary sprang up and locked eyes with her sister. A look that defied words passed between them, and after a moment, Mary bent down and began to scrape up the dirty stew into an empty dish with the shards of the pot.

"Finally you see fit to help me, my sister!" She could not resist, though she immediately regretted speaking because she was sure that the courtyard echoed her words. She ran back into the kitchen. The Master knelt to help Mary. His men looked at one another. One of them, who was both tall and portly and whom Reumah decided must be Simon Peter, stood up, and noticed her. Thinking she was one of the servants, he motioned for her to come immediately. The Master and Mary and Reumah carried the ruined dish into the kitchen where Martha had retreated.

"Lord...do you not care that my sister has left me to do all the work? See now she helps...because you are!" It was as if a month's toil and exhaustion and resentment had suddenly found a vent, and it would not be closed. She turned her back to the Master, who stood near her, and her hands twisted the cloth from which the pot had spilled. Mary quickly and quietly busied herself with the fruit baskets, and Reumah went over on the pretense of assisting her, but she could not take her eyes off the Master as he stood there.

"Martha," he said to her back.

"It seems she will do nothing unless you bid her, Lord."

"Martha," he said again.

"Tell her to come help me!" She spat the words out.

"You would command *me* now?"

At this Martha turned to him. The room was so silent Reumah could hear her breathing.

"Not so, Lord. May it never be. I wish only to serve you."

"You are my friend, Martha! You are my dear friend—and yet you are worried about so many things that you cannot enjoy my company. Mary chose what is most necessary—she chose to fellowship with me while I am still here." He sighed deeply, and for a moment looked so aggrieved that he could not speak.

"I will not take that away from her."

Martha's eyes gleamed. "Forgive me, Lord. I am a foolish woman. I made you feel honored—but not loved."

They stood, looking at one another, in silence. Mary and Reumah stood immobile, hardly daring to breathe, holding large melons in their hands. Yet the lapse between Martha and her lord was not awkward, but simply a pause that rendered words unnecessary, because a perfect understanding had passed between them.

"Now come…be seated among us. Dine with me. And let the others in too, for you have made enough food to feed the entire village."

"The others, my Lord?"

"Yes, the others…the ones at the gate. Let them come in…let them all come in."

Afterward Martha spoke of how she had felt fresh strength pour into her body. It was as if, when she opened the gate and bade the huddled, hungry strangers to come into the feast, a gate inside her opened as well, and her energy was renewed and her heart was lightened.

Afterward, Mary spoke of how the food never seemed to run out... how the bread baskets remained full and the platters never became empty.

"No one...not one...went away hungry," she whispered, after the gate had closed on the last sleepy guest.

And Reumah never forgot the look that was exchanged between the Lord, as she now called him, and Martha. It filled her with the deepest longing she had ever known. His words, "She chose what is most necessary; I shall not take it away from her," echoed over and over in her mind, and sank into her heart, and made her forget everything else for a time.

Even the missing vial of perfume.

25

"I wish it would snow," says Kevin.

He does not say it gazing wistfully out the window, as Jennifer would have done at his age. He says it during a TV commercial, about snow tires. The commercial features vehicles of all shapes and sizes with their tires spinning and skidding on ice, followed by shots of cars flung into snow piles and overturned in deep, snow-piled ditches. Then one car rides safely through the mayhem. *"There's only one tire than can stand up to Mother Nature,"* says a deep, authoritative voice-over, and the driver with the correct tires steers with his left hand, and rests his right arm on the back of the passenger seat in a relaxed manner. He glances in his rearview mirror at a pig-tailed toddler, sleepy and nestled safely in her car seat.

"We haven't had a lot of snow this winter, have we?" says Jennifer.

She sits beside him on her couch, not too close, since he is not a snuggler. He keeps his eyes on the screen, watching a schmaltzy movie about a boy who rescues a family of dolphins from an evil and exploitative theme park investor. In these movies the bad people are always easy to spot: the investor is fat. He has greasy lips and squinty eyes and blows cigar smoke into people's faces. He has money, and he wants to make more money, which is always evil in these movies. In contrast, the quiet, misunderstood hippie film maker who befriends the fatherless boy and helps him save the dolphins looks like one of the Bee Gees. He is short of cash, but his brown eyes are filled with kindness and his white jeans never seem to get dirty. When his neighbors get busted for growing pot, he says to the boy, "It's an organic substance…why do they make such a big deal about it?" He has a tanned, shapely girlfriend who wears a different bikini in every scene and seems to have perpetually wet hair. By the end of the movie, his documentary film about dolphins wins an award and helps him to get a generous grant from the government to conduct further research, and the viewer is left to assume that the film maker and his girlfriend will look out for the boy, and be his protective big buddies forever.

Yeah, right, Jennifer thinks. In real life, the hippie guy would introduce the boy to pot and the boy would start selling it to his junior high friends. In real life, the kid would flunk out of school and do time in a juvenile detention center. In real life, she had never met a guy who used recreational drugs and had what she considered a normal, productive life. Jeb's life was productive, but you could hardly call it normal. *You buying this crap?* She wants to ask Kevin.

"Do you like dolphins?" Jennifer asks instead when the credits are rolling. She has no idea what to talk about. She wishes the boys from downstairs would come up at that moment and engage him in some boyish game or activity. She has never paid close attention to the quieter games that boys play. They involve objects that hold no interest for her: marbles or cards or dice or jacks and small rubber balls.

"Naw," says Kevin. "They're girly. Like unicorns." He looks down at his hands, and begins to pick at a wart on his index finger.

"Oh don't do that, sweetie," Jennifer says, adopting the tone of the girlfriend in the movie, who was maternal and nurturing, despite her centerfold body. "You might make it bleed."

"I like makin' it bleed. I do it all the time in school, and then I get to go to the nurse for a Band-Aid."

"Oh dear. Well...I better check and make sure I have some Band-Aids then." She can't remember the last time she needed a Band-Aid. She thinks about going downstairs, on the pretense of asking for one or two. She could take Kevin with her, and the boys would perhaps invite him in to do something. They seem like the kind of boys who would be friendly enough to do that. Then what would Jennifer do? She would admire the new bookcase, she supposed. Maybe Rebecca would offer her a cup of tea? Then what? What would they talk about?

A momentary panic rises within her, which is quickly replaced by anger. She stares at her reflection in the mirror.

It's your own damn fault for not saying no when you had the chance. Why can't you stand up to her? Here it is, Friday night, and you're stuck babysitting her kid, so she can monopolize Jeb and have him die on her watch.

She had never seen Vina so mollified, so willing to play on her sympathy, so willing to look *weak*. It had caught her off guard. She got sucked in.

"I've been stressing, you know? All his shit...all the paperwork... I'm trying to sell some of his earlier work to collectors to pay for the funeral, you know? It's not going so good. They all want his later stuff and I'm trying to hold on to it until...well...you know. Once he's gone I can triple the asking price, you know?"

She sits down on the couch and crosses her legs and pulls a cigarette out of her purse, puts it into her mouth, then takes it out again, remembering that Jennifer doesn't allow smoking.

"Anyways...I'm sorry about last time...I was stressed, honey...I was rather short with you and of course I realized afterward you were just trying to help...of course he called you when I couldn't come. God, he never wants me to leave, but what can I do? I have a business to run." She waves the unlit cigarette around while she speaks, not looking at Jennifer, but at the clock on the opposite wall. It is one of those sunburst clocks, with pointy, brass rays emitting from the frame around the face. It's a piece of junk, as far as Jennifer is concerned, but it still works, and her mother was fond of it, because it had been a wedding present.

"And a kid..."

"Pardon?"

"Um...you have a business to run...and Kevin."

Vina puts the cigarette up to her mouth for a split second before remembering that it's not lit. She takes a deep breath anyway.

"Which is another thing...my ex is being a prick, as usual." She looks directly at Jennifer. "I could really use a babysitter this weekend."

Which is how Jennifer ended up with Kevin, but she had negotiated with Vina, and she felt proud of herself for it:

You stay with him tonight and I stay with him tomorrow night. Otherwise…no deal.

Vina had agreed, without arguing, and Jennifer had enjoyed a moment of exultation, as her visitor rose to leave.

"Nice clock, that. Vintage. I might want to buy it off you."

Jennifer glanced at the sunburst clock, and then back at Vina, who had a small, tight-lipped smile on her lips. She was never sure if Vina was being serious or sarcastic.

So it's only nine o'clock, and the kid is already tired of TV, and bored, and Jennifer slams her medicine cabinet shut. She has no Band-Aids.

God help me.

When she comes out of the bathroom he has discovered her book about William Bentley and his snowflake photographs. Normally she keeps the book on the coffee table, because it had been a gift from her mother for her eighth-grade graduation, and like most coffee table books, she has never read it, but only stared at the photographs. She has small markers in the pages of her favorite ones.

"Are these real snowflakes?" Kevin asks, leafing slowly through the pages. There are dozens of original snowflake photographs, arrayed in rows and columns, like diamond brooches on black velvet, each different from the rest.

"Yep. Amazing, aren't they?" She suddenly feels like some happy creature has been released from a cage inside her. She hands him all her snow globes, one by one, to look at and then retrieves her scrapbook, which contains her snowflake drawings and stickers and Christmas ornaments made out of white and silver and blue pipe cleaners and school reports and her story about the Snow god. Kevin says little but remains subdued and engaged. He has forgotten his wart but picks his nose a few times and wipes his finger abstractedly on her couch, but she doesn't care because she is suffused with affection for him now. She has finally converted someone to faith in the Snow god. In a moment of epiphany she excavates Jeb's drawing from the closet and shows it to Kevin. He contemplates it for a long time, which for a kid his age, is about a minute.

"It looks like a church statue of Jesus. Only with snow coming out of the holes in his hands."

"Yes. And no cross."

"I like him."

"Me too." She places the sketch on the coffee table next to the couch, where she has made a bed for him. "Would you like me to leave this here?"

"Yeah," says Kevin. "I'm gonna pray to him before I go to sleep."

"Really?" She feels a bit guilty that Kevin's faith has now apparently surpassed her own. "What will you say?"

"I'm gonna ask him for snow, of course."

"Oh, honey…um…it's like forty-five degrees out there. Not really cold enough to snow, I'm afraid."

His face darkens for a moment, and then clears. "If he's real…if he's a real god, he can make it snow. He doesn't have to send a lot. Just enough for me to make a snowball. Enough for me to believe."

She sighs and leaves him then, with the Snow god picture and a glass of water and a nightlight. She wants a glass of wine to take to bed along with a magazine. With the fridge open she wavers between orange juice, and the bottle of cabernet. She closes the door of the fridge, and then opens it again. She pours half a glass of cabernet, and puts an ice cube in it, to subdue her guilt. She tastes it, frowns, and tops up the glass. When she is settled in her bed another disconcerting thought seeps into her brain.

Christ, what would his mother think?

She bolts out of bed, semiconscious, and knocks over the empty wine bottle, which somehow ended up next to her bed. Her brain feels like a washing machine on its spin cycle. She lunges into the living room.

Kevin is screaming.

She fights the urge to scream herself, and her hands are shaking when she reaches for the switch on the lamp next to the couch.

The boy is sitting upright, his face bright with red patches from the exertion of his screams, and his eyes fixed on the corner of her living room. She actually turns around, expecting to see a spectral horror, but it is only the half-empty wastepaper basket, with a pile of assorted footwear next to it and her pocketbook. The key rack is on the wall above it.

"Kevin! Kevin! It's OK! It's a dream, honey...c'mon, shake it off..." but to her horror, his screams intensify and he looks at her with wide-eyed terror, as if she is now part of whatever it is.

Christ almighty...

She must have said it aloud because he screams even louder at the sound of her voice, or maybe it is the knocking that makes it worse, because someone is knocking at the door, which turns out to be Rebecca, from downstairs.

"I'm couldn't help but overhear—"

"Oh, god! I don't know what happened—"

Rebecca steps over to him and takes his hand in hers. He snatches it away, and she then sits behind him and begins to rub his back. "What's his name?" she mouths, looking at Jen.

"Kevin..." her mouth is so dry she can hardly get the word out.

"Kevin...Kevin..." Rebecca says, in a soft, singsong voice, and then she begins a song, very low, right next to his face, not in English. Jennifer hears something like "Barucha" and "Yeshua" in the song. Maybe it's Yiddish. Or Hebrew. Whatever it is, it seems to work, and Kevin stops screaming, and his eyes become refocused on Rebecca.

"It's all gone now, Kevin...it's OK. You can sleep now."

"It was the Snow god..." he says, his voice quavering, and Jennifer has the sensation of a rock settling in her intestines. She prays Rebecca won't ask. Or see the sketch.

"Well, it's gone now..."

"He had no snow, though...just blood. Blood dripping out of his hands..." and his eyes become wide and fierce again and he sits up.

"Sweetie...sweetie...whatever it was...it's gone. All gone, OK?"

"OK." He lays down again, and Rebecca smooths his hair and then rises and heads toward the door. Jen follows her.

"God, I don't know what to say...guess it woke everyone up, huh? I'm sorry...his mom told me once he gets night terrors or something... didn't think it would happen on my watch, though..."

"It's OK...I was still awake...and I came right up. You look like you've seen a ghost too..." She smiles gently. "You OK?"

For a split second their eyes meet, and Jennifer is struck by the beauty of her large gray eyes behind her glasses. They have a tranquil quality, like a misty lake at dawn.

"Oh…I'll be fine. Stuff like that happens all the time at work… patients on pain meds…I'm just not used to it here…in my apartment, you know? Kinda caught me off guard."

"Of course. Hey, come for breakfast? We're making cinnamon rolls. It'll be fun."

"Um—uh…OK." She agrees because she doesn't know what else to say. For a whole minute she stands in the middle of the room after Rebecca leaves, and tries to pinpoint what's bothering her. She looks over at Kevin—his breathing is even and deep, and his eyes are closed. She looks at the sunburst clock, and fails to discover whatever vintage appeal or kitschy charm Vina had discerned in it. The clock ticks on, benignly. She thinks of Rebecca, so calm and efficient, arriving just in time, and so soothing and nurturing and *maternal*.

Who am I trying to kid? I don't have it. I don't have what it takes… he would have screamed all night if it was left to me to soothe him.

She quietly steps over to the coffee table and rerolls the Snow god sketch carefully. She removes her old scrapbook and the heavy, hardbound snowflake book and hides everything in the closet, leaving no evidence of the Snow god anywhere. Unless it actually snows, he will probably forget everything, and if he remembers anything, it will be like a dream.

There is no snow anywhere, and Kevin says nothing. He has become shy, and is reluctant to go downstairs with her for cinnamon rolls.

"No thanks. Do you have Pop-Tarts? Or waffles?"

She is on the verge of calling Rebecca to make a polite excuse for them, when the younger Peterson boy appears at the door.

"Hi," he says to Jennifer, and then looks at Kevin. "Ya comin' down?"

Jennifer is relieved to see that the cinnamon rolls are not made entirely from scratch…they are made from store-bought refrigerator dough, but then Rebecca and the kids dip them in butter and roll them in cinnamon sugar. They stick walnuts in some and raisins in others before they go into the oven. The rule is you have to eat cereal or fresh fruit or a hard-boiled egg, while the rolls are baking, "so there is some nutritious component," says Rebecca. Everyone squeezes the sticky packets of white frosting onto the rolls when they come out, and the boys eat twice as many as the girls, because they don't sip coffee with theirs. The little girl in the high chair—Bee-Bee, they call her—stares solemnly at Jennifer, holding a grayish-white undershirt to her nose and ignoring her cinnamon roll. The oldest girl, Sarah, sips tea out of a china cup, and looks disdainfully at her brothers, who fight over the last roll and gulp down big glasses of milk. David, Jennifer thinks it's David, barely stifles a burp, and then, red-faced, asks if they can be excused. The other boy nudges Kevin and says, "Come on…"

When the boys leave, Jennifer glances around the room, frantically searching for a topic of conversation. The southern windows are crowded with potted flowers, and so she says, "I guess you're big into plants, huh?"

"Um…not really. My hubby has the green thumb. He actually inherited those from his mom. Prize orchids. They're quite beautiful…but so delicate. I'm afraid to breathe on them." She refills Jennifer's coffee cup.

"Thanks," Jennifer says, wondering if she should tell her that she shouldn't be drinking coffee, and why. "And thanks again…for last night…for coming up. I really didn't know what to do."

"Honestly, I think it's that song. It works all the time for my kids."

"You'll have to teach it to me." They lock eyes then, across the table, and suddenly Jennifer perceives that Rebecca knows. Maybe Clay saw the books on the coffee table, and maybe he told her, or maybe she could just tell by looking at Jennifer, but she nods in an assenting way, and this reassures Jen, as if they have joined forces, one mother with another, to combat the terrors of childhood.

An hour later she goes to summon Kevin from the freezer room, as they call it. He is laughing and fooling around with the other boys, and his clothes and face and hair are wet and there are large puddles on the floor.

"What in the world are you guys doing?" she says, with the image of Vina's irate expression springing up in her brain.

"Look, Jen. They froze it! Cool, huh?" He plunges his hand into a large Tupperware container of snow. "They have more in the freezer."

"That's my brother's dumb idea. He wants to freeze a bunch of it and then sell it in the summer," the older boy says, rolling his eyes derisively.

"Wow. What a clever idea! I'll buy the first snowball, OK?" She smiles, and then looks over at Kevin, whose mother is coming in fifteen minutes to retrieve him.

"I guess he's real after all," Kevin says.

"What?"

"The Snow god...remember? Last night?" He seems annoyed at her sudden amnesia.

"Of course...yes." She says it in a nonchalant manner, as if she is used to having the Snow god answer her prayers all the time, and she pushes the incident far back into her brain until Vina is driving away with Kevin, who gives her a thumbs-up from the back window, as if to remind her of their secret faith. Jennifer cannot help but be affected... as if a tiny ray has been transmitted into her soul from the unmistakable sparkle of hope in the boy's eyes.

XXVI

*I*n the few moments before Reumah wakes, she dreams of her father. She dreams that she is back in his house, that he has allowed her to enter his chamber because he is close to death, and she kneels at his bedside, and returns the alabaster vial to him, unbroken, its contents as unadulterated by air or human contact as the day it was sealed. She dreams that he weeps with joy at the sight of her, and by the honor of her tribute. She dreams that he places his hand on her head, and whispers to her that her sins are pardoned, and he will remember them no more. He calls her *my lamb*, and tells her that she has always been *"the apple of my eye."* She can hear the hired mourners assembling in the courtyard, and the encroaching scent of death in the house, and her eyes and her heart are so heavy with grief that she wants to stay by his side forever, with his hand growing cold on her head, and follow him to the place of Sheol.

But when she is fully awake, the truth swoops on her like a vulture: it is not her father, but Lazarus, and it is not her father's hand but Mary's that smooths her hair to wake her. In less than a month, the house of Lazarus has gone from a house of feasting to a house of mourning. It is as if a massive cloud cover has erased even the memory of light from the sky; the festive banquet given in the Master's honor now seems a faded memory, eclipsed by the anguish that followed only a week later.

She perceives the truth before it is uttered.

"He is gone from us," Mary whispers. Her eyes are swollen from the grief of her bedside vigil.

The tears of her dream that were appointed for her father she now sheds for Lazarus and his sisters. They weep together quietly for a few moments before Reumah speaks.

"Sleep, my friend. Take my place here, and rest. I will tend to things…"

"No, I must help Martha…"

"You cannot! You are weary with grief and sleeplessness. Let me go to Martha…I will do whatever she bids me. She must rest too."

"It's too much…too much to ask of you."

"Do not deny me the honor of serving the ones who have become my sisters…and he…likewise…has been more of a brother to me than ever were my own."

This produces a fresh torrent of weeping for both women, and they cling to one another before Mary finally lies down and closes her eyes. The rays of the morning filter through the shuttered casement and create a design on the floor: small squares of light between dark bands that form crosses. Reumah fixes her eyes on the pattern. She takes a deep breath and whispers a prayer.

"Yaweh Sabaoth…have mercy on us. Grant us the strength to face this day."

The pain of her brother's death, and the anguish of the days before it, fill Mary's mind with such darkness that it cannot give way to the sweet release of either prayer or sleep. There are too many unanswered questions that lead to more perplexing problems that roll over each other in her brain, dislodging the anchor of hope in her heart.

Why—it was beyond ironic—had Lazarus given up his own vial to redeem Reumah's?

She had spoken privately to her brother of Reumah's loss in the euphoric days immediately following the feast, and her brother, ever generous to a fault, had insisted his own specially prepared vial be used to redeem Reumah's. Of course Mary had resisted the idea at first.

"You can't, brother! By your own hands it has been specially prepared for your burial, may it not be for many years."

"True…which means I can prepare another in its place. But Reumah's vial was a gift from her esteemed father, who, from what you've told me, is estranged from her. Come now. What else does she have? Look around you...I have no end of resources to prepare another vial for myself."

"But it took years for you to distill and prepare that ointment!"

"This is true, but think again of your friend. Her most precious possession has been taken from her by the man who betrayed her, and she will never have it again if we do not intervene. We cannot force him to recompense her, as we have no proof of the theft, and as long as he remains one of our Master's friends we cannot shun him. He is a businessman; let us hope that he has not sold it already. We will barter with him: my vial for hers. He will not care whose vial it is, as long as he has one in his possession that is of equal value, for reasons known only to himself. He is, after all, the treasurer among the Master's disciples; let us assume that his motives are honorable. Perhaps he means to use it for a just cause in the Master's service."

"He stole it from Reumah! How can his motives be honorable?"

"Perhaps he did. Or perhaps he meant to safeguard it, in case others tried to steal it."

"Nay, brother. You are far too generous. He is a thief and a liar." She knew more of Judas's conduct toward Reumah than did Lazarus, for this had been the subject of much late-night whispering between the two young women.

"Mary! You must not speak ill of one who has been chosen by our Lord to be among his disciples."

At this she had sighed heavily, and then nodded. "You're right, of course. Perhaps there is some divine role for which he has been chosen, known only to the Master, who makes no mistakes and can read the intent of a man's heart. We must believe that all will be made right at the appointed time."

"All right, then. Leave him to me. I shall arrange everything. I shall summon him this day."

Still her nerves felt fraught with tension, and she arranged for herself and Reumah to be about the village all the following day, visiting the sick and the poor, in an effort to avoid any direct contact with Judas. Such precaution proved unnecessary: he came from the city, under the cover of night, and met her brother in a shadowy corner of the courtyard, away from the blaze of the fire where the servants warmed themselves. He was gone before the servants arose to light the cooking fires. The vial—Reumah's treasured vial—was the first thing that Mary's eyes beheld when she opened them. Lazarus had placed it on a small table by the window, and the beautiful alabaster gleamed with moonlike luminosity, reflecting the sun's first rays. She found it difficult to look at anything else, or to pray, as was her daily habit, in her excitement for Reumah to awaken.

"How? How can this be?" Reumah rubbed the sleep from her eyes, and held the vial in disbelief. It was smooth and intact, and its seal was unmolested. She felt giddy with the relief of holding it again, and she discovered that the joy of reclaiming it was even greater than the joy of receiving it as a gift the first time.

"I...cannot say. I can only tell you that a friend—who asks to remain nameless—has redeemed it for you."

Reumah knelt at her side. "Please...please tell me...I am indebted to him or her for the rest of my life...please tell me who it is...and...at what cost was it redeemed?"

"I'm sorry, Reumah. I can't. Just accept it as from the hand of the Almighty, and live out your days in gratitude to him."

Reumah had caressed the vial adoringly, and with her finger traced the small inscription at its base, which was engraved with the insignia: Lazarus of Bethany. She remembered reading the insignia for the first time, and trying to imagine the faceless stranger whom her father had commissioned to prepare the vial. Lazarus was hardly a stranger to her now, and she wondered what her father would say if he knew that his daughter had become a member of his household, and gratefully served his family along with his sisters, every day.

She wondered if the one who had created the vial of perfume was, in fact, its redeemer as well. Her heart whispered the truth.

These were her musings on that bright morning, and she shared them with Mary, who laughed gently alongside her, sitting next to her amid the pillows and saying little, but sharing her joy. She would share it still, if her brother had not suddenly taken ill two days later. The questions now raged unanswered in her mind, the loudest one being that which had Martha voiced, gazing out at the hills of Judea beyond her window, and it was the same question that now echoed relentlessly in the chambers of Mary's heart, which had become devoid of every emotion except a rising tide of fear and grief.

Why does the Master not come?

They had sent word to him, of course. In a bizarre turn of events that defied human understanding, her brother's extreme act of generosity was seemingly repaid by the fatal fever that took hold of him only one week after the feast, and two days after he had given up his own funereal vial in exchange for Reumah's. They had wasted no time dispatching Phineas, their brother's personal servant, to summon the Lord.

"Tell him, 'Please come quickly! Your dear friend Lazarus is sick,'" Martha had instructed Phineas. Mary stood next to her when she said it. At that moment she had been so infused with faith, and so convinced that the Lord would immediately return to rebuke the fever once and for all, that she had actually smiled at the thought of him receiving the news.

"Nay," she told Phineas. "Say simply, 'Lord, the one you love has taken ill.' He will know. He will come."

But Phineas had returned without him.

"He has gone to Perea," he told them.

"But surely you gave him our message?"

"Indeed, mistresses, I did. And he told me, and the others standing nearby, that the sickness would not end in death, but that it would be for the glory of God and his Son."

The sisters stared at him for a moment, and then looked at each other, as if daring the other to press on in faith.

"It is the word of the Lord," said Martha firmly. "We will not doubt it. I will go tell our brother."

Mary went out to the courtyard where the Lord had been only days before. She knelt down at the couch where he had reclined, and placed her head on her arms where his feet had been. She longed to tell him what his words meant to her: it was as if he had lit a small lamp in front of her, which did nothing to illuminate the long road of her life, but merely a spot on the path before her feet, enabling her to take the next step.

She must have dozed, because abruptly she finds herself awake and momentarily confused, before the tumult of the house closes in on her. She sits up. Martha is standing next to her bed.

"Mary...I'm sorry to wake you...but I don't know what to think."

"What is it? Sit here...sit down for a moment."

Martha does so. This in itself is so unexpected that Mary is engulfed by a cloud of fear. She is not accustomed to seeing her sister become unraveled or weary, for the entire family and surrounding village regard Martha as a valiant woman who can be relied on in any crisis. Now she sits heavily on the bed and closes her eyes, and takes a deep breath, as if summoning strength from a hidden source.

"What is it?"

"His vial. We began assembling the materials to prepare his body... his vial is missing. I have looked everywhere. No one seems to know where it is. Caliah is hysterical."

As if on cue, the voices of Caliah and Naomi and the other servants and mourners suddenly increase in volume and pitch, and soon the lament is taken up in other parts of the village as well.

"How they loved him," Martha whispers. Her eyes fill.

The sisters sit in silence, listening as the piercing wails of the women inundate them and are echoed in the courtyard and village beyond. They allow themselves the luxury of grieving privately. After a few minutes, Martha composes herself.

"Do you know where it is? His vial?"

And Mary tells her sister the bitter truth. Martha is silent for some time, as if she is choosing her words with great care.

After a few moments she says, "Is it not fitting? He died as he lived, and the final act of his life is one of such supreme generosity that he compromised his own burial as a result. God will reward him. I am sure of it. He will recompense him in a way that we cannot now know. This is not the time for recrimination or regret. Nor must we question of the will of Yaweh in this matter or any other. He could have prevented the trade of our brother's vial for Reumah's...He could have prevented the death of our brother—He chose not to. It is enough that he grants us wisdom and strength to take the next step."

"How can you be so steadfast?! I have not half your faith!!" She stands and begins to pace the small room. In her agitation, she makes a fist of one hand, and grinds it into the other as she speaks. "I cannot fathom the ways of our God, or his son, our Master! The hope that his words first gave me has been torn away…and left a wound inside me that I fear will never heal!" Anger now replaces grief. Martha tries to soothe her but Mary waves her outstretched hand aside. "Oh, Martha…I cannot accept it! I cannot accept that he did not come to us, especially when he said the sickness wouldn't end in death! How could he have misled us? The one who has affirmed his love to us, and called us his dear friends?"

"Stop. Stop! The time for questions and explanations and reassurances will come, but not today. Today we must do right by our brother, and honor him in death as best we can. We must embalm him. You must help me decide what to do."

Mary stands still and closes her eyes. Out of sheer love and respect for her siblings, she wills herself to focus on the present, and leave her burning questions to smolder. After a moment she opens her eyes and looks at Martha.

"There must be spikenard. It is chief among the anointing oils." Her voice is flat, and Martha's eyes widen a little at the sound of it.

"Yes, but…we have not the skill to make it. Even if we could, it would take months to procure the plants for the distillation…and then there is the cost…"

"We will use mine. My vial is unsealed, because I have used many drops to anoint the women in service to the Master."

"And so you will need it for that noble purpose for a long time to come."

Mary shakes her head resolutely. "There can be no more nobler purpose than the anointing of my brother on the third day of his burial, as is our tradition. The poor, the sick, and the destitute will be always with us, but my brother will die once; we will not have the opportunity to honor him again in this life." There was a bitter edge in her voice that Martha could not fail to notice.

"Oh, Mary. I fear that your anger will overtake you, and will cause you to become bitter against the Master who loves us. Think of all that he has done for you, and for our family!"

Mary turns away from her sister, and reaches for a beautifully carved chest, in which she keeps her perfumes and cosmetics. She removes her own alabaster vial from its appointed place, and carefully opens its seal. Almost immediately the air of the room is changed, but it is not the fragrance they expected. The sisters look at each other in horror, and hurriedly Mary grabs a small saucer and pours the ointment into it. Both sisters gasp in revulsion: a small, dead insect, beautifully preserved, floats in the rancid oil.

"Well…that settles it," Martha says finally. "We will use what we have…herbs and spices…these will have to suffice. We cannot delay."

But the sight of the fly in the precious ointment is too grievous a sight for the younger sister, and she collapses onto her bed. The grief of her brother's death now seems less than the horror of the ruined ointment. Throughout all the hours that Reumah tends her, and stays at her side as the sole witness of the travail of her soul, Mary cannot explain why.

27

*C*live sits in his car for twenty minutes trying to decide what to do. It's too early to go for dinner at his brother's house, although he knows he'd be welcomed there. But it would be awkward. He doesn't really know Rebecca, although she seems to be a kind, quiet sort of person, not unlike Clay, and he doesn't know his nieces and nephews, and would have to think hard to remember their names. He feels some guilt about this. His ideas about the role of an uncle are sketchy: his father's two brothers did not live in New Jersey. The younger one, Joe, had been an independent contractor in Harrisburg. To amuse the family, he would do imitations of the Amish men conducting business in town, and these were a source of uproarious laughter, although Clive never understood what was so funny. The only thing he knew about the Amish was that they were very religious, and somehow their faith was connected to them all dressing alike, not using electricity, owning lots of property, and helping each other build barns and houses. He could think of worse ways to make a living. The older uncle, Richie, had lived in Florida and owned a boat. He did not know what Richie's business had been, and apparently no one else did either. Both uncles were dead now, but years ago when they visited they would sit around and drink and laugh and argue and play poker with his dad into the early morning hours. They would smoke cigars on the back porch (ironic that his chain-smoking mother refused to allow them to smoke indoors), and they would drive to Point Pleasant for obscenely expensive lobster dinners. Sometimes his older brothers had been included in these activities, but Clive was too young, and other than rustling his hair or slapping him on the back and asking him if he had a girlfriend, the uncles did not pay much attention to him. There were some transient aunts that were connected to them, but he does not remember any of those ladies. On his mother's side there was one brother, Uncle Cedric, a librarian and collector of rare books, who lived in Manhattan. He had never visited, but sent a large platter of assorted dried fruit every Christmas. No one in the family ever ate the fruit, and his mother would leave the unwrapped platter under the tree for a few days, then rip off the tag and give it to the cleaning lady. Clive would sometimes keep the tag, which had his uncle's name signed on it, and use it as a bookmark—almost out of a sense of loyalty to the uncle he had never seen. Even now, if he read "May contain pits" on a package of dried fruit, he thought of his Uncle Cedric. He did not have any other thoughts of him.

So by those standards, he feels only slightly guilty that he is not more involved with his brother's children, and he feels no compulsion to rush over there to see them, because he is not in the mood for making small talk or answering any awkward questions that children tend to ask. But he feels a twinge of regret about his brother. He would like to be more connected to Clay, and by extension, his family, because he feels like this would probably mean a lot to Clay. But he has no idea how to go about it. His brother dwells in a realm of existence that includes sermon-making and going to church and praying and homeschooling and sleeping beside the same person every night, and Clive cannot relate to any of it, although he is happy for his brother, as long as his brother is happy. Earlier today, when he saw Clay, he didn't look so happy. He looked tired and stressed and sad. Also thinner. He wonders if this is why he hasn't already made some excuse to bow out of dinner and then jump on the parkway and head back to the office.

But then there's Jeb too.

The act of offering forgiveness—last rites, in a sense—to the dying man, even under the pretense of being some other man, has created within Clive a sense of connection that he cannot shake off. He decides he should stick around for the weekend. He has never seen a person die, up close, in real life, and he thinks that Jeb's demise might be a good first experience, since it wouldn't be too traumatic for him, but still have some drama and poignancy, which are two qualities he feels his life is greatly lacking.

So he finds himself driving around the small town, looking for an off-season bed-and-breakfast that will accommodate him for the night. He drives slowly, carefully scrutinizing the numerous Victorian-era inns, each arrayed in Easter-egg colors and festooned with gingerbread molding and stenciled shutters, and yet each so uniquely charming that any of them could be on the cover of *America's Finest Historic Inns*. An obnoxious honk from a car directly in front of him causes him to realize that he is driving the wrong way down a one-way street, and this causes him to loudly say, "Christ almighty," while he is backing up, which makes him think that Christ may have something to do with him then bashing into two large metal trashcans, which make a clanging, clattering sound and cause a number of people to peer down out of second-story windows. He begins to rethink his decision to stay the night. He gets out of his car to inspect the damage to his rear fender. He lifts a severely dented trashcan and then notices that he is standing in front of the Shiloh Seaside Inn, which has a small hinged sign that says, *Vacancies*.

Next to the large paneled doors another sign reads, *Alice Paul slept here, circa 1915*. He has no idea who Alice Paul is. He only hopes that the innkeeper will not add a replacement fee for the damaged trash can to his bill.

To his relief he discovers that the owners of the establishment are currently in Naples, and the hostess, an older lady whose voice is deeply roughened from decades of tobacco use, waves away his apology for the trash can, and shows him to his room, which contains a queen-size bed with a brass headboard, and far too many ruffled pillows. There is a musty, mothball odor in the air, and the wallpaper is overly congested, in his view, with burgundy roses. The floorboards creak painfully with his slightest move. He checks the bathroom, which is so small that it must have surely been birthed from a closet. It occurs to him that he could use the toilet and shave at the same time, which makes him think that he should probably get some toiletries for the night.

At the local drugstore he runs into someone he feels he should know, because he has seen her before, and knows that she is connected to

Jeb. The woman has one of those posh Italian bags with the designer's logo absurdly printed all over it, and is buying cigarettes and hair spray and a pack of spearmint gum. There is a boy with her, presumably her son, because he is wheedling her to buy him a toy Ninja. Clive clears his throat and says, "That's a lovely bag…" and the woman turns to look at him.

She looks at him carefully for a few seconds and then she says, "Ah…I think we've met…"

"Clive Peterson…I'm embarrassed to say I don't—"

"Vina. I'm his manager."

"Of course…well…I saw Mr. Kellon today, actually and—"

"Yes?"

"He…I…was shocked, frankly. Um…"

"We should talk. Are you free tomorrow?"

"Uh, yes. Yes, I am."

"Good. There's a café on Main Street called Ground Zero. Can you be there at noon?"

"Sure."

"Perfect." When she says "perfect," she smiles and he catches a glimpse of her teeth, which are small and tidy, although stained. This bothers him, for some reason. As she is exiting the store, with her whiny kid still bugging her, she turns to him and says, "Are you staying in town?" and he says he is.

"Do me a little favor, will you? Can you check in on him sometime this evening?" She hands Clive her card, which has two large, violet intersecting V's on it.

"Just call me…if you think he's in any danger…you know." She gives him a knowing look, but he's not sure what for. It occurs to him afterward that he has said yes to everything a woman whom he doesn't even know has asked him to do.

He washes his face, neck, and armpits and brushes his teeth and slaps on some cheap cologne that he bought in the drugstore, not having his own more expensive stuff with him. He dons a fresh shirt and tie from the stash he keeps in the trunk of his car for such emergencies, having had a few mishaps with spilled soup in the past. He is knotting his tie when he thinks how ridiculous it is to be wearing it to his brother's house. He removes the tie, deciding to save it for his meeting with that Vina-person tomorrow. When he arrives at his brother's house, he painstakingly parallel parks in front of their house, and then realizes he should have brought a bottle of wine or some flowers or dessert. He wonders if Clay's religious convictions now prevent him from drinking beer, and his mind goes blank momentarily. In any case, the sale of alcohol is prohibited in Ocean Grove, but he can't remember why. He pulls out again, and heads to a florist on Main Street, where he purchases a bouquet of yellow tulips for Rebecca, which he places gently on his backseat. Then he returns to the drugstore across the street, and buys a large box of chocolates. Back at his brother's house, the two older boys, apparently on the lookout for his arrival, saunter out to greet him. He shakes hands with the older son, whose name he can't remember, and turns to the younger son to do the same. At the same moment the older boy says, "Nathan!" in an embarrassed way, because Nathan has discovered the box of chocolates on the passenger side.

"These for us?" he says, grinning up at Clive.

"Sure thing," Clive says, "but you better check—"

Nathan is already running into the house with the chocolates, and Clive smiles in an amused way at the older son, wondering if he should be so bold as to ask him his name.

"I'm David, by the way," the boy says abruptly, and in Clive's eyes, he suddenly grows five inches.

"Hey, David...I'm—"

"I know. Uncle Clive. My dad's kid brother."

"Well...it's nice to see you guys...it's been awhile."

"Three years, come Thanksgiving."

They go into the house and he is unprepared for how normal everything seems. He wasn't sure what to expect: religious icons on the walls, or a shrine to Jesus, or something weird like a "prayer plant." He has heard of such things. But there are toys on the floor, as well as a litter box. The table is set, but not too formally. His brother's wife has an apron on. He tries to think if he has ever seen a woman (other than a waitress) wear an apron. She hugs him in a friendly way and gives his coat to the older girl, who looks to be about fourteen, and is very pretty in an uncontrived way.

"You remember Rachel, I think?"

"Of course…you had pigtails…and wore overalls the last time I was here…" He can feel himself starting to relax.

Rachel laughs shyly and says hello with the sophistication of a much older girl. Her voice sounds exactly like her mother's. She goes to hang his coat somewhere.

"We're so glad you could come," Rebecca says, looking directly at him, and smiling. She means it.

To his surprise, Clay offers *him* a beer, and they clink bottles in the family room, with Clay holding the littlest one, a girl, in his other arm.

"Bee-Bee, this is Uncle Clive," he says, and she stares gravely at Clive with large brown eyes under a halo of fuzzy curls. Her left eye lists ever so slightly, giving the impression that she can see auras or peer into souls.

"Hello, sweetheart," Clive says, and she immediately tucks her face into her daddy's shirt.

They sit on a large, yielding couch that reminds Clive of a sloppy, heavy-set girlfriend he once had. The couch has denim slipcovers and a hodgepodge of throw pillows in primary colors, and he glances around the room, which could be mistaken for a library. The one wall that is not covered by bookshelves has framed handprints and artwork of his nieces and nephews, also in primary colors. He concludes, correctly, that his brother and nephews have constructed the simple frames. He glances down at the rug, which looks very recently vacuumed, and suddenly there is a small boy at his knee holding a large, live turtle with both hands.

"See my turtle?" the youngster says, only when he says *turtle* it sounds more like *total*. The boy and the turtle blink at him at the same time. Clive is utterly charmed.

He actually forgets the rest of his life for a while. His brother's kids make him chuckle. They seem to have just the right blend of politeness and verve. To his relief, Clay drinks two beers. Rebecca serves pot roast and he tastes red wine in the gravy. There are small chunks of chopped garlic in her salad dressing.

"Is there sour cream in these mashed potatoes? I'm kind of addicted to sour cream," he says, now quite jovial. He is on his third helping.

"My grandmother put sour cream in everything," she says, smiling.

They are eating dessert, which is strawberry frozen yogurt accompanied by assorted chocolates, when he sees the woman of his dreams for the first time. He doesn't realize that she is the woman of his dreams when he first sees her, because he is so caught off guard, but afterward, when he is asleep at the Shiloh Seaside Inn, he has a dream about her. In his dream she doesn't speak at all, but the first time he sees her in real life she says, "Excuse me…I'm sorry to bother you guys, but my car is kind of blocked by one of yours…"

But he is not immediately aware that she is referring to his car, or that Clay and Rebecca glance over to him expectantly, because the woman is utterly beautiful in a vulnerable way. She smiles apologetically, and he notices that she has lovely teeth. She sticks her hair behind her ear in a self-conscious gesture, and he notices she is wearing dangling gold and blue feather earrings. She glances over the family in a bashful way, and he notices her eyes are hazel, and moist, as if she has been crying recently, but she has applied a lot of mascara and eyeliner to hide the fact. He notices she is wearing a shiny, clinging black blouse over a pair of jeans, and he decides it is the sexiest outfit he has ever seen on a woman. The top four buttons are unbuttoned and make a low V of her neckline and he can hardly keep from staring at her décolletage. It reminds him of vanilla custard.

"I can move it," Clay says, rising, and then, "Where are your keys, bro?"

"Pardon?"

"Clive…this is Jennifer. Our landlady." Rebecca's voice penetrates his brain.

"Oh! I'm sorry…I didn't realize—"

There is a scramble for his keys, which are in his coat pocket, which Rachel has put in an upstairs bedroom. In the end both Clay and Clive find themselves on the front lawn, watching Jennifer drive away. The sun is setting, and the temperature has dipped, and neither of them has a coat, yet for some reason they stand there, exhaling garlic-scented clouds in the nippy air.

"Nice lookin' lady," says Clive, jiggling his keys in his pocket.

"Yep," Clay answers. "And owns property too."

"She married? Divorced?"

"Nope. Neither one, as far as I know."

"Jesus. Why the hell not?"

"Guess she hasn't found the right guy." Clay grins at him.

"Shit! I said *Jesus*. Sorry 'bout that."

Clay laughs softly. "Only Jesus knows why she's not married...think that's what you meant to say, huh?"

"Yeah, that's it." Clive laughs a bit too, and his laugh comes out sounding exactly like Clay's. They stand there for another minute and a multitude of unspoken thoughts pass between them.

"You have a beautiful family, bro. You done good here."

Clay shifts back and forth on his feet and crosses his arms. He wishes he had a cigarette now. He feels awkward with empty hands.

"Hey, thanks. That means a lot to me. You saying that, I mean." He looks directly at his brother's face, and unexpectedly perceives traces of a much younger boy, pale with fear after a nightmare, staring back at him in the waning light.

"I miss you, bro. I miss you a whole heckuva lot." Saying it aloud releases the lock on a vault deep within him that he didn't even know existed until this moment. It catches him off guard and he is grateful for a speeding car that suddenly passes.

"Me too, me too. I'd like to come again. Soon, I mean...not three years from now."

He is absolutely in a good mood when he says good night to his brother's family. He promises to come by again tomorrow afternoon. He promises. They all stand on the porch and, with the exception of little Bee-Bee, who solemnly regards him with a sagelike countenance from her daddy's shoulder, wave him off as he drives away.

He is actually whistling when he pulls up to the Shiloh Seaside Inn. He is still whistling while he uses the tiny lavatory of his room, and then he stops whistling when he remembers that he promised that Vina-lady that he would check on Jeb. He promised.

He knows she will ask him. He could always lie. Prevarication is one of his many talents, especially in business. But then what if the man died? What if the man died at, say, seven-thirty in the evening, and he didn't know, and told her that he'd been there at eight?

So he drives over to Jeb's, and for the rest of the night and many days to follow, he wishes he hadn't.

He wishes he hadn't, because when he approaches the dying man's bedside, he is shocked to see a woman lying next to him, her arms encircling his feeble form, and her long hair splayed across the pillow. Even in his state of shock he is struck by her angelic beauty, and it takes him a moment to regain his equilibrium. He clears his throat.

They both open their eyes and contemplate him. Her eyes widen at the sight of him. No one speaks but the air feels heavily disturbed.

"I...um...was asked by a friend...to look in on you...see how you're doing." He finds himself whispering.

"Sylvain." Jeb's voice is frail, as if his vocal cords are made of tissue paper.

Clive clears his throat again, and sits tenuously on the bed to hear him better.

"Yes, Jeb."

"My fiancé...Jennifer..."

"Oh?" He looks at her and she blushes heavily.

"And the mother of my child."

"Ah! Well. Jesus. That's surprising news. Very." He stands up and takes a turn around the room, trying to think quickly. He is surprised to find Jennifer standing behind him.

"Do you know any judges in the area? He wants to get married... as soon as possible. You know...so the child has a legal father. It's his last wish."

And he actually promises to see what he can do. Another promise to another woman he doesn't know. He promises her because he is pretty sure he is in love with her, despite the fact that she is inexplicably linked to a weird guy dying from a wasting disease. It makes no sense.

That night he dreams that they are embracing one another in the ocean. The waves are jostling them, and he kisses her. He can taste salt on her lips. The dream makes him wake up, sweaty. It feels so real that he has to get out of his bed to clear his head. He pulls the curtain open and looks out and sees the Great Auditorium with the cross on top, like a sentinel standing watch over the whole town. The cross is not lit up, but he can see it in the encroaching light of the sun rising across the ocean, and he finds the sight vaguely reassuring, although he has no idea why, having never been religious.

On his way to get the paper he goes by Jeb's place and sees her car still parked there. When he comes out with the paper he notices the yellow tulips, still wrapped, on the backseat of his car. He stares at them for one whole minute, and then he has an epiphany.

On his way back to the inn he leaves the bouquet on her windshield, with a small note tucked inside: *For the bride.*

XXVIII

L ike a flock of goats descending from Gilead, Reumah thinks, hearing the phrase in her father's voice.

As soon as the news reaches Jerusalem, a steady stream of visitors begins arriving to comfort the family, for Lazarus had been held in high regard by many of the merchants, and his name is known to all the leading men of the city. But it is The Fragrant Ones that Reumah recognizes most readily, and she cannot help but smile as she watches them approach the village, carefully picking their way along the hilly descent, carrying large bundles, their veils and cloaks billowing like wings behind them. She can see that the senior Mary is in the lead, and it is she who enters the courtyard first. The older woman greets Martha with a kiss, and some private words of comfort, and then steps away while the others gather around her, like a flock of doves. As the scent of their perfume fills the air, the mourners and guests become quiet, almost as if the aroma is an invisible presence that permeates each soul, causing their grief to become more acute, but bringing also the promise of eternal life within reach. The ethereal scent, mingled with the sound of the women's murmuring voices, provides a soothing contrast to the wailing of the hired mourners, and Reumah is immediately comforted by their presence. Mary Magdalene's eyes scan the courtyard, and alight on Reumah. She stretches forth her hands, and Reumah goes toward her, bows low, and kisses them.

"My dear girl—I can see two things immediately: One, that you are weary beyond words, and two—that you have proven to be a faithful friend and comforter to our sisters here."

"Were that but true, my mother!" The word *mother* escapes her lips before she has time to wonder if it is appropriate. She flushes, but the older woman seems to read her mind.

"Go on, my daughter."

"That I am weary, I can't deny…but no more so than my sisters… that I have been a comfort, I am less sure. I have failed to bring light or hope to my sweet friend's heart."

"How does it go with her?"

"She does not eat or drink. She is beyond tears. She remains despondent, and I cannot find the words to soothe her pain, it seems."

The older woman turns to find a couch, and then seats herself. Reumah remains standing until Mary of Magdala pats the seat on her right side. Reumah sits next to her, suddenly self-conscious at finding herself in a position of honor. She waits for the lady to speak.

"When you first came to us, I was not sure of your role among us. I sought the guidance of Yaweh himself, and it seemed best to me that you simply remain at her side. Now I know why. He has appointed you to help her bear this heavy trial."

"I have not left her side until now, when I heard you all arriving. But truly, I have not comforted her in any obvious way."

"When the occasion is joyous, one has no lack of friends to join in the celebration. But you have been her companion in sorrow, and mostly silent, which is appropriate, since her sorrow goes beyond words. Would that the comforters of Job had done the same!"

Reumah sighs. She is weary, it's true, of her long vigil at Mary's side, but she is also conscious of an overwhelming anxiety that is darkly tinged with guilt. The entire household has discovered the irony of their master's missing vial. His burial cloths were laden with pounds of spices and crushed herbs, but the third day—the day of anointing— is quickly passing, and the one who spent the best years of his life preparing rare and exotic perfumes for others, now lays in his grave, without the anointing of spikenard or any other costly aromatics. No one is pretending that this was done according to plan, and a hundred unanswered questions hang in the air, and are whispered among the servants, which only add pain to the grieving sisters, and especially to

Mary. It is agony to sit with her, but Reumah does so, not knowing what else she can do.

"Take me to her." The voice of Mary Magdalene breaks through her dark reflections.

When the two women enter her chamber, she looks up without surprise, and without words. She kisses the older woman's hand, and leads her to a cushioned seat before returning to her bed. The three sit in silence for some time, conscious of the lengthening shadows of dusk. Presently Reumah stands.

"I shall fetch a lamp," she says. When she returns, and sets the lamp on a small table, the eyes of each woman turn on it, and suddenly Mary speaks.

"'Call me *Mara*,'" she said, quoting from the ancient book of Ruth, "'because the Almighty has dealt bitterly with me.' So I was aptly named at my birth, and to such I shall return."

At once the older woman comes to her. "Nay, my daughter. 'He knows my way, and when he has tested me, I shall come forth as gold...'"

"Ah. You quote our ancient patriarch to me. Here, I think, is one more fitting: 'How I long for the months gone by, for the days when God watched over me...when by his light I walked through the darkness!'"

"My child...you must not despair. Your faith is being tested, and you will prevail. As a babe in the womb cannot see the light of day, so you are in darkness now, but this is not the end. The light will come, indeed, he is on his way."

Mary stares at her, slowly swallowing her words.

"How do you know this? That the 'light will come,' as you say? Have you heard that the Master is coming?"

"I have not heard with my ears, but my spirit knows it. He will come, my daughter."

Mary turns away and shrugs.

"No matter. It's too late."

"I cannot pretend to know why he delayed his coming. I only know his ways are perfect. He makes no mistakes. When he comes, you shall know it too."

Mary shrugs again. After a few more minutes of painful silence, she thanks the older woman for her words of consolation, and then asks to be left alone. Reumah stays, but she bids her go as well.

"Leave me, Reumah. Do not fret over me. I shall sleep, and be better tomorrow. Please. Let me be."

But when she is alone, she does not sleep. She gazes listlessly at the flickering lamp, her thoughts spiraling downward, as dark as the shadows on the wall. Time passes, and her mind is resolved: she will not see him, even if he arrives tomorrow. She cries bitterly for a minute or two, and then blows out the flame. Darkness overtakes her.

Close to midnight a blanket of stillness falls on the entire household. The mourners have gone home, and most of the visitors have likewise gone in search of lodging, or have made pallets in the courtyards and alcoves or on the couches of the sprawling home of Lazarus.

Reumah has arranged a bed for herself near the latched door of her friend. She keeps a little basket of dates and bread near her, in case Mary should decide to break her fast, but a knot of worry grows like a tumor inside her. Her concern for her friend's bodily strength is only eclipsed by her dread of the bitterness that has engulfed Mary's soul. Waves of fear flow over her, and she is struck by her sense of powerless and a surprising amount of anger. The anger, she thinks, is her defense against the resentment she suspects is building in Mary's heart toward her, because it was her vial that was redeemed, and because Reumah has made no counteroffering of it to ensure that Lazarus is properly buried.

But I cannot...I cannot! It's not my fault that they used his to redeem mine! I didn't ask them to do it! And surely she cannot expect me to part with the only vestige of my own father's love!

Sleep eludes her.

Thus is our friendship already being tested...and a nobler friend I have never had. What shall I do if she casts me off, in the end? Or tolerates my presence out of pity, but without any true attachment? And what of the other women? Will they accept me when they know the truth? That I would not give up my vial, not even for Lazarus, who so generously gave up his for me? Will they not despise me for my weakness and call me greedy?

She sits with her back against the wall, listening to the noises of the house, her eyes seeing only the dim square of light from a far-off window. She tries to pray, but no words form on her lips. The Almighty seems to have hid himself behind a thick cloud. She sighs deeply, and then is abruptly jolted by the loud wail of a child.

She strains her eyes in the darkness. The child's cries are closer, and Reumah suddenly realizes that it is Jabez, the youngest child of Lazarus, who sometimes walks in his sleep. The boy is eight or nine years of age, and his health is delicate due to the travails of his birth.

"Jabez! Come to me!" she reaches out to the boy in the darkness and takes hold of him.

The child's eyes are wide and uncomprehending, but he recognizes the familiarity of Reumah's voice. He collapses into her arms, sobbing noisily, and soon her tunic is damp.

"Hush, sweet boy. Hush…you will wake the others…"

Jabez is awake now, and his weeping is coming from a more conscious source. He buries his face in her cloak, and she permits him to vent his grief. After a few minutes he turns toward her, and even in the dim light she can see his eyes are swollen in despair.

"Abba…I want my abba…" the words are almost incomprehensible amid his choking sobs, but spoken, as they are, so starkly in the darkness, they perfectly embody the longing of her own heart, and surely the longing of every soul in the world, throughout the ages, who hungers for the love of a father. She holds the child tightly.

"Yes…as do I."

Her own grief overtakes the boy's.

She must have slept.

She must have slept because Jochabed, one of the children's nurses, has to wake her, and she cannot immediately comprehend the girl's words.

"Reumah…there is a man here to see Mary. I don't know what to do. He says it is urgent."

"What man?" she says, trying not to disturb the sleeping boy at her side.

"I don't know. He claims to be from among the Master's disciples, and I think it's true. But he wouldn't give his name."

Reumah takes a deep breath, trying to decide if she should wake Mary. There is no sound from behind her door.

"Where is the man? Can you watch the boy...or bring him to his mother?"

"I will keep watch over the boy. The man is in the far corner of the courtyard. You will need a lamp to find him...and take care you don't trip over the others sleeping there."

She goes first to the kitchen to get a lamp, carefully feeling her way along the walls, trying to stay quiet and not trip over any sleeping forms. She wonders who would come at such an hour, and why his business could not at least wait until the light of day. She wonders if she should go back and wake Mary, or if she can take care of the matter herself. She decides she must try. It will be a small thing she can do...to be of service to her friend, and give her one less thing to worry about. Probably the man is a relative or friend who could not find lodging, or perhaps someone has taken ill. But why bother to wake Mary? Why not just have the servants take care of it?

By the time she has made her way to the courtyard, now carrying a lamp, she has decided that it is probably the servant of an anxious father from the village whose wife is in labor and cannot bring forth the baby. A sense of apprehension envelopes her, and she wonders how quickly she will be able to rouse Naomi, Caliah's doula, at this hour. The light from her lamp trembles slightly as it illuminates the ground ahead of her bare feet.

But it is not a servant sent to summon help, nor a harried relative in need of lodging. In the darkest corner of the courtyard stands a cloaked figure whose form is very familiar. It is Judas.

29

Jennifer squints against the brilliance of the morning after the dank darkness of Jeb's house. The unmistakable scent of spring air—earthy and moist, with a hint of grass—assails her the moment she steps outside. She grips the porch railing and breathes deeply. Giddiness and morning sickness combine to make her feel almost faint, but this is quickly followed by a heady realization that she is in her own version of a fairy tale, and she half expects a butterfly to land on her shoulder, or a rainbow to grace the horizon. She is hardly surprised, then, to find a bouquet of yellow tulips on her windshield, and by the time she has plunged her nose into their dewy heads, she is actually laughing.

An older gentleman who lives down the block and walks his dachshund past Jeb's house three times a day scrutinizes her intently and frowns. Jennifer sees him and waves. He shakes his head at her. He is truly shocked at how brazen she has become, spending the night at the vulgar artist's house, without a thought of propriety. He has heard rumors that the artist is a sodomite and that he has made tons of money painting filthy pictures on the walls of discotheques and other decadent places all over Europe. Furthermore, he has heard that the artist is dying of some kind of pneumonia that only sodomites get, and he knows that this is God's way of punishing him and showing all the other sodomites how revolted he is by their sin. The older gentleman is outraged that the town council has allowed the vulgar artist, with his deadly disease, to continue living here despite his repeated attempts to have him evicted, and so every time he walks by the vulgar artist's house, he prays fervently that the artist will die soon and burn in hell forever, as he deserves.

"Hi, Mr. Shackleford," Jennifer says, stepping into her car. Her coat is open and he can see that there are too many buttons undone on her blouse.

"Your mother would have been ashamed of you, young lady," he replies.

At the mention of her mother, he notes with satisfaction that her smile disappears. Clearly there is some hope for the girl...she seems to have a shred of conscience, no doubt because of her late mother's good influence.

"You should be in church!" he says, thrusting his index finger in her direction. His remaining fingers clutch a small plastic bag full of Dinky's poop.

Jennifer slams her car door pointedly, and rolls down her window.

"Be careful, Mr. Shackleford. You might drop your breakfast." She quickly pulls away from the curb. She can see him in the rearview mirror, still shaking the poop bag at her, and rebuking her soundly, but she can't hear him because she is laughing so loudly now she is sure the neighbors will wake up if they haven't already.

She can't remember the last time she felt so pleased with herself.

She sits for twenty minutes in her car, outside her house, trying to decide what to do first. Jeb had told her to find a judge or someone legal that could perform a bedside ceremony. And a ring! He told her to find herself a ring, and when she asked him who would pay for it, he told her that his accountant would reimburse her. Neither of them mentioned Vina. He told her to hurry up, and of course she knew that. But she needs time to think.

First she thinks, happily, of Jeb altering his will. Apparently that's why Clive Peterson was there. She can only hope that he has enough strength, with Jean-Denis assisting, for him to sign whatever he is supposed to sign. She hopes that he is considered "of sound mind," and that the whole thing will work out, and give reason and meaning to his death, because he will die as her husband and the father of her child, and no one will ever be the wiser. She has begun to think of his death as sacrificial—as if he is actually giving up his life for her and the child, saving them both, in essence, from insignificant lives of mediocrity, and by the time the baby is born, she knows it will be true. She will make it true.

Next she tries to think who might have left the yellow tulips on her windshield, with a little note that says, "For the bride." She decides that it must be Clive Peterson, Jeb's attorney, because who else could have known so quickly? She decides that Clive must have some class, and that this is all part of her fairy tale, and that God is somehow involved, and the tulips are a sign that she should expect Clive to play the role of fairy godfather. She had prayed to Jesus, sincerely prayed, and somehow that had been the right thing to do, and now Jesus—or God, his Father, she isn't sure who—is happy with her, and making good things happen. Her dream is coming true. If only she had tried this five years ago. If only she had prayed more conscientiously, God or Jesus might have saved her mother.

The thought of her mother produces a spasm of regret, and she hastily gets out of her car.

I know it's not how you would have wanted it, Mommy. But I'm doing the best I can with what I have. Just try to be happy for me, OK?

Upstairs in her apartment she places the tulips in a vase and calls Clive, using his business card, but of course she gets the answering machine at his office since it's Sunday. While she is in the shower, she remembers that he is staying at the Shiloh, so after she is dressed she calls over there and leaves a message for him to call her. She puts the kettle on for tea and goes into the bathroom to put on some makeup. While she is applying mascara, two things happen at the same time: Clive calls back, and she decides that she must get a special dress for her wedding. She can't believe that she didn't think of it already. She is so excited about the dress that when she answers the phone she is almost breathless.

"Hello?"

"Jennifer? Clive Peterson here. You called?"

"Hi! Um, yes...thanks. We were wondering—Jeb and I—if you knew of anyone in the area that could perform—um—some kind of bedside ceremony."

He wishes she were in the room. He wants to see her say "perform some kind of bedside ceremony" in person. He can picture her blushing. On second thought, it's probably better for him that she's on the phone.

"What did you have in mind?" He sees himself in the mirror behind the front desk, smiling into the phone.

"Oh, I don't know. It doesn't matter, as long as it's legit."

He clears his throat. "Well, I can get the paperwork together; it's not very complicated. You just need someone official to sign it. Like a judge."

"Oh. Well…I know a couple of priests…but I don't think they'd do it. Jeb isn't Catholic, for one."

"Well, you need a license. And I don't know if we can get a justice of the peace out here on such short notice. Plus, it's Sunday."

Her fairy tale is starting to unravel. It's as if there's an unnamed villain in the story now, opposing her, keeping her from her prince, as villains always do, and intent on her destruction. The dress and the bouquet are ebbing away and further down the line, the dream of birthing his baby, with newspaper reporters standing by in the hospital lobby, fades into a mist.

She seats herself on a kitchen chair. She has to figure out a way to make it happen. Or maybe not.

Jesus…can you hear me? Can you help me?

"Hey, wait a sec. My brother's a minister."

"What?"

"My brother, Clay. I think he is licensed to marry by his denomination."

"What's his denomination?"

"I have no idea. But I think he could do it. Just ask him. And then tomorrow you can just get a license from city hall to make it legit."

By the time they hang up, Jennifer is so wound up she can hardly think what she will say to ask Clay. And Clive can't believe how bizarre the whole thing is. Back in his room, he flops back on the bed and stares up at the ceiling and can't believe how happy he is, because he made her happy. It's as if he has suddenly discovered the reason for his existence. He hopes Jeb Kellon dies soon.

It takes her ten minutes to explain the whole thing to Clay in a long note, which she leaves in an envelope taped to their mailbox, because of course they all went to their church in Asbury Park. She has never figured out why they go to a church in Asbury Park when there are a number of well-established churches right here in town, but that is hardly her concern at the moment. She has no idea what kind of church it is, or what kind of minister Clay is. She just hopes he can do it. *I hope you can do it*, she writes in the note, which begins with *Your brother tells me that you have a license to marry in the state of New Jersey…* and ends with *You will be making his dying wish come true*.

She sits in her car again, gathering her thoughts, trying to decide where she can get a dress and a ring in a hurry, and the most obvious choice is Red Bank, but as soon as she thinks of Red Bank, she thinks of Vina, and suddenly she realizes who the wicked witch in her fairy tale is. She can't drive fast enough.

Her note sits on Clay's desk, unopened. He is sure he knows what it's about, and he can't deal with it. Not today.

Today is Sunday, and as usual, he wants to collapse after church. He wants to collapse because he feels exhausted by the weight of the people of his church, whom he truly loves. He loves the way they sing and pray, with upraised hands, and cry out to God with tears running down their faces; he loves the way they serve each other and embrace each other and give their money so generously when most of them have hardly anything to spare; he loves how they teach Sunday school and make platters of food for the homeless and comfort crying babies in the nursery and visit old people and sick people and family members who have ended up in jail. He thinks of his church as a giant hand, Christ's hand, in fact, and the people of the church as Christ's fingers. He has taught them all that, about being the hand of Christ; he has taught them in various ways, using various verses and metaphors and stories from the Bible, and the more he has taught them, the more they have become it. And so he loves them all, but he is exhausted, nonetheless, by the weight of them. Every Sunday he comes home carrying their lives in his head—their petty arguments and complaints and infidelities and financial woes and rebellious children and loneliness and depression and addictions and their illnesses, God, so many illnesses: chronic back and joint problems and diabetes and hypertension and cancer and Lyme disease and glaucoma and gout. Half of them are way too fat, and he becomes so angry, watching them eat doughnuts during the fellowship hour, watching their fat *children* eat doughnuts, that he has to put down his coffee and walk out the door to breathe, where a cluster of them are outside, smoking. Sometimes he fantasizes about smoking with them, to make a point. But he's not sure what his point would be, and they'd probably miss it anyway, because they'd be aghast that he was smoking. Without turning around he can feel his wife observing him with anxious eyes.

"Can't we get rid of the doughnuts?" he asks Rebecca on the way home. Rebecca sighs.

"Honey…"

"No, seriously. It's revolting. That little Levon…what is he, four years old? He had *three*. And his mother sitting right there…with the chair ready to collapse under her humongous butt…not doing a thing."

"She was praying over the Costanzia baby."

"Not the whole time. She was eating doughnuts too! Why are we spending money on *doughnuts*? Why don't we pass out syringes too, while we're at it? Or condoms?"

In the rearview he sees his two eldest children glance at each other, smirking.

"I love doughnuts," says John-Mark, from his car seat, only he says L with a Y sound, so it sounds like *yove*. He pops his thumb out of his mouth to speak, and then replaces it. No one else says a word the rest of the way home.

An hour or so later, his brother is on the phone. Clay takes the call in his office. Jennifer's letter remains unopened on his desk.

"Hey, bro. Sorry I'm not going to make it back to the house…I'm tied up with my client and your landlady's business…"

"What?"

"Your landlady. Jennifer. Didn't she talk to you?"

"Uh—no. I mean, she left a letter. I haven't had a chance to read it yet."

"Read it, for god's sakes. She wants to get married—quickly—and she wants you to do it."

"What?"

"Good god, just read the letter."

Clay is already opening it. His eyes scan her large, tidy cursive script. She must have gone to Catholic school. The *I*'s are dotted with tiny circles. The facts of her letter, and her request, leave him stupefied. After a moment he begins to laugh, and turns in his chair to face Rebecca.

"She's not kicking us out."

"OK. And you're laughing...because you're so relieved?"

"I don't know why I'm laughing." He stops laughing. "She wants to get married. She wants me to do it. Las Vegas-style."

She watches him for a moment, in her usual way, leaning against the doorway, with her hands behind her and her head cocked to one side.

"You're not seriously going to do it?"

"Why not? The groom's almost dead."

"All the more reason! She's not thinking straight, obviously."

"I don't see what difference it makes, at this point. Apparently she's carrying his child."

"Honey...you told me in seminary you would never marry a couple unless they had had comprehensive premarital counseling and understood the seriousness of the step they were about to take."

He feels himself getting angry at her. He hates himself for it.

"We're not in seminary. This is the real world, Becca."

"Marriage is still a covenant!"

He shoves Jennifer's letter in a drawer and stands. He feels besieged by a fit of unaccountable anger that he is powerless to stop, like a wrecking ball about to smash his house with his family inside. He looks at her, still standing at the door, with questions in her eyes.

"Yes. I went to seminary. I'm an ordained minister. I think I know what marriage is."

She reaches out for him, but he brushes past her, into the hall, into the living room, where he grabs his coat, and heads out the front door.

She feels a sudden draft. It's as if his words, still hanging over her, had been coated with ice.

Clive arrives at Ground Zero eight minutes after twelve because he couldn't find a parking space anywhere close by. It's as if the entire population of the town woke up, went to church, and decided to stay out afterward, not wanting to be inside on such a lovely day. Prior to that he had mistakenly put on the same tie that he had on yesterday when he saw Vina, so he had to take it off and start again with the other.

"Sorry I'm late..." he says, sliding his briefcase under the table. "The parking—"

"—is horrendous. I know." She motions to the waiter, and he can't help but feel a little intimidated at the way that she finishes his sentence and commandeers the waitstaff. He decides he must be cautious.

"Hello, Frank. The usual." She says this to the waiter, and then she and Frank look expectedly at Clive, who of course has not even seen a menu yet.

"Um—is this lunch?"

"Whatever you like. My treat."

"What do you recommend?"

"The chocolate soup."

"'Chocolate soup'? That sounds decadent."

"Oh, it's quite sinful." She winks and smiles at him and then turns to Frank. "Put extra whipped cream on his."

Clive decides she is going to be nice after all, and begins to lower his guard. He would like to exchange more pleasantries—perhaps even flirt a bit—but by the time Frank has returned with his "soup"—which turns out to be thick hot cocoa, almost like a mousse, but warm, served in a bowl with a hefty dollop of whipped cream and packages of minimarshmallows and graham wafers on the side—she is asking him about Jeb.

"Well, he's got me scrambling now, obviously." He dunks a graham wafer into the silky chocolate-and-cream mixture and slides it into his mouth. For a moment he can't speak while his tongue has an orgasm.

"My god, this is wonderful," he says, his mouth full of chocolate-sodden wafer.

"What do you mean, 'scrambling'?"

"You know. Altering his will. To provide for the wife and the kid."

He notices that she has not taken a sip of her cappuccino, but just keeps stirring it. The biscotti remains in its cellophane wrapper. He decides she must be one of those women who pretends to enjoy sophisticated food. He has dated such women—svelte, well-groomed ladies who order tiramisu or pate foie gras or endive salad and leave it untouched, on the plate. He usually despises them before dinner is over. He sincerely hopes Jennifer is not like that, because he definitely intends to date her.

"Interesting. I've never met his wife."

He is struck by how crisply the words come out of her mouth. It's as if she is having trouble forming them.

"You know what I mean. His fiancé. Jennifer. They're getting married this afternoon. You must have met her?"

He stops slurping for a moment because she suddenly seems unwell. One hand is on her chest and the other one reaches for her cigarettes. She is taking deep breaths.

"You OK?"

"I'm—no. It's too warm in here. I'm sorry, but I'm going to have to leave. I'm coming down with something. Here—" she says, taking a twenty-dollar bill out of her bag and placing it on the table. "Call me… when you find out for sure about the wedding. He should have invited me, don't you think? Apart from our business arrangement, I'm his best friend!"

She leaves Clive staring after her curiously, but she doesn't care. She slams into her car and takes off down the main street toward Jeb's house on Heck Avenue. Her hands are gripping the wheel and she is unaware of how fast she is driving or how loudly she is speaking.

"Die, you son of a bitch. If you don't die soon—I'll kill you."

XXX

She approaches him with the stealth of a lioness. If she were alone, she might have fled on seeing him, but surrounded, as she is, by her newly adopted household, she is bolstered by a surge of valor and a desire to protect her friend. She raises her lamp and fixes her eyes on his.

He stares at her for a moment before the corners of his mouth turn downward in displeasure.

"I sent for Mary of Bethany."

She is not dismayed or surprised by his resentful tone, but by his appearance. His face seems to have aged by years instead of months. His flashing eyes, which she found so mesmerizing in times past, now smolder with anger, and his lustrous hair, which captivated her long ago, now hangs limply about his hollowed cheeks.

"There was a time when a glimpse of my face would have elicited a warmer response from you." In so saying, she is surprised to realize that she feels little resentment toward him, but a small amount of pity.

"Since you speak of time, allow me to tell you plainly that you are wasting mine. I am here to speak to your mistress, and every moment that you delay will bring further loss and sadness to her."

She is certain that he must bring a message from the Master himself for Mary, no doubt extending to her his condolences and assuring her of his imminent arrival. But why the Master would choose Judas from among his other companions to be his messenger is beyond her ken.

Aloud she says, "Allow me to tell *you* that she has become my dearest friend and closest companion, no thanks to you. At present she is unwell, and cannot be seen. You must know that the entire household is in mourning and does not wish to be disturbed, especially at this hour."

He suddenly grasps her wrist, which holds the lamp, and draws it closer to both their faces. His face is so close now she can smell his breath, which is foul.

"I know very well the family is in mourning. I would not presume to disturb any of them unless my business was urgent, which it is, and it is with Mary, and Mary alone." His words are like the hissing of a serpent. "Now go, and let me assure you, that if your 'dearest friend' discovers that you were the impediment to the pleasure that I have in my power to grant her, she will undoubtedly despise you. As I do." He drops her hand abruptly and oil from the lamp splashes onto her foot.

She closes her eyes and makes herself breathe. Whatever spirit had emboldened her a moment ago has suddenly left her, like the oil spilled from the lamp. Her heart pounds so loudly she is sure he can hear it. She reaches out for the stone wall to support herself.

"You—you despise me?"

"Yes. As a man despises anything that costs him nothing to procure."

Regardless of his cruelty, she cannot resist the truth of his words. It's as if they are the words of a much wiser, nobler man, and Judas is simply repeating them because they now suit his purpose. In a flash of insight, she realizes they were probably spoken first by his Master, and the words themselves bring the voice of the Master into her head. A sense of his presence envelops her, as if he is watching her from across the courtyard to see what she will do. She gazes down on the lamp in her hand. Despite being shaken, its flame is rekindled.

"I forgive you," she says simply. "In the name of Yeshua, our Master, I forgive you."

His eyes widen and she detects something else in his expression. Shock, perhaps, or even fear, if that were possible, although he seems to fear nothing. The look—such as it is—passes quickly, and his grim, dark expression returns.

"You're wasting precious time, woman."

"I am going."

"Make haste!"

She returns to her pallet. Jabez is nowhere to be seen; presumably Jochabed has returned him to his mother's rooms. She steps toward Mary's door and knocks gently. There is no answer, but to her surprise, she finds the door unlatched.

At the edge of Mary's bed she lifts her lamp. Her friend's face is more peaceful in sleep than it has been for many days. She reaches down to shake Mary's shoulder in an attempt to waken her gently, and her hand stops in midair, almost as if another restrains it.

Merciful God, You have granted sleep to the one you love, and I dare not wake her from it. But what must I do to spare her from seeing the one that neither of us trusts?

She stands in the middle of the room, poised uncertainly, still holding the flickering lamp. She imagines Judas out in the courtyard, shifting impatiently, growing angrier by the minute, and uncontrollable shivers take hold of her. She looks around for her cloak and realizes it is still on her pallet outside the door. She goes to retrieve it, and to her dismay it is gone—no doubt with Jabez wrapped in it and sleeping somewhere near his mother. She returns to Mary's bedside and in an instant she realizes what she must do. After searching frantically about the room, she finds a discarded robe of Mary's, meant for laundering. She sets the lamp down to remove her own robe and tunic, and she puts Mary's robe on instead. After another hurried search she finds one of her friend's headscarves, and this she carefully arranges about her head, just as she has watched her friend do numerous times. Lastly and most painstakingly she removes the cloak that is gathered about Mary's sleeping form, and replaces it with her own clothing, which she tucks about her carefully.

The aroma of Mary's clothes—infused with her perfume—overwhelms Reumah with a sense of her dignity and nobility, as if the vestments possessed a magical capacity to imbue her with the spirit of her friend. She would like to linger for a moment, and look in the mirror. She would like to see herself in Mary's richly embroidered robe, belted with the scarlet sash, and draped with the dark, heavy, well-spun cloak. The cloak reaches almost to the floor, but not quite, since she is taller than her friend. But the thought of Judas, and his ominous threats, spurs her on.

As she turns to leave the room, the light from her lamp suddenly causes something to glimmer on a small table, near Mary's bed. She steps closer to it and sees her bracelets and earrings, no doubt removed because she is in mourning. Then her eyes alight on a large gold ring, inlaid with rubies, which she has always admired and secretly coveted. Without another thought, she slides it onto her right index finger, just as Mary wears it.

Yaweh Saboath—blind him to what I must hide. Cause him see only what I wish to reveal.

In the courtyard, the servants' fires in the braziers have been reduced to smoldering embers, too weak to give off much light or warmth. In a far corner, Judas has seated himself against the wall, his cloak and arms wrapped around himself, now and then his head touching down on his chest in slumber, but then jerking up again, as if his anger will not allow him to rest.

Return what you have unlawfully taken, lest your son be taken from you.

The words of the Master surge through his brain, unrelenting as waves on the sand. He had become accustomed to tuning out the Master's instructions, because he felt that most of it did not apply to himself, but rather to the thick-headed followers from Galilee, who needed much repetition and review.

But these words were spoken to Judas alone, only days after his infant son had fallen prey to a fever. His wife, whose name was Beulah, had been driven to hysterics by the piteous cries of her firstborn, who had become too weak to nurse. The entire household seemed choked with a paralyzing fear of divine judgment, as if they were all somehow responsible for the baby boy's sickness. She had prostrated herself at her husband's feet, pleading with him not to leave her, but he could not bear the dark cloud of despair that blanketed his house. He had returned to the Master, against his better judgment, to request aid at this time of crisis. Rather than offer words of healing and hope, the Master had spoken what was little else than a threat of divine retribution.

At first he had wondered who had informed the Master about the vial. He guessed that it had been Lazarus himself, probably seeking to have his returned, but this did not make sense, since the Master had left for Perea before Lazarus had given Judas his vial. He came to realize that it must have been Reumah or Mary, and perhaps they had told some of the other "Fragrant Ones" as well. His lip curls in scorn at the thought of them.

Judas hates most women, but especially the women who have devoted their lives to the Master. The widows and cast-off wives who live with Mary Magdalene amid the stench of the fishmongers are a small group of a multitude largely comprised of the undereducated and the disenfranchised: bastards and orphans, foreigners, impoverished stragglers, simpletons, sluggards, shepherds, drunkards, prostitutes, tax collectors, sodomites, and Samaritans. All these the Master has befriended and fed and touched and healed of their distress. Forgiveness he extends to them; food and raiment are given when needed; bags of coins are passed into their hands; even tools and seeds and animals for those able and willing to work. Occasionally he and his men are invited to the banquets of the leading men of the city, and these Judas eagerly attends, but more often than not, the Master is content to dine with the sordid company of the streets, and Judas makes his excuses, and returns to his own home rather than dine with such riffraff. He is deeply aware that the Master's reputation is being stained by the company he chooses to keep. He is equally incapable of making the Master care, though he has done his best to reason with him.

He is not stupid, however. He understands why: they follow him because they are poor, and ignorant; loveless and loathly undesirables with little else to live for. But he cannot fathom why the ones who are intelligent and wealthy, like Lazarus of Bethany or Joanna, the wife of Cuza, would offer up their money and their services to an undistinguished itinerant preacher from Nazareth, of all places. Regardless of his persuasive powers and personal charisma, he has neither property nor prestige, and they have nothing to gain, Judas reasons, by being his disciples. Furthermore, the foundation of his Master's government, Judas has apprehended, will be based on the merits of the twelve disciples that he has already chosen, of whom Judas is clearly the most educated and accomplished. He is certain that most of the Master's friends, at least those that have any sense, must surely recognize this, and so he is especially piqued that one of them, more than likely Mary of Bethany, has informed the Master of the stolen vial, and incriminated him unnecessarily. Doubtless Reumah had told her. He had not counted on the two of them becoming friends, and now bears a special hatred for both women. They have purposely schemed against him out of Reumah's desire for revenge. And now, because of the Master's threat, he finds himself in the humiliating position of having to return the brother's vial, like a repentant thief. But he is hardly so.

The entire household is barefoot out of respect for the dead, so he does not hear the footsteps of an approaching servant girl. His eyes are closed and his head leans against the wall behind him and snaps forward at the sound of her voice.

"Excuse me, sir…"

"Stupid girl! What do you mean, waking me out of a dead sleep?"

"A thousand pardons, sir. I came only to tell you that the one you seek is seated yonder."

"Why did she not come to me?"

"She is weakened from her lamentation, sir, and must remain seated."

On a narrow bench sits a woman, cloaked and hooded, with her head lowered. He takes her hand into his, bows low, and kisses it in greeting. She does not look up at his approach or his greeting, but only shifts slightly in her seat.

"You will forgive me, sir…"

"Speak up, dear woman. I cannot hear you."

"I'm sorry…my voice is weak from lamentation. I cannot speak above a whisper."

"Very well, then. I shall have to sit closer to you than is customarily proper, in order to say all that is in my heart."

She moves slightly to make room for him. The scent of her perfume fills the air around him and he notices she is trembling slightly. He smiles at this, but she does not see it.

"Now, then…let me begin by offering you my condolences on behalf of the Master and his chosen ones."

"Thank you, sir. That is kind. Is the master far off? We had hoped to see him…but of course I knew he would send word before long…and here you are."

"To be sure, we were at a loss to know why he did not come sooner, especially when he was informed of your brother's demise."

"I suppose he was delayed by some unexpected weather or hardship."

"I assure you he was not."

There is a pause, followed by an uncomfortable silence. "I don't understand," she whispers.

"The Master insisted that your brother would not die. He purposely chose to tarry where he was. It is entirely baffling to me. I would have thought that he, of all people, who heals every hapless invalid that crosses his path, would have come immediately, as soon as he was made aware of his cherished friend's illness."

Again there is a pause before she speaks, as if she is weighing her words carefully.

"You seem to imply that he was negligent in this matter. Callous, in a word, toward us."

He moves closer to her.

"If I may speak plainly…that is precisely what I meant to imply. For I have long suspected that he is not the man of compassion and truth that so many assume him to be. Indeed, I have found, from my personal association with him and by virtue of our close connection, that he has many faults, and negligence of his friends and their deepest concerns is but the least of them."

She is visibly trembling now.

"Surely you are mistaken, sir. Surely you do not know him as well as you think. Perhaps you have become bitter toward him because of some perceived offense—"

"I am not mistaken, I assure you. I have spent the better part of three years in his company, and I have seen a side to him that few people have."

"And this—this is what you came to tell me? Reumah spoke of something good you wished to impart to me. This is hardly good."

"I beg your pardon. Far be it from me to add to your grief. Let me assure you my intentions are honorable. Indeed, I came to warn you, it's true, against trusting too implicitly in the Master's friendship and kind regard. The truth is, I don't know if he is coming at all. He seems determined to pursue his own agenda, regardless of the anguish of his friends. As your friend, I cannot help but put you on your guard."

"I will not believe it. This is merely your opinion and one that I do not share."

"Very well. But please—allow me to give you a token of my good will and noble intent." He withdraws for a moment, as if removing part of his vestment, and then turns toward her, laying a small bundle on the bench beside her.

She gazes at the object for a moment, as if it contains a poisonous snake.

"Open it," he commands.

She knows before she unwraps it fully that it is Lazarus's vial.

"You were wrong to take it from us! And yet—I am relieved beyond words that you have returned it!"

"You are mistaken in me, dear woman. I merely kept it as collateral, until I knew that Reumah's had been safely returned to her. And then, when I heard of your brother's death, I came as quickly as I could, knowing that it would be needed. I am only sorry that I didn't get here sooner."

"What? That is not true. You stole Reumah's!"

"How sadly you have misjudged me! I kept Reumah's only until I could properly return it. It would have been stolen by others had I not rescued it for safekeeping."

Her head remains bowed, and her face is veiled up to her eyes, which are downcast, but he can tell by her trembling that his words have taken effect.

"I cannot believe you. You're a thief and a liar."

"And this is how I am to be thanked for returning your brother's vial at great inconvenience to myself? Do you have any idea how dangerous it is to traverse the hills after nightfall?" He speaks lightly, as if he is indifferent to her opinion; nonetheless, there is a dark edge in his tone.

"For returning what rightfully belonged to my brother, may he now rest in Abraham's bosom, I thank you. But for the lies that you have spoken against my Master, I will not forgive you."

He draws close to her head once more—much too close for her comfort.

"It is I who must forgive *you*, for you have accused me without cause. I am not a liar—or a thief for that matter. If I was, I would have kept this, rather than return it now to you." So saying, he pulls her hand away from her face, and drops something into it.

It is Mary's gold ring, imbedded with rubies.

She gasps, and he rises to his feet.

"I'm rather surprised that you would wear such an elaborate ring at this time of mourning."

She is clearly agitated.

"It was a gift...from my brother. I could not bear to remove it."

"Perhaps you should guard it more carefully, then." He stares at her hands for a moment, as if he has not noticed them before. He stares at them as if they are known to him. She hurriedly replaces the ring and tucks her hands beneath the cloak.

He bows low once more.

"I bid you good night. I extend to your entire family my condolences. I am sorry for your loss, and sorrier for your refusal to embrace the hard truth when you are directly confronted with it."

He leaves her, tremulous on the bench in the courtyard, straining her eyes in the dark after him. He leaves the home of Lazarus, in a mood of dark triumph, but even the discovery, hours later, that his infant son had been entirely healed from that point on, will not eradicate the bitterness that poisons his every thought.

31

Jennifer locks her car and scurries along the sidewalk, muttering "sorry" to the dozen people she has to brush against because they are too slow. By the time she reaches the main stretch of boutiques along Broad Street she is almost running. She ventures into *Isabella's Bridal Couture* and an elegant woman in her late thirties, wearing crisp black pants and a mauve silk blouse with matching fingernails, approaches her.

"May I help you?"

"Oh, hi. Um...I'm in a hurry. I need to find something today. Something off-the-rack. Do you have anything I can look at?"

The consultant drops her eyes down to Jennifer's waist for the barest second and then quickly looks up again. Jennifer notices. But she doesn't care.

"You're the bride, of course?"

"Of course."

"Congratulations...I'm Adrienne, by the way. I can help you with everything you need. What's the date?"

"The date?"

"Of the wedding."

"Oh. Well...um...maybe tonight...or tomorrow...as soon as possible, actually."

"I see." Her dark face assumes a mask of businesslike civility, as if she has quickly realized that Jennifer's purchase will not net a great deal of commission. She hurriedly paces toward the back wall of the large store, her heels clicking on the linoleum with professional efficiency.

She begins to file through a rack of long, clear plastic sheaths which remind Jennifer, eerily, of body bags. Each gown hangs on a life-size plastic bust, as if the bags are filled with nameless, preformed brides, swathed in ivory and cream-colored fabric in seemingly endless combinations of satin, tulle, taffeta, and lace, waiting to be born.

"Size? Price range?" Adrienne says over her shoulder. When Jennifer doesn't answer, she turns around.

Off to the side of the sales floor is a carpeted dais, like a small stage, surrounded by triple-pane floor-to-length mirrors. A young woman, younger than Jennifer, with an auburn ponytail is standing before the mirrors, swishing the skirt of her voluminous gown for the benefit of her attendants. The three of them, one of them clearly a sister, murmur admiringly around her, like a cluster of doves. But Jennifer has noticed the mother, who stands a few feet away. The older woman is red-cheeked and freckly. She clutches a shabby pocketbook with both hands and gazes with deep-blue glimmering eyes at her daughter in the mirror. The eyes of the bride and her mother meet, and a look passes between them…the mother bestowing her approval without a word; the daughter receiving it with a self-assured smile before turning back to her attendants.

"It's lovely," the mother says to their hovering consultant. Her accent is decidedly Irish.

"Miss? Excuse me?"

"What?" Jennifer's trance is broken by Adrienne.

"How much were you planning to spend?"

"I—uh—I'm sorry. I can't do this."

"Are you all right? Do you need to sit down?"

"No…I just realized…I don't know what I was thinking…" She hurriedly backs toward the door. "I can't do this without my mother…"

She can hear Adrienne saying something about being open till six, but she is already on the sidewalk, walking as quickly as she can, past another boutique and then a florist and then turning down an alley where she leans heavily against a brick wall. It's as if it happened yesterday. It's as if the stark news that came to her through the phone at the front desk, her coworkers standing around in respectful silence, the hum of the fluorescent lights suddenly so loud when they told her that she couldn't speak and couldn't cry and couldn't comprehend. She remembers staring at the clock above the desk but the time did not register on her brain.

It's as if it just happened. She closes her eyes and leans her head against the bricks: an orphan, abandoned in the wilderness, crying for her mother.

Vina's father had owned a stationery and office-supply store called Vinito's. After his third wife had left him (Vina's mother was the second one), there had only been enough money, her father told her, to send her brother to college. "Your goal is to marry rich," he told her. "With your looks, that shouldn't be too hard." So Vito, her twin brother and a spoiled punk, got into Rutgers University by the skin of his teeth, and Vina stayed home and went to trade school to train as a paralegal, even though she was much smarter than her brother and actually read thick volumes of art history, for *fun*. Not long after Vito had flunked out of Rutgers due to excessive partying, her father told her there was no money left in the college fund. He also told her that nice girls lived at home till they got married, and he would not pay for her wedding if she moved out, and she asked him why he would pay for a wedding but not school.

"A wedding is cheaper," he explained to her. "And you don't need to become a lawyer! Just marry one. Marry a lawyer and you'll be set for life." She hated him after that. She hated the word *cheaper* in connection with any aspect of her life.

She was always efficient and polished, and at nineteen years old she carried herself more like twenty-four. Her classmates loathed her, but her teachers gave her excellent references, and she landed a job right out of the paralegal school with a well-established law firm. Soon after, she told her father that she needed to move closer to work because of the long hours, which was partly true. She also became the mistress of one of the partners of the firm, but that piece of information she kept to herself, and when her father asked her how she could afford her new Chrysler, she told him it was from her "Christmas bonus" and he believed her. Now he was proud of her, and ashamed of Vito, who lived at home, occasionally sold cars, and played pool all day. But it was too late. There was nothing he could say that mattered to her, although she did take his advice about "marrying rich." She made sure that her father went into debt paying for her wedding, and the marriage lasted long enough to confirm her suspicions about men: they were stupid, but useful. Her experience of two husbands and numerous paramours only served to substantiate her theory, and by the time she had met Jeb she had become skilled at separating men from their money. She had worked very hard to gain control of his assets and was damned if she was going to lose everything now to Jennifer.

"I'll be damned...I'll be damned if that dumb-ass, devious bitch thinks she can come in now and steal everything I've worked for—" she says, with her fist hitting the steering wheel for emphasis. She is hardly paying attention to a large Buick backing out from one of the diagonal parking spaces that some idiotic town planner had absurdly placed along Main Street. She is momentarily shocked into silence when the Buick smashes into the passenger side of her car.

The driver of the Buick is a grandmother who is five foot two and has no business whatsoever, in Vina's opinion, driving a car that size. She is obviously a grandmother because, aside from the two inches of gray-whitish roots that part her dark hair like a skunk's back, her grandson is strapped into a car seat in the backseat.

"You should have known better! You got a kid in the back! I had the right of way!" Vina screams at her, right in front of the officer, who has a difficult time getting the facts from either of them, because Vina is so enraged, and the grandmother never stops crying the whole time the officer tries to get her account of the collision. She tightly holds the little boy, who looks to be about two. The little boy keeps saying, "Car go boom, Gamma, car go boom." He had been jolted awake at the moment of impact, and now appears to be, miraculously, unharmed.

"Oh my god, oh my GOD!" Vina says, like a mantra, pacing the sidewalk, although she doesn't acknowledge any official god or subscribe to any religion. She was a lapsed Catholic in her younger years, and then after her first divorce she met Tonya. Tonya had convinced her that Eve was the pinnacle of creation, and that lesbian sex was "transcendent," whereas any sex involving the male organ is essentially rape, and most of all, there was a goddess named Sophia, who ran the whole universe, but permitted the male gods, including the God of the Bible, to occasionally exert their influence on the created order in the interest of maintaining cosmic harmony.

Tonya was five foot ten without heels, and dark and mystical, like a goddess herself. She owned a store that sold bright pottery and various artisan crafts, and she wore turquoise or deep-purple-shaded turbans and multiple pairs of silver hoop earrings and lived in Greenwich Village. She was over forty back then but she seemed ageless, and possessed a shimmering sensuality that attracted both men and women. Vina was easily converted. She would probably still be an avowed devotee of the goddess were it not for the retreat in the Poconos: she and Tonya had gathered with about twenty other wor-shippers of Sophia (*Sophites*, they called themselves) for an expensive weekend of vegetarian meals (meat was of the domain of men), ritual-istic bathing, incantations, meditation, and of course, tantric sex, which was obviously the way to "become one" with the goddess. Vina had never felt more alive and open to the spiritual realm, nor so in love with Tonya. But it was not to be: Tonya developed a sticky yeast infection a few days before the event. She ate copious amounts of yogurt but neither that, nor some of the women laying hands on her crotch and pleading with the Supreme Mother for healing, cleared it up. Tonya became stoic and philosophical. Clearly, she told Vina, the goddess was not permitting her to "engage in carnal worship." She spent most of the weekend in their room on her yoga mat. From behind her sun-glasses, Vina watched the other women making out. They attended the worship sessions all flushed and glowing from their transcendent "nonphallic" lovemaking, and she felt bitterness rise inside her like vomit. A few of the women invited her to join them in a *ménage à trois*, but she declined. Her body and soul craved Tonya. She tried to participate, as they sang and chanted in their saris and sarongs, but without Tonya the whole thing suddenly seemed laughable. She glanced around the circle of women. In the light of day they looked squat and stupid and undignified, a ragtag bunch sitting in the lotus position, each contemplating her *yoni* in a hand-held mirror, caught up in a haze of self-worship. In the last session someone passed around a pipe, and a loud and rancorous debate broke out concerning the use of marijuana during worship. The weekend ended on a sour note, with the pro-weed coalition vowing to have its own retreat next time. This brought Vina to her senses, and effectively ended her relationship with Tonya and the goddess.

After that she decided she wanted to believe in a more powerful being, and she became fascinated with Lucifer, who was actually an angel, she discovered, but then a few terrifying things happened to her in the dead of night that she could neither explain nor account for. She had been driven back, temporarily, to the Catholic church. When the fear of God or Satan or whatever it was wore off, she returned, unscathed, to her first love: money. Money was safe and predictable and comforting. You owned *it*, not the other way around. And there was no limit to how much one could accrue. She believed in the spiritual realm—she couldn't doubt it now—but she lived in the comforting, material world of dollars and cents, or dollars and *sense*, as she had been known to write to business associates, and she realizes now that, practically speaking, it would take her less than ten minutes to walk to Jeb's house from here, less time if she ran, but she would have to take her heels off and run in her stockings.

"Oh my gaw, oh my gaw," the little boy repeats after her, watching her from the inside of his grandmother's car. She stares at him for a moment, and he grins at her. There are traces of chocolate around his mouth. She is about to say something castigating to the grandmother, who is sitting in a slumped position in the driver's seat dabbing her eyes, when Clive suddenly appears in her line of vision, walking along the sidewalk and wiping his mouth with a paper napkin.

"Oh my god, Clive! Get over here!"

"Good god, what happened? Is that your car?"

"Never mind that now. You have to get to Jeb immediately."

"I was just heading over there. Do you want me to tell—"

"Hell, no. Just stop that marriage from taking place!"

"I beg your pardon?"

"Jennifer. You have to keep her away from him. She's lethal!"

"I don't understand." He truly doesn't. He only knows that the woman standing in front of him, who appeared completely rational and self-controlled only twenty minutes ago in the café now seems about to explode, like the old movies in which a wine glass shatters at the climax of a soprano's aria.

"I don't have time to explain. She's about to seize his assets. Everything. You must have figured that out. I mean, come on! Marrying a man on his deathbed!"

"I understand she's carrying his child."

"Impossible! Utterly impossible." She steps closer and whispers something in his ear, and his eyes widen slightly. Perhaps it's true. Perhaps Jennifer is actually not pregnant, which would of course make things less complicated since he plans to date her, down the road.

"Legally I can only go by what Mr. Kellon says. He seems convinced that she is carrying his child, and wishes to claim it as his legal heir."

"There is no way he could have fathered that child!"

"It's really none of our business—" But she is two inches from his face now, and thrusts her index finger, which has some kind of Egyptian scarab ring on it, into his tie.

"His business *is* your business! You need to get over there now. You need to stop the marriage from taking place. Do whatever you have to do."

Clive paces hurriedly to his car, his mind working as quickly as his feet. By the time he is in the driver's seat he has already decided that he has no intention of preventing the marriage, because he has no intention of depriving Jennifer of Jeb Kellon's assets, none the least being that he may end up marrying her himself, baby or not.

If it weren't for Bee-Bee, Clay would have certainly started smoking again by now. If it weren't for the fact she has a strange, sensory-impaired relationship with the people around her, especially when it comes to scents and odors, he would definitely have started smoking cigars, at the very least. The entire family has stopped using scented toiletries, because his wife had done research and discovered sources of specially formulated, unscented detergents and cleaning products through some homeschooling connection. The organic products cost twice as much as regular products but nobody, least of all Clay, protested. His little girl has made the space where his shoulder merges into his neck a sort of refuge, and she would frequently seek solace there from the world of harsh scents and sensory dissonance. She would be the first to notice if he became tainted with the scent of tobacco.

He had slammed out of the house, annoyed at his wife for non-specific reasons but unwilling to relent of his anger, which seems to have turned into something of a caged animal: tense but controlled for the time being. He cannot account for it. He walks quickly toward the beach, but then, on an impulse, turns back toward town, intending to walk along Main Street in search of new sights or new people, but with the glum expression of a man who expects nothing but what has always been. He looks up briefly to notice that there has been a minor car accident and one woman who he has occasionally seen around town is yelling at the top of her lungs at another woman, who holds a young boy. He bypasses the curious onlookers and crosses the street to a newsstand, thinking he might buy the *Times* and make an effort to complete the crossword, but this would be foolhardy without Rebecca, and he knows it.

Attempting to navigate any difficult challenge in his life without Rebecca at his side would be foolhardy, and he decides that this must be the reason for his growing resentment toward her. *You're afraid of needing her*, he tells himself. *You're even afraid of admitting that you need her.* He says it a few times, to allow it to sink in, and then feels relieved that he has figured this out about himself. It makes him feel mature, as if an older, saner version of himself has given his younger, more impulsive self some wise counsel, and now both are better for it. He will be OK. He's not stupid! He will not destroy his life and his marriage and his family and his pastoral ministry as long as he has these little counseling sessions with himself. He is almost ready to go back home, explain himself to Rebecca, apologize for his anger, and allow her to commend him for his self-awareness and honesty.

I'll admit I was wrong, and that it's my issue.

But first, as a small reward for his humility, he decides to treat himself to a cup of coffee at Ground Zero. A large basket situated by the entrance of the café is specifically intended to be filled with the pre-owned magazines of customers, with a view to sharing and reusing rather than discarding and wasting. He shuffles through the magazines and picks up a back issue of *Rolling Stone*, which is a private, guilty indulgence left over from his seminary days. A dark, cosmeticized young man is on the front cover. He has a one-syllable name, *Prince*, with no surname. Like *Cher*. Clay has never heard of him, but he has no doubt that the young man and his music are well-known to a large segment of his congregation, and he is therefore justified in reading the article, with a view to being relevant. He can envision the surprised faces of the young people in his congregation when he intones the musician's name to make some point in his sermon next week.

He finishes the lengthy article, has his cup refilled twice by a waiter, and then turns back to read the letters from readers, again with a view to staying current and relevant. He is about to read the editor's page when something—like the compulsion to glance at one's watch or check a rearview mirror—causes him to look up. David, his twelve-year old son, is standing in the door of the café. They stare at each other for a moment—the father, surprised at the unexpected appearance of the son, and the son, with a hint of disdain crossing his face, which has the effect of producing a stab of guilt, like the jab of a penknife, in his lower bowels. He places the magazine on the chair next to him.

"What's up?" he says as David approaches.

"We didn't know where you were."

"Oh. Well, your mother's home, no?"

"She went to Red Bank. It's Sunday."

"Oh, geez. I forgot about that. Her coffee house thing. Sorry. You guys OK?"

"Just come home, will ya?" His son is decidedly angry. By the time Clay pays for his coffee and leaves a tip, David is already fifty paces ahead of him, apparently determined not to walk alongside his father. He slips into the house ahead of his dad, and Clay knows instinctively that he is reporting to Rachel and Nathan: *Found him sitting there reading a magazine in Ground Zero…*

Clay feels the caged animal rising within him. He begins a lecture, in his mind, designed to take his older son down a few pegs. His major points will be "the need for me to be alone periodically" and "it might look like a magazine to you but, believe it or not, I was actually preparing for next week's sermon," but the words die in his head when he walks into the house.

There is cat litter all over the floor, because John-Mark decided that the litter box needed replenishing, but the large bag of litter proved too cumbersome for the boy. Nathan's left eyelid is swollen shut, but neither he nor his older brother is forthcoming with an explanation. The air is permeated with the caustic odor of burnt popcorn. And Bee-Bee—

Bee-Bee has moved to a place beyond grief. Her anguished, relentless wailing is so pervasive that his entire family, minus Rebecca, has been hijacked by it. They appear to be on the verge of mutiny. Rachel's mascara runs in black streaks down her cheeks. David slumps on the couch, his arms crossed rigidly, regarding Clay from a great distance. Nathan sits opposite David, his eyes cast to the floor, and he cracks his knuckles in anxious frustration. John-Mark, seeking comfort and distraction, disappears behind the freezer door in search of an ice pop. And Bee-Bee—

At the sight of Clay, Bee-Bee scrambles off her sister's lap and flies to him. He picks her up and instantly her wet face soaks the neckline of his T-shirt and her tiny frame shudders with sobbing hiccups. His other children gradually drift away, like small sparrows venturing out for worms after a storm. Only Bee-Bee is inclined to stay with him, and wordlessly offers him her full and free forgiveness, although if asked, he would not be able to consciously identify what sin he has committed.

Nevertheless, he holds her for a long time.

XXXII

*M*ary's eyelids open suddenly, as if they cannot endure another moment of sleep. She stares into the darkness above her bed, trying to make sense of her dream.

The dream was of a great white seabird, lying dead on the floor of a dark cave, ravaged by the ocean's fury. Despite the darkness, she could clearly see the bird, and her stomach churned with revulsion at the sight of its torn, muddied wings and neck, twisted in unnatural angles, its crooked claws, and the sightless eyes. But as the first rays of dawn penetrated the gloomy dankness of the cave, a breeze stirred the bloody feathers of the dead bird, giving it the appearance of movement. Then there was no mistake; the bird moved. Its eyes blinked and became alert and focused, and a moment later it shuffled to its feet, shook out its wings, and then hopped to the entrance of the cave, which was situated on a beach. Large rocks and pieces of driftwood blocked the cave's entrance, and they suddenly fell away, like the sand caving into the bottom of an hourglass. On the beach the great seabird extended its mighty wings, shaking away the last traces of blood and debris accrued in its death struggle. It cawed exultantly and then abruptly took to flight, gliding and swooping triumphantly over the very sea that had destroyed it, catching and eating a fish for breakfast, and then rising on the wind. Soon it soared above some low-lying clouds, a dark and majestic shape in the rays of the rising sun, which gleamed and danced on the great sea. The sight was at once beautiful and blinding. In her dream, Mary stood at the edge of the water and strained her eyes to watch the magnificent bird fly into the heavens until she could not see it anymore nor bear the light of the sun. And then she awoke.

The Sea of Galilee, she whispers in the darkness, although she has only seen it a few times in her life. She sighs deeply, longing to go there, wishing she could ride on the wings of the great bird and leave behind the overwhelming sadness of her house, and the stench of death.

She rises on her elbow, trying to gauge the hour of the night by the shadows in the garden outside her window. She becomes conscious of someone stirring in the hall, and then a flickering lamp emerges from behind her door. Not surprisingly, it is Reumah.

The two women gaze at each other in the wan light of the lamp. Reumah is the first to speak.

"I did not think to find you awake. I hope I did not disturb you?"

"I had a dream, like a vision." Mary sits up. "I am trying to make sense of it."

"Please tell me," Reumah replies. She is so relieved to see her friend awake, and in her right mind, she immediately sits down across from her on the sleeping platform, forgetting, for the moment, that she is wearing Mary's robes and ring.

Mary tells her of the seabird. Her voice is low and her tone is sad despite the joyous beauty of her dream, as if it belongs to another sleeper, and holds no meaning for her. Her eyes are fixed on the pale light of the window, but she seems unmindful of the approaching day.

"Surely it is from the Lord himself," Reumah whispers when the retelling is done.

"Perhaps. What can it mean?"

"A vision intended to comfort you in your deepest grief. No doubt the bird represents your brother's spirit, which lives on and has soared to the Almighty. He is beyond the reach of death."

Mary sighs again. "Perhaps. And yet...I feel no comfort...only sadness that I am left behind on the shore, and must face the waves of darkness and destruction now without my brother's protective care. How can I be comforted in that? *One day I shall go to him...He will not come to me.*" She quotes the words of Israel's ancient shepherd king as an afterthought, with little emotion.

They are silent for some time, watching the morning light infiltrate the room and dispel the shadows. Reumah wishes she could find the words to relieve the heavy despair of her friend's mind, but no words come to her now, except for the words of Mary's song, Mary the mother of their Lord. She wishes she could sing the song now. She wishes that she possessed a voice like *that* Mary, and could sing the song that stirred into her soul a deeper hope and longing than she had ever known before. But she is certain her voice would quaver and fall flat, and the result would be laughable. She remains silent.

The room becomes lighter and suddenly Mary says, "I am hungry. Famished, actually. And thirsty as well. I feel I will faint—"

Her thought is not finished before Reumah places a small basket of ripe figs and bread and cheese into her friend's lap.

"I will fetch some wine as well."

"Yes. And water for washing."

When Reumah returns, the room is brighter and she looks into Mary's eyes, hoping to see a light of hope there as well. But she is disappointed. Mary chews her bread slowly, and for a few awkward minutes scrutinizes Reumah, as if seeing her for the first time after many days.

"You are wearing my robes."

"I beg your pardon. But I had good reason to put these on."

Mary stops chewing. "I can't imagine."

Reumah takes a deep breath and begins to tell Mary about Judas. She speaks slowly, carefully choosing her words, with a strong instinct to protect her friend in her vulnerable emotional state from the worst of his words.

"Why did you not wake me?"

"I thought it best to let you sleep. You seemed so…peaceful. I could not bear to have you disturbed after so much agony. Was I wrong?"

"I understand you wanting to let me rest, and it does you credit. But I would have liked to hear for myself what Judas had to say. He was, after all, chosen by the Master to bear the message of condolence to me, personally. These are now second- and third-hand tidings."

Reumah is struck at once by Mary's abrupt tone. A sharp pang pierces her intestines.

"I'm sorry! I thought I did well in not disturbing you. Perhaps I judged poorly."

Mary takes a piece of bread and rips it apart. She puts some of it in her mouth, and says, chewing with uncharacteristic rudeness, "What else did he say?"

"I have saved the best for last. He gave me this." So saying she places the vial, still enclosed in its cloth wrapping, before her on the bed. Mary stops chewing, and then spits the bread from her mouth into her hand and throws it to the floor.

"Too late…Alas, too late! We are cursed! The Master doesn't come in time to save my brother's life, and his vial arrives too late for the day of his anointing!" Mary rises from the bed and tears her robe and begins a loud, extended lamentation. In the hallway outside her door Reumah can hear a group gathering and murmuring.

Reumah hurriedly bars the door and turns toward Mary.

"Please, Mary. Please, my dearest friend. Only think—we have his vial, his very own anointing oil made with his own hands. Surely that will be a treasured reminder of him for years to come?"

Mary wipes her face and her hands and picks up the vial. She grasps it tightly, almost greedily, as if terrified of losing it again, and Reumah observes a dark expression pass over her face, like a sinister cloud passing over the moon, before she looks over at Reumah.

"You're lying to me."

"What?"

"Judas did not freely give this to you. You contrived to get it from him—in exchange for—"

"What are you saying?"

"I know it all. It came to me now. You—standing there in my clothes! Wearing my ring!! How dare you? You gave yourself to him, only he thought you were me! You impersonated me! And in exchange he gave you back the vial! I see it all before me now!"

"Stop! Stop, Mary! You don't know what you're saying! Your grief has—has—addled your senses!" Reumah is weeping now, and a tide of hysteria rises between the two women, like floodwaters washing away a pathway between two houses, creating a miry pit of treacherous mud.

A sharp incessant knocking causes them both to look toward the door.

"Who is it?" Mary says, sharply.

"It is I, Martha. Please let me in. You are waking the entire household."

Mary opens the door and bolts it again as soon as Martha is in the room. The older sister glances back and forth at both of them, but before she can ask them anything Mary speaks.

"A terrible thing has occurred, my sister. Last night, while I slept in the exhaustion of my grief, this woman—who calls herself my friend—gave herself to the man, Judas. Gave herself! Wearing my clothes and my ring, so that he would be deceived into thinking it was me that he slept with! In exchange for her favors, he gave us back the vial of our brother. Such is the woman we have allowed into our home!"

"Mary—Mary! You are crazed with grief—you speak the words of a mad woman—"

"The entire region knows of my reputation for purity! Everyone knows I am a virgin, and wish to remain so in service to our God! No wonder Judas was willing to pay such a price in exchange for my favors! We all know his character and reputation. Don't you see? Don't you see the damage that has been done by this imposter? She contrived the scheme to get back the vial, no doubt because she felt so guilty that she had received hers in exchange for our brother's, but then would not share hers when it was most needed! Worthless, filthy girl!" Here she turns, with angry tears springing from her eyes, to Reumah.

"The Lord himself will know that he was a fool to name you *A Fragrant One*." She turns her back abruptly on Reumah.

For Reumah, the room is spinning and she would have fallen if Martha had not taken hold of her. She surveys her sister's clothes on Reumah, and the bright ruby ring, which now catches the morning's light. There is deep consternation on her face until she looks into Reumah's eyes.

"Please…please, mistress…believe me…it was not like that… please…" Her words are mouthed more than spoken. Mary does not hear them.

"I cannot pretend to understand what transpired here last night. God knows the truth, and will reveal it in his time. For now, Reumah, you must change these clothes, and remove yourself to another part of the house until this matter can be resolved."

They leave her then, and go out to where the rest of the family is gathering in the courtyard for the first meal of the day. With trembling hands, Reumah quickly removes Mary's clothes, and puts on her own again, all the while hearing the words of Mary echoing in her mind.

The Lord himself will know that he was a fool to name you A Fragrant One.

The words slither down and coil around her heart like a python, squeezing the breath of hope out of her. She sinks to her knees by the window, with only the conviction of her blamelessness giving her the strength to pray.

"Yaweh Sabaoth...you are my shield and my strong tower...my only hope. You know all things...you know I have been a sinful woman. But in this matter I am innocent. I will die of grief if you do not come to my defense."

She chooses the shade of the garden for her refuge. For over a week no servants have been there to pluck the blooms, since all work has stopped out of respect for the dead. She removes some of the roses that droop heavily on their stems, being careful of their thorns, and cups them beneath her nose. Their fruity scent, along with the freshness of the morning air, fills her with a painful and unexpected longing for her father's house. On mornings such as these she would find him and her brothers on low benches in the shade of their dwelling, and she would creep over and sit at her father's feet. The flow of his teaching was never interrupted, nor would he protest if she let her head rest on his knee in the rising heat of the day. Her brothers would scowl at her, particularly if they erred in reply to their father's questions as he taught them, and especially if she tried to answer them herself.

"Father, it is not fitting that she is taught with us...a mere child and a girl. I will not learn my lessons if she remains," her elder brother said one day, crossing his arms, and the other nodded in agreement.

She learned to be silent and stay out of sight while he taught them, and afterward, when they were gone, she would approach him quietly while he sat in prayer, and wait until he opened his eyes, which were always filled with delight at the sight of her.

"Yes, my lamb. Were you listening?"

"Every word, Abba! Ask me, ask me!"

One time her mother came out carrying some clothes for laundering and a bowl of table scraps for the dogs. The bowl slipped from her grasp and clattered on the stones, which sent the dogs yowling in dismayed surprise. She turned and wagged her finger at both of them.

"Your daughter eats the bread of idleness and you say nothing to rebuke her."

"She has a mind for learning"

"You will make her unfit for any husband. Men want wives who are hardworking and diligent, not useless and lazy."

Her rebuke hung in the air like smoke from a fire and stung her eyes. She never forgot it, nor how her father's hand, in the next moment, came to rest warmly on her head, and stayed for a moment in a reassuring way before he nudged her to go in and help her mother. It eased the sting of her mother's words.

Abba, my abba...how you loved me...

She closes her eyes to remember his face and to quash the wave of grief that rises in her soul. Perhaps the love of a father surpasses the love of a friend or a husband, she thinks. It is like being loved by God himself. The thought is so surprising to her that she opens her eyes, and is immediately confronted by a tiny hummingbird, its emerald feathers resplendent in the morning sun, hovering over the scarlet roses in her hands. The sight is so delightful she cannot help but smile. She cannot help but think that is a sign of her father's love, even now, hovering over her in her dark hour.

The moments turn into an hour, and then two. Perhaps she dozes in the rising heat of midday; in any case, her shaded spot is gone and she is heated and dizzy as she stands. She turns toward the gate leading to courtyard, suddenly conscious of a commotion. Wishing to avoid the scrutiny of a crowd, she heads back toward the cooking area, seeking sustenance and with a desire to be useful to Martha. She taps the shoulder of a servant.

"Where is the mistress?"

"She is not here."

"What? Did she leave?"

"Yes, yes! Only minutes ago. She ran out the gate as soon as she heard."

"Heard what?"

The servant stares at her, as if she is dense or deaf.

"The Lord himself is approaching the village. The entire household has been roused."

Her heart beats faster and something small and hopeful begins to grow and gather inside her, like the first raindrops that fall after a drought. She taps the servant again.

"What of her sister? Did she go too?"

The servant clucks her tongue.

"No. She is not pleased with anything today. Not even the news of the Master arriving. She has locked herself in her room, and says she is not to be disturbed. Very troubling it is for all of us, to be sure."

Reumah stands still and quiet for a moment, saddened by the servant's words, and conscious that she, unwittingly, has contributed to Mary's travails. But just as quickly the surmounting joy at the prospect of seeing the Lord overtakes her.

"Here—let me help." She takes the small bellows, unmindful of the heat, and begins to fan the flame under the oven.

The news of his arrival—the very mention of his name—has caused the few raindrops that fell inside her heart to turn into a summer shower, refreshing and cooling the parched places within.

33

On the sidewalk outside Pages, Rebecca contemplates a handwritten sign on the door that reads, *Closed due to burst pipe.* Underneath the message someone else, probably Pasqual, has written:

Visit us again soon to discuss more important matters...

She smiles briefly, and then sighs. It would have been nice if Rita or Pasqual had called to let her know before she drove all the way from the Grove. Maybe it just happened. Maybe it happened in the last half hour, and they panicked and left until they could figure out what to do. That would be like them: capable of wrestling with the larger questions of existence, but utterly daunted by the sudden appearance of puddles next to the toilet. She can picture them, looking askance, each hoping the other would know what to do, and then calling Sappho, their daughter, to handle it.

Rebecca glances at her reflection in the window: a medium-tall woman with large, calm eyes and a braid draped over the left shoulder of her long trench coat. Wrapped around her neck is a scarf that her mother made for her four years ago when she went through a knitting phase. The scarf is ridiculously long but she loves its colors: soft greens and blues and yellows. On her right lapel she wears a brooch in the shape of a fish. The fish gleams with inlaid peridots and topaz, and it belonged to her father's mother. She is not particularly fond of the brooch, but Bee-Bee is, and she will make a fuss if Rebecca tries to remove it.

She takes a step closer and peers into the small bookshop and café, but there is no sign of life, or water damage, for that matter. The

chairs are on top of the tables and only the dim lights above the counter are on, barely illuminating the counter on which sits an industrial-
sized cappuccino maker, which was imported from Italy, and which cost
more than two months' rent to purchase and install. At least that's what
Rita told her. The cappuccino maker, in Rebecca's imagination, is like
the Buddha at the center of a shrine: without it the café would cease
to exist.

Rita and Pasquale had bought the cappuccino maker because they
believed that cappuccino should be enjoyed by the masses, along with
baklava, and *mille fueilles*, and various other European pastries involving phyllo dough. They had lived and traveled extensively in Europe,
and had discovered their mission and purpose in life while riding in a
taxi in Moscow. The taxi driver had quoted Dostoyevsky, and Pasqual
had turned to Rita in amazement.

"He quoted Dostoyevsky."

"Yes. In English, no less."

"A mere taxi driver," he said, his voice lowered.

"Can you imagine? It would be like a cabbie in New York quoting
Whitman or Ferlinghetti."

They decided then that they must return to the States, and educate
"the people." They decided that they must bring what they referred
to as "the European world view" to America, and also that they must
become dispensers of knowledge, and feed the souls of the unedu-
cated and philosophically illiterate throngs with the enduring wisdom
of past sages. They decided that higher education was overrated, and
overpriced; nevertheless, knowledge must not be kept from the "huddled masses yearning to be free" simply because they could not afford
it. They decided to open a bookstore, which Pasqual wanted to call
Pages of Sages to make it more poetical, but everyone, including Rita,
felt the name was too cutesy for the urbane Red Bank crowd.

The bookstore enclosed a small café. Or a café, which was surrounded by shelves of books, depending on how you looked at it.
Pasqual and Rita were utterly fervent in their mission, and quit their
teaching jobs (they were teaching English in Prague at the time) and
sold most of their possessions, including their car, to return to the
States and open Pages. They now lived upstairs from the café, and

Rebecca had never been in their apartment, although she had heard their daughter refer to it wryly as "a library with beds."

The bookshelves of the café are heavily laden with everything that Rita and Pasqual consider "classic" or "an essential contribution to the Great Dialogue"; mostly purchased secondhand from poor or disillusioned university students. Often the books are sold again, mostly to poor and disillusioned university students, because, admittedly, it is rare to have a cab driver or hair stylist or meter reader come into the shop deliberately searching for a volume of Homer or Machiavelli or Proust, for that matter. Nevertheless Rita insists on prominently featuring the works of those brilliant minds, along with those of Freud, Hegel, Nietzsche, and others (depending on her mood), in dignified, albeit dusty, window displays. A patron venturing inside the shop could also find volumes of fiction and poetry and philosophy from authors who are actually still alive, and these had been collected over the years by Rita and Pasqual throughout their travels, and were the works of authors that they had met or with whom they had become acquainted, which is how Rebecca had come to know them.

In Paris, Rita had gone into a bookshop and demanded to know what "the people" were reading. It was the same question she asked of all bookshop owners, in every city she visited.

"*Les Fragrantes*," said the owner. "It's a translation. The Muslim women from *la Sorbonne* especially are asking for it. I can't keep it on the shelf."

Rita was intrigued. It took her two days to read half of it in French, so she gave up and bought it in the English. She finished the book in five hours. When she returned to the States, she contacted Rebecca and told her "it was a lovely story" and that she would like to meet her for lunch.

"Why the Muslim women, do you think?" Rita wanted to know. She had been pleased with the fact that Rebecca had lived in Israel, and was fond of falafel and tahini, which they were now eating.

"Well...obviously there are some cultural similarities."

"Yes, but...your story unabashedly portrays Jesus as divine."

Rebecca had smiled. "True. And the Savior of all, including women."

"Ah," nodded Rita. "A fairytale, in essence, to the female minds living within the framework of a repressive, male-dominated culture. Christ as the archetypal Prince."

The lunch had resulted in Rita inviting Rebecca to become part of their monthly symposiums, which were held on Sunday evenings in the cafe, to represent the "Judeo-Christian" perspective on whichever topic was being discussed. Usually the topics were along the lines of "What is Evil?" or "Are Human Beings Evolving?" but occasionally the entire audience (which, on a good night, was about fifteen people) veered off into uncharted territory, and ended up debating whether one of the women present should nurse her baby openly in the café, or whether Rita and Pasqual should be considered a married couple, even though, legally, they were not.

They had met in their twenties and had been together for over forty years, and their union had produced one daughter whom they had named Sappho, in earnest hope that the carefully selected moniker would inspire their daughter to become a passionate lover of poetry and philosophy. Alas, the name and its possessor seemed almost comically mismatched. The girl had left her parents' home (which was in Madrid at the time) at age nineteen, and returned to the States to join the National Guard. This so shocked and dismayed her parents they remained estranged for a number of years, until Sappho had been mysteriously discharged from the service. No one knew why, although it was whispered that she had had an illicit affair with a senior *female* officer that had resulted in that officer committing suicide, but this was merely a rumor. Sometime after they had returned to the States, she had reconciled with her parents, and now, at age thirty-eight, owned a small business that was contracted by the state and local governments to remove the pulverized carcasses of unfortunate animals along all the major highways of New Jersey. Her parents summoned her for almost every practical need they had, and Rebecca is not the least surprised to see, parked outside the shop, Sappho's truck, with the name *Reliant Removal Co., Expert Carcass and Animal Debris Removal* painted on the outside.

Rebecca lingers for a moment before turning back in the direction of her car. She spent most of the drive to Red Bank engaged in a prayerful dialogue with the Almighty regarding her husband and his erratic behavior, and followed this with a fervent prayer for wisdom and discernment, which she typically prayed before heading into the café for the symposium. It occurs to her now that God might have some other purpose for her being in Red Bank, and for that reason she hesitates.

She decides to stroll along the sidewalk, and is immediately confronted by the appearance of Sappho, who is carrying a carefully coiled plumber's snake.

"Wasn't even a pipe. Just a blocked toilet. Good god," Sappho mutters, noisily cramming the snake into the back of her truck.

"Oh...well...thank God they have you," Rebecca ventures. She has never had more than a polite conversation with Sappho.

"You gotta love 'em but let's face it: they are so checked out." She pushes her sunglasses onto the top of her head, and looks at Rebecca more pointedly, as if noticing her now. "I guess you came for the symposium, huh?"

"I did. Should I go up and say hi?"

"Nah. I wouldn't bother. Rita's in one of her moods. She's on antidepressants now and they can't seem to get her dosage right. And dad's a bit sloshed, if you really want to know."

"Oh. I'm sorry..." Rebecca is at a loss. She contemplates the only child of Rita and Pasqual, standing hesitatingly beside her truck, her thick dark hair perpetually pulled back in a severe bun, probably a habit left over from her military service; her large lovely eyes (very like her mother's except without the false eyelashes Rita wears behind thick glasses), which tended, in conversations, to gaze into the distance, apparently seeking something better than whatever was directly before her. Rebecca is not a hugger, but she feels a maternal, protective instinct rise up inside her.

"I'm sorry, Sappho," she says again. "It must be...difficult...to always feel like you need to take care of them."

Sappho lets out a long sigh before going around and pulling open the driver's door. She turns to Rebecca before climbing in.

"I hate to admit it, but I forget your name."

"Rebecca."

"Right. They like you. I can see why. You're a good person. Take care, Rebecca." She rolls up her window and pulls out into the street, and Rebecca is left wondering, again, if she should head home.

The late-day sun has imbued the sky in shades of lavender and fuchsia and deep turquoise, like a giant celestial baby shower, and Rebecca finds herself walking again, walking toward the colors, and alternately worshipping and wondering, conscious of a restless longing. She cannot escape the sense that she is meant to be here, at this time, and she is therefore not the least surprised to see a woman in a side alley, her back turned to the street, weeping.

She is not surprised, but almost relieved, to realize that the woman is Jennifer. She steps toward her and taps her gently on the shoulder.

"It's just me," she says, when Jennifer turns, startled.

Neither woman says anything for a few minutes. Rebecca finds some tissues in her bag and hands them to Jennifer, who blows her nose and wipes her eyes.

"I'm OK…really. I'm fine."

"Please let me help you."

"I'll be fine. It's just…hormones, I guess. Everything seems…I don't know…worse than it is."

"Why are you here?"

Jennifer blows her nose again and tells her. Rebecca probes. Jennifer tells her some more, and while she is talking, Rebecca has an epiphany, although she would not have been quick to label it as such if she had been retelling the incident to, say, Clay. She suddenly sees, in her mind, a certain dress in the window of a consignment shop on the next street. She passed it a half hour ago on her way to the café. She hopes the shop is still open.

"Come," she says firmly to Jennifer. "I need to show you something."

The shop caters to a younger clientele of mostly hip urban women with a taste for vintage clothing. The dress in the window is not a wedding gown, but a knee-length, fitted frock, with capped sleeves and obviously designed to enhance an hourglass figure. Rebecca and Jennifer contemplate the dress for a few minutes.

"It's pretty," says Jennifer. "But I don't know. It's not really a wedding dress." The dress is cream-colored, overlaid in lace. It reminds Jennifer of something Jackie Kennedy might have worn, with matching coat, hat, and pearls, to mass on Easter.

"Just try it on. Come on."

Rebecca's eyes alight on the jewelry counter while Jennifer is in the fitting room. She leans down on it, mentally carrying on a conversation with God while she surveys a large collection of faux pearls and rhinestone brooches. Her lips move sometimes, unconsciously, and she is unaware of the clerk glancing at her aloofly before going back to her magazine.

When Jennifer opens the curtain, she has the dress on, and she is crying again, only softly. Rebecca goes over to her.

"It looks beautiful on you." She is not exaggerating.

"It has snowflakes." Jennifer begins to cry harder.

"Snowflakes?"

"The lace…the lace is like tiny snowflakes…all sewn together."

"Is…that good?"

"Oh yes," says Jennifer. "Yes. It's perfect. It's as perfect as it could be."

After the dress is purchased they discuss the ring. Rebecca asks if Jennifer's mother had any rings that could be used, and Jennifer thinks.

"Of course…my mother's wedding ring. It's just a band…my dad was poor at the time. But it would do in the meantime…"

"Yes…and it seems appropriate, doesn't it? In the absence of your parents, you nevertheless have a symbol of them as you take this important step…"

Jennifer stops walking and turns to Rebecca.

"What it is?" Rebecca says. She hopes she hasn't offended.

"I—um—I never thought of it like that. But I like it. Thanks." She is frankly amazed at Rebecca's capacity to see things in such a different light.

They walk back to Jennifer's car, and Jennifer hangs the dress, now cloaked in a plastic sheath, inside the car. She suddenly feels self-conscious with a sense of indebtedness to Rebecca.

"Well...I don't know how to thank you. I feel so much better now. I feel like...you were meant to be here...to help me." Her cheeks redden slightly.

"I feel that way too. It was no coincidence."

"Um...what were *you* doing here, if you don't mind me asking?"

Rebecca explains about café, and the symposium, with a brief mention of her book.

"You wrote a book?" Jennifer says.

"A novel, yes. Years ago."

"Wow. What was it called?"

Rebecca smiles. "I doubt you'd have heard of it. It wasn't a best seller. It's titled *The Fragrant Ones*. Pages is one of the few places that—" she stops because Jennifer's mouth has dropped open.

"You wrote *The Fragrant Ones*?"

"You've read it?"

"My mother did...right before she died. And I—um—just picked it up. Just started it," she lies. She decides that she must read the book immediately. Tonight, if possible. She decides that somehow her mother and Rebecca are connected, spiritually at least, and that an outside force, God probably, is bringing the pieces of her life together.

"Well, that's interesting. I hope you enjoy it. I hope your mother did too."

They say good-bye, Jennifer volunteering a shy hug, which Rebecca warmly returns before heading back to her car. Along the way she thinks how Clay will not miss the irony of her questioning his decision to perform a quickie marriage ceremony, only to help the bride pick out her dress a couple hours later.

She walks faster, as if propelled by an indwelling force, her brain expanding like an elastic band to include this latest incident, and muse on its significance. There are events and matters that are unfathomable: she has spent tearful nights agonizing over the Holocaust, for instance, or the ninth chapter of the book of Romans. There are questions that she has raised, on sleepless nights, before the throne of Yaweh, and by morning still received no answer, but only a renewed conviction that he is the one to ask. This was followed by a strange peace that overshadowed her despair and moved her to worship him.

"How unsearchable are your ways…"

But then, every so often, like this latest incident with Jennifer, the opposite occurs: she is given a glimpse of a vast script, a clear indication that there exists a great overarching drama with eternal origins, a metanarrative that is played out on earth and in heaven and includes the sad, weary daughters of ailing or absent parents, and their appointed comforters as well. Her role is small, but it is crucial.

The sky is darker now, but still contains the pale rosy traces of the setting sun. She turns toward it before getting into her car.

"Thank you…thank you…thank you."

XXXIV

The news of the Master's arrival is like a cooling north wind that sweeps into the house, scattering the dust and darkness and stench of death. Or so Reumah imagines. She does not actually feel any wind, but rather its effect. The servants rush here and there, the family members are roused and summoned, and throughout the house there is a sense of hushed anticipation, as if the imminent arrival of a long-awaited bridegroom has just been announced.

For a moment she stands very still, remembering.

She remembers Elias, her father's steward, telling her father, who then told her mother that Zerah was approaching the village with a noisy procession of friends and family members, carrying banners and tambourines. She remembers the look of panic in her mother's eyes, but it was unnecessary, for she had already bathed, and her oldest aunt—who was the village midwife—had completed the prenuptial rite of the "Scenting of the Seven Orifices." She knew that discreet messages had gone back and forth between doulas in both households to ensure that the bridegroom would arrive at the height of the bride's cycle, and not at the time of her uncleanness, but these, of course, were never mentioned, only assumed. Her mother had placed a sachet of myrrh around her neck so that it rested between her breasts and its scent filled her nostrils and caused her head to swim with murky visions of lovemaking, which brought the face and form of Judas into her mind. Her heart pounded but she quickly put all thoughts of him aside: she was determined to have eyes for Zerah alone. Her grandmother and her aunts and her cousins and her friends had been summoned to help her dress, and the fussing and fixing and amendments to hair and veils and jewelry taxed her to the utmost but made her laugh as well. None of the women ate, least of all Reumah, although the servants plied them with dates and cheese and wine.

Most of all she remembers the sudden silence of the room when her father came in and beheld her for the last time before her departure under the canopy. The eyes of every woman were on him as he contemplated his only daughter's dark, thickly lashed eyes and carefully arranged tresses. Chains of small glittering coins adorned her forehead and neck and wrists, and golden rings gleamed in her earlobes and nose. He gazed at her with a mixture of awe and sadness and love.

"Today I shall rejoice over you with singing..." he said simply.

The women of her life, even her mother, wiped their eyes and sighed, and Reumah, arrayed in her bridal splendor, knelt before him like a child. He placed his hands on her veiled head.

"'Who is this who appears as the dawn, fair as the moon, bright as the noonday sun, regal as the stars in procession?' No longer will you be called the daughter of Nicodemus...today you become the wife of Zerah. May the Lord bless you and keep you, my daughter...may he grant you peace and prosperity and many children in the home of your husband, and may he bless your coming and going, both now and forever more. Amen."

She had kissed her father's hands. She remembers her heart swelling as he spoke his blessing on her, but always the guilt for her sin with Judas tinged every feeling of joy, like the dark kohl that stained the tears that fell from her eyes.

She wipes her eyes and is conscious of the silence around her. She turns to see that the entire courtyard has been quieted by the appearance of Mary, who seats herself on a cushioned bench with the dignity of a queen. Reumah catches her breath at the sight of her.

Mary has done much to improve her appearance. She has changed her robes, and arranged her hair. She wears no jewelry or flowers, but her face is filled with anxious anticipation, like a bride who is unsure of her intended husband's devotion, and expects to be disappointed. No one speaks, and Reumah is conscious of tension, like the air before a thunderstorm.

"Where is my sister?" Mary inquires, imperiously.

"Mistress, she has gone to meet the Master." This is Tobias, who bows as he speaks.

"Why was I not informed of her departure?"

"We did not think it wise to disturb you."

Mary opens her mouth to respond, but is interrupted by a stirring at the entrance of the courtyard, followed by the appearance of Martha, who almost runs across the paving stones toward her sister.

"Mary! He has come at last. I have seen him. I have seen the Lord!"

"Yes? Did he account for his delay?" Mary's jaw is set at an angle. She looks down and rearranges an imagined fold in her robe, as if buying time. Reumah is close enough to perceive the anger in her glittering eyes.

"Mary! He loves us. You know he does! He is asking for you. You must go to him!"

"I, go to him? Why does he not come to us? What manner of love is that?" There is a tremor in her voice and blotches appear on her throat and cheeks.

Martha's face darkens. Reumah edges closer, along with the rest of the crowd. All eyes are on the sisters now, as if each person is trying to choose between the faith of the one, and the reproach of the other.

"Our rulers and teachers in Jerusalem care nothing for him. Without any basis they accuse him of wanting to destroy the temple and undermine our traditions. They want to do away with him! You know this! Only two months ago they picked up rocks to stone him! Their spies are everywhere, and he cannot move about freely as he once did."

This is news to Reumah, who gasps at the idea of anyone wanting to destroy the Master. The idea that he has enemies is almost as unsettling as the resolute anger of Mary's demeanor.

Martha takes hold of her sister, almost roughly.

"The words he spoke to me now on the pathway…were more than mere words of consolation. He spoke to me of the resurrection! He spoke words…of life. Yes, life-giving words. How can you harden your heart against him?"

Her voice almost trembles with outrage now, and she turns to look at all of them, including Reumah.

"I cannot pretend to know all the ways of the Lord, nor the reason for his delay. I only know this: he is the Anointed One! He is greater than my brother's death, and he will not be shunned. He will be honored by our house today, and you know my brother would have it so as well! Do it for the sake of his memory if nothing else." She turns back to Mary, and the two sisters lock eyes.

"I tell you he is here. And asking for you."

Without another word, Mary gets up and leaves the courtyard. The entire crowd of comforters, including Reumah, follows her, murmuring.

"Will she go to him?"

"Perhaps to the tomb?"

"Did you see the look she gave her sister?"

They follow her out the gate and down the path to the outskirts of the village. Minutes pass, and no one speaks, but at the sight of the Master, waiting at the end of the path, Mary breaks into a run, as if an invisible cord has pulled her toward him against her will. She falls to her knees before him.

"Lord, Lord…" she begins, but she is overtaken by her sobs. The Master says nothing, only looks down on her. The men behind him are silent. The crowd of onlookers, made up of family members, visitors from the city, and further back, some of the servants, falls silent as well. It is as if the entire countryside has stopped moving for a moment: even the birds are silent, and nothing is heard except the loud cries of Mary at his feet.

"Lord…if you had only been here…if you had only been here…" She looks up at him with unabashed grief and reproach.

"…my brother would not have died!"

The words of Mary, at least to Reumah's ears, are a thinly cloaked accusation, and they unleash a flood of anguished weeping throughout the entire crowd. It is as if Mary has spoken for them all. The Master takes his eyes off Mary for a moment, and he surveys the crowd.

Reumah is shocked by his expression.

There is sorrow, yes, but something more—something like a deep anger. At the moment she imagines he must be angry at Death itself. She imagines he must think of Death as the ultimate enemy of all those he loves, and in this case, victorious in battle.

A few years later she would find out the truth of that moment: she would find out from John, the master's dearest friend, that the Master was not angry in the face of Death at all, but only at their lack of faith in believing he was more powerful than Death. But at the moment, she thinks as she does, and her heart sinks at the expression of his anger.

The eyes of all, including Mary, are on him, and it seems he must summon strength to keep his emotions in check. In a restrained voice he asks to be taken to the grave.

By this time Martha has come up as well, and together the sisters, followed by Caliah and the rest of the family, approach the cave where they have buried Lazarus. At the sight of the tomb, they all begin to weep afresh. As the cries of the children rise up, the Master suddenly sways, unable to prevent himself from partaking in their grief. Reumah gasps at the sight of tears running down his cheeks.

After a few moments of unrestrained weeping, he takes a step toward the cave.

"Remove it...remove the stone," he says in a choked voice, turning to some of the men.

"No, Lord!" Martha calls out. Mary is standing beside her, but Reumah is behind them, and cannot see their faces. "Lord, it is the fourth day since his death...please...the stench will be overwhelming."

"Martha..."

"Lord...we are honored that you have come to console us, and wish to pay homage to our brother at his tomb. But please...exposing his remains would be a desecration, would it not?" At this she steps over to him, whispering words that no one but the Lord hears, but Reumah imagines they have something to do with the lack of appropriate ointments to anoint his body.

He turns back from the men by the tomb and looks at her directly.

"Did I not tell you before...only believe? Believe and you will see the glory of God." He then motions for them to move the stone.

After that everything happened so quickly that it is difficult to remember. Much later she would tell John that it had been like a dream, and he would say yes, and if there hadn't been so many witnesses no one would have believed them. She would always remember the women and most of the men covering their noses and mouths with headscarves as the men began to roll the heavy stone. She remembered some of the women and children staring in horror, and Caliah kneeling down and clutching her youngest. She remembers being surprised that no ghastly odor assaulted them when the stone was rolled away, and simultaneously seeing Martha lower her veil from her face in astonishment.

She remembered the Master looking up to heaven, and giving thanks in a loud voice, which seemed odd, in the face of death. He called the Almighty *Abba*, and she was so struck by that that she barely heard anything else he said.

His prayer was brief, and as soon as he was done he commanded Lazarus, in a voice loud enough for the throng to hear, to come forth from the tomb. He commanded it as if he expected to be obeyed—as if Lazarus had been simply detained for a few days, and was waiting patiently for permission to rejoin his family.

And then Lazarus appeared, at the entrance of the tomb.

Lazarus appeared, swathed in burial linens, and with a cloth about his head. The entire crowd, including Reumah, was immobilized. No one even breathed.

The Master surveyed them in wonder, as if surprised at their reaction. He stepped toward Martha and Mary. From behind the sisters, Reumah could see that Mary's entire form was trembling. Martha fell to his feet, but he drew her up.

"My Lord...my God—" she began, but it appeared that she was about to swoon.

"What are you waiting for? Take off the grave clothes! Release him!"

After this, so many things happened at once that it would take days and days of all of them retelling what they had witnessed to have any sense of the event.

Lazarus, when they asked him, always said that it was as if he had been caught between earth and heaven...that he had felt himself drawn toward a bright light, unafraid, but that something detained him.

"I felt at peace, as if I was asleep...and could not move from my bed."

Martha was the one who had unwound his headcloth, laughing and crying at once. Caliah and the children embraced him, almost fearfully.

No one could utter a sensible word. Everyone reached out to touch him as he went through the crowd, holding Jabez in his arms. There was such a cacophony of joyous exclamations that very few people noticed the Master and his disciples slipping away.

But one man, whom no one seemed to know, Reumah saw, did not share in the joy of the occasion. He seemed bent on some other sinister purpose, and slipped away quickly, toward the city. Reumah wondered if he was one of the spies of the Pharisees. She suddenly felt cold with dread. Her attention was soon diverted though, toward Mary.

At the moment of Lazarus's appearing, Mary had fainted, but no one had noticed in all the excitement that followed, and she would have been trampled had it not been for Tobias, who caught hold of her when she collapsed, and laid her on his cloak. He was now was fanning her with a large palm frond. Reumah ran over and knelt beside them.

"Mary, my friend...my sister..." She took hold of Mary's hands and rubbed them in her own, forgetting, amid the exhilaration of the event, her friend's anger toward her.

After a moment, Mary's eyes opened, and she stared at Reumah, who smiled at her uncertainly.

"Please say something...please tell us you are all right."

Mary looked at Tobias and then back at Reumah again.

"It was true...my dream of the seabird..."

"Indeed. It was from the Giver of Dreams himself."

"And yet...I did not believe it. I did not believe him..." she covered her face with her hands.

"He is merciful and kind. He will forgive you."

"After all he has done for me...I chose to believe the worst...

"He will forgive you."

Mary looked at Reumah, as if noticing her for the first time.

"And you! I chose to believe the worst of you as well! My faithful friend, who remained at my side throughout the valley of the shadow of death...I humiliated and accused you in the vilest way!"

"All is forgiven, my friend. The Master will not withhold his forgiveness; why would I?"

Mary put out her hands, and Tobias pulled her to her feet. She turned to Reumah and embraced her, unmindful of the lingering onlookers. The two women clung to each other and their act of extending and receiving forgiveness was like a vial of perfume that had been broken open and poured out lavishly, its fragrance now rising and filling the air. All who witnessed the scene could not help but remark at the irony—life had replaced death, hope had replaced despair, and forgiveness had replaced strife: such was the fragrance that lingered in the places and paths where the Master trod.

35

"Not long now."

Jean-Denis glances toward them as he says it, and then replaces his stethoscope into his ears and onto Jeb's chest again. Of the three of them—Clive, Vina, and Jean-Denis—the dark man seems the most despondent. He sighs deeply and makes the sign of the cross over himself after he removes the stethoscope.

Vina looks at Clive.

"No need for you to be here, is there?"

"Um…well, I suppose not. I guess you'll be calling me…"

"Of course. You'll be the first on my list."

"And are you…staying?"

Vina settles herself into the ugly puce-colored chair next to Jeb's bed. She kicks off her shoes and places her feet up on the bed close to the dying man. A faint, cheesy odor is emitted from them, but Clive is too polite to indicate that he has noticed. Vina crosses her ankles and her arms and looks up at him.

"To the bitter end."

But instead of returning to the Shiloh Inn, Clive finds himself parked in front of his brother's home. He sits in his car trying to figure out where Jennifer might be, since he can't see her car parked anywhere along the street. He thinks of going inside to say hi to his brother and the family. That would be an appropriate, uncle-ish thing to do, he thinks, when Jennifer pulls up in her little Toyota. He waves at her.

He manages to open her door just as she is getting out of her car, and feels bolstered by his gallantry. She looks up at him with some surprise.

"I've just seen your fiancé." He is relieved to have something important to discuss with her, and is pleased that he has her immediate attention.

"Is he—still—um—is he OK?" In the semidarkness of the early evening her eyes seem large with fear and something else—like a person who surmounts a small hill and confronts an endless vista. She seems slightly dazed.

He hates that he can't just say it. There must be a way to tell her gently. His brother would know what to say. His brother's wife would know what to say. What the hell is the matter with him? Her eyes have that wet look again, or maybe he just imagines it. Her lips are soft and shaped into an expectant smile and he has to look away to keep from grabbing her and kissing them.

He glances toward her car and sees a garment bag hanging in the back.

"Hey…is that *the dress*?"

"Yes. I just got it. How's my groom? Really?"

"He's—um—well…let's just say…it can't happen soon enough."

"Really?"

"Really."

"OK, then. Tomorrow morning. Nine o'clock. Will that work for you?"

"Sure. Sure, I'll be there."

"Thanks. I'll go make sure Clay's on board."

"I can take care of that. I'm heading in there now. I'll square it away with him."

"Oh, would you? That'd be great! Thanks. I'm kind of tired."

"No problem. Here, let me get that."

He follows her into the house, carrying the dress, watching her rounded derriere—compressed attractively in tight jeans—shimmy back and forth as she walks, and at that moment there seems to be nothing about her that isn't perfect, except that she is marrying another man.

Who is almost dead, he reminds himself, smiling, with the assurance of a man who believes the only real obstacle to his happiness is about to be permanently removed.

Jennifer hangs the dress on the door of the closet near her bed. She thinks Clive might have a little crush on her, but then again, she has thought that of his brother Clay as well, but dismisses it, because it seems impossible now that she knows Rebecca better. Rebecca is remarkable, Jennifer thinks. She would have liked Rebecca to be her bridesmaid, sort of, but she felt too shy to ask.

Rebecca is one of those people who can inspire people to love the whole world, and want to do good things, which is why Jennifer chooses tea instead of wine to drink while she reads Rebecca's book. She feels that Rebecca's book should be read with a sense of reverence, like the prayer book in a church pew, and she is determined to read as much of it as she can. She hopes that it is more interesting than a prayer book.

She brushes her teeth and puts on clean, pink-striped pajamas that she bought herself for Christmas, which she does every year, whether she needs them or not, because her mother always bought her pajamas for Christmas. She gets into bed, and reads the first chapter: it is about a prostitute who lived in Bible times, apparently. She can't help but wonder what her mother was thinking when she read this.

She takes a sip of tea, and feels so happy she can almost weep, because the pieces of her life are coming together magnificently: she is getting married tomorrow to the only man she has ever loved. True, her groom is slipping away, but he will leave his name and his money to her and her unborn child, which has greatly lessened the sadness of his passing. And a new friend helped her find the perfect wedding dress. And now she is reading the book that this friend wrote, and her mother loved, and her mother, somehow, must be smiling over all of this, sitting on her porch in heaven and probably right next to Jesus, who, she imagines, is telling her mother not to worry; he is working it all out.

At precisely eight o'clock the next morning her alarm goes off and she has to think for a minute. She has to think for a few minutes, because her brain is foggy from lack of sleep and so full of images from Rebecca's book that she is having trouble reconnecting her mind to her real life.

The book is a story about a girl named Reumah who becomes involved with Judas, the disciple who betrays Jesus, and who ends up betraying her as well. She remembers Judas of course—even a lapsed Catholic would—but she can't remember what happened to him after he betrayed Jesus, and she also can't remember if Reumah is a real person in the Bible. There are other people in the story that are right out of the Bible, but it's been years since she read about them, and the details of their Biblical roles are hazy. She feels a bit embarrassed by this. She feels that she should remember more of what she learned back then, but it was brain-numbingly tedious at the time, and the noisy boys at the back of the class who said bad words and made her laugh and teased her were so distracting. Sister Yolanda would tell them that they would all end up in hell if they didn't settle down and pay attention, and this would subdue her giggling, temporarily at least, but the boys didn't seem to care.

She turns her head and sees the pale dress hanging on the closet door. In the diffused light of the drapes it cannot help but remind her of a ghost or an angel, hovering just beyond her bedside. She hopes it is an angel. In Rebecca's story there was a dream of a seabird being resurrected, which was a portent. It was followed by the actual resurrection of Lazarus, which is the last thing she read before she fell asleep at two-thirty in the morning, and the first thing she thought of when she woke up. She knows the story of Lazarus is in the Bible: Rebecca didn't make that up. She decides she should try and find it in the Bible and read it again. She could ask Rebecca where it is, but then Rebecca would know that she had not paid close attention to the Bible stories in catechism class, or her own mother's funeral, for that matter.

In the shower she closes her eyes and the water streams over her hair and her face, and she thinks again of Rebecca's made-up story, and how she put it together, somehow, with what really happened, according to the Bible, and how those ordinary men and women living back then probably had no idea that they'd end up in the Bible, and probably they would have laughed at the idea of anyone speculating or writing stories about them two millennia later. It would be like some writer saying to her, today, that he was going to write a story of her life, and it would be read and mused about far, far in the future and for all eternity.

Just go on and do whatever you're planning to do, but I already know how it all works out.

That's what the writer would say.

She wishes it were true. She wishes there were an author who was writing her life, and already knew how everything would turn out, and could somehow assure her, however obliquely, that her story would be happy, and never really end, because it was part of a great universal story, made up of all the other stories, like a rope of a thousand cords, bound together and going on forever.

The jangling of the phone in his dream and next to his bed rouses Clay from sleep. In his dream it is Bob calling, as usual, but Clay doesn't realize it's a dream when he answers the phone.

"Hey, buddy," he says into the mouthpiece.

There is a pause, followed by Clive saying, "Uh—how'd you know it was me?"

It takes Clay a second to realize that it is not Bob on the phone, and it will never again be Bob on the phone. His head flops back onto the pillow, and his mouth goes on autopilot to have a brief conversation with his brother; his eyes remain closed, unprepared as yet to take in the bright sunrays mounting the wall beyond the bed. When he hangs up, he is filled with an odd mixture of dread and disappointment. He knows he should pray for strength. He knows this. He has preached it to his people.

"*God's mercies are new every morning,*" he has told his people. "*That should affect your entire outlook from the moment you open your eyes...mercy is not getting the punishment you deserve...it's the policeman not giving you the ticket after all...it's the lab report coming back negative...*"

He has told them all this, and many similar truths. He can craft a sermon now from a few verses of Scripture and a story from *Reader's Digest*, as easily he can construct a shelf or a step stool.

He tries to put his brain into prayer mode and hears the water from the shower upstairs running through the old pipes in the walls, and for a few seconds he permits himself to imagine Jennifer with her eyes closed and her hair slicked back and her naked breasts, slippery-wet, after which he feels so guilty that he turns his head toward Rebecca's pillow, and is relieved to see the bed empty.

It amazes him how little sleep she needs to function, whereas he requires a full eight hours a night and supplementary naps.

He can hear her slippers padding about in the kitchen. She is making coffee and toast and cheesy eggs, probably, or maybe Cream of Wheat with butter and cinnamon sugar; the kind of breakfasts his mother would have never cooked, not if she lived a hundred years.

"You don't know how blessed you are," he tells his kids at the table, about twenty minutes later, looking especially at the older boys. "Having a mother cook a hot breakfast for you every day…" They stare at him blankly, looking up from their cereal bowls. They glance at each other and then resume eating.

Dad's in a weird mood.

That's what their glances mean. He knows it. He did it too, with his brothers.

She smiles at him over their heads. She is humming and the kitchen is warm with sunbeams and the smell of buttered toast and coffee, and he knows he should be happy. He should be happy and thankful and eternally grateful.

"Hold on, guys…let's say grace," Rebecca says, looking at him. Bee-Bee, sitting next to him in her high chair, watches him solemnly, her index finger delicately plying her left nostril. He feels a tightening in his chest.

I can't. It won't mean anything.

But of course he does. He says the same old thing: *Father, thanks for this food and for Mommy making it for us, and a good night's rest and for all you give us,* and so on. It satisfies them.

It satisfies his kids, but he can feel his wife's eyes on him. She pours coffee into his cup, and he grabs her other hand and kisses it, as if to reassure her.

He feels like a complete imposter.

The hum of the ventilator lulled them both to sleep, apparently, but Vina is first to awaken. She looks at the clock on the dresser, which says 8:35, and then at his chest, which is still, somehow, moving up and down in a herky-jerky way, as if being forced to move against its will.

Ridiculous.

She heads into the bathroom and pees and then confronts herself in the mirror. *Ridiculous*, she says again. *He should be dead.*

She thinks over all the reasons why he should be dead, and they are all good reasons. Furthermore, she can't think of one good reason why he should be kept alive, barely breathing on a machine.

I know him, she says to her face in the mirror, which is puffy from lack of sleep, and has a thick red line along the cheek which was imprinted by a seam in the puce-colored chair.

I know him enough to know that he would not want this.

She washes her face and gazes, clear-eyed, at her reflection, mentally asking a question.

Can you do it?

Jean-Denis's head rests on his arms on the bed next to Jeb. His face is turned toward her, and she can see a small amount of spittle dangling from his open mouth.

She glances again at the clock, which now says 8:42.

Five minutes. Just give him five minutes.

She unplugs the ventilator and watches the clock. She forces herself to watch the clock and nothing else, and the pulse in her head is so loud she can't hear anything else.

At 8:47 she plugs the ventilator back in.

At 8:49 she wakes Jean-Denis.

"I think we've lost him," she says, in a low voice as smooth as caramel.

Jean-Denis stares at her and then looks at Jeb.

"Saint Marie!" he says and fumbles for his stethoscope, and then "Merde!" in softer tones. He puts his head in his hands for a whole minute, while Vina stands behind him, crossing and uncrossing her arms, and tapping her foot. She wishes it were already a week from now. She wants to clean up and clear out of here and get on with everything else.

She goes into the living room to make calls. When Clive and Clay and Jennifer arrive at precisely 8:55—Jennifer absurdly attired in an ivory lace dress and carrying a bouquet of yellow tulips—she is still on the phone, and it is Jean-Denis who opens the door to them, and Jean-Denis who tells them.

"He is gone..." he says. "I'm so sorry."

XXXVI

*A*n earsplitting clap of thunder over the house of Simon silences the entire company. A fierce wind blows through the lattices, causing them to rattle violently, and extinguishes the flames of most of the lamps. The few flickering lamps that remain create large, unnatural shadows on the walls of the large upper room before they smolder and expire. The pelting rain becomes deafening. A few stifled screams from the women are heard and some of the men laugh uncomfortably, as if trying not to panic.

Judas is much more annoyed than alarmed. His scheme for the evening has been effectively thwarted by the unexpected storm. As one accustomed to conducting business at night, his eyes, out of habit, immediately seek the dim light of the nearest window. The blackness of the room now makes the lightning flashes more ominous and present, like arrows propelled by fierce demons with a view to sabotaging the festive gathering, illuminating the wary faces of the guests. Some, but not all, are slightly drunk; most shift about nervously. Judas sits perfectly still, sober and alert as an owl waiting to pounce on its prey. In the darkness he cannot sense the eyes of the Master on him, and so he has come to welcome the darkness as one would welcome a heavy cloak on a cold night.

"To the lamps!" shouts their host in an abrupt, infuriated tone, and two servants, their faces flushed with exertion, rush about relighting the lamps surrounding the couches. Gradually the room becomes golden-bright again, and the entire company relaxes and resumes eating and talking. More servants pass with baskets of fresh bread and salted fish and olives, and a wine steward comes forward to refill the cups, begin-ning with the guest of honor and his friends, and then the host, who is called Simon the Leper.

Judas has done business with Simon—that is, he had gone back sev-eral times to call on him, and remind him of his obligation to the Master. Each time he had a received generous donation. This was, of course, done covertly, without the Master's consent, nor any of the men who accom-panied him. Judas did not feel it was necessary for the others to know all the ways he was able to provide for their upkeep. They seemed more like ignorant youths than grown men, and he felt that it was beneath himself to disclose his business dealings with such small minds.

His host is called Simon the Leper because he had the dreaded dis-ease for many years, and lived on the outskirts of the town, as the law required, in a small but richly appointed shelter. He lived there as an outcast, yet his wealth and family were not diminished, for he owned extensive vineyards, and every day his trusted stewards and servants came with his food and reports of his produce as well as news of his wife and children. But one day, shortly after Mary, the sister of Lazarus, had been healed of her affliction (he was told that her mind and her face were put to rights in the same instance), he saw the Master com-ing up the road leading into Bethany, and, gathering his robes, he ran out to meet him. He prostrated himself in the dust of the road before the Master and his disciples.

"Rabbi, I beg you to heal me. Please make me whole, and I will give you a tithe of everything I own." In his mind Judas immediately began to assess what a tithe of Simon's wealth might be. He was disap-pointed, but not surprised, when he heard the Master's response.

"Simon of Bethany, you cannot buy what God alone can give."

"Then, Master, I beg of you...grant to me what only God can give, and I will give a tithe to the temple."

"There is no cure that can be bought for the disease you have; the word of God alone can heal you."

At that moment Simon had lifted his swollen face from the dust, and stared up at the Master. A small crowd of onlookers had gathered, and Simon became flustered.

"Lord, I know...I have heard...I believe...that if you say the word, I will be healed."

"You have heard correctly. God has healed you...go in peace."

The Master had called him Simon of Bethany and pronounced him healed, which he was from that moment, but the name of Simon the Leper remained, largely because its owner sought to distinguish himself from Simon the tax collector, who also lived at the edge of town, close by the road near his tax collection booth. Despite his wealth, the tax collector is a pariah, whose clothes reek of cumin and whose fingernails grow to obscene lengths. He is the only man of wealth in the town who has not been invited to Simon's banquet.

The banquet was Judas's idea, although he of course does not take credit for this. It was not difficult to persuade Simon to hold the feast in honor of the Master, because the wealthy man had long desired to display his riches as well as his gratitude for the healing. Judas had had another motive for requesting the banquet, and the timing of it was crucial: it was two days before the Feast of Unleavened Bread, and he was hoping to take care of some distasteful but necessary business before the Feast, because what he had to do might cause an unpleasant scene, and if it were during the Feast, the unpleasant scene might escalate into a riot, which would put him in an awkward position. He much preferred to conduct his business covertly. The unforeseen storm had put an end to his plan, which is why he now sits, in sober contemplation, trying to drown out the idle prattle of the other guests, and the annoying voice of his host, in order to devise an alternate way to accomplish his purpose.

Simon sits close to the Master at the long, low table, and when the lights have been relit, he raises his cup and his voice so that the entire room hears his words.

"Good Teacher, clearly you have no fear of darkness or storms. Let us now drink in praise of your courage!"

The guests drink and murmur approvingly. Most are in awe of Simon's wealth and lavish feast, and are inclined to commend anything their host will say. Throughout the banquet he has been repeating similar praises in honor of the Master, so that the entire room can hear.

The Master's eyes scan the room wearily, and those closest to him observe him sigh, aware that he would much prefer to converse with true friends rather than listen, all evening, to the praise of flattering lips. After a moment he speaks.

"I fear neither darkness nor light, for they are as one to me. In the light, men honor me with their lips, but in the darkness, their hearts are far from me."

Perhaps his remarks are meant for their host—it would not be the first time the Master has made blunt comments to the host of a banquet, apparently unconcerned as to whether he is invited back again. But to Judas it seems lately that every word that falls from the Master's lips is designed to sear his heart, or rouse in him a sort of guilt or conviction; if the Master were truly wise he would know the truth—that his words are falling on deaf ears, and if any emotion is aroused within the heart of Judas it is that of disappointment, not guilt.

In truth, he is profoundly disillusioned.

He has spent the last three years of his life accompanying the Master around the entire Judean countryside, sleeping often on the cold, damp earth, like a foul-smelling shepherd, with little but stale bread and salted fish to eat. He has spent weeks of his life in the company of some of the most stupid men he has ever known, and he has had to scrounge and shift about to get money in the most discomforting ways. True, they have been invited to many lavish banquets, such as this one, and had been welcomed into some wealthy homes, but the Master, for inexplicable reasons, rarely seems to gravitate to men of great wealth or influence or position, and has, in fact, made enemies of the very people with whom Judas would most desire to ingratiate himself. Judas had hoped to gain much in attaching himself to the Master, but after three years he has come to see that it has all been a cunning ruse, an illusion on the part of the Master to ensnare him and the others to do his will and fulfill his own purpose. As a rule, Judas admires ambitious men; he understands, more than most, that occasionally it is necessary to exploit others for one's own gain or to accomplish one's own agenda, but in this instance he cannot excuse or forgive the Master for using him, and he has, over time, allowed the seeds of sedition to grow unchecked within his heart.

"You, sir, did not seem afraid of the dark just now," says a smooth female voice above him, pulling him out of his dark contemplation. A servant girl, pausing to refill his cup, smiles down at him. Judas smiles back at her, without offering his cup.

"Clearly you are not lacking in boldness either...what is your name?"

"I am Sariah. I was not afraid as I stood next to you, sir, and sensed your bravery in the dark."

Judas laughs nonchalantly, as one accustomed to having women flirt with him. She is a pretty girl, with full lips and a large bosom. Her charms are not lost on him.

"Well, then...I shall hope, my dear, that we soon have another spell of darkness...perhaps you will discover more things about me that will please you." The young woman laughs and gives him a knowing look before she moves on to another guest's cup; he knows instinctively that she will be back. When she moves away, he perceives the eyes of Lazarus on him, who sits across the room, and the smile that played on his lips for the girl's benefit is replaced by a scowl.

Judas has reason to believe that Lazarus is a spy for the Master as well as an informant. He wishes the man had stayed dead; his resurrection occurred at a very inconvenient time and he is aware of a plot now to kill Lazarus as well as the Master. His intention is to deliver the Master right into the hands of those who seek to destroy him, for a fee, of course. It will not be too difficult to deliver Lazarus to them as well, for an additional fee. But the storm has curtailed—temporarily—his plans.

If he had known that they wanted Lazarus dead as well he could have arranged it four nights ago, when he was at another banquet, held in the Master's honor by Lazarus himself. As it was he had been distracted—unhappily—by Mary, the sister of Lazarus, who, in what must have been a fit of manic hysteria such as is common to silly young women, had poured an entire vial of spikenard on the Master's feet as he reclined, weeping over him as if he were already dead. She went so far as to unveil her head, and applied her long hair, like a towel, to wipe his feet. It was almost obscene. He was not the only one present who had been stunned that the Master had not reproved her. Thereafter the entire house reeked of the perfume for days, and even now the scent lingered on the Master and his closest friends and all their clothes, despite the rain and wind.

Judas had been at a loss to know why the woman would so stupidly waste such a costly substance, and he was particularly incensed to discover afterward, on examining the empty vial, that it had been the same vial he had recently returned to her. He could not remain silent.

"What a waste!" he said, glaring pointedly at her, and loudly enough for Lazarus to hear as well, for he felt it was largely the fault of the older brother for not supervising her more strictly. "This perfume could have been sold, and much money given to the poor!"

The others, for once, agreed with him, and most of them castigated her as well for her careless waste. Lazarus remained silent, but the Master, of course, had spoken up.

"Leave her alone," he said to them all. "She was saving this perfume to be used as it was intended…for my burial." He looked at her in a knowing way, as if they shared a conspiracy, and Judas could stand it no more. "As to the poor…" he went on, but Judas could not bear to hear anymore.

He had left the room, only to see Reumah standing near the door. She held onto the frame of the door, as if needing support because of the shock induced by Mary's careless act. He had watched her for a moment, trying to gauge her reaction, and then quietly edged over to where she was standing.

"No doubt you see the lunacy of that wasteful act, do you not? You are a wiser girl, I think…you would never allow your precious vial to be expended in such a thoughtless way. She is obviously vying for attention."

Reumah turned to him, with a dazed expression on her face.

"No," she said. "She did it because she loves him so dearly, and had not the words to express it."

Judas made a grim, disgusted face, as if he had just come across a pile of dung or an open wound.

"In truth, there is not a man or woman on earth that could induce me to waste so extravagantly."

"I do not doubt your words," she answered. He perceived a reproof in the arch of her back as she turned away from him, but he did not care.

He pretends not to notice the eyes of Lazarus on him, although, in fact, he is deeply insulted by the man's scrutiny, and he resolves to abet his assassination in any way he can. A deep anger churns within him, and he rises from his place at the banquet, on the pretense of going out to relieve himself. The servant girl, Sariah, catches his eye before he descends one of the narrow staircases leading from the banquet hall, and she winks at him, but he does not return her look. He needs time to think before she comes to find him in one of the lower rooms.

His reasoning is this: clearly the Master has some supernatural power, for Judas himself has seen the miracles and witnessed his power over hunger, disease, death, demons, and even the elements. What is not so obvious, at least to Judas, is the source of the power. He is determined, therefore, to hand the Master over to those who would destroy him. If the Master is divinely appointed by God himself, surely God will not let his own die. But if not, if the Master's power is from the devil or a demon, as many of the Pharisees hold to be true, then he will die, and should die, for claiming to be the son of God and deceiving so many hapless and unsuspecting souls. The genius of Judas's plan warms and comforts him; it has become the central purpose of his otherwise miserable life, like the gleam of gold in a murky stream.

He is hardly surprised, after a quarter of an hour or so, to see a veiled woman enter one of the lower rooms of Simon's large house, passing a number of goats and some oxen that are being sheltered there against the storm. The lower rooms are narrow and dimly lit, and filled with the smells of warm animals and fodder. Toward the back, where the kitchens are, there is a platform, piled with straw. A group of children are sleeping on it, no doubt the offspring of some of the household servants.

He rises to meet the woman, taking a lamp in his hand, and is taken aback at the sight of her dripping cloak.

"You need not have exposed yourself to the storm on my behalf, my dear girl—" But then he stops suddenly when she removes her veil.

It is Reumah. In the dim light of the lamp, they stare at each other in awkward embarrassment, as if the circumstances have caused them both to remember their clandestine meetings on the roof of Zerah's house. Reumah glances down quickly and then looks up at him, refusing to be daunted by his presence.

He perceives immediately that she has come to the banquet, uninvited, and with a specific purpose. On further appraisal, he discovers that she is clutching her vial against her bosom, and his brain instantly apprehends why she is there.

"Surely not," he whispers. "Surely you will not fall prey to the same lunacy that seized your friend the other night."

"What some call lunacy, she—and others—would recognize as worship."

"No one in their right mind will call it *worship*, I assure you."

"The one who is worshiped will surely know what it is, for he discerns the motives of our hearts. As to the others—their opinions are nothing to me."

He takes a deep breath, trying to gain time, and convinced that he has come to her at precisely the right moment. He is determined to thwart her. He is appalled and exasperated at the stupidity of these women; how easily they allow themselves to be duped by the Master, pursuing him like senseless sheep after a shepherd. At the same time, he cannot give vent to his irritation, for fear of driving her away and making her more determined to defy him.

"Reumah—"

"Do not attempt to dissuade me."

He wets his lips and chooses his words carefully.

"Please! Listen for one moment, I beg of you."

"Why should I listen to anything you tell me?"

"Quite right. I have not always dealt with you—uh—in the most judicious manner."

"Your words mean nothing. You are wasting my time. Let me pass."

"Reumah, I beg of you. For your own sake, do not do it! You will live to regret it." He pauses for a moment, and looks around him, as if to ensure that no others are listening. Then he leans close to her.

"I did not wish to make it known to you, but perhaps you are already aware that the Master has many enemies, and it's very likely he will soon be…arrested."

"Impossible. Even if that were true—he has done nothing wrong. The charges would be dismissed."

"I wish it were so, but you must believe me. Not only will the charges *not* be dismissed, but more likely he will be sentenced—to death."

"You speak lies to frighten me."

"Lies? You heard him the other night, did you not? He spoke of your friend Mary anointing him for his *burial*."

At this she flinches. He swiftly pursues his point. "The charges against him have to do with our laws, which he continually subverts."

"Liar!" she almost screams the word but he quickly grabs her by the arms.

"Would you call your father a liar?"

"What?"

"Your father and our esteemed leaders and the entire Sanhedrin have branded him an insurgent of Roman law, and a blasphemer, both charges worthy of the death penalty!"

"You can't prove it!"

"Listen…" he says, pulling her close. He can see her fingers, white-knuckled, clutching the vial to her chest.

"What would your father say if you were to take this priceless gift of his and waste it on a criminal, condemned to die?"

They lock eyes, and he is certain he has convinced her. In the bowels of Simon's house, the sounds of the storm are muffled and distant. He can hear her breathing. He can hear the animals breathing and the sleeping children breathing, and the sound of it makes him edgy and claustrophobic, as if the hapless creatures are sucking away the air he requires to breathe. Reumah, however, is acutely aware of the contrast between the ruthless storm outside, and this warm, softly lit room, filled with the breath of sleeping children and blameless animals, as if a spirit of shalom has descended on it. She gazes, for a moment, at the little ones on the straw, wrapped in their mothers' cloaks and spooned against one another for warmth. A surge of longing fills her—to be free of her past, to put aside every reminder of it, and to move toward a future that dawns with hope. Reluctantly she looks up to Judas again.

"I know my father. If he truly believes the Master deserves to die, then it can only be because he does not know him as I know him. But if he does know him, then he will not only forgive this expenditure, but will commend me for it."

He sucks in his breath. He gazes at her in disbelief, and then his lips curl into a sneer.

"You are a bigger fool than I thought: the Master shall pay for his subversion, I assure you, and you will come to rue this night, when you and your friends have become poor and persecuted. Since you will not heed me now, I will not heed your cries for mercy later. I am done with you."

He turns his back on her and pulls his cloak about him, intending to head into the night, but is thwarted, again, by the tempestuous rain. With an irate sigh he turns toward the stairs, having no other recourse but to return to the banquet. Next to the lower steps is a stack of cages filled with turtledoves that have been placed there to shelter the birds from the storm. In a fit of anger he flings the topmost cage to the floor. The shrill cries of the birds and frantic whir of their wings fill his ears as he ascends, but his act of violence does nothing to assuage the venomous fury of his heart.

It is as if the Master expected her—as if the true worshiper that he had sought throughout the duration of the banquet had finally appeared before him, for he immediately sat upright, smiled warmly, and inclined his ear toward her as she drew near.

And so she drew near, she whispered something to him, which no one heard save the Master himself, and then she broke her vial open and poured the perfume onto his head, so that it ran down, down, on his hair and beard and shoulders and robe...*like precious oil...running down on Aaron's beard...like the dew of Hermon falling on Mt. Zion*, he said, and laughed joyously as if he were enjoying a good joke, and the entire house and every soul present breathed in the smell of spikenard.

At first there was silence. Many were stunned and then outraged at the sight of a striking, young, wet-haired woman, her luminous eyes lined with kohl, her earrings and nose-ring sparkling in the lamplight, pouring perfume onto his head, pouring it on while she laughed as he laughed, and cried with relief, as one whose love had been suppressed too long but now had been declared to all.

Then there was murmuring, which became louder.

"Obviously drunk," they sneered.

"A harlot…and yet he permits her to touch him…in front of us all! How disgusting!"

"He should know better."

But his words toward her eclipsed the harsh comments of the guests, and the insensitive rebukes of his friends, and were the only words she remembered from that night.

"Let her alone, let her alone. Why are you bothering her? She has done a beautiful thing to me…such a beautiful thing…"

"Such useless waste. First Mary, now this woman." The men around him spoke to each other, but loudly enough for the Master to hear. "We could have taken both their vials and fed an entire city of beggars!"

"You will always have the poor. You can help them anytime." He looked at them earnestly, and said, in a quieter voice, "You will not always have me."

Then he looked at Reumah again, and a look passed between them, as if they had an understanding.

"She did what she could."

The Master's voice rang out again in her defense.

"I tell you the truth: wherever the good news is preached throughout the entire world, what she has done will also be told, in her memory."

Simon the leper despised him from that moment on. He was appalled that the strange act of lewdness of this unnamed, uninvited woman obviously carried more merit with the Master than the honor and generosity of his sumptuous banquet. He felt the full insult of it, and resolved never to invite him again, nor to give any more "donations" to his friend Judas.

Judas shut out his words. He rose from his place, and gathered his cloak around him, and went down the stairs and into the night. His anger and his hatred were like a hard shell about him, and made him impervious to the rain.

The one called John, who was known as the Master's closest friend, sat nearby. He alone had remained quiet, and had observed her with the Master the entire time. From the moment she broke the vial, using her teeth to unstop the seal, he loved Reumah.

He loved her with his whole heart from that time on.

37

The words of Jean-Denis are immediately absorbed by Clive and Clay.

Clive says, "Ah…" and presses his lips together, determined to say nothing until he can think of the right thing to say.

Clay crosses his arms for a second, and then rests his right elbow on his left hand; his right hand rubs his chin thoughtfully. He suddenly feels very conscious of his body language. He exchanges glances with his brother, then they both looked at Jennifer.

It's as if Jean-Denis has spoken a foreign language that only the two men understand. She stands perfectly still, staring at Jean-Denis, with the tulips clutched in her hands.

"What?"

"I'm sorry, dear lady. He is gone from us."

She looks at Clive, and then Clay. She pushes past Jean-Denis into the living room. Vina, on the phone, shakes her head at Jennifer, and then turns away.

Jennifer runs into the bedroom.

They hear her say, *No!* very loudly.

They hear her say, "No-no-no-no-no…" over and over again. She sounds more angry than distressed. She sounds furious, actually.

She comes out glaring at Jean-Denis.

"What happened?"

She does not wait for him to answer. She turns to Clive.

"You told me he was OK. You told me he was eager for us to get married!" She is yelling now. None of them have ever heard this strident voice before. It occurs to Clive that even though his rival is conveniently dead, he might still have to compete with him in her memory. He had not foreseen this.

She goes into the living room and Vina, still on the phone, mouths the words, "I'm so sorry…" to her.

She grabs the phone out of Vina's hand and throws it onto the couch.

"What the hell?" Vina yells at her, but she is not half as loud or angry as Jennifer, who has turned into a comet with a searing tail. Unconsciously they all back away from her.

She approaches Clay now, brandishing the bouquet of tulips.

"You. You're God's man here."

"Jennifer—"

"No, come on. You believe the Bible, don't you?"

"Of course."

"In the Bible, Lazarus came back to life."

"Yes, he did."

"Don't you believe the Bible??" she is standing right in front of him, her hand on her hip, her other hand still clutching the tulips, which he can smell. He decides some words of Scripture might calm her.

"Jennifer, it says in that story that *Jesus wept*—" but at the name of *Jesus* her eyes widen and blaze, and his mind goes blank.

"Jesus raised Lazarus! It's in your wife's book too! Don't you believe in Jesus?"

"Her book is a fictional account of Jesus—"

"So you *don't* believe in Jesus?"

"It's not that simple—"

"Can Jesus raise Jeb back to life?"

"Theoretically, yes, but—"

"Then, just ask him. Can't you do that? Can't you just ask him for me?"

"Jennifer—please—you're very upset right now—"

"Ask him. Ask him! Don't you believe in him? Why can't you pray to him? You're a fucking useless minister!" She bashes the tulips against his chest, crying now, and Clive, Jean-Denis, and Vina carefully sit down, as if they are taking their seats at a play after the houselights are down and the show has started.

Yellow petals scatter on the rug, and some stick to Clay's sweater. He can hear his pulse, along with the phrase, *fucking useless minister* ringing in his ears, and he knows instinctively that her words have permanently dented his brain. His armpits and back are prickly with heat. He resists the impulse to slap her back to reality, and then bound out of the house and never come back. He actually loathes Jennifer now and decides he has a moral obligation to move himself and his family out of her house at the earliest possible opportunity. It occurs to him that Rebecca has mentioned Jennifer's late-night crying spells, along with the empty wine bottles in the back alley, but he was not overly troubled about it, or the effect her obviously immoral lifestyle might have on his children. In a moment of clarity he realizes that his landlady is not only a drunken slut, but also mentally unbalanced, and he is appalled at himself for ignoring her vices until now.

She stands in the middle of the room, and her eyes, smeared with wet mascara, flash back and forth between them. Then she settles on Clay again, who remains standing with his arms crossed, refusing to be intimidated by her.

"You're a phony. But I believe. I believe in Jesus. I didn't always, but I do now, no thanks to you."

She turns away and heads into Jeb's room, somewhat unsteady on her heels. Clive, despite the circumstances, is struck by the abrupt change in her personality. It's as if she has gone from sex kitten to tigress, and the vision of her in the high-heeled pumps and clingy white dress, bashing the tulips into his brother's chest, strikes him as particularly compelling, to the point of being intimidating. He senses that he is losing some ground. He wonders if he should follow her into the dead man's room, and make an effort to comfort her. He stands awkwardly, but realizes he has no idea of what he should do or say. He sits again.

Clay collapses onto a chair, with a deep sigh, as if he is kindly concerned about Jennifer's fragile state of mind. Nothing could be further from the truth: in his view she almost contrived the event to humiliate him.

Vina digs a cigarette out of her handbag in an effort to keep from laughing. She is secretly delighted that now everyone can see plainly what an idiot Jennifer is. Her part, for now, is to bide her time, and wait for the smoke to clear, and try not to look to exultant. Her lighter expended, she looks around for a light, and Clive quickly obliges. She gets up and walks toward the window, trailing a puff of smoke.

Jean-Denis clears his throat, and takes a pen out of his breast pocket and begins to fill out some forms. Hospice procedure requires him to make some phone calls but he feels compelled, out of defer-ence to the grieving girlfriend, to wait respectfully. In a moment, they can hear Jennifer praying.

They can hear her asking Jesus to make Jeb alive.

Clay shakes his head, and rolls his eyes at Clive, who shrugs, looks down at his hands, and discovers a cuticle that requires his immediate attention. Clay hopes that his brother will not mistakenly place him and Jennifer in the same category of believers in Jesus. His is a historically bolstered, intellectually vigorous faith; the product of calcified ortho-doxy and seminary-trained hermeneutics. Whereas Jennifer…he has plenty of women like her in his congregation: they would not be able to recite the Apostles' Creed to save their lives, but they are the first to go forward at altar calls, and speak in tongues, and yell "hallelujah" after every verse of Scripture quoted from the pulpit, no matter what. They are the first on the dance floor at every wedding, and the last to leave the graveside at every funeral. He can hear their voices, loudest of all, in every worship chorus, and without turning around from his front pew he knows their hands are upraised, and tears are coursing down their cheeks, just as surely as there are crescent stains in their armpits, and pink underwear peeking out of the top of their pants to the amusement of those sitting in the pew behind them.

"The *Flagrant* Ones," he once said to his wife, on the way home from church. "God love 'em," he added, laughing at his spin on her book's title. He is glad they are in the church; they are useful and fer-vent. They *mean* well. There is room at the table for all, but he is also glad he is not anything like them. Rebecca smiled obligingly, and then she looked out the window.

"What does *flagrant* mean?" Nathan asked from the seat behind.

"Sloppy. Indiscreet. Embarrassing, as far as I'm concerned," his father replied. Rebecca turned to look at Nathan.

"Maybe so. But they are also *The Fragrant Ones*. To my way of thinking."

He thinks of these women now, listening to Jennifer calling on Jesus to raise her dead fiancé, and wishes he could explain it to his brother. He wishes he could explain that believers in Jesus express their faith in different ways, and that not everybody cries and sings loudly and is so damn *blatant*, and that there are many who are less embarrassing, and more self-restrained: quiet worshipers who lend dignity to Christ's body on earth and do not check their common sense and self-respect at the door when they enter the kingdom of God.

He clears his throat, and is about to say something—anything—when there is a sudden pause in her praying, followed by a strange sensation, almost like an electric shock, which passes through the room. Jean-Denis looks up from his paperwork. Clive glances up from picking at his fingernails. Vina turns from the window. Clay looks toward the bedroom. Clay is the first to see.

Jeb is standing there.

Jeb is standing at the door of his room, looking at them, his expression a mixture of annoyance and mild curiosity, as when one opens the front door and is confronted by well-dressed proselytizers distributing literature. He glances around the room, and then his eyes rest on Clay.

"Who the hell are you?" he says to Clay.

A few things happen at precisely the same time: Jean-Denis's clipboard falls to the floor, Clive rises from his seat on the couch with a cry of alarm, and Vina utters "Oh my God!" and collapses onto a chair by the window.

Clay stares at Jeb, framed by the door, and is struck by how tall he is. Despite his wispy hair and mottled skin and gaunt frame, he appears larger than life, like an actor with uncontainable stage presence. Clay tries to speak but his mouth doesn't work. It's as if he has forgotten his own name.

Jeb surveys the room. All of the canvases have been packed for shipping, and most of his furniture and personal belongings have disappeared. His expression is that of a man who has returned home after a long trip, and finds his house taken over by squatters.

"Vultures," says Jeb.

"Christ almighty," says Clive.

"*Seigneur...*" says Jean-Denis. "You—you—are alive and well!"

"Damn right," says Jeb. He saunters into the living room. In his sagging pajama bottoms and dirty white undershirt he looks scruffy and disgruntled, like a man rising from a long nap.

"You—" he says to Vina, who is breathing so quickly she is about to hyperventilate. Her hand is spread out on her chest, as if she is afraid her heart will stop.

"You're the queen of the vultures. You wanted me dead more than that flake over here," he says, turning to Clive. "You both can get the hell out of my house."

They oblige him. Vina's hands tremble while she finds her car keys and sunglasses in her handbag. Clay sees them, on the sidewalk outside, talking at the same time. He sees them shake hands before they get into their separate cars and drive away. He wonders when he will see his brother again.

"Who the hell are you?" Jeb says to Clay again.

"I'm—um—Clay Peterson." After a pause he boldly adds, "I'm a minister of the gospel of Jesus Christ," but his tone is that of a man introducing himself at a twelve-step program; as if being a minister of the gospel of Jesus Christ is an addiction he must battle for the rest of his life. His throat is closing up.

"Good for you. What were you doing here? Last rites?"

"I—uh—came to marry you and Jennifer."

"I don't want to marry Jennifer." He turns, and she is standing behind him.

"Jesus made you alive so we can get married," she says to Jeb, in the voice of a very young girl.

Jeb laughs.

"Jesus made me alive because he didn't know what else to do with me. He had one hand on top of me to keep me out of heaven. And he had one hand below me to keep me out of hell. I swear to God, I saw the scars and everything."

"I prayed that he would make you alive and he did. He's giving you another chance."

He steps over to her and pulls her toward him.

"They wanted me dead. You wanted me alive. You all tried to use me. Jesus probably wants to use me. You just want a poppa for your bastard kid."

She is crying again.

"Maybe so. But I love you."

"No, you don't. You love your idea of me."

They do not marry. She returns to her house, and stands in her apartment. She is conscious that her life has abruptly changed course, and she has to stand still for a moment to get her bearings. She goes into her room and removes her dress and slip and stockings and high heels, leaving them in a pile on the floor. The entire outfit seems utterly irrelevant now, as if it belongs to an event that took place a long time ago. She sees Rebecca's book next to her bed and stands motionless, thinking. Then she puts on jeans and sneakers and a turquoise sweat-shirt that says *Ocean Groove*, and goes back downstairs. She knocks at the side door, leading to the kitchen. She hopes Clay is not there. He had left Jeb's house minutes after her.

Nathan answers the door, eying her curiously.

"Hi. Is your mom there?" She glances behind him.

Rebecca comes toward her, her eyes scanning Jennifer's face. She is holding Bee-Bee, who gazes at Jennifer with large cautious eyes. Jennifer suddenly realizes that her face is streaked with mas-cara and lip gloss, and she is still wearing the pearl earrings of her bridal attire.

"I'm sorry to bother you—"

"Not at all. I was just wondering how it went."

"We didn't get married."

"What happened?"

"You'll never believe it."

"Try me. Start at the beginning."

So Jennifer tells Rebecca. She tells her the entire story, including the part about Lazarus. She even tells her what she said to Clay. In her entire life she has never divulged so much information about her life to anyone. Rebecca listens. Bee-Bee falls asleep on her shoulder.

"Do you believe me?" Jennifer says when she is done.

Rebecca does not answer immediately. It's as if she is at the edge of a cliff. She would like to get Clay's version of the event before she jumps. But he has not returned home. She decides to leap, and trust that Jesus will catch her somewhere below the precipice.

"I believe you," she says simply. "I believe you, because I know Jesus. And that sounds just like him."

Clive arrives back at the Shiloh Inn, unmindful of how he got there. At the front desk there are eight messages from his office. The hostess has copied them down carefully, including three that say, *Where the hell are you?* from Roger, his partner at the firm. He gives her a ten-dollar bill. He returns to his room to gather his stuff, and instead sits on his bed with his head in his hands to try to get a hold of himself. He can't believe that Jeb is alive and somehow Jennifer did it with Jesus's help or Jesus did it with Jennifer's help and now Jeb will marry Jennifer and he will never see her again. He cannot imagine how he will live out the rest of his days, knowing that Jeb will wake up beside her soft, beautiful self every morning, and not him.

He calls the office and tells his secretary that he is extremely ill with the flu. He knows Roger will not buy this, but he doesn't care. Then he drives into Asbury Park to find a bar, but none are open at this hour. He finds a liquor store and buys a bottle of gin. Then he goes into a convenience store and buys a pork roll, egg and cheese sandwich, two chocolate bars, and a large bottle of 7 Up.

He drives down to the beach and parks near the boardwalk. He stares out at the ocean, as if noticing it for the first time, alternately guzzling from the 7 Up bottle and the gin, and after a while, just the gin.

He wakes up, hours later, on the large, flaccid couch in his brother's family room. His throat is dry and his head is pounding and he has had a horrible nightmare. Clay's face is hanging over him. The stench of his vomit rises between them. He has no idea how he got there.

Upstairs again, Jennifer reads the next chapter of Rebecca's book, as if it contains the key to her life. She reads the last part of it twice, trying to imagine herself pouring perfume on Jesus's head, like Reumah in the book. She wishes she could do something similar to Jesus.

She closes the book and lies back on her bed and closes her eyes, trying to picture him, watching her. Waiting for her. After a moment, she gets up and finds Jeb's sketch of the Snow-god, and she spreads it out on her bed so that Jesus can look at it too. She rummages through a drawer in the kitchen until she finds a permanent marker, which she uses to draw a cross behind the figure. She adds two large black dots, like nails, into his hands, and then places another one over his feet. Then she goes into the bathroom and finds a bottle of nail polish. The polish is the color of raw salmon but it will do. She carefully paints nail polish oozing out of his palms instead of the snow. She stands up then, next to the bed, so that she and Jesus can look at it.

"It was you," she says quietly. "It was you—all along."

Suddenly it's so quiet she can hear the ocean. She opens her window. From this angle she cannot see the ocean, but she can hear it, the sound of the wind blowing over the waves toward the land, picking up the scents of early spring—wet earth and crocuses and baby grass and tree buds—blowing onto her through the window and filling the room with freshness, with a nuanced fragrance that humans could never produce.

XXXVIII

The morning after the first night of Passover, the clouds do not contain the promise of more rain, but rather hang ominously over the horizon, like a portent. Reumah only thinks of this later, of course, after everything had happened. For now, she merely notices the clouds, as she notes the sky on any morning, while passing through the courtyard toward the cooking fires, to find some breakfast and see what she can do to help clean up after the Feast.

It is Mary who tells her.

Mary draws her aside, out of earshot of the servants, and whispers, "They have taken the Lord."

Reumah does not understand at first.

"Our leaders had him arrested late last night at his favorite retreat—the garden where they press the olives. It was a huge mob—armed with swords and clubs, as if he were leading a throng of Zealots!"

"How did they find him?"

Mary looks away for a moment. "Can you not guess? He was betrayed...by one of his own."

The small barley loaf Reumah is about to eat falls to the ground, and she sits on a bench.

"No. No...it cannot be true. How can we be sure of these things?" She can feel her intestines tightening, like the strings of a sack being pulled together.

Mary sits next to her.

"Indeed...it is true. A young Greek named Dimitri came to tell us. He is a household servant who helped serve the Passover supper to the Master and his disciples. He followed them out to the Mount of Olives afterward, because his heart was so stirred by the Master and his words that he wanted to hear more. When they began to lead the Master away, Dimitri took hold of him and tried to loose the rope binding his hands, so they grabbed him as well, but he managed to break free, alas, without his garment. He had been wearing only a loin cloth. Brave, sweet boy! John, the Master's dearest friend, took pity on him, and gave him his cloak, and his staff, and told him to come to us and tell us what happened. The young man is still asleep, and the cloak around him is John's, as is the staff. I recognized it."

"Surely it will come to nothing! The Master has done nothing wrong! Surely our leaders would not condemn an innocent man!" Of course she is thinking of her father.

"As to his innocence, there can be no doubt. As to a fair trial from our leaders, I am far less confident. Caiphas, the high priest, is known more for his caprice than his mercy. Few of our leaders have any high regard for our Master, Reumah. In their eyes he is a usurper of their authority and a blasphemer."

They sit for a few moments in silence, each one awash in her own anxious thoughts. Presently they are joined by Martha.

"We must not lose heart," she says quietly. "He would not have us give in to fear."

"True," Mary answers. "I can almost hear him saying, 'Woman, where is your faith?'" She smiles, a bit sadly. "But what can we do?" Her question is Reumah's as well.

"We must pray and keep watch. Lazarus will send Tobias with Dimitri back to the city. He will find out how the trial progresses and send us word. Hopefully our Master will be vindicated before sundown, and it will all come to naught."

No sooner are these words spoken when Reumah knows what she must do. It comes to her, like an arrow shot from a hidden bow—she must go to the house of Mary Magdalene in the city.

"But why?" Both sisters question her.

Reumah thinks for a moment, and then she turns to Mary. "Mary of Magdala told me that I was appointed to stay at your side when you were grieving for your brother, as a companion through the dark trial of your soul. Perhaps now I am needed for the same reason in Jerusalem."

Mary nodded. "I know now that God placed you beside me as a quiet reminder of his presence...to show me that I was never alone in my trial, despite how badly I felt. In times of grief or pain God often refreshes our spirits by the acts of kindness and gentle words of our loved ones. But...to whom will you go? All of our friends in the city must be anxious now, as we are."

There is no doubt in Reumah's mind. Without hesitation she says, "I cannot stop thinking of the two other Marys, especially his mother. What fear must be in her heart at this moment?"

"The pain of birth is nothing compared to the pain of death."
Her son, Yeshua, looked right at her when he said it. She had been telling the story of his birth, or retelling it, as was the case, to the other women as they prepared the Passover. He had slipped into the courtyard, unnoticed, and taken a seat on a bench near the wall, eating a handful of ripe figs, his favorite, which he found on a table nearby. He had heard her tell the story many times, of course, and was not about to interrupt her, although his time was short. He knew it was one of their favorite stories, and no one could tell it but her, for they loved how she told it. It was filled with details that only a mother could remember: the long, arduous walk from Nazareth to Bethlehem; the old man, who could barely walk himself, who had given up his place in an oxcart for her; and the lack of money that prevented them from getting a room in any of the inns.

She was preparing the bitter herbs to eat with the lamb, which was already on the brazier, and she put the pestle down for a moment, and wiped her brow, before she continued. *"They took one look at us, in our sweaty, dusty clothes and worn sandals, and asked from whence we had come. 'Nazareth,' my betrothed answered, for he wouldn't lie. And then they knew we could barely afford even a space in their lower rooms, where the animals are kept. 'Sorry, we have no room,' all the innkeepers told us, but we knew they were just keeping the rooms open for those who would pay more. Joseph pleaded with them, on account of my condition: by this time, I was having shooting pains through my* back as well, and kept having to double over, but they were greedy and heartless. Finally he took hold of one man, almost violently, and said, through his teeth, 'Can you not see her time is nigh? For God's sake, have mercy!' The man must have seen something fearsome in my Joseph's eyes, for he quickly directed us to an abandoned stable across the field. At that point we didn't care. We found the structure, it was dilapidated; the only way we knew that it had been a stable was because of the manger—hewn from stone—that still stood in the center of the dirt floor. Joseph made a pallet for me out of our bedrolls, and then he set to work, building a fire and using the broken beams and old planks to construct a shelter over us. He seemed relieved to have something to do while the pains increased on me.

"Not long after, a woman came out to us. She had been summoned by her young son, who had seen us at the door of the inn. She herself had almost died in childbirth a few years before, and her son had never forgotten it...when he saw me laboring, he ran and told his mother of our plight. She brought a lamp and a large water jug and rags for cleansing. Soon another woman came, and then another. In my pain and distraction, I did not retain their names...God knows who they are...they left their husbands and their warm beds and their little ones and came to attend me. The second one came with myrrh and cloves and oil and salt; the third brought a stool and a large woven mat for the afterbirth. I was in my sixteenth year...a strong girl, normally, but now I could barely stand from exhaustion of our journey and my labor. The women held me up, one on either side, and the third below me, on the stool, and when the baby came forth, we laughed and cried, these women and I, as if I had always known them. He had a great deal of dark hair, and his first cry seemed louder to my ears than any other noise of man or beast. From Joseph they took a flint knife, to cut the cord, and then they rubbed him with salt and cleansed him... how he screamed in protest! I thought my heart would break. I could not take my eyes off his tiny form convulsing and shivering in the cold. It was agony to lie there, wanting only to hold and comfort him, while the eldest woman massaged my belly to extract the afterbirth. At that moment I knew that the human heart can know no greater pain than watching one's own child suffer. They took the cloths I had brought, *and they showed me how to swaddle him. Then they presented him to Joseph, whose eyes glistened in the firelight as he gazed earnestly on the babe for a long moment. 'Please...' I begged my betrothed. 'Please let me have him!' Finally I held him, and placed him on my breast for the first time, and he immediately suckled, and my heart was so filled with joy and relief I could not speak.*

"I looked up through the planks of the shelter my betrothed had built, in gratitude to the Almighty. The sky was clear and the night was cold, and the stars were so bright it was as if the heavenly beings were watching us from a great distance. One of the women cleaned the spiders and debris out of the manger where it stood. 'Do not let him lie on the ground next to you...' she told me. 'Snakes...' I shuddered and placed him in the ancient manger and stroked his warm little head, and kissed his tiny face, puckered and so yielding, until my fingertips and lips had memorized his features. We ate the last of our bread, and Joseph kept watch by the fire, and I slept.

"At the break of day, some shepherds came, looking for the baby. They told me that angels had appeared to them, in the sky, telling them of his birth, and singing, and when I asked them when the angels had appeared, they said it was during the second watch of the night, when my son had been born. I asked them about the song, and when they sang some of it I knew that it was the very same song that I had received the night he was conceived within my womb. It was the song I tried to sing to Joseph when I first told him I was pregnant, but he would not listen until after the Lord had spoken to him in a dream. It was the song I could not stop singing all the time my baby grew inside of me, and I sang it to him many, many times after he was born. 'Mother, can you sing my song to me?' he would say, climbing on my lap."

At that point she picked up the pestle again, and began to sing, and the other women, most of whom knew the song, joined her. It was a song that, once heard, could never be forgotten, and must be shared. It was a song that would soothe him, in his boyhood, and ease the pain of nightmares and dark thoughts that would come to him, unbidden, and had plagued him his whole life. He put his head down and closed his eyes while the women sang the angels' song, wishing that the moment would not pass, and the singing would not end, but of course it must.

"The pain of birth is nothing compared to the pain of death," he said aloud, looking at his mother. The entire group fell silent, turning toward him, suddenly aware of his presence. He rose from the bench, and was instantly surrounded with greetings and exclamations.

"You have stayed away too long," said Salome, embracing him in a maternal fashion. "Ah, the scent of spikenard is sweet on you, as if you were a groom just married!"

"Yes, but a groom would not have such an unkempt beard," said another.

"And his hair! Like a Nazarite!"

"You are too thin, Yeshua. Here, take some bread!"

"Do you never sleep? Look at his eyes, how sunken..."

He grinned, meekly accepting their coddling and the food they pressed on him. He looked at each of them, as if he were memorizing their faces. He thanked them for their concern. He motioned to his mother, who followed him into Mary Magdalene's home. Once inside, he turned to her. She had never seen him look so troubled. There was an air of heaviness about him, as evident as the scent of Reumah's perfume, which still emanated from his hair and clothes.

"My son...do you speak of *my* death?"

"No. You shall live out your days in peace, in the home of John, my dearest friend and the one who understands me better than anyone on this earth. You will end your days in the arms of his wife who will care for you until you have taken your last breath. She will be like a daughter to you."

She smiled at him, a bit skeptically.

"I know every word you speak must be true...but you are aware that your best friend is not married, nor ever has been?"

He ignored this, as not being relevant.

"You spoke of my birth...I must speak of my death."

She turned away. "I will not hear this. What mother could? Please, Yeshua. Please. I cannot have this discussion."

"You must listen!" He took her by the shoulders, almost roughly. When she looked up at him in surprise his hands dropped from her shoulders, and he ran them over his head, an old gesture she recognized from his boyhood, as if he were trying to erase some ugly truth from his mind.

"Mother, no one can take my life from me."

"Yes, I know this. You have told me this before."

"When I suffer, it will be because I choose to, because it is the will of the One who sent me, not because it can't be helped."

At this her eyes began to fill. "Why must you suffer at all?"

"You were just now preparing the Passover, and you ask me this? You know why, Mother. For this purpose I came."

She nodded in sad recognition of the truth he spoke. "Old Simeon's words…'a sword will pierce your heart…' have haunted me since you were eight days old, and now they are coming true." She began to sob quietly. He took her face in his hands.

"You will see me again. If it were not true I would not say it. You will not see me for a little while, and then you will see me again. Do not forget these words I have spoken, and do not fear."

"Why? Where are you going? What will they do to you?"

He did not answer. Instead, he kissed her, and then slipped out as quietly as he had come.

The next morning she is roused by Mary Magdalene, who has been awake and in prayer since the cock's third crow.

"John is here to see you," the older woman whispers to her, gently shaking her.

Yeshua's best friend is a quiet, earnest man, not handsome, with a heavy brow and deep-set eyes. His presence is always comforting, however, and she is never sorry to see him. He kisses her hand in greeting, and wastes no time with pleasantries.

"They are taking him before Herod even as we speak," he tells her. "They arrested him last night in Gethsemane. They convened the court and tried him through the night—callous wolves!—and arranged for him to appear before Pilate already this morning. I waited through the night to see what would happen. I did not wish to alarm you unnecessarily, but…I fear it is not going well for him. They want to be rid of him, and do it quickly before there is a riot in the city."

"Pilate? Herod? Why must he appear before them? He has done nothing wrong! And certainly nothing deserving a death sentence!"

"Pilate is like is a rag doll in the hands of our leaders. He seeks to appease them. He will pretend to judge impartially, but he will likely do whatever they want."

"So…they will have him imprisoned by Pilate?"

He does not answer her. He only looks to the door, indicating their need to depart quickly.

But she is seized with sudden fear, and becomes so weak she must sit down.

"They mean to have him crucified…that's it, isn't it?" She begins to weep aloud, and the other women, roused by the sound of her crying, quickly enter the courtyard.

"Surely not," says Mary of Magdala. "They reserve that punishment for the worst of criminals in order to make an example of them…those who cause revolts and insurgencies against Rome." In her younger, pagan days, when she had served Rome with her dark gift, she had been responsible for sending a few innocent men to this most gruesome death. She keeps this to herself, however, for it causes her much pain. "That is hardly our Master! Come, come! We must not give way to fear." Her words calm the other women, but not his mother. She is trembling now.

Her mind recalls. Yeshua was in his fourteenth or fifteenth year and they were on their way home from the temple. They passed an ugly place outside the city; it was a place where the Romans would execute their criminals on crosses, and the stench of death rose up before their nostrils, as if the gates of hell had been flung open. They suddenly came to a dozen ravaged skeletons hanging from the crossbeams, almost unrecognizable as human, because the ravens had feasted on their decomposing flesh. She had screamed in horror, and told him not to look while she quickly covered the eyes of the younger children, but it was too late; he did not turn away. Days later she had seen him, lying out in a field behind their house. Joseph had gone out to fit an ox with a yoke, and Yeshua had taken some beams that he had been working on to make a joist. He had placed them, like a cross, on the ground, and was now laying on them, with his arms outstretched. She stifled her scream when she saw him. His eyes were fixed on the sky and his lips were moving; she saw that he was praying earnestly on the beams. Deborah had called for her then, and she returned to the house, drying her eyes lest the other children see her weeping.

"They shall crucify him," she says now. Her voice is so weak they can hardly hear her. "He knows it. He has always known it."

Mary of Magdala takes hold of her hands and looks earnestly into her eyes. "Remember the words of our patriarch, my sister: 'He shall not abandon his Holy One to the grave, or let him see decay.'" Her words are not without effect, and Mary, the mother of Yeshua, now stands, as if strengthened by an inner force.

"I will follow him to the cross," she says.

"You shall not be alone."

Perhaps if they had known how appalling it would be, they would have stayed away, but once they had joined the throng that followed him out of the city to the Place of the Skull, as it was called, there was no turning back. There were hordes of flies throughout the streets, and above their heads large black birds circled, for the entire city was permeated with the stench of lamb carcasses, the blood of which swelled the brook of Kidron as they passed over it. Reumah was struck by the putrid odor, and also the deafening sound of a thousand women wailing in lamentation behind the Master as the soldiers urged him on. Reumah was certain that her friends, and his mother, were in this crowd of women. When he repeatedly collapsed from exhaustion and loss of blood, the women chanted, "Mercy on him!" and the hardened soldiers, as if awed by their numbers and the volume of their pleas, took hold of a bystander and forced him to bear their master's crossbeam to the place of execution. As soon as the cross had been removed from his bloodied back he stood up, albeit unsteadily, and turned to the women. He addressed them, but Reumah was too far back to hear the words. Her entire purpose was to not lose sight of Dimitri and Tobias, who were trying to find John, or any of the Master's friends, in the multitude. At last they came to John, who stood with some others near the crosses. Dimitri immediately went over to him, and, after he had bowed down, as a servant, and returned his cloak and his staff, he stepped over to the Master's cross, and raising himself on his toes, kissed the Master's bloody feet. He was immediately thrown back by one of the soldiers, who threatened him with the same fate if he stepped up again.

Reumah, who had promised herself she would not look, fixed her eyes on the ground beneath his cross. The earth was soaked with his blood, turning it into red clay, and she felt something burst inside of her, like a wineskin stretched to the limit of its capacity. She fell on her knees. Suddenly he cried out in the anguish of his torment, and without thinking, she looked up. His face was so swollen and gruesome it bore no resemblance to his former visage. His body, completely covered in blood, writhed in relentless torture. The iron spikes, driven between the bones of his forearms, caused his hands to curl up like the talons of a bird.

Darkness and heat and a dizzying thirst swept over her, as if the gates of Hades had suddenly opened before her, and the cries of the men on the crosses became, in her ringing ears, the screams of a multitude of condemned souls, doomed forever to reside in unappeasable flames.

"Make atonement for us!" she cried out to her beloved Master, and then fainted.

John watched her, and caught her as she swooned.

He carried her over to the Fragrant Ones, who had gathered about a stone's throw from the foot of his cross, and gently placed her among them. They had torn their garments and covered their hair with dust, and sat, huddled around his mother, in silent agony. They had chosen not to wail any longer, lest their lamentation cause him greater agony then he now bore.

"Sir, may we have his robe as a keepsake?" Mary of Magdala boldly asked one of the soldiers, for they had stripped him, and two others besides. "It was our gift to him."

But when the soldiers saw that the women kept their heads down, and would not look on their Master's nakedness, they refused.

And when Mary, his mother, saw John carry Reumah, and saw how he looked at her with love as he lay her gently among them, she suddenly recalled the words of her son, who had predicted that John would have a wife, and that his wife would become like a daughter to her. Thus in the midst of her horror she found hope, because she knew that her son's words were true, and that this tenderhearted girl, Reumah, would surely become John's wife, and everything that her son had spoken to her would come to pass, as he had promised.

The women bathed Reumah's face with water, and gave her a drink. She sat up, and Mary held out her hands to her.

"John, who carried you now to us, has told us how you anointed my son with your own precious vial of perfume. Do you know he heard the soldiers say that they could still smell spikenard on his hair and beard even after they tortured him? He was like a fragrant lily emitting its last scent even as it is crushed…" She broke off, unable to continue.

"It was all I had," said Reumah, her eyes filling, and completely at a loss to know how to comfort his mother. "I only wish I could have done more." She had been crushed with guilt for hours now, because she hadn't warned the Master of Judas's slanderous inclinations when she had the chance.

His mother shook her head.

"No, child. You have done what you could, and done it beautifully. And now you have come, at just the right time. Someday you will understand how much your presence has comforted me today."

The two of them embraced then, like a mother and daughter, surrounded by the others, all of them offering the only comfort they could: the solace of shared grief for the one they loved so dearly. They stayed until the sky became black and they could hardly see, until the one they loved exhaled his final breath, and dismissed his spirit. Then they straggled back to the home of Mary Magdalene, in the darkness, and clung to one another through the night, like their ancient ancestors in faraway Egypt, waiting for the Angel of Death to pass over.

39

"Yₒu're supposed to eat it, Bee-Bee," Nathan tells her.

Bee-Bee holds the parts of a small blue plastic egg in her hands, scrutinizing the yellow chick inside it, as if it were an actual live specimen, and not a marshmallow representative. Last Easter she was in the hospital, so this is her first experience of egg hunting, but aside from the blue egg with its sugary chick, she has displayed little interest in the festivities or in the bright, beribboned basket containing a chocolate bunny and jelly beans that sits on the blanket next to her.

It was Rachel's idea to have the egg hunt at the beach, their own yard being too small; the larger "official" town hunt that took place in the park outside the auditorium, they all agreed, would be too crowded with young, overzealous egg hunters. John-Mark, though only a toddler himself at the time, had accidently trampled a younger child last year; Bee-Bee would have been petrified by the noise and confusion.

"Watch...like this," Nathan instructs, and pops the yellow chick from Bee-Bee's egg into his mouth. For a split second she stares at her brother's mouth, chewing, and then her eyes pool and her mouth opens in a wail of abject despair.

With tremendous effort Clay restrains himself from smacking his third child across the back of his head. Lately Nathan's behavior has become more exasperating than usual, for no obvious reason other than the fact that he had recently turned eleven. Clay grabs his arm with considerably more force than necessary.

"Ouch, Dad! You're killing me!"

"Lookit her. She's inconsolable. What were you thinking?"

"I was just showing her you're supposed to eat 'em—"

Rebecca glances at her husband, as if reminding him that they have an audience.

Clay clears his throat.

"Um…thanks for that, Nathan. But next time use one of your own chicks, OK?"

"Ate 'em all."

Clay grits his teeth. "OK, just find me another. Quickly."

Nathan glances toward his mother, and Jennifer and Clive, who are grouped on the blanket near Bee-Bee, and his ears redden. Clive winks at him, and he pulls a marshmallow chick out of Rachel's basket, which sits on the blanket in front of him, and surreptitiously hands it to Nathan, who then hands it to his father. With some wrangling Clay pretends to pull it out of Nathan's mouth, and then places it into the blue egg.

"There it is, sweetheart," he says to Bee-Bee, who is still sniffling. "All better."

She looks at him skeptically and he wonders how many years he'll have before she doesn't believe in him. He wants her to keep believing in him as long as possible. She daintily sniffs the chick in its blue cup, leaving some yellow sugar granules on the bridge of her nose. She smiles at him. He wishes that all his problems were so easily solved.

Clive stands and stretches with studied nonchalance, glancing down hopefully at Jennifer, but she is watching Bee-Bee with Clay.

"She just adores you, doesn't she?" she says to Clay. *A kid needs a dad. What the hell am I thinking?*

"I guess so." He grins. "For better or for worse."

"Kids need fathers," Jennifer says, looking out to the ocean. "They need two parents. It's how God designed it." Rebecca and Clay and Clive lean closer to hear her. They are still not used to this open, forthright Jennifer, who, in the last month, has become much more adept at speaking her mind. No one says anything; they don't want to interrupt her. But she says nothing more.

"I need her too," says Clay, after a pause.

"Really? Like, how?"

He looks out to the ocean, as if consulting the waves, before he turns back to her.

"Well, like just now. The way she looked at me...she makes me want to be that person...the person she thinks I am. When I'm with Bee-Bee, I'm the best version of myself." He can feel himself inexplicably choking up, so he quickly gets to his feet and dusts the sand off his jeans.

"I'm gonna test the water...see when we can start swimming," he says in a jocular way.

Rebecca follows him down to the water's edge.

Bee-Bee looks after them, as if she will follow, but Jennifer suddenly makes a tiny *peep-peep-peep* sound, looking down at the yellow chick, and Bee-Bee's eyes widen.

"I think the chicky is hungry," she says to Bee-Bee. "Shall we find it some lunch?" She holds her hand out to Bee-Bee, who shakes her head, and points to her parents. Ten yards away a seagull squawks, and she abruptly turns to look at it.

"Come on, Bee-Bee," says Clive. "That big bossy bird is getting all the grub. Don't you want to get some for your chicky?"

His voice is like her daddy's, or maybe his hand feels the same, but to Jennifer's surprise she takes his hand and they begin to walk down the beach together, Clive glancing back at her, inviting her to follow. She wants to. She likes the picture they make: his large, lumbering form walking slowly to accommodate the tiny girl's steps. She feels connected to them, even though she's not, technically. But she feels like she is. It's a good feeling. She hoists herself off the blanket, already feeling more pregnant than she is, and follows after them.

At the water's edge Rebecca puts her arms around Clay from behind, and her head on his shoulder.

"You OK?" she asks.

He has been different, ever since that day. Quieter. On that day she had found him, like this, at the edge of the ocean an hour after he had fled from Jeb's house. She had found him, staring out at the waves. She could see he had been crying. They sat there for five minutes without speaking, and she rubbed his back, waiting.

"I betrayed the Lord," he had said, finally. "Like Judas." His eyes filled again.

"No, you didn't."

"I did. You weren't there."

"You denied him. More like Peter."

"How do you know? What did she tell you?"

"I know because you're here. You want him to forgive you. That's not Judas."

"He's already forgiven me. It's me that has to forgive him."

She smiled then, sadly, because she understood. She had had to forgive Jesus too, more than once. Not for anything bad he actually did, but for the painful things she couldn't account for, like the months of torturous legal wrangling they had endured, while adopting John-Mark, when his mother, who had abandoned him in a taxicab when he was ten days old, decided she wanted him back. Like the seizures that racked Bee-Bee's tiny body because her mother had used crack the whole time she carried her. Like the Crusades and pogroms and the Holocaust. She had had to stop holding on to the pain of these things, and stop holding them against Jesus.

"I've been angry at Jesus," Clay told her that day. "All this time. But I miss him. I miss Jesus. I can't live without him. I thought it was Bobby that I missed, but now I realize it's Jesus. I feel like I'm dying inside."

She had said nothing; she just put her arm around him and prayed for him silently, while he put his head down and worked it out with Jesus. They sat for a while, and then they talked, and planned. He would take a leave of absence from the pulpit; he was getting more construction work now anyway, and they both felt the change was needed. They sat until the boys came to get them, and told them the police had showed up, and that Uncle Clive was passed out in a car in Asbury Park. They went and got Clive, and brought him back to the house, and somehow he and Rebecca and David had managed to carry him inside and lay him on the family room couch. And when Clive woke up—from a bad dream—Clay had been there, with the light on, as he had always been. And Clive felt horribly embarrassed, and sick, and thirsty, but also joyously relieved, because he knew he was getting his brother back.

"It's about cleansing," Clay says to her now.

"Hmmm?"

"Last year we sat here and you asked us how the ocean is like God. Remember?"

She laughs lightly. "I remember. We turned to you for your answer, and you said, 'You could drown in it.' Yeah. I remember."

He laughs now too.

"God wasn't trying to drown me. He was trying to cleanse me."

"Wow! That's good. You should use that."

He embraces her, and kisses her mouth, because she is so gentle and strong and perfect for him. A few days ago he had seen her journal, tucked under her bed, and he had read *God help me to keep forgiving him, no matter what*...and he knew it was about him. He refused to read any more, because he didn't want to know what he had done that needed to be forgiven. He pushed it out of his mind until later that night, when he was sitting on the edge of their bed, and she was standing between his knees, her long fingers unbuttoning her blouse in the tantalizing way she had, and his hands sliding up her thighs under her skirt, and it came to him, like a voice in his head, *This is her forgiveness...this is what it feels like*...and when she shook out her braid so that her hair spilled down onto her bare shoulders and breasts, he felt so grateful it almost hurt. He had covered her with kisses, pressing his face into her flesh, smelling and tasting her, like a prisoner who had been deprived of a woman's body for years, now set free to love, half-mad with exhilaration. Afterward he had lain there, expended and exultant; richer than Solomon.

They sit down together, by the water's edge, and alternately watch the ocean, and their kids. Rachel is up on the boardwalk, laughing and chatting with some friends from town—there are a few boys, they notice. David and Nathan have consumed the entire contents of their Easter baskets and have filled the plastic eggs with sand, which they are now throwing around in a newly devised game. Some other boys have joined them. Jean-Mark is sitting with his legs astride a pile of seaweed and driftwood, hunting for skate egg cases and crab shells, which he places in his basket alongside the candy. Bee-Bee is a small figure next to Jennifer and Clive, who are now making their way back. After a while they perceive that Clive is carrying her on his shoulders.

"Wow," says Clay, "that's rather remarkable…"

"Clive and Jennifer? Or Clive carrying Bee-Bee?"

He grins at her.

"Both."

Jennifer is irresistible to Clive, but he is not so to her, and he is confronted with this hard fact whenever they are together, which is fairly often, thanks to the open hospitality of his brother and Rebecca. He has been down to see them every weekend since that day, that weird horrible day, and each time he finds in her new charms to admire, not the least because she seems to be changing, in an indefinable way. It's as if her soul is expanding, along with her expectant body, as if she is becoming more truly herself, or perhaps it is just because he is getting to know her better, so she is occupying more and more space in his brain.

At the same time there is something that keeps her from loving him back; an invisible force that he can't identify. Toward him she is consistently friendly and sweet and attentive, but always a bit preoccupied, as if someone else is drawing her affections away from him, but he is uncertain who this invisible rival is, and can only assume it is still Jeb. He looks far out into the ocean for a second and sucks in some salty air, as if to bolster himself.

"So…do you miss Jeb?"

She looks at him in surprise. A piece of hair blows across her face and he resists the urge to brush it off her cheek. They are walking slowly because of Bee-Bee; it's like walking in a museum with a lot of exhibits. She keeps stopping to show them things that she picks up. Finally Jennifer realizes that she is trying to determine what to "feed" her chick, and plays along.

"Um…not really. What makes you ask?"

"I don't know. Just wondered. I mean, you were going to marry him."

She laughs slightly. "And so I was. Thank God, he had other plans."

"God had other plans? Or Jeb?"

"Well both, apparently. I don't know where Jeb is. He moved out right after."

Clive is silent. He knows where Jeb is, because he has been in touch with him, for business reasons, albeit briefly. He wonders if he should tell her. He wants to, in the interest of full disclosure. But he is afraid. He is afraid she will contact him, or worse, go to him, and he will forever lose her.

"So…you don't miss him? You don't think of him?"

"Of course I do. It's hard not to. I pass his house every day, on my way out of town. I pray for him when I go by. I hope he's OK."

He bends down and puts a small shell up to the beak of Bee-Bee's marshmallow chick. He is buying time, trying to decide.

"I think the chicky likes these, Bee-Bee," he says. "They taste like cookies." He makes the chick bob up and down excitedly, and imitates some chewing sounds. She watches, fascinated. He hands her the shell but she hands it back to him. She wants him to do it.

"She wants you to do it," Jennifer says, laughing. "She's letting you feed her pet…that's a big deal."

It feels like a big deal. It feels like a door that could open and lead to more doors, but he's not sure why.

"He's in the Cayman Islands," he says, squinting up at her from his squatting position on the sand, while he continues to "feed" Bee-Bee's chick. "He's with that nurse, Jean-Denis. He shaved his head, apparently, and he's going around under another name."

Jennifer laughs. She laughs and laughs and Bee-Bee smiles too. Bee-Bee is delighted that her chick is eating. She wrings her hands together and hops from one foot to the other. Clive is utterly confused by Jennifer's reaction.

"What's so funny?"

She is still laughing, and when she tries to stop, she laughs more.

"I don't know exactly. Just you…squatting on the beach…trying to feed a marshmallow chick some shells, being all serious, with your straight-edge haircut and crisp Dockers…it's just funny to me."

"Ha. OK. You may also be interested to know that he has brought charges of embezzlement against Vina, and there's a good chance they will stick. She may be doing some time in the slammer, how about that? After she gets done with her therapy, that is."

"What? What therapy?"

"She hit a tree that day, speeding. Busted up her patella. It's a mess. Gonna require multiple surgeries and months of PT. It happened in Deal…when she came to she was trapped in her car, with cops and EMT workers trying to get her out of the wreckage, and about a hundred Hasidic Jews standing on the sidewalk, watching. You can just imagine."

She stops laughing.

"OK. That explains it."

"What's that?" He stands up now, after assuring Bee-Bee that the chick's tummy is full.

"Her ex-husband left me a message the other day…about possibly babysitting Kevin. He said he got my number from Vina."

"He's got full custody of the kid for now…she's on pain-killers all the time and can barely function."

The former Jennifer would have felt smugly satisfied. She would have said, *Oh well, Vina,* and taken her time returning the call. But Jennifer was different now; the main difference was she did not have to be her old self. She felt she had the power to rise above her old self, like an airplane, empowered to defy gravity. She resolved to call Kevin's father as soon as she got home, and have Kevin come over at the first opportunity.

"You're smiling," Clive says to her. "You hated her, huh?"

"No, not at all," she says. "I'm smiling because I like Kevin. It will be nice to see him."

"You're gonna do it?"

"Of course. Why wouldn't I? It's not their fault that Vina was irresponsible." She feels unaccountably happy, as if her heart, swelled by one act of kindness, now has room for more.

"I may even go see Vina sometime, who knows?" She stops to watch Bee-Bee, who has become fatigued by the long walk.

"Wow," he says, in awe of her gracious attitude. It makes him love her more. It makes him want her more. He hopes she shines on him, in the same way, and lets him in. He hopes the dream he had of her in the

Shiloh Inn will come true. It occurs to him now that the invisible rival is not Jeb, but probably Jesus, and how can he compete with Jesus? He no longer doubts the existence of Jesus—not after that day—but he has a healthy fear of him, the way most people view the ocean. For now he is content to walk along the edge; not wade in too deeply.

"I think she needs to be carried," Jennifer says, and Clive scoops up Bee-Bee and sets her on his shoulders, and Jennifer decides that Clive is quite handsome in his own way. She hopes Jesus gets a hold of him. She hopes Jesus gets a hold of Vina too, and Kevin, and of course Jeb, because she is convinced that he wants them, just as much as he wanted her. She will pray for them all, just as her mother prayed for her, while she read *The Fragrant Ones*, and, she has discovered recently, Rebecca was praying too. She is confident that Jesus will make it happen somehow because she is reading all about Jesus in the Gospels and she is starting to know him now, like Reumah. Like Rebecca. Like Mary and Martha and all the other *Fragrant Ones*.

Clive fetches the blanket and they wrap Bee-Bee in it. They put her in the middle of their small group, and she falls asleep.

"She's like the center of a flower, and we're the petals," says Jennifer. The others laugh.

They sit peacefully, enjoying the hour, receiving it like a gift. They sit, in quiet awareness of the Resurrection, and the power of renewed life. They sit, the sun warm on their backs, until the tide comes in, and flows over their feet good-naturedly, as if the Sea-maker himself had appointed its movement to wash the feet of his disciples.

XL

True to her word, Reumah has remained with Mary, the Lord's mother. They have barely eaten or spoken, only staying near one another, and the other women, like refugees of a war or catastrophe, each one heavy-laden with her own sense of loss; each one remembering the words of her last conversation with him; what he had said, how he had looked, the expression in his eyes. Because of the lateness of the hour, and the exhaustion of grief, most of the women have dozed off, and Reumah, roused by the sounds of scurrying feet and excited voices from at the door, reluctantly opens her eyelids, swollen as they are from weeping and lack of sleep.

"We have seen where they have laid him," announces Mary of Magdala, going straight toward his mother and taking her hands. "A man named Joseph of Arimathea petitioned the governor for his body. He has great wealth, and is a member of the Sanhedrin who opposed the decision of the court, and has been secret disciple all this time. Can you imagine?"

"And Pilate agreed?" Mary slowly pulls herself up off the large cushion on which she reclined.

"Indeed he did. Pilate is reluctant to refuse anyone who has wealth or influence; this we know."

"I do not know this Joseph…how can I properly thank him?"

"There is more," says Mary of Magdala, her eyes bright with fervent devotion, despite the lines of fatigue in her face. "This man, Joseph, also bought new linen, and laid the Master's body in his own family tomb. Think of that! And—where is Reumah?—I must tell her this," she turns to look at Reumah, who is still absorbing this latest report.

"Another man was with him...can you guess who?"

Judas? Had he repented? But she is unwilling to speak aloud the name of her Lord's betrayer.

"I—I cannot imagine who you mean..."

"Can you not? My dear—it was your own father, Rabbi Nicodemus."

Reumah stares at the older woman in stunned surprise.

"My father...is a disciple of our Lord? Can it be? All this time?" her voice falters and the other women reach out to her. The Lord's mother takes her hand.

"There is no doubt about it," says Mary of Magdala. "Your own father brought a great quantity of myrrh and aloes, which the two men and their servants pressed into the linen while they wrapped him. It was done speedily, before sundown, but with no lack of devotion, as if he was their own dear son."

Fresh tears glisten in the eyes of both his mother and Reumah, and some of the other women as well.

"So do not fret," says Mary of Magdala. "However inglorious his death, he was buried with nobility...and utmost respect and devotion."

With what little energy they possess they prepare spices and anointing oils, intending, when the Sabbath is over, to return to the tomb, and anoint his body one last time.

"Now we must rest, as the Law requires," says Mary Magdalene, after the preparations have been made. "He would have it so."

Reumah turns to look at the mother of the Master, asleep on the pallet. Of all of them, she has wept the least, and some of them have whispered that she has become numb with grief, and shut off all her feelings.

"She is shutting down," one of them whispers to Reumah, despondently. "She will not sing again for a long time." Reumah attends the lady carefully, praying that she will not give into despair, as did her friend after Lazarus's death. Later in the day she finds her standing alone in the inner room next to the long table where they sometimes eat or sew, lost in thought. Reumah watches her from the doorway. Mary turns to her.

"He stood here. Right here...he took my face in his hands, and he told me not to forget his words...he said that I would see him again..."

Yes, Reumah thinks. *At the end of time, at the Resurrection, we will all see him...*

"Of course," she says to his mother. "All his words are true. We will see him again."

"Soon," says his mother, her eyes wide, and a smile forming on her lips. "Not years from now. Soon."

Reumah, observing the strange light in her eyes, has a sickening thought that makes her heart sink.

Her intense grief has caused her mind to become addled...

Thereafter Mary begins to hum, and sing bits of songs beneath her breath, as if she is reluctant to disturb her fellow mourners, but can't help the music that flows up from inside her. Behind her back the other women look at one another and shake their heads. Mary Magdalene approaches her, privately.

"My dear...we are all concerned for you...I wish you would rest..."

"I am as well as can be expected, my friend. Do not trouble yourself on my account."

"I am thinking—perhaps—it would be better if you did not come to the tomb tomorrow..."

"Quite right. I will stay here...and he will come to me at his convenience."

Few things shock or surprise Mary of Magdala at this point in her life, but this statement from her Lord's mother renders her speechless, as if she had suddenly beheld a leper, removing his shroud, exposing, for a moment, his ravaged face. She smiles gently at her friend, and embraces her wistfully. Then she leaves her and finds the other women in the courtyard.

"It is as we fear," she says to them with great sadness. "She is losing her mind."

"They think we are out of our minds!" Salome's outraged voice shakes Reumah from her sleep. Beside her, on the sleeping platform, the Lord's mother stirs as well. The door to their chamber bursts open and Salome, who is a large woman, stands before them, breathing heavily. The women who accompanied her and Mary of Magdala to the tomb are behind her.

"A thousand pardons, my dears, for waking you...but you will not be sorry when I tell you the news." She crosses the room and kneels by Mary.

"What do you think? He is not there...your son! The stone had been rolled away, and his body was not there!"

His mother says nothing, only sits up slowly. All the women watch her now, and Reumah finds herself trembling.

"What are you saying, Salome? Please...explain it to us."

"We rose before dawn. We went back to the place where they had laid him. On the way there we tried to figure out how we would open the tomb, for a huge rock had been placed there to seal it. Suddenly there was an earthquake and we fell to the ground. Afterward Mary said, 'Perhaps the Lord sent the earthquake, so that we could get inside the tomb.' We got up and ran to the place...and...and..." she stopped to draw her breath. None of the women moved.

"A huge being...huge...taller than this house...stood on the rock. I know it's unbelievable, but we are all witnesses...we could not see his face, and his form was so bright we could not look on it. It was like sunlight beaming off a mirror. We fell to our knees in terror, but he told us not to be afraid. I do not know how much time passed; it was as if we had turned to stone. After a time we looked up, and the being was gone, or else had been changed into something more like a man. He stood in the tomb and bade us see that the Master's body was gone...and to tell his disciples to meet him in Galilee. I tell you the Master has been raised to life!"

All the women begin to talk at once, their eyes wide, their hands gesticulating, each giving her own account of what she had seen. Reumah looks from one to another, unsure of what to say or do. Mary, the Lord's mother, sitting next to her, breathes deeply, as if she is patiently waiting for them to finish.

"Where is my son now?" she says, when they stop speaking for a moment.

"We do not know," says Salome. "We only know that we were told to tell the men to meet him in Galilee. And they don't believe us...they think we are out of our minds!"

"And...where is our sister Mary?"

"She hurried to tell John. Then she said she would return to the garden where they had laid him. She is determined to find him, and she declared she would not return home until she had seen him."

"You said...a man was in the tomb?" this was Reumah, whose mind is greatly troubled by the story.

"Yes...his appearance was like that of a man, and yet not so, for he seemed otherworldly," says Salome.

"And the tomb was empty?"

"Yes! Only the grave clothes were there...like the cocoon of a cat-erpillar. It was very strange."

"You yourselves did not see the Master?"

"No...no we have not seen him. But we saw the bright being...and the peculiar man who spoke with us...and beheld the tomb, empty. That much is certain."

Reumah's mind absorbs the facts...she wants to believe...but her heart is full of doubt.

She helps prepare breakfast for herself and his mother and the other women, all of whom plan to return to look for him. She tries to settle her mind. She thinks of Mary and Martha, and wonders when she should return to them and what they will say to all this. No doubt they are wondering what has happened. She thinks of her father, loving the Master as she did, setting him apart as the anointed one of Israel, and yet having to bury him. She would give anything now to know what his thoughts were at the time. She cannot help but wonder if he would forgive and accept her now. Her mind is thus occupied even as her hands go through the motions of preparing the bread. As they sit down to eat, there is a knock at the door, and in a moment John, the Master's best friend, appears before them in the courtyard. He walks straight over to Mary.

"Blessed mother," he says, taking her hand in his.

"My son," says Mary, and the others look at one another.

"Have you heard the news?"

"I have. Where is he?"

"I have not seen him, in truth," John says, lowering his head. "But I came to give you this..." He hands her a large cloth, like a napkin, neatly folded. She takes it in her hands, and holds it to her face. The women gather around them.

"It was the headcloth...lying separate, from the rest of the burial cloths...neatly folded. As if he were laying down his napkin in the middle of a meal, as a way of telling us that he would be gone for a moment, but not to clear his away his food, for he would be back. What other meaning could it have? I have dined with him enough times to know his ways...I believe he is alive, though I myself have not seen him nor can I explain it."

Reumah stares at his eyes, and his face, and sees he is in earnest. She longs to believe wholeheartedly, as he does. It occurs to her now that Mary's mind is not addled, but simply grounded in unwavering faith.

"Thank you, my son," says Mary. "Your words greatly comfort me, more than you can know." She clutches the cloth tenderly, and she stands. "Now...have you met Reumah? She has become like a daughter to me."

Reumah lowers her eyes, and bows slightly. She waits for him to speak.

"It is an honor to meet someone who loves with actions and in truth. Shalom, my sister." He inclines his head in a bow.

For a brief moment their eyes meet, and he smiles at her. She smiles back, and something stirs inside her, like a small bird, shaking out its feathers after a rainstorm; as if the force of his faith compels her doubts to be dispelled.

No wonder the Master chose him as his closest friend, Reumah thinks to herself. *I would love him too...he has great faith, and an abiding peace.*

Mary watches them. She sees the look they exchange. Reumah's eyelashes are darkly wet, and her eyes are shining and soft, as if her many tears have made them more luminous; her lips are full and sweet when she smiles up at him. These charms are not lost on John, and so Mary smiles to herself, and the others see her smiling, thinking for sure that she is becoming out of touch.

*His words are coming to pass...*his mother whispers to no one but herself.

About an hour after John leaves, Mary Magdalene enters the court-yard, completely out of breath, her face red with exertion, her hair and clothes in disarray, as if she had rushed back to them.

"I have seen the Lord," she says. She sinks onto a bench, to catch her breath, and someone brings her a cup of diluted wine. Mary, the Lord's mother, goes to her, and sits beside her on the bench, as if determined not to miss one word of whatever she will say. The other women gather round her, about twenty in all. She takes a long drink, and then begins her account.

"After we saw the angel and the empty tomb, I ran and told John. Peter was with him. My words were not proof enough for them; they must see for themselves. Whereas we all reacted with shock and then joy, they were silent and dismayed. They outran me, and when I got there, Peter had gone inside. He came out, looking more dejected than ever I have seen him, as if the disappearance of the Master's body is worse than his death. The strange man whom we had seen inside, who told us the Master was not there, was nowhere to be seen, and clearly they did not believe me. 'Perhaps you were mistaken, and saw a gardener or someone spying for the Sanhedrin,' said John to me. Peter was more to the point. When he came out of the tomb, he said, 'There is no body.' Then he looked directly at me and added, 'And certainly no angel.'

"'I would not lie,' I said to him.

"'I would not accuse you,' he said to me. "'But at times like this, our minds become unclear, and we dream of things we wish were true.'

"'We were not dreaming! You think we do not know what is true? Or real?'"

"'I can only speak for myself...' said Peter, turning away. "'And I no longer know what is true, or what is real.' He picked up a rock, and threw it into the dark tomb. We heard it rattle against the stone inside. Then he looked at John.

"'I'm going back to Galilee,' he said.

"Meanwhile, John retrieved the headcloth, intending to bring it to you. Has he been here?"

They show her the headcloth. She holds it for a minute against her cheek. Her eyes close, and for a moment she seems lost in her reflections and unwilling to speak further. His mother clears her throat gently, and Mary opens her eyes.

"In truth, my sorrow was all the greater for their skepticism. I blessed you all, my friends, who had loved and stayed by the Master in his final hours, and I scorned the men who had left him to die alone, except for John. God forbid that I become bitter toward them, especially Peter, whom we all thought was so brave and bold! I know I must forgive him, for the Master would have it so, but at that moment I felt engulfed by spite and anger.

"'God, have mercy on us all!' I cried aloud, and suddenly a light shone from the tomb, as if someone had lit a lamp inside. I bent forward, and saw two men instead of one, dressed in white linen as before, seated on the ledge where the Master's body had lain.

"'Why are you crying?' one of them asked.

"I began to tell them my sorrow, when I heard a noise behind me, like someone approaching me carefully..." She stops speaking again, as if it pains her to continue. The women shift around, some of them sit down on the benches nearby. No one speaks.

"It was a man, in the shabby garb of a vinedresser. His robe was tied up, so that his legs would not be encumbered...for...he was somewhat lame...his feet seemed not quite right, and his hands, likewise, were misshapen, like claws." Again she stops, and the women gaze on her, hardly breathing.

"Who? Who was it?" The Master's mother cries out.

Mary of Magdala closes her eyes, and holds up her hand, as if she is uttering an oracle.

"'Why are you crying, woman?' He spoke so softly that the coos of the mourning doves in the trees around us almost drowned out his voice. 'Who is it you are seeking? Maybe I can help.'

"'Sir!'" I told him. 'If you have taken him away...please...please tell me where you have put him! Please!'

"He lowered the scarf around his head...and...I gasped to see him...his face was severely...deformed...the brows were mashed down over his eyes, which could hardly be seen, and his cheeks, mouth and nose, likewise, were scarred and misshapen, as if they had been broken and beaten and had not properly healed. He had almost no hair on his head or chin; it was as if it had all been shaved off recently. I thought at first that he was leprous, but his skin was not tumorous or scaly, but had rather a stark, ethereal quality, as if it had been drained of blood or pigment. I could not help but stare.

"'Forgive me, sir,' I said to him, 'but your appearance'—and then—then—he said one word, this time more loudly. He said my name. He said, 'Mary.'" Her eyes opened and she turned to look at the Master's mother.

"No," says his mother. "Let it not be so…" She begins to cry. The other women, likewise, begin to weep softly.

"I knew his voice. It was him. I screamed when I knew it, and took hold of him."

"No, no…" said his mother, taking hold of the headcloth again, and putting it against her face. Reumah takes hold of her.

"Listen," says Mary Magdalene. "Listen to me, all of you…his appearance is grotesquely altered, it is true…you will not know him at first when you see him…but his voice is the same, and his spirit is joyous! A smile played about his lips all the while that he spoke to me, as if he could not contain his joy, and he told me he wants to see us…all of us…before he returns to our God. Think of it!"

Salome has left the room, and returns now with a bundle of cloth, which she unfolds.

"What are you doing, Salome?"

"What do you think? He will need a new robe, of course," she says, matter-of-factly. "Immediately. Come…all of you. We must work quickly."

"Yes," says his mother, wiping her eyes. "With a hood."

"Your brother is about to be married. Go back to your father's house, and all will be forgiven."

He spoke the words to Reumah directly, in the presence of Mary and Martha, and they rejoiced with her, like sisters. He also told her that she would become a wife, and bear children, and her face grew warm even as her mind wondered. He spoke of many things to all those who came to him, to all who loved him, in groups large and small, in secluded gardens and groves, away from public scrutiny. They were shocked at first, at the sight of him, but as soon as he spoke they recognized his voice, and they were comforted greatly. They stayed near him, like sheep resting in the shade near their shepherd, taking hold of his last words, like children of an aged father, eager to hear his blessings and admonishments before his final departure.

"I have told you all these things, so that when they come to pass, you will know that every word I have spoken to you is true."

He said this again and again to them, and so they hung on to his words all the more. Some even wrote them down, but most of them, like Reumah, held them sacred in their hearts, never to be forgotten, and taught them to their children and their grandchildren, and for a generation not yet born.

"Your father is not the same man," her mother told her. "Perhaps your return will revive his spirit." She spoke the words with a sense of resignation, and even bitterness, but they proved to be true. Her father stood up and welcomed her with outstretched arms. They did not speak while they embraced, and Reumah buried her face in his robe to hide her tears and her shock at how much he had aged. They spoke very little at first, sitting together in the small garden next to his house, watching the sun set over the hills. A thousand questions rose up in her mind to ask him, but she waited, as always, for him to choose the topics, and for now, his mind was only on the Master.

"There was so much blood," he told her. His voice, to her ears, sounded like that of a much older man. "Reumah, you cannot imagine how much blood there was. It was caked in his hair, on his beard, all over his body. We did our best to wash him, but the sun was about to set, and in the end, we had to shave his head and his face...there was so little time."

"Abba, what were your thoughts as you prepared him for burial?"

He sighed deeply. "The words of the prophet Zechariah came to me, my lamb...'They shall look on the one they have pierced, and grieve bitterly for him, like for a firstborn son...'" His voice broke off and she saw he was weeping. "In truth, I wept for my own sins and blindness...that I had not known him until that moment." He began to sway slightly, as if he were praying, or grieving.

"And what do you think, Reumah? While we shaved and cleansed him, the scent of spikenard, the sweetest of all fragrances, rose up from his body, broken and pierced as it was, as if his spirit had already taken up residence in paradise." He wiped his eyes.

She gasped at the implication of his words. In time she would tell him about the vial—she knew now he would love to know the story—but for now she wanted only to be near him. She squeezed his hand playfully, suddenly filled with joy.

"Abba, no more tears. We must rejoice! Our Lord is alive forever-more, your son is about to take a bride, and your daughter has returned to you. Look, the musicians have arrived to begin the procession." In the courtyard they could hear the sounds of lyres and tambourines and harps and drums. The clash of cymbals caused her heart to race with exhilaration.

"Yes, yes, you are right in saying so, my daughter. The time of sorrow has passed, for now...it is time to rejoice. Go...go and dance before the Lord with all your might."

And Reumah danced.

Made in the USA
Middletown, DE
03 October 2015